365
Stories for Girls
A Story a Day

DiSNEP PRESS
New York · Los Angeles

JANUARY 1

Once Upon a Flower

Once upon a time, in a land far away, a single drop of sunlight fell to the ground. The sunlight soon grew into a magical golden flower that possessed healing powers.

The only person who knew the location of the flower was a vain and selfish woman named Mother Gothel. She used it to keep herself looking young and beautiful.

As the centuries passed, a glorious kingdom was built close to the cliff where the flower grew. One day the kingdom's beloved queen fell gravely ill. The king's subject's had heard stories about a magical flower with healing powers. They searched far and wide until, at last, they found the golden flower.

As Mother Gothel looked on in horror, a royal guard dug up the flower and took it back to the palace. The queen drank a potion containing the flower and instantly recovered!

Soon after, the queen gave birth to a beautiful baby girl. The whole kingdom launched flying lanterns into the sky to celebrate the princess's birth.

One night, an aged and vengeful Mother Gothel crept into the nursery. As she stroked the baby's hair and sang softly, Mother Gothel became young again! The flower's magic still lived in the baby.

Mother Gothel greedily cut off a lock of the girl's hair, but it instantly turned brown and lost its power. The only way Mother Gothel could remain young was to keep the child with her, always. And so she snatched the baby and vanished into the night.

Everyone in the kingdom searched, but no one could find the princess. Although the king and queen were heartbroken, they remained hopeful that one day their daughter would return to them. Each year on the princess's birthday, they released lanterns into the night sky. They hoped their light would guide their daughter home.

Meanwhile, Mother Gothel raised the princess, whom she named Rapunzel, in a soaring tower in a hidden valley. She loved the girl only for her hair and treated Rapunzel as a prized possession.

Would the lost princess ever be found?

A Fairy Tale Kiss

Once upon a time in New Orleans, there lived two unlikely friends named Tiana and Charlotte. Charlotte believed in fairy tales and wishing on stars, while Tiana knew that she had to work hard to make her dreams come true.

Tiana often visited Charlotte's house with her mother, Eudora, who worked as a seamstress for the family. One night, as Tiana's mother was sewing a new dress, she told the two girls a fairy tale about a prince who had been turned into a frog. This was Charlotte's favorite story.

". . . and the beautiful princess was so moved by his desperate pleas that she stooped down, picked up the frog . . ."

"Here comes my favorite part," Charlotte said, whispering in Tiana's ear.

". . . raised him to her lips and . . ."

"Yes, do it, princess!" whispered Charlotte under her breath.

No, don't do it! thought Tiana, looking disgusted.

". . . kissed that little frog! Then, the frog was transformed into a handsome prince. They were married and lived happily ever after!" said Eudora with a smile.

"Yay!" cried Charlotte. "Read it again! Read it again!"

But it was time for Tiana to go home.

As Eudora was putting away her sewing things, Tiana said to Charlotte, "There is no way in this whole wide world I would ever, ever, ever—I mean never—kiss a frog!"

Charlotte picked up a frog puppet and put it on the head of her kitten. The little animal tried to get away, but Charlotte held it up to Tiana, saying, "Well, here's your prince charming, Tia. Go on, kiss him!"

"Yuck!" protested Tiana.

"I would do it," said Charlotte. "I would kiss a frog. I would kiss a hundred frogs if I could marry a prince and be a princess!" she said. And with that, she planted a big kiss on the nose of the kitten, who leaped away in horror.

The two girls rolled around on the floor laughing. They had no idea of the adventures the future would bring.

The Sleepover

"Comfortable, Piglet?" Pooh asked. The two friends were having a sleepover at Pooh's house.

"Oh, yes," Piglet replied. "Good night, Pooh Bear."

Piglet lay in the darkness of Pooh's room. The darkness at Pooh's house was much, much darker than it was at Piglet's house. Pooh's bedroom was also much quieter than his own room at night.

"Pooh Bear?" Piglet whispered. There was no answer.

Piglet heard a soft, low rumbling. The sound grew louder and then softer, over and over again! Is that the sound of a heffalump? Piglet wondered.

"Oh dear!" Piglet shouted, running to Pooh's bed. "Wake up! P-p-please, P-P-Pooh!"

"Hmm?" Pooh said drowsily, sitting up. Piglet was hiding under the covers in Pooh's bed. "Why, Piglet," said Pooh. "What's the matter?"

"It's that horrible n-n-noise, Pooh," he stammered. Piglet listened for the noise, then realized he couldn't hear it. "That's funny," said Piglet. "The noise stopped as soon as you woke up, Pooh."

"Hmm," said Pooh. He shrugged. Then he yawned. "I guess that means we can go back to sleep."

"Pooh Bear," said Piglet timidly, "could we, well, have the rest of our sleepover another night? I'm just used to sleeping in my own house."

Pooh put his arm around Piglet. "I understand, Piglet," he said. He helped Piglet gather his things and then, hand in hand, they walked to Piglet's house.

Piglet was happy to be at home. "Thank you so much for understanding," he said. "I suppose you'll need to get home to bed now?"

"That does sound like the thing to do," Pooh replied. "But first I might sit down for a little rest."

While Piglet put away his things, Pooh sat down in a chair. By the time Piglet came back, Pooh was making a soft, low rumbling sound. But in the comfort of his own house, it didn't strike Piglet as anything other than the sound of one sleeping bear snoring.

"Sweet dreams, Pooh Bear," he whispered. Piglet climbed into his own bed and drifted off to sleep. It seemed that he and Pooh were having their best-friend sleepover after all.

Tinker Bell Is Born

One winter's day in London, a baby laughed for the very first time. That laugh floated up and away to meet its destiny. It would become a fairy, just like all first laughs.

The laugh floated toward Never Land, where it landed in magical place called Pixie Hollow, home of the fairies. Vidia, a fast-flying fairy, guided the arrival into the Pixie Dust Tree. The other fairies were waiting. As the laugh settled, a dust-keeper named Terence sprinkled it with pixie dust. Soon the laugh took the shape of a small fairy.

Queen Clarion waved her hand and several toadstools sprung up around the new fairy. Fairies of all different talents fluttered forward to place objects on the pedestals. Rosetta, a garden fairy, brought a flower. Silvermist, a water fairy, carried a droplet of water. Iridessa, a light fairy, placed a lamp on her toadstool.

Each of the items began to glow. "They will help you find your talent," the queen explained to the new fairy.

The fairy timidly placed her hand on a beautiful flower. Its glow instantly faded. She reached for a water droplet, but that, too, faded. The fairy moved on without touching anything else. She was afraid to fail again. Then, suddenly, something amazing happened. As she passed by a hammer, it began to glow even more brightly. It rose up from its toadstool and flew straight at the new arrival!

"I've never seen one glow that much before," said Silvermist.

"Tinker fairies," called the queen. "Welcome the newest member of your talent guild—Tinker Bell!"

A large fairy named Clank and a bespectacled fairy named Bobble came forward to greet Tinker Bell. Then they whisked her off for a flying tour of Pixie Hollow. It was almost time for the changing of the seasons, and they could see everyone getting ready.

Finally, the trio landed at Tinkers' Nook. Tink looked around and saw fairies fixing all kinds of amazing, useful objects. She couldn't wait to learn all about her unique fairy talent!

I Choose Archery!

Merida was a young, adventurous princess. She lived in the Scottish Highlands, in a kingdom called DunBroch. Merida's mother, Queen Elinor, wanted Merida to marry the son of a lord from a neighboring clan. This would help to keep peace between the lands.

But Merida didn't want to get married. She wanted to go on great adventures and follow her own path.

Soon, the clans' ships sailed into DunBroch. Queen Elinor dressed Merida in a formal gown to greet them.

"I can't move," Merida complained. "It's too tight."

"It's perfect," her mother said, smiling. But Merida wasn't happy at all.

The royal family welcomed the lords and their clans in the castle's Great Hall. Lord MacGuffin, Lord Macintosh, and Lord Dingwall, the heads of each clan, stepped forward to present their sons. The three were to compete for Merida's hand in marriage.

Queen Elinor stepped forward and clarified the rules of the competition. Only the first-born of each house could participate. The princess herself would determine the challenge.

First born? Merida's eyes lit up as an idea formed in her head. She leaped to her feet, crying, "I choose archery!"

The competition began at high noon. Young MacGuffin took the first shot—and nearly missed the target completely. Young Macintosh's shot was slightly better. His attitude, however, was not. He stomped angrily on his bow. Wee Dingwall was the clumsiest of them all. But to everyone's amazement, he hit the bull's-eye!

Just then, Merida strode onto the field. "I am the first-born descendant of Clan DunBroch!" she declared before the stunned crowd. "And I'll be shooting for my own hand!"

"Merida! I forbid it!" the queen cried. But Merida ignored her mother.

One by one, she fired her arrows at the targets. She hit all three bull's-eyes. Queen Elinor was furious! Merida might have just ruined the peace between the clans.

Young Mike Wazowski

Mike Wazowski couldn't wait. His class was going on a trip to Monsters, Inc.

Mike was the smallest monster at Frighton Elementary—and the least popular—so it was not surprising that when his teacher told everyone to pair up, Mike ended up alone.

"Well, Michael, looks like it's you and me again," said the teacher, taking Mike's hand.

A tour guide met the class and took them inside. "We're entering a very dangerous area," he warned. "This is where we collect the scream energy to power our whole world."

The guide warned the little monsters to stay in the viewing area and never cross the red safety line marked on the floor.

But that didn't stop Mike. He followed one of the Scarers into the human world!

Mike watched as the Scarer crept up to the sleeping child and frightened him. It was the most exciting thing the little monster had ever seen!

It was then that Mike decided he wanted to be a Scarer when he grew up.

The years passed and Mike grew old enough to attend college. He decided to go to Monsters University to study Scaring.

On Mike's first day, a group of monsters called the Smile Squad greeted Mike happily. They helped him to register and told him all about the university. Soon Mike was touring the campus.

As Mike walked through the quad, the Greek Council handed him a leaflet. "We sponsor the annual Scare Games. It's a super-intense scaring competition where you get a chance to prove you're the best!"

Mike liked the sound of that!

Finally he reached his dorm. Inside, he met his roommate, Randy. He was a friendly eight-legged monster who could disappear without warning. It was a great talent, even if his glasses *did* give him away.

Mike started to unpack. His dream was about to come true. All he needed to do now was graduate with honors and become the greatest Scarer ever.

"Aren't you even a little nervous?" Randy asked.

"No," said Mike. He had been waiting for this moment his whole life.

A Day Without Pumbaa

"Mmm!" said Timon. "Breakfast time!" Timon was showing Simba how to catch some very sneaky bugs in the jungle. "Too bad Pumbaa has to miss out. I haven't seen him. Have you? Ooh! There's a good one!" Timon crouched behind a log and was about to pounce, when—

"AAAHHH!" Pumbaa swooped out of the trees, swinging wildly on a vine. He crashed straight into Timon.

"Oops! Sorry, Timon," Pumbaa said.

"Sorry?" shouted Timon.

"It wasn't on purpose," Pumbaa said.

"You never do anything on purpose," Timon replied. "You're a disaster! You couldn't catch a bug if it flew into your mouth."

"That's not true!" Pumbaa protested. "I'll prove it." The clumsy warthog lunged for a grub, only to fall headfirst into a puddle. Mud splattered Simba and Timon from head to toe.

"That's it!" cried Timon. "I've had it!"

Pumbaa hung his head. "It would be better if I just left," he said. And with that, he plodded back into the jungle.

Just then, Simba saw lightning. He looked up at the threatening clouds. "Timon, we can't let him go!"

But Timon was too mad at his friend to worry about him. He went back to bug-hunting.

The storm came and went. And then so did lunchtime—but still, no Pumbaa.

"You shouldn't have been so hard on him," Simba said. "I wonder if he's okay."

"He's fine," snapped Timon. "Besides, he walked out on *us*, remember?"

Just then, the friends heard a rustling sound coming from the riverbank. *Wham!* Pumbaa tumbled out of the jungle, knocking into Timon and Simba. All three of them crashed into a large tree trunk. Pumbaa had brought bugs for his friends, but they went flying into the air.

"I'm back!" Pumbaa said.

"So we see," mumbled Timon, trapped under the warthog.

Embarrassed, Pumbaa stood up. "I came back to say I missed you," he said. "But now look what I've done! I'm the worst friend ever."

"Now, wait one minute!" cried Timon. "That's just not true!"

"You're a wonderful friend, and we missed you, too!" Simba said. "Welcome back."

"We even missed your disasters," Timon added. Pumbaa smiled.

A Visit in the Night

It's not easy to read with a broken arm! Alone in his room, young Carl was trying to turn a page without letting go of his flashlight.

Suddenly, he heard a small squeaking noise. Then a blue balloon forced its way through his bedroom curtains! A merry little face framed by a mop of red hair appeared at the window and Carl let out a cry.

"Hey, kid. Thought you might need a little cheerin' up!" whispered Ellie, his new friend, before she leaped down onto the floor. She slipped quickly under the cover that Carl had made into a tent and sat down.

Ellie pulled out her notebook. "I am about to let you see something I have never shown to another human being. You'll have to swear you will not tell anyone."

Carl promised, and Ellie opened up the book. A photo of the explorer Charles Muntz had been stuck on the first page.

"My adventure book!" Ellie cried. "When I get big, I'm going where he's going: South America. Paradise Falls!"

Carl looked admiringly at the beautiful waterfall, next to which Ellie had drawn the little house where they'd met each other that same afternoon.

"I'm going to move my clubhouse there and park it right next to the falls!"

Without saying a word, Carl's eyes drifted up to the shelf where his collection of miniature airships stood, including a model of Muntz's *Spirit of Adventure*. Ellie immediately understood.

"That's it!" she cried out. "You can take us there in a blimp! Swear you'll take us. Cross your heart."

Carl promised. He could see no reason not to. It was clear that Ellie was a true adventuress!

"See you tomorrow," she said, getting up. "You know, you don't talk very much. I like you," she added, laughing, before climbing out the window and disappearing into the night.

"Wow!" murmured Carl, totally bowled over by his new friend. Just ten minutes in Ellie's company was one of the biggest adventures of his life!

That night, as he slept, he dreamed of a colorful little house perched atop of Paradise Falls. One day he would get there. . . .

Grumpy Rajah

It wasn't always easy being the daughter of a sultan. Sometimes Jasmine thought she would be the loneliest girl in Agrabah if not for Rajah, her pet tiger (and best friend).

But apparently, it wasn't always easy being a tiger, either. Rajah was having a bad day.

"What's gotten into you?" Jasmine asked him.

But Rajah just looked at her and growled again.

"Hmm," Jasmine said thoughtfully. She hated it when Rajah was down. But what could she do to cheer him up?

As a princess, Jasmine wasn't allowed to do much. But one thing she could do was be a good friend to Rajah, and she was determined to do just that.

"You know what you need?" Jasmine asked.

Rajah paced back and forth.

"You need to try to relax!" Jasmine told him.

Rajah just looked at her.

"You know," Jasmine explained, "loosen up, have a good time."

Rajah began to growl again.

"All right, all right!" Jasmine held up her hands in surrender. "I'll stop."

But she just couldn't let it go. She really wanted Rajah to be happy!

Jasmine patted her tiger on the back. "You know, Rajah, I wouldn't be saying this if I didn't care about you. You have to enjoy life, not growl at it! Look at me—I spend all my time talking to the brainless, unpleasant princes my father brings around. But I still try to have fun whenever I can!"

Rajah lay down and put his paws over his ears.

Finally Jasmine understood. "You're jealous of all those princes!" she said.

Rajah looked up. Jasmine was right. He *was* sick and tired of all those princes coming around.

Jasmine lovingly scratched Rajah behind the ear. "Jealousy isn't very becoming," she teased him, "even in tigers. I know I haven't been spending much time with you lately, Rajah. But it's not like I have a choice. The law says I have to find a prince to marry."

Princes, Rajah thought. Yuck!

"But you know," Jasmine continued, hugging her tiger around his big furry neck, "I like you better than any prince."

Rajah began to purr. Jasmine smiled. "Princes!" Jasmine said. "Yuck!"

Just Desserts

Belle walked to the village, thinking about the wonderful book she had just finished reading. It was full of fire-breathing dragons, magical wizards, and brave princesses.

All of a sudden, Belle's thoughts were interrupted by a great crashing noise. Even before he spoke a word, Belle knew who was walking behind her. She would recognize that stomp anywhere.

"Gaston," Belle muttered.

"Belle, is it true?" Gaston said. "Have you come out from behind a book?"

"*Bonjour*, Gaston," Belle said. She was tempted to open her book again on the spot.

"Off to market, eh? I shall accompany you," Gaston announced.

Gaston followed Belle into shop after shop, keeping up a steady stream of chatter about himself and his exploits.

"My, Gaston, you certainly do boast well," Belle said in a flattering tone.

"Yes! Thank you!" Gaston said—before realizing that Belle was not complimenting him. His smile disappeared briefly as he opened the door to the bakery.

Belle stepped inside and quickly asked for an apple tart before Gaston could begin speaking again. When the tart was in her basket, she waved to Gaston and the shopkeeper. "Good-bye!" she called, walking quickly toward the forest path.

"Belle, wait." Gaston caught her arm.

"I really have no time to linger, Gaston," Belle replied. "I must get home to make dinner."

"I can walk you home," Gaston said, puffing out his massive chest. "I insist upon it. You need protection."

Belle laughed. "Protection from what? These woods are my backyard!"

"From predators. Monsters. Thieves," Gaston said dramatically.

Belle sighed and shook her head.

Just then, the two heard something coming from the path ahead. Something large!

Quickly, Gaston pushed Belle out of harm's way. Belle tumbled to the ground. Her basket went flying.

"Look out!" Belle yelled. But it was too late.

The "predator" emerged. It was her father's horse, Phillipe! For the first time that she could remember, Belle smiled at the sight of Gaston. The apple tart had landed right on top of his head!

The Induction

Nemo still had a satisfied smile on his face from the previous night's induction ceremony. I'm part of the club! he thought.

After being kidnapped from the reef where he lived with his dad, Nemo had been brought to live in a fish tank in a dentist's office. The tank's other residents had a secret club, and they had accepted Nemo as one of them! They had even given him a cool nickname: Shark Bait.

"So, Shark Bait, what did you think of the ceremony?" Gill asked.

"It was the best!" Nemo exclaimed.

"If only we could get Flo to be part of it sometime," Deb mused. "But she never seems to want to come out at night."

"Nemo, what was your favorite part?" Jacques wanted to know.

"I think it was swimming to the top of Mount Wanna . . . wannaha . . . ha . . ." Nemo tried unsuccessfully to pronounce it.

"Wannahockaloogie," Bloat said.

"Yeah," Peach reminisced. "I have a soft spot for my first climb, too."

"I wonder," Nemo said, "who came up with that name?"

Bubbles pointed at Gurgle, who pointed at Bloat, who pointed at Peach, who pointed at Deb, who pointed at Flo.

Deb shrugged. "I guess we came up with it together," she said.

"Why do they call it the Ring of Fire if there's no fire?" Nemo asked.

"Well, you see, it's like this—I don't know," Peach had to admit.

"But who made it up?" Nemo asked.

"I think Bubbles came up with the Ring of Fire," Gurgle offered.

"Aren't they beautiful?" Bubbles mused.

"I find it very unsanitary to swim through others' bubbles," Gurgle complained. "Which is why I came up with the chanting part of the ceremony. It's very cleansing both for the body and the mind, and circulates carbon dioxide through the gills."

"That makes sense," Nemo agreed, although it really didn't.

"What can I do in the next ceremony?" he asked eagerly.

"Hopefully, we won't have another one. Not if we break out of here first, Shark Bait," Gill answered.

"Well, you never know," Deb said forlornly. "Maybe Flo will come around."

Everyone rolled their eyes, including Nemo.

Fish-in-the-Box

"**A**riel?" Flounder called out timidly, poking his head inside Ariel's secret grotto. Ariel had told Flounder to meet her there, but she hadn't arrived yet. "I guess I'll wait for her inside," he said to himself.

He swam around slowly, gazing at Ariel's collection of things from the human world. The rock ledges were filled with various objects the princess had found in sunken ships and up at the surface. It was Ariel's favorite place. But without Ariel there, Flounder found the place lonely . . . and quiet . . . and creepy.

Flounder swam past one object that he had never noticed before—a square metal box with a handle on one side.

"I wonder what that thing does," said Flounder, staring at the handle. After a few moments' hesitation, Flounder summoned his courage. By flapping his tail fin and pushing the handle with his nose, he managed to turn it around once . . . twice . . . three times. Nothing happened. Flounder was halfway into the fourth turn when—*Boing!* The latch to the top of

the jack-in-the-box released and the spring-loaded jester inside popped out and lunged at Flounder.

"Ahhhhhhhhhhhh!" Flounder screamed as he raced backward away from the jack-in-the-box and collided with the lid of an open treasure chest. The force of the collision caused the lid of the chest to slam shut, trapping Flounder inside.

Moments later, Ariel swam into the secret grotto.

"Flounder?" she called. "Are you here yet?"

From inside the chest, Flounder yelled to Ariel. "*Mm-nn-eer!*" came the muffled cry.

Ariel followed the sound of his voice and swam over to the chest. Lifting the lid, she found her friend inside. "What are you doing in there?" Ariel asked with a giggle.

Thinking quickly, Flounder replied, "I'm about to do my imitation of that thing." He pointed at the jack-in-the-box. Then Flounder sprang suddenly out of the chest, raced out the door, and kept on swimming. He'd had enough of Ariel's secret grotto for one day!

A Tinker's Talent

Tinker Bell had just arrived in Pixie Hollow and was being shown around her new home.

Fairy Mary looked Tinker Bell over. Noticing the new fairy's dainty hands, she said, "Don't worry, dear, we'll build up those tinker muscles in no time." Then, reminding Clank and Bobble to make their deliveries, she was gone.

Soon, Tink, Clank, and Bobble set off to deliver supplies to the other fairies. Cheese the mouse pulled their loaded wagon. Inside were rainbow tubes for Iridessa and pussy-willow brushes for Rosetta. Iridessa explained that she used the tubes to roll up rainbows and take them to the mainland.

"What's the mainland?" Tink asked.

"It's where we're gonna go change winter to spring," replied Silvermist.

Next the tinkers stopped at the Flower Meadow, where Vidia was vacuuming the pollen out of flowers.

"Hi! What's your talent?" Tink asked.

"I am a fast-flying fairy. Fairies of every talent depend on me," Vidia answered, making it clear that she didn't think much of tinker fairies.

Tink was insulted. "When I go to the mainland, I'll prove just how important we are!" she replied.

Angry, Tink flew off to the beach, where she discovered wonderful treasures buried in the sand! When she arrived at Tinker's Nook with her treasures, Clank explained they were Lost Things, items that washed up on Never Land from time to time. But Fairy Mary whisked the trinkets away. The queen's review of the springtime preparations was that night, and there was a lot to do. There was no time to waste with Lost Things.

That evening, the Minister of Spring welcomed Queen Clarion to the review ceremony. Suddenly, Tinker Bell interrupted the proceedings. "I came up with some fantastic things for tinkers to use when we go to the mainland!" she told the queen.

"Has no one explained?" Queen Clarion said gently. "Tinker fairies don't go to the mainland."

Tinker Bell was devastated. Only nature fairies went to the mainland! And so Tink decided, she would just have to become a nature fairy!

Imagine That!

The carnival was in town and Pinocchio couldn't wait to see it. He grabbed his friend Jiminy Cricket, and off they went!

Pinocchio was amazed by the marvelous sights. "That elephant is amazing!" he cried.

"I suppose," said Jiminy politely.

Next they came to a lion's cage. The big cat opened his mouth and roared.

"Look at those teeth!" Pinocchio marveled.

Jiminy Cricket nodded. "They're pretty big, it's true."

Then they saw a giraffe.

"What a long neck!" Pinocchio exclaimed.

"Giraffes are all right, I guess," said Jiminy with a shrug.

Pinocchio was confused. "If you don't like elephants, lions, or giraffes, what kind of carnival animals do you like?" Pinocchio asked.

"Fleas," said Jiminy.

"Fleas?" Pinocchio said, even more confused.

"Come on! I'll show you," said Jiminy.

Jiminy led Pinocchio to a tent with a sign that read FLEA CIRCUS. Inside, Pinocchio saw a tiny merry-go-round and little swings. There were small animal cages and a little trapeze. There was even a tiny big top with three miniature rings. But no matter how hard he looked, Pinocchio could not see any fleas.

"That's because there aren't any fleas," Jiminy explained.

"What's the point, then?" Pinocchio asked.

"The point is imagination," said Jiminy. "Why, you can do anything with your imagination. You can even see the fleas at the flea circus."

Pinocchio laughed and joined in the game. "That flea is going to jump through a ring of fire," he said. "I hope he makes it!"

"Now the fleas are doing acrobatics," Jiminy declared.

"Look! They've made a flea pyramid," said Pinocchio. "And the flea on top is standing on his hands!"

After they had watched the flea circus for a long while, it was time to go home.

"What did you think of the Flea Circus?" asked Jiminy Cricket.

"It was the most amazing circus I've ever seen, and I didn't really see it at all!" Pinocchio replied.

"Yes, indeed. You imagined it," said Jiminy Cricket. "Imagine that!"

Soup's On

Mulan stood in the kitchen, moodily stirring a pot of soup for supper. Grandmother Fa sat at the table, sorting through grains of rice. Neither one of them spoke.

They were both lost in thought at the recent news they had received: Mulan's father, Fa Zhou, had been ordered to join the Chinese army in order to help protect the Emperor from the invading Huns. Mulan was distraught, for she knew that if her father joined the army and went into battle, he would surely die.

"Why must my father fight?" Mulan asked her grandmother suddenly. "He is but one man, and the Emperor would never know the difference if he didn't join. Yet what a difference to our family it would be if he were to die!" She sighed heavily.

Her grandmother also sighed and continued to sort the rice silently for a few moments. Then she stopped and turned to Mulan. "You are partly correct. One grain of rice, such as this one that I have in my hand, is small and insignificant." Then she held out her hand and tipped the grain into the large bowl of rice she had been sorting. "Yet together, you know, all the grains of rice in this bowl could feed many people. The Emperor needs an army of many, many people in order to defeat the invaders."

Mulan shook her head miserably, afraid that if she spoke she would cry. Grandmother Fa was just as unhappy as Mulan, but the older woman realized that it was useless to protest against some things. She stood up and walked silently out of the kitchen.

Mulan continued to stir the soup, even though it didn't need stirring. Next to the pot sat a small bowl, which contained a peppery red spice. She picked up the small bowl and looked at it thoughtfully. "One grain of rice is small and insignificant," she said to herself. "And yet, a tiny pinch of the spice from this little bowl could change the flavor of this whole pot of soup. Perhaps," she went on, "one person can make a difference, if she follows her heart."

Mulan dumped the whole bowl of spice into the pot and smiled.

"Soup's on!" she cried.

Sleepless Beauty

"Oh, there, there, little Aurora. There, there," cooed Flora, trying to calm the crying, fussy baby princess. Flora and her fellow fairies, Fauna and Merryweather, stood huddled over the cradle of tiny Aurora and looked down anxiously and helplessly at their royal charge.

The three good fairies had taken the princess from the castle after the evil fairy Maleficent had put a curse on her. Perhaps if Maleficent couldn't find the girl, the curse would not work. But the baby had not stopped crying since Flora, Fauna, and Merryweather had arrived with her at the secluded cottage in the woods.

"Oh, goodness!" cried Fauna. "What have we gotten ourselves into? We don't know the first thing about taking care of human babies!"

Flora gave Fauna a comforting pat on the back. "Now, now, don't panic, Fauna," Flora said. "It may be harder than we expected. But this is the only way to keep the princess safe from Maleficent."

Merryweather and Fauna knew Flora was right. So, one after another, they tried different things to try to get the baby to stop crying and go to sleep.

"Well," said Flora, "fairy babies are soothed by a sprig of dandelion root placed in their cradle. Let's try that!" Flora hurried out of the cottage and returned minutes later with the sprig. She laid it at the baby's feet. But the princess cried on.

"Perhaps she needs to be entertained!" suggested Fauna. Flora, Fauna, and Merryweather locked arms and danced a little jig. But baby Aurora took no notice—and kept on crying.

As the fairies fought over how to calm the baby, Flora accidentally nudged Aurora's cradle, causing it to rock gently back and forth. Soothed by the rocking, the baby's cries slowly grew softer and softer.

"Fauna!" cried Flora. "You've done it!"

"Look how much she likes the rocking!" added Merryweather.

The three fairies continued to rock the cradle gently back and forth, and soon Aurora drifted off to sleep.

"Well," Fauna whispered to the others, once the baby was sleeping soundly, "that wasn't so hard, now, was it?"

Smitten

Robin Hood straightened his hat and smoothed his whiskers. "How do I look, Little John?" he asked.

"You look like you always do," John replied with a wave of his hand. "Like a regular Casanova."

Robin grinned. "Let's hope Maid Marian agrees with you." He put a hand over his heart. "I just hope she still remembers me."

Robin Hood was nervous. Maid Marian was the cleverest and most beautiful maiden in the land. But she had been living in London for the past few years.

What if she didn't remember her childhood sweetheart?

"Get going," Little John said.

Robin nodded and set off through the forest. Soon he was outside the castle gate. He could hear voices—female voices—laughing and talking. Maybe one of them was Marian's!

Robin's heart pounded in his chest. He had to see! He looked around and spotted a large tree with branches that reached inside the castle grounds. Perfect!

Robin leaped gracefully up to the first branch, grabbed hold, and began to climb. When he was nice and high, he worked his way out onto a branch. Now he was inside the castle grounds. Robin moved a branch and leaned forward to see who was talking.

It was Marian! She was playing badminton with Lady Cluck. And she was a good shot!

"Nice one, Maid Marian," Lady Cluck said as Marian won a point.

Robin gazed down at the sight below. Maid Marian was so lovely, and so talented!

"Oops!" Marian said as the birdie sailed off the court completely.

Robin saw it fly toward his hiding place. It landed in the tree just above him! He got to his feet and reached up to retrieve it for Marian. But he lost his balance and fell just as the birdie came loose. The two landed on the ground at the same time.

"Oof!" Robin didn't mean to make an entrance like this!

"What was that?" Lady Cluck asked as Robin scrambled away, leaping over the fence.

"I do believe it was an outlaw," Maid Marian said with a smile.

A Gammy Spell

Deep in the ancient Scottish Highlands, in a kingdom called DunBroch, lived a princess called Merida. Her mother, Queen Elinor, wanted Merida to marry a son from one of the neighboring clans. But Merida didn't wish to marry. She wanted to choose her own destiny.

When the suitors came to compete for her hand, Merida decided that the challenge should be archery. Then, surprising everyone, she joined the competition and beat all the suitors!

"You don't know what you've done," the queen told Merida.

Merida was very angry. She slashed her family tapestry between the images of her and her mother. Then she fled into the woods on her horse, Angus.

Suddenly, Angus stopped. The two were inside a ring of giant stones. Strange blue lights were flickering nearby—the legendary will-o'-the-wisps! The lights seemed to beckon Merida forward, forming a chain that led deep into the forest. Merida followed the blue lights to a small cottage in the woods.

The cottage belonged to an old woman who appeared to be a wood-carver. But it didn't take long for Merida to realize the woman was actually a witch.

"I want a spell to change my mum. That will change my fate!" Merida told the woman.

The witch hesitantly agreed, throwing things into her cauldron. When the spell was done, the Witch pulled a cake out of the cauldron and handed it to Merida.

Back at the castle, Merida apologized to her mother and gave her the cake. Elinor took a bite. "Now, why don't we go upstairs to the Lords and put this whole kerfuffle to rest," Elinor said.

Just then, Elinor stumbled. She was feeling dizzy. Merida helped her mother upstairs and into bed. The next thing Merida knew, a huge shape rose up from the sheets!

"Mum, you're a bear!" Merida cried. "That scaffy witch gave me a gammy spell."

Elinor-Bear let out an angry roar. Merida had wanted to change her mother's mind, but the spell had changed Queen Elinor completely!

Merida was horrified. She had to save her mother from the witch's spell!

A Mouse in the House

Alice was a daydreamer. Once, she dreamed of a silly place called Wonderland.

When Alice awakened, her sister suggested they have some tea.

Sitting at the dining room table, Alice began to tell her sister all about Wonderland. "I know I was only dreaming," said Alice, "but it all seemed so real! I attended the strangest tea party, at which the Mad Hatter and the March Hare—they were the hosts of the party—kept offering me tea, but refused to serve me any." Alice picked up the teapot to refill her own cup. "And you won't believe it, but inside the teapot lived a little . . ."

Just then, the lid of the pot Alice was holding flew open and a little whiskered face popped out.

"Eek!" Alice yelled, slamming down the lid. Her mind raced. How could the Dormouse from her dream have crossed over into her real life?

Alice finished her tea and cookies as quickly as possible. When her sister went to pour more tea, Alice grabbed the pot away and insisted,

"I'm sorry, but there isn't any more!"

"My goodness!" Alice's sister declared. "Now you're acting like the Mad Hatter and the March Hare!"

Alice slipped outside with the teapot as soon as she could. "Maybe if I doze off again I can dream this little fellow back where he belongs," she said.

But Alice couldn't fall asleep. Finally, she lifted the lid of the pot. "I'm sorry," she told the Dormouse. "I'm not sure what else to do." But the Dormouse knew. He jumped out of the teapot—and was chased by Alice's kitten! The Dormouse ran into the stump that led to the rabbit hole of Alice's dream, but the kitten stayed behind. The inside of the stump looked too dark and scary to the little cat.

Alice waited, but the Dormouse did not come out again.

That night, as she slept, Alice dreamed of Wonderland again. She was back at the un-birthday party, waiting to be served a cup of tea. The Dormouse threw open the teapot and gave Alice a sleepy grin. "Thank you, miss!" he said. "And whatever you do, please don't dream about your cat!"

Mike Meets Sulley

Mike Wazowski had been the smallest monster at Frighton Elementary School, and the least popular. Now Mike was all grown up. He was still small and he was still unpopular, but he didn't care. He had made it to Monsters University and was about to begin studying at the best Scare Program in the world!

On the first day of classes, Mike and his roommate Randy entered the Scare School lecture hall. As their teacher, Professor Knight, was greeting them, Dean Hardscrabble swooped in. The Dean was in charge of the Scare Program.

"At the end of the semester, there will be an exam," said Hardscrabble. "Fail that and you are out of the program."

After Dean Hardscrabble left, Professor Knight asked, "Who can tell me the properties of an effective roar?"

Mike's hand shot up. He was giving his answer when an enormous "*ROAR!*" erupted from the back of the classroom.

It was James P. Sullivan—Sulley for short. Sulley was a huge blue monster, and the son of legendary Scarer Bill Sullivan.

"I expect big things from you," Professor Knight told Sulley.

After class, Mike went back to his room, but his peace was disturbed by a creature flying through his window. It was Archie the Scare Pig. Archie was the mascot of rival university Fear Tech. Sulley had stolen him!

Mike just wanted to be left alone, but Archie grabbed his lucky hat. Mike took off after him, with Sulley close behind.

Finally Mike caught the Scare Pig. Sulley scooped them both up and held them triumphantly above his head. Everyone thought Sulley was a hero!

The top club on campus, Roar Omega Roar, was impressed. They wanted Sulley to join them.

Mike tried to explain what had really happened, but the RORs wouldn't listen. Their president told Mike to go and hang out with the losers' club, the Oozma Kappas. Sulley laughed and told Mike that ROR was for Scare students who had a chance.

"My chances are as good as yours!" Mike said angrily, and he promised Sulley he would out-scare him in every way in coming year. The challenge was on!

An Excellent Cook

Tiana and her father loved to cook. One night, Tiana decided that she wanted to make dinner all by herself.

"What are you going to make for us, sweetheart?" asked her mother.

"Gumbo!" replied Tiana. This was her father's specialty. He even had an enormous pot that he kept especially for his gumbo!

Little Tiana sat perched on a stool stirring, seasoning, and tasting. "I think it's done," she announced finally.

"Okay," said James as he tasted a spoonful. "This is the *best* gumbo I've ever tasted!

"Eudora, our little girl's got a gift," James continued. "A gift this special just gotta be shared."

And so the family decided to invite their neighbors to enjoy the gumbo on the back porch. Soon the night air was filled with the sounds of clinking spoons, conversation, and laughter.

"You know, the thing about good food," said Tiana's father, "it brings folks together from all walks of life. It warms them right up and puts smiles on their faces."

When bedtime arrived, Tiana's mother and father came to tuck her in. Tiana leaned out her window and made a wish on the evening star.

"But remember," added James, "you've got to help it along with some hard work of your own." Then, thinking of the night filled with good food, family, and friends, he said, "Just never lose sight of what's really important."

Tiana looked at the picture that her father had once given her of the restaurant he wanted to open. It was her father's dream to open a restaurant in the old sugar mill, and now it was Tiana's dream, too. She was ready to work hard to achieve it—with the help of the evening star, of course.

Tiana's father gave her a kiss good night, and then left her room. As he shut the door, Tiana looked out at the evening star. "Please, please, please!" she whispered.

I will make our dream come true, Tiana promised herself as she went to sleep that night. And with that, she fell asleep peacefully, knowing she would have the courage to succeed.

The Perfect Birthday

Mother Gothel was a wicked woman. She had stolen a princess named Rapunzel when she was just a baby and kept her locked in a tower. Though she pretended to love the girl, she truly only loved Rapunzel's magical hair, which kept the woman forever young.

Being stuck in a tower didn't dampen Rapunzel's spirit. She and her friend Pascal, a chameleon, kept busy doing all sorts of things. They cooked, they sewed, they brushed and brushed Rapunzel's hair, and best of all, they painted! Rapunzel loved to paint more than anything else. But, Rapunzel still had one dream that she longed to make come true.

Every year on Rapunzel's birthday, strange lights floated up into the night sky. Rapunzel couldn't help but feel like they were especially for her. More than anything, she wanted Mother Gothel to take her to see them.

On the day before her eighteenth birthday, with Pascal urging her on, Rapunzel decided to tell Mother Gothel what she really wanted as a gift.

"I want to see the floating lights!" she blurted out, revealing a painting she had done of them.

"Oh, you mean the stars," Mother Gothel lied. She wanted Rapunzel to forget her wish.

"That's the thing," countered Rapunzel. "I've charted stars, and they're always constant. But these? They appear every year on my birthday, Mother—only on my birthday. And I can't help but feel like they're meant for me. I have to know what they are."

Mother Gothel had always said that the world outside was far too scary for a weak girl. There were ruffians, quicksand, and snakes! Now, she said, "Rapunzel, don't ever ask to leave this tower again!"

Rapunzel fell silent. She put her arms around Mother Gothel's neck and hugged her. She understood why her mother wanted to protect her.

Unseen by Rapunzel, the wicked woman gave a sly smile.

Rapunzel sighed and smiled weakly. She knew that she should have been happy with what she had. But she just couldn't give up on her dream.

Little Lost Sheep

Woody was relaxing on Andy's bed when Bo Peep came running over. "Oh, Woody! It's my sheep!" Bo cried. "I can't find them anywhere!"

"Are you sure?" asked Woody. "Where did you see them last?"

Bo explained that her sheep had been with her earlier that day, but now they were missing.

Woody put his hand on Bo's shoulder. "We won't rest until those sheep are safe with you! Right, everyone?" he called. All the toys in Andy's room shouted their agreement.

Soon the toys were searching the whole house. "Please, find them!" called Bo Peep. Then she sat down. She looked like she was about to cry.

Suddenly, the baby monitor crackled on the dresser. Andy's mother had left it in his room when she picked up the laundry that morning. The sound of Sarge's voice came from the speaker.

"This is Sarge reporting from the baby's room. There are not any sheep in here. Over and out."

"Oh, dear," said Bo. "Where could they be?"

Woody and Buzz came back into Andy's room with RC and Wheezy behind them. "Kitchen is clear," Buzz said. "No sheep there."

At that moment, the toys heard the sound of bleating sheep. Bo Peep gasped. Then she looked at the sheep more closely. "These aren't my sheep," she said.

Woody lifted a cotton ball off a little green head. It was the Aliens! They had just wanted to help.

Bo Peep thanked them, but she was still upset that her sheep were missing.

Suddenly, Hamm called out, "Andy's mother is coming!"

All the toys went limp as Andy's mom walked into the room. She placed a basket on the bed and started folding Andy's clothes. After a few minutes, she laughed. She'd found Bo Peep's sheep in her basket!

"Hey there, little guys!" she said. "I hope you enjoyed your bath." Finding Bo Peep on the shelf, she placed the sheep beside her. "I bet you missed these," she said, laughing. "Little Bo Peep has lost her sheep," she sang.

When the toys knew it was safe to move, they burst out laughing!

Float Like a Butterfly

One day, Dumbo's best friend, Timothy Q. Mouse, found Dumbo looking sad.

"What's the matter, little guy?" the mouse asked the elephant. "Have people been teasing you about your ears again?"

Dumbo nodded. The little elephant looked totally miserable.

Timothy was trying to think of a way to cheer up his dear friend when he saw something. "Look, Dumbo!" he cried, racing over to a nearby fence post. "It's a butterfly cocoon!" Timothy said excitedly.

Dumbo came over to examine it.

"And look—it's about to hatch into a butterfly," said Timothy. He looked thoughtful for a moment, and then he turned to Dumbo. "You know what? You're a lot like the little caterpillar that made this cocoon."

Dumbo looked at Timothy, confused.

"Yep, it's true. You see, a caterpillar is something nobody really wants around much. They think it's kind of plain-looking, and it can't really do anything very interesting. But then one day, the caterpillar turns into a beautiful butterfly, and everyone loves it. And you know what? I think you're going to be that way, too. When you get older, everyone is going to admire you rather than tease you!"

Dumbo smiled gratefully at his friend and wiped away a tear with one of his long ears.

Suddenly, it started to rain.

"Oh, no!" cried Timothy. "The butterfly is going to get its new wings all wet. It won't be able to fly if it gets rained on. What'll we do? We need an umbrella!"

As Timothy looked this way and that for an umbrella, Dumbo smiled and unfurled his long ears. He draped them over the fence post so that they made a lovely roof for the insect, protecting it from the falling droplets of rain.

"Great idea!" said Timothy admiringly. The two friends stood there during the downpour, which didn't last very long. While they waited, they watched the beautiful new butterfly emerge from its cocoon and unfurl its colorful wings. When the rain stopped, the butterfly spread its wings (which were quite dry, thanks to Dumbo) and flew away.

A Tiny New Friend

It had been a week since Cinderella's stepmother had forced her to move out of her bedroom and into the attic of the old house, but Cinderella was still not used to her new sleeping quarters. The only other soul around to keep Cinderella company was a skittish little mouse who she had seen scurrying in and out of a hole in the corner.

One day, at suppertime, Cinderella slipped a piece of cheese into her apron pocket. That evening, when her work was finished, Cinderella hurried up to her room and pulled out her sewing basket. She used some scraps of fabric to make a mouse-size suit of clothing: a red shirt and cap, a tiny orange coat, and two brown slippers.

Cinderella carried the clothes over to the mouse hole and knelt before it. She pulled the cheese out of her pocket and placed it, with the clothes, in the palm of her hand. Then she laid her open hand just in front of the mouse hole.

"Hello in there!" she called.

The mouse cautiously poked his head out of the hole and sniffed the air. Seeing the cheese, he inched out of the hole and over to Cinderella's hand. He paused and looked up at her.

"Go ahead," she said kindly. "They're a gift just for you."

The mouse scampered onto her palm, picked up the cheese and the clothes, and hurried back into the mouse hole.

Cinderella waited patiently for a few minutes, still kneeling in front of the hole.

"Well," she called after a short while, "let me see how they look on you!"

Timidly, the mouse came out in his new outfit. Cinderella clapped her hands.

"Perfect!" she said. "Do you like them?"

The mouse nodded. Then he jumped, as if an idea had just occurred to him and scurried back into the mouse hole. Cinderella frowned. Had she frightened him?

But her worries vanished when the mouse reappeared—along with several other mice, who followed timidly behind him.

"More friends!" Cinderella cried. She hurried to get her sewing basket, delighted to have found the warmth of friendship in the cold attic room.

Dream Tales

One morning, Snow White got up early and prepared a special breakfast for the Dwarfs—fresh cinnamon porridge!

"Good morning!" Snow White greeted the Dwarfs. "Did everyone sleep well?"

"Bike a lady," Doc replied. "Er, I mean, like a baby. What about you, Princess?"

Snow White shook her head. "I had a bad dream," she said. "I dreamed my stepmother, the wicked Queen, was coming to get me."

"Oh, no!" Happy cried. "If she's coming, you'd better hide!"

"And quick!" Grumpy added. "That Queen is trouble, mark my words!"

The other Dwarfs nodded and looked nervous. Dopey even hid under the table.

Snow White laughed. "Why are you hiding?" she exclaimed. "Why, you should know that dreams aren't real!" She smiled at the Dwarfs. "What about all of you? Did you dream about anything last night?"

Happy laughed cheerfully. "I dreamed about the things that make me happy."

"Like what?" Snow White asked.

Happy paused for a moment. "Friends and work and sunny days . . . well, gosh, I guess all sorts of things," he replied. "Just about everything makes me smile."

Just then, a butterfly flew in the window and landed on Happy's nose. The Dwarf smiled widely.

"What about you, Sneezy? Do you remember your dream?" asked Snow White.

"*Aaaa-choo!*" Sneezy sneezed. "I dreamed I kept sneezing flowers. And every time I sneezed more flowers, they made me sneeze even more," Sneezy said.

"Dopey?" Snow White said. "Did you dream about anything last night?"

Dopey shook his head, looking sheepish.

Grumpy rolled his eyes. "Of course he did," he snapped. "He dreams he's the wisest ruler ever to sit upon a throne."

"That sounds like a marvelous dream, Dopey!" Snow White said, clapping her hands.

"But what about your dream, Princess?" Bashful asked quietly. "Aren't you scared?"

"Not a bit," Snow White replied. "Remember, dreams are just make-believe. They disappear as soon as you wake up!"

"I think it's time to make this breakfast disappear," grumbled Grumpy.

And that's just what they did.

Carl and Ellie's House

After their first meeting, Carl and Ellie became best friends. Every day they met at Ellie's clubhouse to play and dream together about exploring the world.

One sunny morning, as the friends looked at Ellie's adventure book, they made an important decision. One day they would go to South America and live next to Paradise Falls.

As the years passed, Carl and Ellie's friendship grew into love. Eventually they married. They bought the little house they had played in as children and set up a home there.

One morning, Ellie decided to paint the mailbox. She had hardly given the metal its first bit of color when Carl leaned carelessly against it!

Ellie burst out laughing at the big mark left by his hand. She then pressed her own hand to the side of the box. When she lifted it off, the two prints seemed to be joining as if to hold hands.

Carl and Ellie's life together was perfect. But they still dreamed of going to Paradise Falls. To earn enough money for their journey to South America, the couple found jobs at the town zoo. Ellie looked after the animals, and Carl sold balloons to the children. When they returned home in the evening, they were pleased to get back to their pretty house.

Ellie painted a superb picture of Paradise Falls, which she stuck above the fireplace. In front of it she placed a piece of pottery and a small statue of a tropical bird. Carl added a pair of binoculars and a model airship. Then he put a jar on a table in which, every month, they put aside some money for their trip.

Unfortunately, whatever they managed to save steadily disappeared! They had to buy new tires for the car, pay for a cast for Carl, and then replace the roof of the house.

But over the years they continued to dream, enjoy themselves, and, in the evenings, dance together in their living room. Neither of them was worried. They knew that one day they'd leave their little town and live out their big adventure.

Ariel and the Sea Horse Race

"Ariel!" King Triton's voice thundered. "Why would you want to sign up for the Annual Sea Horse Race? No mermaid has ever competed in it. It's for mermen only."

Ariel raised her chin defiantly. "Mermaids ride sea horses, too, Daddy," she said. "And Stormy may be small, but he's fast."

"No, Ariel. I forbid you to enter the race!" he said. "It's too dangerous!"

Ariel moped around the racecourse all week long. Her best friend, Flounder, tried to cheer her up, but it was no use.

"That's it!" cried Ariel. "I'll pretend to be a merman!"

Ariel swam around the palace, looking for a racing uniform and helmet.

On the morning of the competition, Ariel hid with Stormy near the starting line, her tail swishing back and forth nervously. When everyone was in position, a spark shot out of the tip of King Triton's trident. The race was on!

The racers steered their sea horses through the water at breakneck speed. When they reached the coral reef, many of the more powerful sea horses could not fit through and had to swim around. But Stormy was small, and Ariel was brave. They zipped in and out of the spiky coral. It was not long before they were in the lead.

The sea horse whipped around the next turn—but this time he was going too fast! Ariel's helmet hit the coral and popped off. Her long red hair streamed out behind her. The whole kingdom could see them now. The crowd gasped as they recognized King Triton's daughter.

Ariel and Stormy crossed the finish line first! Ariel smiled broadly and waved. Then she caught sight of her father. He looked angry. Ariel nervously steered Stormy toward the royal box. There stood King Triton, holding the gleaming trophy.

"Daddy, I—" Ariel began, but she didn't finish, because King Triton hugged her tightly.

"Oh, Ariel, I'm sorry," he said. "I had forgotten how much fun racing could be. Will you forgive me?"

Ariel nodded. Then, proudly, King Triton handed his daughter—the first mermaid ever to win the Annual Sea Horse Race—her trophy.

A Change of Scenery

Dr. Sherman had left for the day when Gill called everyone together for a Tank Gang meeting.

"We need to make some changes around here," Gill began. "We've all been living in this glass box for how long now? And every day we stare at the same scenery—the same volcano, the same sunken ship, the same treasure chest and tiki hut. Well, seeing as how we can't change what's in our tank, I propose we rearrange things a little. Who's with me?"

Everyone agreed.

"All right!" said Gill. "Then how about we start with the tiki hut? Bloat, you hoist it up. Gurgle and I will help you move it. The rest of you guys tell us where you think it should go."

Gill, Bloat, and Gurgle swam over to the tiki hut. Bloat wriggled his body underneath it and blew himself up, hoisting the hut a few inches off the gravel. Meanwhile, Gill and Gurgle stationed themselves on either side of the hut and prepared to push.

"Let's try it over there," said Peach, pointing to a far corner of the tank.

With blown-up Bloat acting as a cart underneath the hut, Gill and Gurgle pushed the tiki hut into the corner.

"Oh, no," said Deb, "that's all wrong. Can we see what it looks like over there?" She pointed to the opposite corner of the tank.

So Gill, Gurgle, and Bloat worked together to move the tiki hut again.

"That's a disaster!" exclaimed Jacques.

Gill, Gurgle, and Bloat were getting worn out by all the moving. "Can we all just agree on where it should go?" said Gill. "And quickly?"

"Ooh! I know!" said Deb. "Bring it over this way." She led Gill, Gurgle, and Bloat over to a shady spot next to some plastic plants. "Put it down here," she said. So they did.

"I like it!" exclaimed Peach.

"The perfect spot," said Jacques.

"Mmm-hmm," said Bubbles.

Gill stepped back and looked around. "Guys, this is where it was in the first place!"

Deb giggled. "Well, no wonder it just seems to fit here!"

The other fish nodded—except for Gill, who sighed in frustration. And that was the end of the tank redecoration for the evening.

JANUARY
30

Tink's Trinkets

Tinker Bell wanted to visit the mainland. But tinker-talent fairies were not allowed to help change the seasons. So Tinker Bell decided to change her talent. She was sure she could learn to be a nature fairy! Tink's friends weren't so sure it was a good idea, but they agreed to help, anyway.

Fawn, one of the animal fairies, tried to show Tink how to teach baby birds to fly. But Tink's baby bird seemed terrified. Silvermist tried to teach Tink how to hang dewdrops on a spiderweb, but the droplets kept popping. Iridessa tried to teach her how to light fireflies, but instead Tink lit herself!

Desperate, Tink went to visit the only fairy she thought might be able to help—Vidia.

But Vidia was in a bad mood. She suggested that Tinker Bell prove she was a garden fairy by capturing the Sprinting Thistles. Tink knew this was her last chance to get to go to the mainland. She tried hard to herd the thistles, but Vidia blew open the corral gate and set them free again. It was a stampede! The Thistles trampled over the carefully organized springtime supplies, ruining months of work. Tink was devastated!

When Queen Clarion saw the mess, she scolded Tinker Bell. Springtime was ruined, and it was all Tink's fault. Tink decided to leave Pixie Hollow. But she couldn't go without one last visit to her workshop.

At the workshop, Tink noticed some trinkets she had found on her first day in Pixie Hollow. Suddenly, she had an idea. . . .

That night, Tink showed the Queen the speedy machines she had created to fix what the Thistles had trampled.

Vidia was furious!

When Queen Clarion realized that the fast-flying fairy was really the one responsible for the mess, she sent Vidia to capture the Thistles. The other fairies worked all night using Tink's machines. By morning, the fairies had more springtime supplies than they had ever seen.

"You did it, Tinker Bell," Queen Clarion told the little fairy.

"We all did it," Tink replied happily. She had finally realized that talent *was* important after all!

Of Mice and Rice

"Cinderella! Help!" shrieked Drizella.

Cinderella dropped the broom she was holding and rushed down the hallway. "What is it, stepsisters?" she called.

"We're stuck!" yelled Anastasia.

Cinderella hurried to the parlor. She barely managed to suppress a giggle at what she saw. Her two stepsisters were stuck in the doorway, so hasty had they both been to leave the room first. With a bit of tugging and pulling, Cinderella managed to get the sisters unwedged.

Smiling to herself, she headed back to the kitchen.

"*Meeeeeowww!*" came a cry.

"What on earth . . . ?" said Cinderella. She hurried into the kitchen. Lucifer the cat was howling at the top of his lungs.

"What's the matter, Lucifer?" she said, running over to the fat feline. "Oh, you silly thing. You've gotten yourself stuck, too!" Cinderella laughed and tugged him out of the mouse hole he had wedged his paw into. With a haughty look at Cinderella, the cat strode away.

Cinderella peeked into the tiny mouse hole. The mice crept cautiously forward.

"You little dears," Cinderella said softly. "Why, you're all shaken up! Well, do you know what I do when I feel sad or afraid? I find happiness in my dreams." She picked up her broom. "You see this broom? I like to pretend it's a handsome prince and the two of us are dancing together!"

Suddenly the mice dashed for their hole—someone was coming! It was Cinderella's stepsisters.

"What on earth are you doing, Cinderella?" asked Drizella.

"I was just, uh, sweeping," Cinderella replied quietly, blushing.

"Well, you looked as though you were having too much fun doing it!" snapped Anastasia.

Then a nasty smile appeared on her face. Picking up a bowl of rice from the table, she dumped it onto the floor.

"Perhaps you need something else to sweep!" she said, and with a mean laugh, the two sisters left.

Cinderella's mouse friends rushed out and began to pick up the grains of rice. Cinderella smiled. "You know," she said, "I think we'll be just fine if we all look out for one another."

Chaos in the Kitchen

"Now, now, dearie," said Aunt Flora to little Aurora, "it's time for your nap." Flora had just given the baby her bottle and settled her in her cradle.

"Time to make supper!" Flora said to Fauna and Merryweather, turning away from the snoozing baby princess and clapping her hands together purposefully.

The three fairies gave each other uneasy grins. It was the first meal they had to prepare in the little cottage in the woods, where they would live until Aurora's sixteenth birthday.

In order to keep Aurora well hidden, the three fairies had vowed to give up their magic wands and live as ordinary humans. But none of them had ever cooked, cleaned, or cared for a baby before. This was going to be quite an adventure!

"I shall cook a stew," said Merryweather. The others thought that was a wonderful idea. Stew sounded hearty and delicious. What a cozy meal for their first night in the cottage!

"I'll bake some blueberry biscuits and mash the potatoes!" said Flora.

"Are you sure you know how?" asked Fauna.

"How hard could it be?" said Flora. "Fauna, why don't you make a salad to go with Merryweather's stew?"

"I'll try!" said Fauna brightly.

Soon Merryweather was chopping meat and vegetables, Flora was mixing flour and water, and Fauna was slicing and dicing the salad vegetables.

An hour later, dinner still wasn't ready. Merryweather's stew smelled like old boots. Flora opened the oven and pulled out her biscuits, which were as flat as pancakes. The mashed potatoes were terribly lumpy. And somehow most of the salad greens had ended up on the floor.

The three fairies looked at one another in dismay. "Back to the drawing board, girls," said Flora. "But let's not be too hard on ourselves— after all, we've got sixteen years to learn how to cook without magic!"

"And that's how long it's going to take!" replied Fauna.

Merryweather laughed. Fauna was obviously joking—wasn't she?

Ariel's Big Rescue

The news was traveling through the undersea world—a human ship had been spotted not too far away.

Ariel was thrilled as she swam to the surface. A captain stood at the bow. On the deck stood a girl who looked like a princess. Suddenly, the ship lurched, causing everyone aboard to stumble and fall. The sailors began scrambling about and shouting. A few minutes later, the captain approached the girl.

"Princess, I'm afraid I have some bad news," Ariel heard him say. "Our ship has hit a reef and sprung a leak. We're close enough to shore that we can make it, but I'm afraid we will have to toss items overboard to lighten the load."

Ariel and Flounder quickly ducked below the surface. "Maybe we can help," Ariel said. The two friends went under the ship and discovered a large hole. Water was rushing into the ship!

"Quick, Flounder!" Ariel said. "Gather all the seaweed you can! We'll stuff it into the hole. It may give them time to get to shore!"

Soon Ariel and Flounder had plugged the hole. The two friends swam beside the ship as it started moving toward land.

"Woo-hoo!" cried Flounder when the ship finally reached the shore. "We did it!"

Relieved, Ariel took one last look at the ship and turned for home. As she swam, she saw a trunk on the ocean floor, overflowing with human clothes.

"Flounder, this must be the princess's trunk!" she exclaimed. Ariel pulled out a long, blue gown. "I've never seen anything so beautiful!" she exclaimed. Carefully, she held it up and smiled.

"Gee, Ariel, you look almost . . . human," Flounder said.

"I know." Ariel sighed. "Isn't it wonderful?"

Then she stopped. "I should really return them to the princess," Ariel said.

"Oh, no!" Flounder replied. "We're not going anywhere near those humans."

But that night, with Flounder by her side, Ariel took the trunk close enough to shore for the tide to wash it up on the beach.

"Maybe someday I'll be able to walk onshore and wear dresses just like hers," Ariel said dreamily. "I'll be a human princess, too."

The Bake Sale

Minnie looked around the Clubhouse and smiled at her friends. "We'd better start baking my cranberry-oatmeal cookies!" she said. "We promised to make a lot of them for today's bake sale."

Minnie's friends nodded and helped her gather ingredients. Then they put on their chefs' hats and aprons. Finally they were ready to bake!

Minnie was so happy to be baking her favorite cookies! She called for ingredients very quickly. "Flour! Sugar! Eggs!" she shouted. "Baking cookies involves a lot of counting and measuring. We are going to make double batches to speed things up. So, Daisy, you need to break four eggs into that bowl. Goofy, you can measure out the oatmeal, flour, and other dry ingredients," said Minnie.

Goofy carefully measured sugar, salt, baking powder, and flour. A tiny speck of flour landed on his nose.

"ACHOO!" Goofy sneezed. The flour went everywhere!

"Gawrsh," said Goofy. "I guess both flowers and flour make me sneeze. I'm sorry, Minnie."

"That's okay, Goofy," said Minnie. "But we have to start again." She tied a towel over Goofy's nose so he wouldn't sneeze. Then they got new dry ingredients and measured them out again.

When all the ingredients were ready, they quickly mixed the dough. Then they scooped the dough for each cookie onto a baking sheet.

"We need to bake the cookies for a little more than twelve minutes," said Minnie. "But I don't have a timer. I exercise for twelve minutes every day. Why don't we all do that while the cookies bake?"

"That's a great idea, Minnie," said Mickey.

Minnie popped the trays into the oven. Then, for the next twelve minutes, she led everyone in sit-ups and jogging in place.

"This is fun!" said Daisy.

"Yeah," said Donald, "and it's probably a good idea to get some exercise if we're going to a bake sale!"

When they finished Minnie's workout, everyone went back to the kitchen. The smell of freshly baked cookies filled the air.

"Let's each have one," said Minnie.

Mickey bit into his cookie. "These are the best cookies ever!" he said.

Snow Day

One cold February day, Belle sat at the window watching the snowflakes swirl outside. She had agreed to stay in the Beast's enchanted castle in exchange for her father's freedom. She knew the Beast tried to be kind to her, but he was gruff and had such a terrible temper.

Suddenly, she jumped. The Beast had appeared, trudging through the snow beneath her window. She thought she saw him glance up at her, but she wasn't certain.

"What on earth is he doing?" she asked out loud. She watched him scoop up an armful of snow and try to form it into a ball, but it fell apart, spraying snow right in his face. Belle giggled to herself. "Why, I think he's trying to build a snowman!" she cried. "But he has no idea how to begin!"

The Beast made a smaller snowball. This one managed to hold together, and he began pushing it around the courtyard. It grew bigger and bigger. Soon it was so big that even the strong Beast could hardly move it. Belle watched as he suddenly fell over the top of the snowball, his enormous feet kicking vainly in the air. At this, Belle let out a peal of laughter. It was the first time she had laughed since she had arrived in this dreary old castle.

A few of the servants heard Belle's laughter and ventured into the hallway outside her room.

"Do you suppose she is starting to like him?" Mrs. Potts whispered to Lumiere.

"I don't know!" he whispered back. "I hardly dare to hope! But just in case, I must arrange for another romantic dinner for two this evening!"

Belle watched the Beast slowly climb to his feet. Scowling, he began to roll another snowball. This time, he slipped on some ice and fell flat on his back.

With another laugh of delight, Belle jumped to her feet and threw on her coat. She raced out of her room and hurried outside to join the Beast. Soon she was showing the Beast how to make a snow angel.

The servants all ran to the window to watch the two new friends play in the snow together. Maybe, just maybe, something good was about to happen!

Elinor-Bear

Merida was a princess. Her mother, Queen Elinor, wanted Merida to marry a neighboring clansman in order to keep peace in the land. But Merida wasn't ready to marry. She wanted to have her own adventures!

Angry at her mother, Merida slashed her family tapestry, tearing it in half. Then she fled the castle to clear her head. Deep in the forest, Merida met a witch, who gave her a magic cake. Merida thought the spell would change her mother's mind about the marriage, but instead it turned her into a bear!

Merida knew that she and her mother had to find the witch. While Merida's three little brothers distracted King Fergus and the clan lords, Merida and Elinor-Bear snuck out through the kitchen. "I'll be back soon," Merida told the triplets.

Merida and Elinor-Bear found the witch's cottage, but it was empty. Only a message remained: "Fate be changed, look inside, mend the bond torn by pride."

Suddenly, a cloud surrounded Elinor and Merida. When it cleared, the cottage was in ruins.

That night, the two slept in the ruins of the witch's cottage. In the morning, they were hungry. Merida caught a fish for breakfast. But Elinor was used to being a queen, and queens have manners, so she refused to eat the fish until it was cooked.

Elinor's manners did not last long. She was too hungry. Soon she was catching fish on her own! Merida and her mother played together in the stream. For the first time in a long while, they enjoyed each other's company. This strange adventure was bringing them closer together.

Then, suddenly, Elinor's eyes turned cold. She sniffed at Merida as if she didn't recognize her. Merida screamed. What had happened to her mother? Then, just as suddenly, the warmth returned to the bear's eyes.

"You changed," Merida told her mother. "Like you were a bear on the inside."

Merida and Elinor were worried. What if Elinor was stuck as a bear for good? Suddenly, their argument didn't seem to matter as much as it did before. They had to save Elinor before it was too late.

Carl's Promise

Carl and Ellie had been best friends since they were young children. As the two grew up, they got married and dreamed of becoming explorers. The years went by, and Carl and Ellie grew older. After Ellie passed away, Carl kept all her things just as they had been, but it wasn't the same. He missed Ellie. To make matters worse, the neighborhood around their beloved home was being torn down to make room for tall, modern buildings.

One day, Carl heard a knock at his door. A boy in a uniform was standing on his porch.

"Good afternoon," said the boy. "My name is Russell, and I am a Wilderness Explorer. Are you in need of any assistance today, sir?"

"No," replied Carl. He didn't want help. He just wanted to be left alone.

But Russell wouldn't leave. He wanted to help Carl so that he could earn his Assisting the Elderly badge. "If I get it, I will become a Senior Wilderness Explorer," Russell explained.

To get rid of Russell, Carl gave him a task. He asked him to find a bird called a snipe. "I think its burrow is two blocks down," Carl said.

Russell eagerly set off to find the bird, not knowing that it didn't really exist. Carl had made the whole thing up!

Not long after that, Carl received some bad news. He was being forced to move out of his house and live in a retirement home. But Carl didn't want to leave his house. All his memories of Ellie were there.

That night, Carl sat in his living room, looking through Ellie's adventure book. He remembered Ellie's dream of going to South America. He had promised her he'd take her there in an airship.

The next morning, two nurses arrived to drive Carl to the retirement home. "I'll meet you at the van," he told them. "I want to say one last good-bye to the old place."

As the nurses walked back to their van, a huge shadow fell over them. They turned to see thousands of balloons tied to Carl's house!

A moment later, the whole house rose into the air!

"So long, boys!" Carl yelled out of the window. He was going to South America!

A Good Team

Mulan could hardly believe she was riding through the woods on her way to join the Emperor's army. But what else could she do? If she didn't take his place, her elderly father would be forced to fight against the Huns.

"It will be all right," she told her horse, Khan. "This is the right thing to do."

The horse snorted. For a second, Mulan thought he was answering her. Then he stopped short, almost sending Mulan tumbling.

"Hey," she said. "What are you doing?"

She kicked at his sides. Instead of moving forward, the mighty warhorse backed up a few steps, his massive body shaking fearfully.

Mulan looked ahead. Just a few yards away, a deep, shadowy ditch crossed the trail.

"Is that what you're afraid of?" Mulan asked the horse. "Don't be silly. It's just a small ditch—step over it, you big chicken."

She kicked again. Still the horse refused to go. He just danced nervously in place.

"Come on!" Mulan shouted impatiently. "You're being ridiculous!"

She kicked him. She slapped him on the neck with her hands. She even grabbed a thin branch from a nearby tree and smacked his hindquarters. But the horse wouldn't take even one step forward.

Mulan didn't know what else to try. She collapsed onto Khan's neck, feeling hopeless. "Now what?" she said.

She didn't seem to have much choice. Sliding down from the horse's back, she walked toward the ditch. To her surprise, Khan followed her.

Mulan gasped. Could it be? Could the big, bold, strong warhorse really be trusting her to lead him over the scary ditch?

"Come on," she said, reaching for his bridle. The horse allowed her to lead him forward. A few more steps and he was standing at the edge of the ditch.

"The last step is the big one," Mulan warned.

Holding the reins, she hopped over the ditch. For a moment, she was afraid he wouldn't follow. Then he jumped. Mulan was yanked forward as Khan landed ten feet past the ditch.

"Good boy." Mulan patted the horse. "I think we might just make a good team after all."

Thrown Out

Mike Wazowski was determined to do well at Monsters University. He had dreamed of becoming a Scarer his whole life, and he was willing to do whatever it took to make his dream come true.

Mike worked harder than anybody else. He read every book he could find on scaring. He practiced making frightening faces in the mirror and studied every Scare technique. His competition, James Sullivan, hardly worked at all. Johnny Worthington, the president of the ROR fraternity, told Sulley that if his grades didn't improve, he would be kicked out of ROR.

On the day of the Scare final exam, Professor Knight explained that each student would enter the scare simulator and perform a Scare on a robot child. Dean Hardscrabble would then decide who would move on in the Scare Program.

While they were waiting, Mike and Sulley began to fight. Before they knew it, they were in a Scare-off. Suddenly, Sulley stumbled into Dean Hardscrabble's record-breaking scream can, knocking it to the floor. The can flew around the room, releasing the scream as it went.

"It was an accident!" Sulley insisted.

Dean Hardscrabble remained calm, but when Mike and Sulley finished their exams, she announced that neither of them would be continuing in the Scare Program.

Mike begged for another chance, but Dean Hardscrabble's decision was final. Mike and Sulley were enrolled in the Scream Can Design Program instead.

"Some say a career as a Scream Can Designer is boring, unchallenging, and a waste of a monster's potential," droned Professor Brandywine.

Mike and Sulley agreed. They had to find a way back into the Scare Program.

Back in his dorm room, Mike threw a book against the wall in frustration. His calendar fell down, revealing a Scare Games flyer. Mike thought back to the day he had been given the flyer.

"It's a super-intense scaring competition where you get a chance to prove you're the best!" a monster had told him.

Mike smiled and grabbed the flyer. The Scare Games were the answer to his problems!

A Tiny Tale

One day, Alice was sitting in the garden, listening to her older sister read a book out loud. As her sister's voice droned on, Alice's mind wandered. She watched a little inchworm climb a blade of grass, its tiny body scrunching and straightening as it moved up the leaf. "What must it be like to be as tiny as that?" Alice wondered to herself.

The next thing she knew, she was that tiny! In an instant, the garden had grown higher and higher until the grass towered over her head, as tall as trees. The inchworm, now half as long as Alice was, waggled its antennae at her and continued its climb.

"Oh, my!" cried Alice. "I must get back to the house. If I don't start out now, I shall never be back in time for tea!"

The garden path, which formerly had seemed to slope ever so gently, now appeared as a mountain in front of her, and the house was not even visible. Suddenly Alice felt herself upended, traveling feetfirst up the path. She looked down and gasped. Three ants were carrying her on their backs!

"Put me down at once!" she said to them crossly, but the ants took no notice of her. With a quick twist of her body, she managed to tumble to the ground. The ants appeared not to realize that their load had vanished, and continued up the hill.

"Well, at any rate I am now a good deal closer to home," said Alice, gazing up at her house. She found herself standing at the edge of a huge puddle. Just then a large leaf blew off a tree and landed in the puddle directly in front of her. She stepped onto the leaf and let the breeze blow her across.

But as she reached the edge of the puddle, a huge bird swooped down and plucked her up by the sleeve of her dress. "Oh, bother. Now I shall never get home for tea," she said.

The next thing she knew, her sister was plucking her sleeve. "Wake up, Alice!" With an exasperated sigh, her sister stood up. "We may as well end the lesson for the day, as it's time to go in and have our tea."

Enormously relieved to be her usual size again, Alice followed her sister up the garden path and into the house.

Pesky Princess

Jasmine's father, the Sultan, was growing impatient. "My dearest daughter," he pleaded, "the law states that you should be married before your sixteenth birthday, and that is coming up soon. Must you be so picky? There are many princes who would love to marry you."

Jasmine sighed. "I promise to try, Father," she said.

The next day, Prince Sultana arrived. "I know you will be pleased to hear that I have selected you as my bride," he told the princess. "Shall we discuss our wedding?"

Jasmine tried to hide her distaste for the prince. "I was just about to take my pet for a little walk around the palace," she said. "He needs his exercise, you see. Why don't we discuss it while we walk him?"

The prince readily agreed.

With a sly smile, Jasmine whistled. Out bounded her pet tiger, Rajah. When he gave a snarl of welcome, the prince ran away.

The next day, another suitor arrived with a group of servants in tow.

"Announcing . . . Prince Habibi!" the footman called out.

Jasmine poked her head out of her bedroom window and called down, "Hi! Sorry, I can't come down. The, uh, stairs are being polished. Do you mind taking my laundry to the Royal cleaners? Catch!"

Prince Habibi stood below the tower, arms outstretched. *Boom!* A big laundry bag knocked him flat. "Harumph!" he cried, and off he went.

The next day, Prince Baklava arrived. "The princess is at the royal pond, sire," the footman said. When Prince Baklava reached the pond, he saw Jasmine reading a book on a little island. All around her, huge hungry-looking alligators waited in the water.

"Hello!" Jasmine called to him. "Would you mind coming out to fetch me?"

Prince Baklava stared at Jasmine and then at the alligators. Then, with a shriek of terror, he turned and ran.

Jasmine giggled and stood up. Then the princess stepped daintily across the pond on the backs of the alligators. "Thanks, guys," she said with a wink as she headed back to the palace.

Homesick

Nemo still couldn't believe everything that had happened to him. First, he'd been snatched up by a scuba diver in the ocean. Then he'd traveled a long way in a big water cooler. Finally, he'd been dumped in a fish tank in a dentist's office.

"Hey, kid," Bloat the blowfish said. "Are you okay? You look a little down in the gills."

"I'll say," said Nigel the seagull.

Peach the starfish glanced over from her spot on the tank wall. "He's just upset," she said. "It's only natural." She smiled kindly at Nemo. "It's okay, hon. We know how you feel."

"How could you know?" he muttered, feeling sorry for himself. "You weren't grabbed out of the ocean, away from your dad."

"Well, no," a fish named Gurgle admitted. "But we all had families back where we came from. We all miss them."

"Really?" Nemo blinked in surprise. He hadn't thought about that.

"Sure," Peach said. "The lady who sold me over the Internet kept lots of us starfish in her basement." She sighed sadly. "I still wonder where all my brothers and sisters ended up."

"I hear you," Bloat agreed. "I was hatched in somebody's garage. They sold me and a whole school of my brothers and sisters and cousins to Bob's Fish Mart. Just when we made friends with the other fish there, he came in and bought me." He waved a fin toward the dentist in the office outside the tank.

A fish named Deb nodded. "I'm lucky he bought me and my sister together. Right, Flo?" She smiled at her own reflection in the glass of the tank. When the reflection didn't answer, Deb shrugged. "I guess Flo is too choked up to talk right now. But I can tell by her smile that she agrees. We don't know what we'd do without each other. But we still miss the rest of our family."

"Wow," Nemo said, looking around at his new tankmates. "I guess you guys *do* know how I feel."

Even though he was sad that the other fish had been taken from their families, too, it made Nemo feel a little less alone. At least they understood how much he wanted to find his way back to his father. Now, a little braver and more determined than ever, Nemo was ready to escape from the tank—no matter what.

Wendy's Music Box

Tinker Bell had been trying to learn a new fairy-talent since she had arrived in Pixie Hollow. She wanted to visit the mainland, but tinker fairies did not go there. Tink tried to be an animal fairy, a light fairy, a water fairy, and a nature fairy. But she was not good at any other talent.

Tinker Bell sat on the beach. "Great," she muttered. "At this rate, I should get to the mainland right about, oh, never!"

Tinker Bell threw a pebble and heard a strange *clunk*! When she went to investigate, she found a broken porcelain box. Soon Tinker Bell was busily putting her discovery back together. The final touch was a lovely ballerina that fit into the lid. Tinker Bell gave the dancer a spin. To her delight, the box played music!

"Don't you even realize what you're doing?" asked Rosetta when she saw Tink fixing the box. "That's tinkering!"

"Who cares about going to the mainland anyway?" Silvermist added.

Later that day, as Tink used her talent to help the fairies make extra springtime supplies, she finally realized that her friends were right. Her talent

was important!

"Queen Clarion," said Silvermist. "Can't Tink come with us to the mainland?"

"It's okay," Tink protested. "My work is here. And I still have so much to do."

But Fairy Mary had other ideas. "Not here, you don't!" she said. She gave a little whistle, and Clank and Bobble brought out Tink's music box. It was all polished and shiny. "I'd imagine there's a little girl out there who's missing this. Perhaps a certain tinker fairy has a job to do after all . . . on the mainland," Fairy Mary continued.

And so Tinker Bell traveled to the mainland with the nature fairies.

Tink found the home where the music box belonged and tapped on the windowpane. A little girl named Wendy Darling poked her head out of the window. Tink watched from her hiding place as Wendy's face filled with happiness at the discovery of her long-lost treasure on the windowsill.

Watching the girl, Tink couldn't wait to get home. She had lots of tinkering to do!

Eeyore's New Old House

One blustery February day in the Hundred-Acre Wood, the wind blew so strongly that it knocked Eeyore's house right over! So Eeyore went to Pooh's house.

"Well, Pooh," Eeyore said, "it seems that February just doesn't like me. Or my house. So I'm afraid I will have to stay here with you. If you don't mind, that is."

Pooh assured Eeyore that he didn't mind and offered him some honey.

"I'd prefer thistles, if you have any, which you probably don't," Eeyore said. "Oh well. Perhaps Rabbit has some."

Rabbit did have some thistles, so Eeyore settled down to stay with Rabbit. But Rabbit's house was so full of vegetables and gardening tools that there was scarcely room in the burrow for Eeyore.

"I suppose Piglet may have more room, though I doubt it," said Eeyore.

Piglet told Eeyore he was welcome to stay with him, and even made Eeyore a little bed next to the pantry, which was full of haycorns. But Eeyore was allergic to haycorns, and soon his sneezing almost knocked Piglet's own house down.

"One house knocked down today is more than—*ah-choo!*— enough," said Eeyore. "I'll just have to try Kanga and Roo."

But Kanga and Roo's house wasn't quite right, either. Eeyore was about to try Owl's house when his friends showed up.

"Eeyore, we've found you the perfect house to live in!" Piglet cried.

"I doubt that," Eeyore said as they led him through the Wood. "The perfect house would have thistles, and enough room, and no haycorns. But where am I going to find a house like that?"

Soon they arrived at a snug little house made of sticks with a pile of thistles in it. "Here it is, Eeyore," said Piglet.

"That's *my* house," said Eeyore, hardly able to believe his eyes. "But my house got knocked down."

"Piglet and I put it back together again," Pooh said.

Eeyore looked at his house and then at his friends. "It looks like February doesn't dislike me so much after all," he told them. "Maybe, that is."

Happy Valentine's Day

"Whatcha doin', Doc?" Happy asked.

Doc was hard at work carving a heart out of a piece of wood. "I'm making a present for Snow White," he replied.

"A present for Snow White?" Happy exclaimed. "Oh, dear! Did I miss her birthday?"

"No, silly," Doc said. "It's Valentine's Day."

"Valentine's Day?" Happy turned to Dopey. "Have you ever heard of Valentine's Day?"

Dopey shook his head.

Doc cleared his throat. "Valentine's Day," he began, "is a very special day that gives people the opportunity to let loved ones know how important they are."

"I'm giving Snow White these handkerchiefs," Sneezy said as he sneezed into one of them. "Well, maybe not *this* one."

"That's very thoughtful," Doc answered. "I'm sure she'll be able to use them."

"If he has any left," Grumpy said.

Then Bashful shyly held out a paper flower he had made.

"Wonderful! And you?" Doc asked Dopey.

Dopey held up a paper airplane he'd just made for Snow White.

"You know what I'm going to do? I'm going to juggle for Snow White for Valentine's Day," Happy said, gathering several apples.

"She'll love that!" Doc said.

Sleepy yawned as he held up a pretty card he'd made.

"And you?" Doc asked Grumpy.

"Well, all right," Grumpy confessed. "I wrote Snow White a poem."

Just then, there was a knock on the door to the cottage. Snow White had arrived!

"Happy Valentine's Day!" the Seven Dwarfs sang, each holding up his gift for Snow White to see.

"What a wonderful surprise!" Snow White exclaimed, giving the Dwarfs the valentines she had brought for *them*, and placing a kiss on each of their cheeks.

The Dwarfs looked at their Valentines. They thought they were the most beautiful valentines they had ever seen. And for once, even Grumpy was pleased.

Bedtime for Gus

Cinderella looked out of her bedroom window as the sun was setting. The clock in the tower of the castle struck eight. Cinderella tapped gently on the walls of her attic room.

"Bedtime, everyone!" she called. Jaq, Suzy, Gus, and the other mice hurried out of their mouse hole.

"Buh-buh-bedtime?" Gus asked. Gus was Cinderella's newest mouse friend. She had just rescued him from a trap that morning.

"Close eyes and fall asleep!" Suzy explained.

Gus looked confused. He closed his eyes and started to tip over. Jaq caught him.

"Not *fall*, Gus-Gus," he said. "Fall asleep. Like this." He put his head on his hands and pretended to snore softly.

Cinderella laughed. "Gus has never lived in a house before. We'll have to teach him about getting ready for bed.

"First, you put on your pajamas." She went to her dresser and pulled out a tiny pair of striped pajamas for Gus.

"Now sleep, Cinderella?" Gus asked.

Cinderella smiled. "Not quite yet," she said. "Now you need to wash your face and brush your teeth. Then I'll kiss you good night, and Suzy will tuck everyone in."

When the mice were all neat and clean, Cinderella kissed each of them good night. "It's time for everyone to go to sleep," she said sweetly.

"Follow me," Jaq told Gus. He ran over to his little bed and hopped in. Then he pointed to the bed next to him. "That's your bed," he said.

Gus grinned and got under the cozy covers.

"Story, Cinderella!" someone cried.

Cinderella smiled. "All right," she said. "Once upon a time, there was a young prince who lived in a castle . . ." She continued the story for a long time. Each time she tried to stop, the mice begged for more. But after a while, they couldn't keep their eyes open any longer.

When the last mouse had fallen asleep, Cinderella tiptoed to her own bed and climbed in. She snuggled against her pillow and yawned. "If only some of my stories would come true. . . ."

Bagheera Bears Up

Mowgli danced around the jungle humming happily to himself.

"What are you doing, Mowgli?" Bagheera asked from his perch in a nearby tree.

"Practicing being a bear," Mowgli told him. "You should try it."

"Well, I'm a panther and I happen to like being one," Bagheera replied. "Why on earth would I want to be a bear?"

"Are you kidding?" Mowgli exclaimed. "Bears have the life! They hang out all day long and they eat ants!"

"Eat ants?" Bagheera asked. "And that's a good thing?"

"Sure!" Mowgli said. "Well, truthfully, they tickle your throat at first. But you get used to it soon enough."

"Have you?" Bagheera asked.

"Not yet," Mowgli confessed. "But I will!"

Mowgli thought for a moment. "And if you were a bear, you would eat fruit and drink coconut juice and you would relax, just like us!"

"If you ask me," Bagheera said, "I don't see anything so bad about being a panther. In fact, I like it very much."

"I think you're scared," Mowgli said.

"Absolutely not!" Bagheera protested. "What on earth would I have to be scared of?" He gracefully jumped out of the tree and onto the ground.

"Exactly," Mowgli said. "So why not try it?"

"You've got to be kidding me!" Bagheera said.

"You know what your problem is?" said Mowgli.

"I'm afraid to ask," Bagheera replied.

"You're like a beehive," Mowgli told him. "You work too hard. Come on, dance with me!" he cried, grabbing Bagheera's paw and prancing around. After a bit, Bagheera began to dance, too.

"Look at that!" said Baloo, joining his friends.

"You know what?" Bagheera admitted. "This isn't so bad after all."

"Now you're getting it!" Mowgli exclaimed. "Now you see why being a bear is so great!" The Man-cub stopped dancing and threw himself on a soft patch of moss. "It's not so bad, is it?"

"Actually," Bagheera said, scratching his back against a rock, "it's sort of fun!"

And with that, he and Baloo danced away.

Flynn Rider

Flynn Rider lowered himself carefully into the throne room. Beneath him was the lost princess's crown.

But Flynn was not alone. With him were his two partners in crime, the Stabbington brothers. Flynn tossed the crown into a satchel, and the three took off running through the forest.

The thieves hoped to get away quickly, but the theft of the princess's crown had not gone unnoticed. The royal guards chased after Flynn and his partners, determined to capture them and throw them in jail.

Suddenly, Flynn stopped in front of a WANTED poster. It had a picture of him on it.

Flynn was not happy to see his picture on the poster. They had gotten his nose all wrong!

Suddenly the royal guards appeared at the top of the hill. The thieves ran off as fast as they could, but soon found themselves trapped in a dead end, up against a stone wall! There was only one way out—to climb over the top. Flynn turned to his accomplices.

"Give me a boost, and I'll pull you up," he said.

But the Stabbingtons didn't trust him. They shook their heads. "Give us the satchel first," they demanded, reaching for the bag.

Flynn pretended to get angry. "I can't believe after all we've been through together you don't trust me," he said. Flynn handed them the satchel, and the Stabbington brothers quickly boosted him up and over the wall.

But when they asked Flynn to help them climb up, he just burst out laughing. "Sorry. My hands are full." He waved the satchel that contained the crown in the air.

The Stabbingtons were furious. Flynn had managed to get ahold of the crown without them seeing! He jumped off the wall, leaving the Stabbington brothers behind.

But Flynn had not left the royal guard behind. They were already hot on his heels. At the front of the pack were the captain of the guard and his horse, Maximus.

How was Flynn going to escape capture now?

Happy to Help

Dumbo was walking toward his train car, looking forward to a long nap, when suddenly he heard someone shout, "Oh, no! My beautiful balloons!"

Dumbo looked up. A bunch of colorful balloons were drifting away from a balloon seller. The elephant quickly sprang into action. He flew after the balloons, grabbed the strings with his trunk, and flew back to the ground.

"You're the best!" the balloon seller said.

Happy to have helped, Dumbo continued to make his way toward his train car to take his overdue nap. As he walked, he saw a crowd gathering. Using his trunk, he politely nudged his way in to see what was going on. A little girl stood crying in the middle of the crowd.

"I think the poor kid is lost," said a magician. "We must help her. But how?"

Dumbo walked over and tapped the girl on the shoulder with his trunk.

"Great idea, Dumbo!" said the juggler. "You could spot the little girl's mom from above!"

He picked up the girl and put her on the elephant's back. Dumbo and the little girl flew up above the circus tents. They looked down at the crowds of people.

"Mommy! There's my mommy!" the girl shouted.

Dumbo landed gently. The girl climbed off his back and ran into her mother's arms.

"Thank you, Dumbo! Thank you!" said the girl's mother.

Dumbo was glad to have been able to help.

Suddenly, a pie went whizzing by!

Dumbo turned to see some circus clowns throwing pink cream pies at one another. They were covered from head to toe!

"What a mess!" said one of the clowns.

"I think it's time for a shower," said another.

Dumbo had an idea! He flew over to the water tank and filled his trunk. Then he sprayed water all over the clowns! The clowns laughed as Dumbo rinsed away the gooey pink pie. Then, smiling, Dumbo went off to finally take his long-awaited nap!

Love Letters

"Ahhh," Ariel sighed dreamily. "Oh, no," Sebastian fretted. "A sigh like that can only mean one thing."

"What?" said Flounder.

"She's obviously writing love poetry for that human she can't stop talking about," Sebastian said.

Ariel was hard at work writing in her seaweed notebook. "How do I love thee . . ." she said out loud.

"Oh, yuck!" Flounder exclaimed.

"You're telling me," Sebastian agreed. "Terribly trite and overused."

"What would you write?" Ariel asked.

"Me? Well, this is just off the top of my head." Sebastian ceremoniously cleared his throat. "But I would write something like, 'Oh, crabby crab, oh, crab of my heart, my crabbiest crab, may our claws never part!'"

"Double yuck!" Flounder exclaimed again.

"What do you know?" Sebastian snapped.

"But he's a total stranger!" Flounder cried, turning back to Ariel.

"What's that supposed to mean?" Now Ariel was offended.

"How can you be in love with someone you don't even know?" Sebastian asked.

"I know him," Ariel protested. "Besides, haven't you ever heard of love at first sight?"

"Flounder is right," Sebastian interrupted. "This human doesn't even know you exist!"

"You don't know that!" Ariel cried, and she went back to work on her poem.

Finally, when she had finished, she cleared her throat dramatically. "How's this sound?" she asked Sebastian and Flounder, and began reading: "'I'm always thinking of you, it sets my heart atwitter. But I'm also easily distracted—ooh!—by things that shine and glitter. Do you remember me? Of me have you thunk? Sorry, I've just got to go see this boat that has just sunk. (Now I'm back!) I love you more than anything, even more than my snarfblatt. I wish this were a song to sing. I'm really much better at that."

"Wow—" Sebastian exclaimed.

"—that's really bad!" Flounder finished.

"True love, indeed!" Sebastian concluded.

Scrooge's Nature

"Would you look at that!" Huey pointed to a picture of a Junior Woodchuck relaxing in a hammock while another camper fished in a nearby lake.

"And that!" Dewey's eyes widened. He pointed at a picture of a star-filled sky in the same brochure.

"Camping at Faraway Lake sure looks fun," Louie agreed. "Do you think Uncle Scrooge would pay for us to go?"

"He *might*," Huey said.

The three boys looked at one another. "Nah!" they said in unison.

"Let's show him, anyway," Huey said. "It's worth a shot."

The other boys followed Huey into their uncle's study. Dewey nudged Huey forward. "Look at this, Uncle Scrooge," Huey said, thrusting the brochure into his uncle's lap.

"Humph." Uncle Scrooge scowled at the glossy photos. "What have we got here, lads?"

"It's a camp, Uncle Scrooge. It's educational," Huey stammered.

"Looks like a waste of my hard-earned money," the old duck said.

"But . . . but we could camp out under the stars," Dewey said.

"And cook over a fire," Louie put in.

"And see nature," Huey added.

Uncle Scrooge's eyes narrowed. He looked from the brochure to his nephews' hopeful faces and back to the brochure. So, they wanted to learn about nature, did they? Scrooge had a plan.

"Here you are, boys," said Uncle Scrooge a short time later. He smiled from the safety of the screened-in back porch. "You have tents"—he said, pointing to the three leaky pup tents set up in the backyard—"and you can see the stars"—which was true, although only one or two stars were visible through the branches of the tree the tents were under—"and you're cooking over a fire," Scrooge finished, pointing at the tiny, smoky little flame.

"This is much better than that Junior Woodchuck nonsense, isn't it, boys?" Uncle Scrooge asked with the smile of a duck who has saved himself a dime.

"Yes, Uncle Scrooge," Huey, Dewey, and Louie said. Then they turned back to the fire.

"I think . . ." said Huey.

". . . next time . . ." continued Dewey.

". . . we ask Uncle Donald!" finished Louie.

Making Dreams Come True

In a time not so long ago, a girl named Tiana lived in New Orleans. She was a very pretty and clever young girl. But Tiana didn't have much time for fun. She worked hard as a waitress, trying to earn as much money as she could. She hoped to one day buy the building where she and her father had dreamed of opening a restaurant.

One morning, Tiana was serving breakfast at Duke's Diner when her best friend Charlotte's father, Big Daddy, came in for a bite to eat.

"Good morning, Mr. LaBouff!" Tiana said. "And congratulations on being voted king of the Mardi Gras parade!"

Big Daddy nodded. "Caught me completely by surprise . . . for the fifth year in a row!" he said with a chuckle. "Now, how about I celebrate with—"

"Some beignets?" guessed Tiana, a full plate of the soft doughnuts already perched on her arm. "They've just come out of the oven!"

Just then, Charlotte burst into the restaurant.

"Oh, Tia! Did you hear the news? Prince Naveen of Maldonia is coming to New Orleans!"

Charlotte showed Tiana a picture of an attractive young man, adding, "And Big Daddy invited the prince to our masquerade ball tonight!"

Charlotte's bright eyes shone with excitement. She would do anything to become a princess . . . including marrying the first prince that came along!

"Oh, Lottie. That's swell," said Tiana. "A little word of advice—my momma always says that the quickest way to a man's heart is through his stomach."

Charlotte turned to her father, who was busy feasting on beignets. He looked as if he was in heaven. Her friend was right! She would catch the prince with some tasty homemade treats. He never needed to know they weren't made at *her* home!

"Oh, Tia, you're a bona fide genius," cried Charlotte. "I'm gonna need about five hundred of your man-catching beignets for my ball tonight."

As Charlotte handed her a bundle of money, Tiana almost exploded with happiness. This was enough to finally allow her to make the first payment on her restaurant!

A Helping Hand

"Oh, Pinocchio!" cried Geppetto. "I can hardly believe that my little puppet is alive!" It was the morning after the Blue Fairy had visited Geppetto's house and brought Pinocchio the wooden puppet to life.

"You must get ready for school, my boy," said Geppetto.

Pinocchio was full of curiosity. "Why must I go to school, Father?" he asked.

"Why, so that you can learn and be wise!" Geppetto replied. "Now be a good boy and go make the bed while I clear away these dishes."

Ever eager to help, Pinocchio sprang up from the breakfast table and ran over to Geppetto's workbench. He found a hammer, a nail, and a piece of wood, and he began to pound loudly with the hammer.

"Pinocchio! Whatever are you doing?" cried Geppetto.

"You asked me to make the bed," said Pinocchio. "So I was starting to make one."

With a little smile, Geppetto said, "Perhaps it would be better for you to put the cat out."

As Geppetto turned back to the breakfast table, Pinocchio jumped up and grabbed a pitcher of water. Hurrying over to Figaro, Pinocchio threw the water onto the cat.

"YEEEEOOWWWW!" shrieked Figaro.

"Pinocchio!" shouted Geppetto. "Why did you do that?"

"You . . . you told me to put the cat out. I thought he had caught fire," said Pinocchio in a small voice.

"Oh, my dear boy, you have much to learn!" Geppetto sighed as he dried off Figaro. "Okay, you can be a helpful boy by helping me to pick up the house a bit before you leave for school."

"All right, Father!" said Pinocchio, and he raced out the front door.

Curious, Geppetto followed Pinocchio outside.

Pinocchio was crouching at the base of the house, trying with all his might to lift it.

"What are you doing, son?" asked Geppetto with a twinkle in his eye.

"Trying to pick up the house, Father," said Pinocchio, his voice straining with effort.

Geppetto chuckled and gently guided Pinocchio back inside. "My boy, the sooner you go to school and learn about the world, the better for us both," he said.

Fairy Medicine

Deep in the forest, in a humble cottage, the three good fairies had been secretly raising Princess Aurora for many years. The king and queen had sent their beloved daughter into hiding to try to protect her from a curse laid on the princess by the evil fairy Maleficent.

One morning, the girl woke up with a terrible cold.

"We must nurse her back to health," said Flora.

Fauna and Merryweather agreed. While Briar Rose stayed in bed, Flora brought her a bowl of soup, Fauna fetched her a cup of tea, and Merryweather gave her a dose of medicine.

"Ooooh!" said Briar Rose, wrinkling her nose. "That tastes awful!"

"Most medicine tastes awful, dear," said Merryweather. "Just drink it down."

"Would you like anything else?" Flora asked.

The princess blew her nose and gazed out her window. "What I really want is to get out of bed," she said.

"Oh, no, dear," said Flora. "You're far too sick."

Then the fairies left Briar Rose and went downstairs.

"I feel bad for the sweet girl," said Fauna. "Staying in bed all day is boring."

"What can we do?" asked Merryweather.

"I know!" cried Flora. "We'll entertain her!"

"Splendid!" said Merryweather. "I'll fetch my wand and conjure up some fireworks, a puppet show, and—"

"No!" Flora cried. "We all agreed to give up our fairy magic until Briar Rose turns sixteen and she's safe from Maleficent's curse. How about if we play card games! That will be fun!"

And so the three fairies then went up to Briar Rose's room and played cards with her all afternoon. Briar Rose won almost every game. After a while, Briar Rose yawned and said she was ready to take a nap. So the fairies went back downstairs.

When Flora went outside to do some gardening, Fauna approached Merryweather.

"Tell me the truth," she whispered. "Did you use magic to let the princess win?"

"I just used mortal magic," confessed Merryweather. "No harm in a little sleight of hand. After all, you must admit, if you're feeling down, winning is the best medicine!"

Nemo's Best Shot

"**C**ome on, Dad! We're going to be late!" cried Nemo. Nemo and Marlin were hurrying through the busy swimming lanes of the colorful Great Barrier Reef.

"Are you sure you want to play pearl volleyball?" Marlin asked nervously. "There are lots of other things you can do. Sponge jumping, for example. Or maybe reef dancing."

"Reef dancing!" cried Nemo, horrified. "No way! That's for babies! I want to play pearl volleyball!"

At Sea Urchin Stadium, Mr. Ray made the opening announcements. "Hello and welcome, everyone! Before we get started, let's give a big thank-you to Ms. Esther Clam for donating today's ball."

Everyone applauded as Esther opened her shell and spat out the pearl.

"Let's play!" cried Mr. Ray.

The players lined up on either side of the sea fan net. Ray's Raiders were on one side, and Nemo's team, the Fighting Planktons, were on the other.

Marlin watched anxiously. He was sure that Nemo wouldn't be able to play as well as the other fish because of his small fin. And Marlin wasn't the only one who had doubts.

Turbot Trout came up to Nemo on the court. "Coach may be letting you play today," Turbot snapped, "but you'd better not mess up the Planktons' winning streak."

Turbot didn't know Nemo had spent many hours smacking around pebbles in a dentist's fish tank!

"Just watch and learn," murmured Nemo.

Suddenly, the pearl came right to Nemo. Smack! Using his good left fin, Nemo sent the pearl flying right over the net. The pearl flew so fast, the other team couldn't return it. Nemo scored his first point for the Planktons!

Nemo played like a pro. He scored again with his good fin, then with his tail. And, just to show his father and Turbot Trout, he scored the winning point with his little fin.

"Go, Short Fin!" cried Turbot Trout. "With a player like you, we're going to go all the way to the Lobster Bowl Clampionship!"

"Wow, Nemo," said Marlin after the game. "That was amazing!"

"Thanks, Dad," said Nemo. "I gave it my best shot, like you said. And we actually won, too!"

No Work for Tinker Bell

The fairies were traveling to the mainland to help bring forth summer, and Tink couldn't wait to get there! Unlike the other seasons, summer needed the fairies' constant attention—which meant that Tink was going to be on the mainland for months instead of days.

Tinker Bell was so excited! She had heard that the fairy camp where they'd be staying was an amazing place.

As the fairies arrived on the mainland, they instantly got to work. Vidia, a fast-flying fairy, created a breeze that made the summer grasses sway softly. Iridessa, a light fairy, bathed flowers in sunshine. Fawn, an animal fairy, painted butterfly wings while Silvermist, a water fairy, frolicked with playful pollywogs. Rosetta, a garden fairy, helped bees find their way to the flowers' sweet nectar.

Tink arrived on the mainland with her friend Terence, a dust-keeper fairy. The two had landed in a pretty little clearing. Tinker Bell looked around, disappointed. She was always dreaming about fantastic adventures. But there was nothing going on here!

Terence walked over to a huge oak tree and pulled back a thick tangle of leaves. "There it is, Tink! Fairy camp," he said, pointing through the leaves.

Tink could hardly believe her eyes. The Fairy Camp was even more incredible than she had imagined! Hidden beneath the tree, an entire fairy community bustled with activity.

Summer was the fairies' busiest season. There was so much to do that the fairies stayed on the mainland all summer. That was why they had set up a base camp!

Tinker Bell couldn't wait to start tinkering! She walked over to a couple of animal fairies painting stripes on bees to see if anything needed to be fixed.

"How's the beeliner workin'?" she asked excitedly.

"Like a dream, Tink! Thanks!"

Everywhere Tink went was the same. Her inventions were working so well that she wasn't needed!

Tinker Bell sighed. She hoped she'd find something to fix soon But in the meantime, she had some Lost Things to search for!

The Scare Games

Mike Wazowski had dreamed of being a Scarer his whole life, but he had failed out of the Scare Program. Now he only had one hope left: he had to win the Scare Games and prove that he had what it took to be a world-class Scarer.

There was just one problem. In order to compete, he had to join a team.

Looking around, Mike found only one option: Oozma Kappa. OK was a fraternity full of students who had also failed out of the Scare Program. But the team still needed one more member.

"The star player has just arrived," said James Sullivan, joining the rest of the Oozma Kappas.

Sulley had done nothing but cause Mike trouble. In fact, he was the reason Mike had been kicked out of the Scare Program. But without Sulley, they wouldn't be able to compete, so Mike had to agree.

Now that he had a full team, Mike proposed a deal to Dean Hardscrabble, the head of the Scaring program. If his team won the Scare Games, she would have to let them all into the Scare Program.

Dean Hardscrabble agreed, but on one condition. If they lost, Mike and Sulley would leave Monsters University for good.

Mike and Sulley moved into OK's fraternity house with the other OKs—Don, Squishy, Terri and Terry, and Art. Soon an invitation to the first Scare Games event arrived. It was called the Toxicity Challenge, and it was to take place that night in the sewers.

When the teams arrived for the first event, they learned that the object of the challenge was to make it through a pitch-black tunnel filled with stinging glow urchins as quickly as possible. The last team to cross the finish line would be eliminated.

The teams took off! Mike and Sulley charged ahead while the other OKs struggled through the urchins. The Roar Omega Roar team stormed through to win, with Mike and Sulley finishing closely behind them. But the rest of the OKs finished last. OK was eliminated.

Just then, the judges discovered that the Jaws Theta Chis had cheated.

They were disqualified. Mike sighed with relief. The OKs were back in the Games!

Rise and Shine

"All right, Dwarfs!" Doc called one morning. "Is everyone ready to leave for work? Let's see. We've got Happy, Dopey, Sneezy, Bashful, Grumpy, and Sleepy." Doc looked around. "Sleepy?" he called. No answer. Sleepy was nowhere to be found.

"Oh no, not again," Doc complained, leading the other Dwarfs up the stairs to their bedroom. There, just as Doc expected, they found Sleepy, dozing peacefully in his bed.

"Oh, this is ridiculous!" exclaimed Grumpy. "We go through this every single morning, dragging Sleepy out of bed, and I'm tired of it."

"I have an idea!" said Doc. "We'll have to take the day off from the diamond mine and stay here today to work on my plan, but I think it will solve our problem—once and for all!"

The Dwarfs gathered into a huddle around Doc as he outlined the details. Then they got their tools and set to work. Soon the bedroom was filled with the sounds of hammering, sawing, and metalworking. All of the activity centered on Sleepy's bed. Despite the racket, Sleepy slept on. . . .

He slept all morning. He slept all afternoon. He slept all evening. He slept through the night.

Then, bright and early the next morning, an alarm clock perched on top of Sleepy's bedside table sprang to life. Its bell jangled noisily, shaking the clock. The clock, which had a rope tied around its handle, bounced across the top of the table until it fell off the edge. The falling clock tugged on the rope, yanking a broomstick at the other end. When the broomstick moved, the large weight it was propping up dropped to the floor, activating a pulley that pulled up sharply on Sleepy's headboard. The head of Sleepy's bed lifted off the floor, and Sleepy slid down, down, down . . . right into a wooden tub filled with cold water. Wide awake, Sleepy sat in the tub, blinking and wondering what had just happened.

The other Dwarfs crowded around the bedroom window and peered down at him, grinning cheerfully

"Good morning, Sleepy!" cried Doc. "Do you like your new alarm clock?"

Paradise Falls

Carl had wanted to be an explorer ever since he was a child. So had his friend and wife, Ellie. Carl had promised her that he'd take her to see Paradise Falls in South America one day. But they were never able to save enough money to go. When they grew older, Ellie passed away and Carl was told he had to move out of his house.

Carl decided he had to keep his promise to Ellie. He tied thousands of balloons to their little house, and slowly it lifted into the sky.

"We're on our way, Ellie," he said happily.

Suddenly, there was a knock at the door.

Carl was shocked. He was thousands of feet up in the air! Who could be at his door?

It was Russell, a Junior Wilderness Explorer who had knocked on his door a few days before. Carl had told him to find a snipe—a bird that didn't really exist—just to get rid of him. Russell had been under Carl's porch, looking for the snipe, when the house lifted off.

Carl hated to stop, but he knew he had to land and send Russell home. He started to cut some of the balloons free.

Meanwhile, Russell was watching the clouds out of the window. "There's a big storm coming," he said. But Carl didn't hear him.

A flash of lightning lit up the room. Carl quickly tried to steer the house away from the storm, but it was too late. The little house tossed in the wind. Carl ran this way and that, trying to save Ellie's belongings. Finally, exhausted, he fell asleep.

When Carl woke up, the storm was over.

As Carl and Russell stepped out onto the porch, the house bounced into the ground and sent them both flying outside. "My house!" Carl cried as the house started to drift up and away from them. Grabbing hold of the garden hose, he and Russell managed to pull the house back down.

Then the fog cleared. There, a short distance ahead, was Paradise Falls! It looked just like the picture Ellie had drawn of it!

"We made it!" Carl shouted. "We could float right over there!"

Carl had finally made the trip he and Ellie had always dreamed about.

Dear Sisters

"I had the strangest dream," Cinderella told her mouse friends one morning. "My Fairy Godmother sprinkled happy dust over Anastasia and Drizella, and they were so nice to me!"

"But that was only a dream," Jaq warned her.

"I know," Cinderella told him, "but it was so nice that I think I'll try to pretend that it really happened. Whenever they are horrid to me, I'll pretend they actually said something sweet and kind."

When Cinderella got downstairs, Drizella threw a pile of laundry at her. "Wash my dresses," she demanded.

"And polish my shoes," said Anastasia, opening her closet door.

"Right away, sisters!" Cinderella sang out, as sweet as you please. "Thank you!"

All day long, Drizella and Anastasia barked orders at Cinderella. But no matter what they asked her to do, Cinderella always sang back, "Right away, sisters!" or "You're too kind!"

Finally, Anastasia pulled Drizella aside. "It makes no sense. No matter what we tell Cinderella to do, she stays happy," Anastasia said.

"Do you think she's gone mad?" Drizella asked.

Anastasia looked worried. "She could be! Who knows just what she's capable of!"

Just then, Cinderella walked in. She stopped, surprised to see her stepsisters looking at her as though she were crazy.

"Why, my dear sisters, whatever can be the matter? I do hope you're not ill," she said.

"D-d-d-dear sisters?" Anastasia stuttered. "You called us your dear sisters?" She and Drizella edged toward the door.

"Of course," said Cinderella. "I adore you both. I'm the luckiest girl in the world to have such kind, caring siblings."

That did it. Convinced that Cinderella had lost her mind, the two stepsisters turned and ran. Cinderella listened as her sisters' doors slammed shut. Then she smiled at Gus and Jaq, who had been watching the whole time.

"They may not actually be caring or good-natured," Cinderella said to the mice, "but they'll be too frightened to come out of their rooms for at least a few hours. Who's up for a game of hide-and-seek while we've got the run of the house?"

Sebastian's Big Day

It was Sebastian's big day. As the official royal composer for the court of King Triton, he had been working very hard on a brand-new piece of music, and that evening he was going to conduct the royal orchestra as they played his song before the kingdom for the first time.

Just before the curtain went up, the musicians began to gather backstage. Music filled the air as the trumpet fish and the conch shell players tuned their instruments. Benny the octopus, the orchestra's drummer, was the last musician to arrive.

"Sebastian!" he exclaimed, rushing over to the conductor. "I—I can't play tonight!"

Sebastian stared at Benny in shock. "What do you mean? You *have* to play!"

"You don't understand," Benny replied. "I *can't*. I took a nap this afternoon and fell asleep on my tentacles, and now they're all tingly! I can't hold my drumsticks!"

"What am I going to do?" Sebastian exclaimed, looking around at the musicians. "My composition calls for eight drums. Benny has eight tentacles—one for each drum. Where will I find enough hands to take his place?"

Just then, Ariel and her six sisters swam backstage to wish Sebastian luck.

"Ariel!" Sebastian cried. "Am I glad to see you!" He explained his problem to Ariel and her sisters. "Could each of you help by playing a drum in the concert?" he asked.

"Of course!" the mermaid sisters replied.

Sebastian breathed a sigh of relief. "Okay, we have seven drummers. We just need one more!"

The musicians stared at Sebastian.

"*Me?*" he said. "But I am the composer and conductor! This is the day my true genius will finally be appreciated! I cannot be hidden in the drum section!"

But there was no other choice. When the curtain went up minutes later, there was Sebastian, drumming away. His day in the spotlight would have to come another time. As he played, he shrugged and smiled.

"Well, you know what they say," he whispered to Ariel.

"The show must go on?" Ariel guessed.

"No," Sebastian replied. "A true genius is never fully appreciated in his own lifetime."

Tuned In

Andy's toys were gathered around the TV in Andy's room. "This again!" Bo Peep said as a super hero show came on. "We watch this every day."

"So?" said Hamm. "He's the defender of the universe! What could be better? I love this show."

Rex picked up the remote control and pressed a button. Suddenly, the channel changed to a real dinosaur show.

"Aggh!" Rex cried, diving under the covers. "Save me!"

The Green Army Men sprang into action. "Eliminate the enemy!" Sarge ordered. "Go! Go! Go!"

The soldiers jumped on the remote, and the channels began to change.

"Oooooh!" cried one of the Aliens as the channels flew by in a blur. "Perhaps this machine can help us return to our planet," they all said together. Bo Peep chuckled.

Buzz walked over. "Sheriff, I think we need to put an end to this channel surfing," he said. Woody agreed.

Sarge called off his troops, and Buzz marched over to the remote control. He told the Aliens that the television couldn't take them back to their home planet. "But the TV *can* take you to plenty of new and exciting places," Buzz said.

This made the toys start talking about their favorite shows. They couldn't decide what to watch, so Bo Peep suggested they watch a little of each channel.

The toys watched super heroes for Hamm. They watched the Animal Channel for Slinky Dog. Then they turned to the Military Channel for Sarge and the Green Army Men. They watched the Cooking Channel for Rex and the Sheepherding Channel for Bo. Then, finally, they turned to the Cowboy Channel for Jessie.

"Howdy, partner!" the toys suddenly heard.

"Could ya keep it down, Woody?" said Hamm. "We're trying to watch something."

"Huh?" said Woody. "I didn't say anything."

"Well, would you look at that!" said Jessie. "Woody and I are on TV!"

The TV was showing an episode of *Woody's Roundup*!

"Now there's a show!" said Woody. Everyone else had to agree!

Such a Shame

Mulan nudged Khan into a gallop and kept her eyes straight ahead. She was on her way to town to go to the market for her family. It was a regular trip for her, but the people working on the sides of the road did not seem to think so.

Without even looking at them, Mulan knew that she was causing whispers. But they weren't just talking about her. They were talking about the man riding with her—Captain Li Shang.

Shang swung down from his horse and offered to go inside to buy the rice. Mulan was about to object—she didn't need Shang's help with the shopping. The only reason she'd brought him along was because he wanted to see more of her town. But Shang was already inside the tiny shop.

Mulan sighed. She held the captain in high esteem. She liked him—she really did. But she always found herself disagreeing with him. Even when she didn't need to.

"Shame!" Across the street, an older woman pointed at Mulan, startling her out of her thoughts. "Shame!" the woman said again. "Don't think I have forgotten you."

Mulan blushed, recognizing the woman. It was the Matchmaker! Mulan looked at the ground as her cheeks grew even hotter, but they were not as hot as they had been on the day that she first met the Matchmaker—the day she accidentally set the woman on fire!

The Matchmaker continued, pointing and screeching at Mulan as she waddled across the street. "You!" she scolded. "Just because China thinks you are a hero does not mean you can escape your fate. I predict you will bring shame to your family. I feel it."

Mulan did not know what to say to the old woman.

"There is not a matchmaker in the world who could ever find a match for you!" the woman screeched.

"Then it is a good thing she will never need a matchmaker," Shang said. As he walked past the Matchmaker, he accidently stepped in a puddle, splashing her from head to toe!

The Matchmaker was speechless, her face twisted into a scowl. Mulan could not think of a thing to say, either. But instead of wearing a scowl, her face was set in a wide smile. For once she agreed with Shang!

Enchanted Stew

Belle hummed to herself as she strolled through the castle. She had been living there for a few months now and was finally beginning to feel at home. Now, she was headed toward the kitchen for a chat with Mrs. Potts and the Stove.

"Well, hello dear!" Mrs. Potts and the Stove called out together as Belle stepped into the large kitchen. The smell of roasting meat and vegetables greeted Belle.

"Hello," Belle replied.

"You're just in time for a spot of tea," Mrs. Potts said.

Belle smiled as Chip hopped across the counter, stopping right in front of her. "I'll be your teacup," he said. "And no bubble tricks, I promise," he added seriously.

"All right, then," Belle agreed.

"How was your morning in the library, dear?" Mrs. Potts asked.

"It was wonderful!" Belle exclaimed. "I finished my book about knights in shining armor and started one about a prince who's disguised as a frog."

"A frog!" the Stove exclaimed. "Oh, my! What a tale!"

Suddenly, black smoke began to seep out of the sides of the oven door.

"Oh, my!" the Stove said again, throwing open the door. Smoke poured into the room. When it finally cleared, Belle spied a scorched roast and crispy black vegetables inside.

"Oh, my!" the Stove exclaimed a third time.

"What are we going to feed the Beast for supper?" Mrs. Potts fretted.

The kitchen door opened, and Lumiere rushed into the room. "What is that awful smell?" he asked. A moment later, he spied the roast. "It's absolutely scorched!" he cried. "We can't possibly feed that to the Beast! What will we do?"

Belle got to her feet. "Enchanted Stew," she said calmly. Taking down a large stew pot and a few vegetables, she began to chop and simmer.

The last ingredient was the scorched roast. "It adds the perfect smoky flavor," she explained.

Just then, the Beast came into the kitchen. "What smells so delicious?" he asked.

"Supper," Belle replied with a smile and a wink at the Stove and Mrs. Potts. "It's called Enchanted Stew, and we cooked it together!"

A New View of the World

Jasmine and Aladdin were taking a ride on the magic carpet. "I have never done anything so exciting!" Jasmine said.

"I'm very glad you're enjoying it, princess," said Aladdin. "It's time for you to see the world."

The carpet zoomed across the desert, which was lit by the stars and the moon. They approached a huge mountain range and hovered above a silvery waterfall.

Next, Aladdin and the princess soared toward the sea. It glittered like glass in the moonlight. Jasmine spied a pod of dolphins leaping out of the waves.

The two flew away from the sea and over a meadow filled with beautiful golden flowers. A breeze blew, and Jasmine breathed in their delicious fragrance. Aladdin steered the carpet down so that could fly just above the flowers. He swept up a handful and presented Jasmine with a beautiful bouquet.

Jasmine stole a look at the mysterious prince. He seemed so familiar, though she was sure she had never met him before. He reminded her of someone she had once met . . . in the market. The princess shrugged. They couldn't possibly be the same person!

Aladdin looked at the beautiful princess. How long could he make her believe that he was a prince, and not just a street boy in disguise? Thanks to the Genie, Aladdin's wish to look like a prince in order to impress Jasmine had come true. But what if she remembered that they had met before? If the princess recognized him as the street boy who had spoken with her that day, all would be lost.

The sun was just rising over the east as Aladdin brought Jasmine back to the palace and said good-bye to her. After he left, Jasmine went inside and threw herself onto her bed, a dreamy look on her face. Rajah, her pet tiger, came over to greet her, and she absently stroked his silky head.

"Oh, Rajah," she said. "I saw the world tonight, and it was beautiful. I think I may have met someone interesting. It's all so wonderful and confusing!" She sat up and looked at Rajah. "I think," she said softly, "I just might be starting to fall in love."

A Bouncy Babysitter

Roo was excited. Tigger was babysitting him!

"Now, Tigger, I know you and Roo like to bounce," said Kanga. "But a good babysitter must know when to put the bouncer to bed."

"Don't worry, Kanga!" said Tigger.

For hours, Tigger and Roo had a fine old time bouncing around. Then Tigger looked at the clock and said, "Time to bounce into bed!"

Roo hopped right into his room. That was easy, Tigger thought to himself. He followed Roo into his bedroom.

"Now I'll just tuck you in and—Hey! I said bounce *into* bed. Not *on* it!" cried Tigger.

But Roo wouldn't stop. So Tigger gave up and started bouncing, too!

Then Tigger remembered what Kanga had said. "Wait a minute! I'm the babysitter," said Tigger. "I'm supposed to be tucking you in!"

"I don't want to be tucked in," said Roo.

"What if I read you a story?" asked Tigger.

"No," said Roo. "I'm not even sleepy. I could bounce all the way to Pooh's house!"

"But it's time for *bed*, not bouncing," said Tigger. "I'll get you some milk. That will make you sleepy."

But when Tigger came back to Roo's bedroom, Roo was gone!

"Uh-oh!" said Tigger. He rushed to Pooh's house.

"I'm sorry, Tigger," said Pooh, "but Roo isn't here."

Tigger returned to Kanga's house. Where could Roo be? Tigger passed Roo's room—and saw Roo in his bed!

"Where were you, Tigger?" asked Roo.

"Where was *I*?" said Tigger. "Where were *you*?"

Roo explained that when Tigger had gone to get the milk, Roo had decided he did want to hear a story. But his favorite book was under the bed.

"You were *under* the bed?" cried Tigger.

"I'm home!" called Kanga at the front door.

Tigger sighed with relief.

"How did it go?" she asked Tigger.

"Kanga," said Tigger, "the wonderful thing about tiggers is bouncing—and from now on, I'm sticking with that. Babysitting just has too many ups and downs!"

The Queen's Way

"Goodness!" Alice took a few steps back. She had no idea a queen could bellow quite so loud! Alice had been excited to meet the Queen of Hearts, but the Queen was always shouting, "Off with his head!" It really wasn't very friendly.

"I guess since she's the queen, she can do what she likes," Alice said to the flamingo croquet mallet she held firmly by the feet.

The flamingo nodded.

Standing back, Alice watched the Queen take her turn. Her Royalness bent over the hedgehog ball, swung her flamingo mallet high into the air, and brought his beak down with a whoosh. The prickly creature was off on a rolling run. He tumbled through wicket after wicket, getting dizzier as he went. He was nearly finished, when one of the wickets bent over the hedgehog's path too late. The hedgehog rolled off course, and the Queen's turn was over.

"Off with his head!" the Queen roared.

"Oh, this is so unfair," Alice lamented to her flamingo. "It wasn't his fault that the hedgehog got dizzy.

And that is no way to treat anyone!"

"It is a way," her mallet whispered, looking terrified. "It's the Queen's way."

Unfortunately, the Queen had heard Alice. She turned to the girl, her face redder than a tomato. Alice knew what was coming. She cowered beside a rosebush and waited for the horrible order.

"Off with her—"

"M-m-my dear." The small king appeared from behind the Queen. "The wickets are out of line." He pointed at the cards that were nervously shuffling themselves off the croquet field.

"Get back here!" the Queen shouted. "I'll have your heads!" Forgetting all about Alice, the Queen marched toward the cards.

Alice breathed a sigh of relief and straightened her collar. "She wants everyone else to lose their heads," she whispered very softly. "But, clearly, she has already lost her own!"

At this, Alice's flamingo laughed so hard, she nearly lost her grip on it.

Alice smiled. The Queen might be a living terror, but at least Alice had a friend in this crazy court—even if her friend was a croquet mallet!

Mend the Bond Torn by Pride

Princess Merida was an adventurous teenager. Merida's mother, Queen Elinor, wanted her to marry in order to keep peace in the land. But Merida wasn't ready to give up her freedom. Elinor told Merida about an ancient prince who had broken tradition and split from his three brothers. Their kingdom had then fallen to ruin.

Angry with her mother, Merida slashed at a tapestry of her family, slicing through it just between the pictures of her and her mother. Soon afterward, Merida had stumbled upon a witch and asked for a spell that would change her mother.

The witch told Merida about a prince who had asked for the strength of ten men. She showed Merida the ring the prince had given her. Two crossed axes were carved into it. The witch told Merida that she would give her a similar spell. But instead of changing Elinor's mind about the marriage, the spell had changed Queen Elinor into a bear!

Now Elinor-Bear and Merida were searching for something to break the spell. Soon, the two came upon an old stone arch with crossed axes carved on it, just like the witch's ring. It led to an ancient ruin.

As they explored, Merida fell through a hole. She found herself in the throne room of a ruined castle. On the ground, Merida saw a stone engraved with the pictures of four princes. The stone had been split in two. The fourth prince was broken off from the rest. Claw marks covered the walls. Suddenly, Merida realized that the witch's prince had lived here—and that he was the same prince of her mother's legend.

"The prince became . . . Mor'du!" she cried.

At that moment, Mor'du appeared. The bear lunged at Merida, but Elinor-Bear pulled her to safety just in time. Mother and daughter raced away from the ruins.

Finally, Merida knew what she had to do. She had to fix the tapestry she had sliced in two.

The witch's spell had shown the princess that she must learn to understand her mother's wishes, and fix what had broken between them. But could she fix her mother?

Strange Animals

Carl Fredricksen and a Junior Wilderness Explorer named Russell had just arrived at Paradise Falls in South America! Carl had dreamed of seeing the falls his whole life. He had promised his wife, Ellie, that he'd take her there one day. Sadly, Ellie had died before they could take the trip.

When Carl was told he had to move out of their home, he decided it was time to keep his promise to Ellie. He tied thousands of balloons to their house, and it lifted up into the air! Carl hadn't planned on taking a companion along—but Russell had been on Carl's porch when the house took off.

"This is fun already, isn't it?" Russell said as they trudged along. "By the time we get there, you're gonna feel so assisted. . . ."

After a while, they stopped to take a break. As Russell nibbled on a chocolate bar, a beak poked out of the bushes and began to nibble on it, too!

"Don't be afraid," Russell told the creature. He used more chocolate to lure it from its hiding spot.

When the creature emerged, Russell gasped. It was the biggest bird he had ever seen! The bird liked chocolate. It liked Russell, too. Russell named the bird Kevin. He couldn't wait to show his new friend to Carl!

"Can we keep him?" Russell asked.

"No," said Carl.

Carl and Russell set off again. But Russell didn't want to leave Kevin behind, so he dropped bits of chocolate for the bird to follow.

They hadn't gone far when they met a dog. "Hi there," said the dog. "My name is Dug."

A talking dog? Carl and Russell were stunned!

"My master made me this collar so that I may talk," Dug explained. "My pack sent me on a special mission. Have you seen a bird? I want to find one. I have been on the scent."

Suddenly, Kevin flew out of the bushes and tackled Dug. "Hey, that is the bird! May I take your bird back to camp as my prisoner?" Dug asked.

"Yes! Take it!" Carl told him. He didn't want to deal with all these strange animals—he just wanted to reach Paradise Falls. But would he ever get there?

The Prince and the Sorcerer

Prince Naveen did not know it, but New Orleans was a city of magic, good and evil. Bad experiences might be waiting just around the corner—particularly if you were a carefree young prince!

Naveen had just arrived in the city and was eager to explore.

"We must go to this masked ball, my prince! Your hosts are waiting for you!" said Lawrence, his valet.

Naveen wanted to experience the city instead . . . until Lawrence reminded him that he had no money.

But Naveen realized there was just one solution: he would have to marry a rich young girl. But marrying would deprive him of his freedom, and he didn't much like the idea of that, either!

Then a sinister character passed by the prince in the street. "What an excellent stroke of luck for me!" he said to himself with a laugh. It was Dr. Facilier, a fearsome sorcerer who had his sights set on taking Naveen's place and seizing his wealth.

Dr. Facilier introduced himself to Prince Naveen. Then he ushered the young prince into an alley.

Dr. Facilier said, "I can read your future. I can change it around some, too. . . . I look deep into your heart and soul, make your wildest dreams come true."

Unaware of the danger, Naveen followed the sorcerer into his den at the end of a dark alleyway. Terrifying whispers haunted the place. Scary masks glared down from the walls, and shadows danced everywhere.

The sorcerer sang to Naveen and Lawrence, promising to give them all they had ever wanted.

Naveen was hearing exactly what he wanted to hear. He was fascinated.

Dr. Facilier took his chance. He waved a magic talisman, pricked Naveen's finger with it, and filled a vial with the prince's blood! Naveen began to shrink and shrink until, finally, he was fully transformed into a frog!

Poor Naveen! It was true; money wouldn't be a problem for him from now on. But what would happen to him? He had no idea what life as a frog would bring.

A Friend in Need

"Whatever could be keeping the Seven Dwarfs?" said Snow White. "They should have been home from work by now!"

Just then, Happy came through the front door looking upset. "Come quickly! A young deer is hurt in the woods."

Snow White followed Happy, and they soon reached a small clearing. Everyone stood in a circle around the deer.

"Thank goodness you're here, Snow White!" said Doc. "This little fella's in trouble!"

"He must be cold," said Snow White, covering him with her long cape.

"Maybe he's just tired," said Sleepy. "A nice long rest should do the trick!"

"Why, you could be right, Sleepy," said Snow White. "But he's not closing his eyes, so I think it might be something else."

"Maybe he has a . . . aahhh . . . aaaahhhhchoooooooo! . . . a cold," said Sneezy.

"I know!" said Happy. "Maybe he's feeling sad and needs a little cheering up!"

"I, uh, don't know for sure," said Bashful softly, "but perhaps he's too shy to let us know what's the matter."

"We all feel shy sometimes, don't we, Bashful?" said Snow White.

Then Dopey started pacing back and forth and pointing over his shoulder.

"Maybe you're right. He could be lost," said Snow White.

"I'll bet I know what happened," said Grumpy. "The wicked Queen probably cast a spell on him! She's always up to no good!"

Suddenly, Doc walked up to the deer. "May I lake a took—er, I mean, take a look?" he asked. Doc knelt down beside the deer. "Well, would you look at that!" cried Doc, pointing at the animal's foot. "The poor deer must have stepped on a thorn."

Doc gently removed the sharp thorn from the deer's hoof. The deer jumped up and licked him.

"Oh, how relieved you must be!" cried Snow White.

The deer licked Snow White's hand and ran off into the forest. Then Snow White and the Seven Dwarfs went home to their little cottage.

"I am so proud of each and every one of you," said Snow White, smiling at her friends. "You each did your best to help a friend in need!"

Avoid the Parent

I t was the day after the first event of the Scare Games at Monsters University, and Mike Wazowski was very upset. His future at the university was dependent on his team winning—and his team members were useless! OK had almost been eliminated in the first event! The only one who had any scaring skills was Sulley, and he was the one who had gotten Mike into this mess in the first place!

Dean Hardscrabble, the head of the Scare Program, had thrown Mike and Sulley out. The Scare Games were their only way back in. If the Oozma Kappas didn't win, Mike had promised to leave the school!

Sulley wanted to ditch the OKs and find another team, but the rules didn't allow it. So Mike insisted that the team do things his way from then on.

The next event was "Avoid the Parent." The competitors had to make their way through the library and capture their team's flag without getting caught by the librarian. If the librarian caught them, she would grab them with her giant tentacles and launch them out of the library.

Mike told his team to move slowly and quietly. He even made them practice tiptoeing.

But Sulley thought he knew better. He climbed a sliding ladder and zipped sideways toward the flag. Suddenly, there was a loud *CRACK!* The ladder broke and Sulley crashed to the floor with a loud crash!

The librarian turned to Sulley, but Don distracted her by making noises with his tentacles. Then Terri and Terry created a distraction to save Don, and Art created a distraction to save Terri and Terry.

Mike didn't know what was going on! The librarian chased the OKs, who escaped through the back door.

"Woo-hoo! We did it!" yelled Art.

"No, we didn't. We forgot the flag!" said Mike.

Just then, Squishy appeared with the flag. The OKs took fourth place.

As the triumphant team walked back home, another team drove up in their car. They asked if the OKs were going to the party with the other teams that night.

The OKs were thrilled. They'd never been invited to a party before! Had their luck finally changed?

MARCH 14

A Salty Surprise

Briar Rose picked up a large basket and stepped out the door. It was a beautiful afternoon, and she couldn't help but sing a little song as she headed into the forest.

Rose had spent many afternoons in the forest and knew exactly where the cherry trees grew. She put her basket down by her favorite tree and began to fill it with juicy cherries. A pair of bluebirds came and landed on her shoulder while she picked. Soon the basket was heavy with fruit.

"That should be more than enough for a pie," she told the bluebirds. She was going to bake her aunts a surprise dessert. Still humming to herself, Rose carried the cherries back to the cottage.

Rose put down the basket and looked around the cozy kitchen. She felt nervous. She had never baked a pie by herself! She wasn't even sure where to find all the ingredients.

"It can't be that hard to find the butter, flour, and sugar," she assured herself.

Taking a deep breath, Briar Rose searched the cupboards. Then she set to work cutting the butter into the flour for the crust. After adding cold water, she gently patted the dough into a ball.

"And now for the tricky part," she said to the bluebirds, who had followed her home. Rose rolled out the dough and set it into the pie tin. It looked perfect.

"Now for the filling," Briar Rose said. She washed the cherries and pitted them. Then she mixed in some spices and sprinkled on spoonfuls of the coarse white sugar.

After dinner, Rose cut four nice-sized pieces of pie. Smiling, everyone dug in. But their smiles almost immediately turned to severe puckers.

Then Rose burst into tears. "Salt!" she cried. "I used salt instead of sugar!"

"There, there, dear," Flora consoled her. "I once made the same mistake with an entire batch of fruitcake—twenty cakes!—and it took a while before anyone would touch my cooking again! But they got over it eventually."

Rose wiped her tears as the good fairies began to giggle. "I remember that!" Merryweather said.

Rose smiled, then giggled, too. After all, she had ruined only *one* pie!

Minnie's Rainbow

Minnie's just finished reading a book. She's asked all her friends to come take a look.

She learned about something you see in the sky, a colorful arc that birds fly right by.

But what makes a rainbow that follows the rain? Let us find out as Minnie explains . . .

Minnie pictures the rainbow in her head and remembers the first color is red.

Red makes a rainbow so fiery bright—it's for strawberries, stop signs, and Mickey's night-light.

Next there is orange. It's cheerful and cute—the color of tigers and sunsets and fruit.

Now look again at the pretty rainbow—you'll find the third color is one that you know!

Yellow gives rainbows their light, happy rays, a reminder of ducklings and warm, sunny days.

Can you name the fourth color? That's right, it is green! Look back at the rainbow, you'll see what I mean.

There's a garden of green in each rainbow you see. It's for pickles and peas and the leaves of a tree.

Inside every rainbow is cool, calming blue, for blue skies and bluebells and your blue jeans, too.

Now look at the rainbow, each colorful strand.

It's clear now that blue is the rainbow's fifth band.

Violet you'll find at the end of the line. It's the color of lilacs and grapes on a vine.

Red, orange, and yellow are one, two, and three. Green is four. Blue is five. Violet's six, as you see.

But there's more to each rainbow you see in the sky. There's a whole spectrum of colors, so let's find out why!

A rainbow is made of the colors of light. When we look at it whole, we can see only white.

But when white light is split, then more colors appear. If you tried counting them, it might take a whole year!

There are not only colors like red, green, and blue. There are some you can't see with your eyes—yes, it's true!

So what makes a rainbow? What is it we see?

All the colored waves that are part of light, naturally!

Marlin's Story

"P. Sherman, 42 Wallaby Way, Sydney . . . P. Sherman, 42 Wallaby Way, Sydney." Dory kept muttering the address to herself. She and Marlin were searching for Marlin's missing son, Nemo.

Marlin had the address memorized and thought he would go crazy if he had to hear it again. "Dory!" he said with a sigh. "I know you just want to be helpful, but do you really need to keep talking?"

"I love to talk," said Dory. "I'm pretty good at it. Hmm . . . what were we talking about?"

"I just want to find my son," Marlin said.

"That's right, your son, Chico," said Dory.

"Nemo! One time, Nemo and I—" Marlin began.

"Go on," Dory said. "Is this going to be exciting?"

"Yes, it's an exciting story," said Marlin, relieved that he had gotten her to stop reciting the address. "Well," Marlin began again, "one time, I took Nemo to the other side of the reef to visit a relative of mine who was known as the fastest swimmer of all the clown fish in his day. But when we visited him, he

was getting on in years."

Dory yawned. "When's the good part?"

Marlin sighed. "I was just about to get to it!" he said. "So, anyway, on the way back home, guess what we ran into?"

"What?" asked Dory.

"A huge jellyfish!"

"Uh-huh," said Dory. She seemed to be trying to remember something. "P. Sherman . . ." she muttered softly.

"For a moment there I thought we were goners," said Marlin. "But then . . . a gigantic sea turtle swam up and swallowed the jellyfish in one gulp!"

"Did you say thank you to the turtle?" asked Dory.

"Well, no," Marlin replied. "I was afraid he would eat us, too, so Nemo and I hurried on our way. But, ever since then, I have been fascinated with turtles. And I hope I never have to meet another jellyfish!"

"Say, I've got a story, too!" said Dory excitedly. "It takes place at 42 Wallaby Way, Sydney. At P. Sherman. Now, at P. Sherman, 42 Wallaby Way, Sydney, there was this, um, fish . . . and . . . well . . ."

Marlin just groaned and kept swimming. At least he couldn't forget where he was going!

Curious Tinker Bell

Tinker Bell and the other fairies had arrived on the mainland to set up summer. But Tinker Bell couldn't find anything that needed to be repaired, so she set out to look for Lost Things.

Just then, a loud *CRACK* echoed through the fairy camp! Startled, Fawn knocked over some paint she was using to decorate butterfly wings. The splattered butterfly took off.

The other fairies hid, but Tinker Bell wanted to see where the noise had come from. Flying to the top of a tree, she saw a car making its way down the winding road. Tinker Bell had never seen a car before and quickly took off after it.

Tink followed the car to an old house in the country. When it stopped, she saw a little girl, her father, and their cat get out.

The little girl pointed to the meadow. "That's where I'm going," she told her father. "Would you like to come?"

"Not now, Lizzy," he said. "I have to update my field journal."

After the three had gone inside, Tink flew under the car to examine it. Suddenly, Vidia appeared. "You shouldn't be this close to the human house!" she scolded.

But Tinker Bell was already poking around the engine. She found an interesting-looking lever and turned it. Outside of the car, Vidia got showered with water! She was furious! Everyone knew fairies couldn't fly with wet wings!

Moments later, Lizzy and her father returned to the car. The fairies froze in fright. Luckily, the humans were busy examining a strange looking butterfly.

"I guess that's just the way the fairies decided to paint it," Lizzy said.

"Fairies do not paint butterfly wings, because, as you know, fairies are not real," Dr. Griffiths insisted as he captured the creature with a net.

Lizzy sighed. She loved fairies, but her father was a scientist. He didn't believe in magic *or* fairies. He was also usually too busy to spend much time with her.

Tinker Bell had heard the humans' conversation. She wanted to prove that fairies existed! But she knew that could be dangerous, so she stayed hidden—for the moment.

A Big Girl Now

Flynn Rider had stolen a royal crown. Now he was running from the palace guards.

Maximus, the captain of the guard's horse, caught up with Flynn and grabbed the satchel holding the crown.

"Give me that!" yelled Flynn. He yanked the satchel free and it went flying into the air. It snagged on a tree branch that extended over a cliff's edge!

That didn't stop Flynn or Maximus. They both made their way out onto the branch. Flynn reached the satchel just ahead of Maximus.

CRACK! The tree branch splintered, and both horse and thief toppled into the canyon below.

On the canyon's floor, Flynn found a hidden entrance to a cave where he could hide from Maximus. Walking through the cave, he soon emerged to an astonishing sight. There, in the center of a hidden valley, stood a single enormous tower.

It was the perfect hiding place!

Using two arrows, Flynn climbed up the tower and through the open window at the top. *CLANG!* Suddenly, everything went black. Rapunzel, the girl who lived in the tower, had seen Flynn climbing through the window and had hit him with a frying pan!

Rapunzel had been locked in the hidden tower her whole life. Mother Gothel, who pretended to be her mother, had told the girl that the outside world was far too dangerous for her.

Using the frying pan, Rapunzel opened the intruder's lips. His teeth weren't pointy. In fact, nothing about this man seemed ugly and scary, as her mother had warned. He was actually very pleasant looking.

Rapunzel stuffed Flynn in her wardrobe and propped a chair against it. Then she stopped to consider her situation. She had just defended herself from an outsider. Surely this act of bravery would prove to Mother Gothel that she could handle herself in the outside world.

"Too weak to handle myself out there, huh, Mother? Well." Rapunzel laughed. "Tell that to my frying pan!" She boldly brandished the frying pan above her head. As she waved it around, *WHAM!* She accidently hit her own head!

"Ouch!" she cried. It was a good thing Mother Gothel hadn't seen that!

Hot on the Trail

"Over here!" Simba said, sniffing the trail. "It's going this way!"

"Yup, this way," Nala said with a nod, sniffing a stick.

"I saw that stick first," Simba said. Nala was a good tracker, but Simba had learned from an expert—his mom. She was one of the best hunters in the pride.

"Hmm," Nala said with a sniff. "So what are we following, then, master tracker? Can you tell me that?"

Simba was silent. They had seen some footprints, but they weren't clear enough to read. They had also seen lots of crushed grass and broken sticks.

"Something that isn't very graceful," Simba said.

"Mmm-hmm." Nala nodded impatiently.

"A rhino!" Simba said confidently.

"A rhino?" Nala rolled onto her back, laughing. "Simba, you crack me up!"

"What?" Simba couldn't hide the hurt in his voice. It might be a rhino!

"The footprints aren't big enough," Nala said. "It's Rafiki, the baboon."

Now it was Simba's turn to laugh. "Rafiki likes the trees; he doesn't use trails like a hyena!"

The giggle died in Simba's throat, and he felt the fur on the back of his neck stand up. Hyenas were clumsy and left light tracks. . . .

Nala didn't say anything, but her fur was standing up a little, too.

The two lions walked in silence. Ahead of them they heard noises—thrashing and grunting.

The young lions crept through the grass on their bellies as quietly as they could. The grunting and thrashing grew louder. Something about the smell and the sound was familiar, but Simba couldn't put his paw on it.

As they crept closer, two bodies came into view by the side of a termite mound. Simba pounced!

"Pumbaa! Timon!" he shouted, landing between his friends.

"Simba!" the warthog said, grinning. Termites dripped out of his muddy mouth. "Want some?"

Timon held a handful of wriggling insects toward Nala. "There are plenty to go around."

"Uh, no, thanks," Nala said as she came out of the grass, giggling. She shot a look at Simba. "I think I'll wait for the master tracker to hunt me up some lunch!"

Lucifer's Bath

Cinderella's stepsisters didn't like the idea of Cinderella going to the Prince's ball, so they decided to keep her busy.

"We need to take our baths," Anastasia said.

"You heard my girls, Cinderella," said the Stepmother. "Get their baths ready at once!"

Cinderella already had far too many jobs to do, but she didn't argue. Once Anastasia and Drizella were soaking in their bubble baths, all Cinderella had to do was mend their clothes, clean the house, wash the curtains, and give Lucifer his bath—then she could get ready for the ball.

Unfortunately, her stepsisters wouldn't leave her alone. Each time her stepsisters called, Cinderella had to stop whatever she was doing and take care of them.

When Drizella called for tea, Cinderella went down to the kitchen and put the kettle on. Then she let Bruno the dog in for a snack. "Oh, Bruno," she said, tossing him a bone, "if my stepsisters don't get out of their bathtubs soon, I'll never get my chores done in time."

Bruno narrowed his eyes. Those stepsisters were the most selfish, lazy, nasty girls he'd ever known—and their cat was just like them. Bruno wanted to help Cinderella, so when the tea was ready, he followed her up the stairs and down the long hallway.

As Cinderella walked up to Drizella's bathroom door, Bruno noticed Lucifer sleeping nearby.

"Woof, woof!" Bruno barked.

With a screeching yowl, Lucifer ran into Drizella's bathroom. Splash! Bruno chased the cat right into Drizella's tub— and then Bruno jumped in himself!

Drizella screamed and Lucifer jumped out. And Bruno chased the cat down the hall and into Anastasia's bathroom.

Splash! Lucifer landed right in Anastasia's tub. Bruno jumped right in after him!

"Get out of your tubs this instant!" Cinderella's stepmother cried. "You don't want to smell like that dog, do you?"

Cinderella sighed in relief. Although she still had many jobs to finish before the ball, at least one job was now done. Thanks to Bruno, Lucifer had had his bath!

A Hair-Raising Experience

Ariel looked at her hair in the mirror and sighed. *Ugh!* It was so straight . . . and red . . . and boring! Ordinarily, it wasn't such a big deal. She'd run a dinglehopper through it and that would be that.

But today, for some reason, she felt like a change. Ariel was still staring at her hair in the mirror when her sisters arrived.

"Hi, Ariel. What are you doing?" the oldest, Aquata, asked.

"Oh, nothing," said Ariel. "Just trying to figure out something new to do with my hair."

"Just parting it on the other side can make a big difference," said Aquata. "Shall I try?"

"Sure!" said Ariel.

But when Aquata had done it, Ariel's sister Andrina shook her head. "Not enough," she declared. "What you need, Ariel, are some curls."

"Okay." Ariel shrugged. She sat patiently as Andrina rolled her hair in curlers and took them out half an hour later.

"Oh, my," said Ariel, gazing into the mirror.

"Still not enough," said another sister, Arista. "Imagine how great your hair would look if we colored it black with squid ink!" And, just to prove her point, that's exactly what she did.

"Well, it certainly is different," said Ariel, looking at her new inky-black hair.

"You know what you need?" said her sister Adella, looking at the finished product. "Braids! Definitely braids! Girls, come and help me."

And before she knew it, Ariel's hair had been divided into ninety-nine tight, twisty braids. Ariel looked in the mirror . . . and then looked away twice as fast!

"What if we just cut it all off?" said her sister Alana.

"Hold it!" said Ariel, suddenly jumping up. "You're *not* cutting off my hair! I wanted a change—not a total reconstruction!" She reached up and began to unbraid her hair.

"Suit yourself," said her sisters. They helped her undo their hard work. Soon Ariel was back to normal, to her great relief. Still, she thought, it had been an interesting experiment. Changing her hair hadn't worked out so well, but what about changing something else?

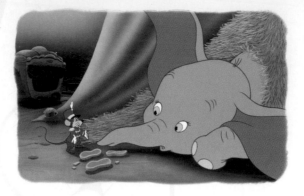

Hide-and-Seek

Dumbo had been the newest baby in the circus for quite a while. Then, one day, the stork arrived with a brand-new delivery—a baby giraffe.

"You know, Dumbo," said his friend Timothy Q. Mouse, "I think we should ask that new baby giraffe to play with us."

Dumbo nodded. He loved making new friends!

"Hello, Mrs. Giraffe," Timothy said. "Can your lovely new baby come out to play?"

Mrs. Giraffe agreed and the three new friends set off.

"Okay, kids," said Timothy, "what do you feel like playing? How about hide-and-seek?"

Dumbo and the giraffe nodded happily as Timothy closed his eyes and counted.

"Ready or not," he said finally, opening his eyes, "here I—Hang on! Don't you guys know you're supposed to hide?"

No, actually, they did not.

Timothy sighed. "Okay, let's take it from the top. When I close my eyes, you guys hide. You find a place where you

can't see me and I can't see you. Like this." Timothy ducked behind a popcorn tub. "Get it?"

Dumbo and the giraffe nodded slowly.

"Okay then, let's try this again. One, two, three . . ." Timothy counted to twenty, then opened his eyes.

"No, no!" he groaned. "You can't hide behind the popcorn tub. You're too big. Let's try this one more time."

Again, he closed his eyes and counted. Then, very slowly, he opened them and looked around.

"Much better!" he said, surprised. Of course, it didn't take him long to find Dumbo's nose sticking out of a pile of hay or the giraffe sticking out from behind the clowns' trunk.

"This time, guys, try to find a place for your whole body to hide," Timothy said.

Dumbo and the giraffe waited for Timothy to close his eyes once more. Then they quietly hid again. But this time they picked places that covered their whole bodies.

And do you know what? They hid so well, Timothy Q. Mouse may still be looking for them to this very day!

A Beastly Makeover

One evening, the Beast was heading toward the dining room when Lumiere suddenly stopped him.

"You can't go to dinner looking like *that*!" Lumiere said.

"Why not?" the Beast demanded. "I'm wearing my best outfit!"

"Clothes aren't enough," Cogsworth chimed in. "You have to make a good impression."

"You always told me looks don't matter," the Beast said.

"There's a difference between looks and style," Lumiere told him.

"And you may have no control over your looks," Cogsworth added, "but you certainly can do something about your style!"

"What's wrong with my style?" the Beast said, looking a bit hurt.

"Very well," Cogsworth began, "let's talk about your hair."

"What's wrong with my hair?" the Beast cried, offended.

"Women like hair long, but neat—not straggly," Cogsworth explained. "When was the last time you combed it?"

"I—" the Beast began.

"You've got it all wrong," Lumiere interrupted. "Women like hair short, closely cropped." He brandished a pair of scissors.

"I don't *want* a haircut!" the Beast said.

"We could always try ringlets," Cogsworth offered, nodding wisely.

"Or braids," Lumiere suggested.

At this, the Beast climbed onto a bookcase that swayed under his weight.

"How about a French twist?" Cogsworth said.

A low growl began in the Beast's throat. Just then, Belle hurried into the room. The candelabrum and mantel clock were brandishing combs and ribbons at the snarling, cornered Beast, who was scrabbling to stay on top of the bookcase. Belle burst out laughing.

"What's going on?" she asked.

"We were just trying to fix his hair," said Lumiere. "It's a dreadful mess!"

"Actually," Belle said, "I happen to like it just the way it is. Now, would you escort me to dinner, Beast?"

"I would be honored," the Beast replied.

Cogsworth and Lumiere looked baffled as the two headed off to the dining room.

"Kids these days!" Cogsworth said.

Choose Your Own Fate

"Mend the bond torn by pride." That was exactly what Princess Merida needed to do, before it was too late!

Merida's mother, Queen Elinor, wanted her daughter to marry in order to keep peace in their kingdom. But Merida was an adventurous teenager. She wasn't ready to marry.

Angry, Merida had slashed a tapestry of her family in half. Then, to make matters worse, she had asked a witch for a spell that would change her mother's mind. But instead, it had changed Elinor into a bear!

Now, Merida and Elinor-Bear needed to find a way to break the spell. The only clue they had was a riddle from the witch: "Fate be changed, look inside, mend the bond torn by pride."

It had taken Merida a long time, but finally she realized what the riddle meant. She needed to mend the family tapestry. With Elinor-Bear close behind, Merida returned to the castle.

Inside the Great Hall, Merida's father, King Fergus, and the other clans were locked in battle—all because Merida refused to marry one of the lords' sons!

Merida looked to her mother for help but there was nothing Elinor-Bear could do. It was up to Merida to stop the fight.

Merida marched into the center of the room. She was about to agree to marry one of the lords' sons when, from the shadows, her mother stopped her. Elinor-Bear mimed what she wanted Merida to say. "The queen feels . . . that we should be free to . . . find love in our own time," Merida translated.

"A grand idea!" Lord Macintosh's son exclaimed happily.

The other lords' sons agreed. They wanted to be free to choose their own fates.

"That settles it," Lord MacGuffin said. "Let these lads try to win her heart before they win her hand."

Elinor-Bear was proud of her daughter. At last she understood her need for freedom, and Merida realized the importance of what her mother had wanted her to do. It had taken a spell that turned Queen Elinor into a bear, but they finally they were seeing eye to eye.

But would it be enough to break the spell?

Look Sharp, Jiminy

"Gosh." Jiminy Cricket scratched his head between his antennae and yawned a big yawn. Climbing into his tiny matchbox bed, he gazed again at the wooden boy, who was fast asleep.

Jiminy still could not believe his eyes—or his luck. It had been a miraculous night. Not every cricket got to witness a wish granted by the Blue Fairy and see a puppet come to life. And not every cricket was chosen to be somebody's conscience!

Jiminy ran his hands down the new jacket hanging by his bed. He picked up the hat and twirled it. "My, my," he said, shaking his head.

Then he couldn't resist any longer. He put on his new shirt, coat, hat, and shoes, and he hopped over to Cleo's fishbowl to see his reflection.

Jiminy whistled low. "Don't you look smart!" he told his reflection. "Smart enough to help that wooden boy. Except for that smudge." Jiminy leaned down to inspect a dull spot on his shoe. He breathed on it and rubbed it with his sleeve until it was shining like new.

Suddenly Geppetto snored loudly.

Jiminy jumped and looked up. Outside the sky was starting to lighten.

"Would you look at that?" Jiminy knew he had to get to bed. A good conscience needed to be alert! He hurried out of his new clothes, hung them up carefully, and tucked himself back into bed.

"Big day tomorrow." He yawned. "Very big day. Yes, indeed!" A moment later the little cricket was chirping in his sleep.

Jiminy woke to the sound of hundreds of cuckoo clocks. He sat up and rubbed his eyes. He barely remembered where he was. Then the events of the evening before flooded back. Why, he had work to do!

"Get up, Pinoke!" Jiminy called toward the big bed. But Pinocchio was already gone. The bed was made, and Geppetto and Figaro were gone, too! Cleo swished nervously in her bowl and pointed toward the door.

"I must have overslept!" Jiminy said, quickly pulling on his new clothes. "I can't let Pinoke start school without me. You don't have to be a conscience to know that's wrong!" And, quick as a flash, Jiminy hopped out the door.

The Masked Ball

Charlotte LaBouff had thrown a masked ball to welcome Prince Naveen of Maldonia to New Orleans. But so far the prince had not shown up.

"It's just not fair! I never get anything I wish for!" Charlotte said.

"There are still a few stragglers," Tiana said, consoling her friend.

"No, my prince is not coming!" sobbed Charlotte. "Maybe I just gotta wish harder."

Tiana let out a sigh. Her friend still believed in fairy tales. Tiana was too practical to believe in wishing on stars.

Suddenly, Tiana spotted the estate agents from whom she was supposed to be buying the restaurant space. Tiana's dream had always been to open her own restaurant, and she had finally earned enough money to buy it!

She greeted them cheerily and asked if they'd brought papers for her to sign so she could buy the sugar mill for her restaurant.

But there was a problem. Someone had offered more money. If Tiana couldn't match the offer, she'd lose the sugar mill!

Tiana was so disappointed that she fell against the food and ruined her costume! Fortunately, Charlotte arrived to help.

"Oh, you poor dear," she consoled her friend, leading her upstairs. "I've got just the dress for ya."

She led the way to her room, and Tiana quickly changed. She looked beautiful, but she was too upset to return to the ballroom with her friend. Instead she went out onto the balcony.

"I was almost there . . ." Tiana whispered to herself, looking at a picture of her dream restaurant. Then she looked up into the sky. "I cannot believe I'm doing this," she said. And she started to wish on the evening star!

She closed her eyes and concentrated. When Tiana opened her eyes again, a frog had appeared on the balcony!

Tiana sighed. "So what now?" she said to the frog. "I reckon you want a kiss?"

"Kissing would be nice, yes!" said the frog, smiling.

Tiana shrieked and ran back into Charlotte's bedroom. First, she had wished on a star, and now she was seeing talking frogs!

Maybe fairy tales could come true, after all!

A Shower of Disasters

Tinker Bell was a very curious tinker fairy. She always wanted to investigate everything—and nothing interested her as much as the mainland. Humans had such unusual inventions!

The fairies had recently arrived to bring summer to the mainland. Almost as soon as Tink arrived, she saw a car speeding down the road. She couldn't help herself. She had to take a closer look. Soon the car stopped in front of a house. The driver got out and went inside with his daughter. This was Tinker Bell's chance. She quickly flitted beneath the car's hood!

"This thing is amazing!" she said. There were all kinds of levers, hoses, springs, and nuts. Tinker Bell quickly realized that this complex system made the car move. She was having a good look at the spark plugs and the battery when Vidia, a fast-flying fairy, soared down.

"Tinker Bell! What are you doing here?" Vidia cried.

"Vidia, this is amazing. It's a carriage that moves by itself!"

Tinker Bell began to investigate a strange metal lever. "Will you stop flitting around in there!" Vidia called.

But Tinker Bell wasn't listening. "I think this must power the whole thing!" she said, pushing a lever.

But what Tink didn't realize was that each time she pushed the lever, Vidia was drenched by a huge splash of cold water!

Tink flew back out and looked Vidia up and down. "You're all wet," she remarked.

"You don't say . . ." Vidia grumbled.

Suddenly, the little girl and her father came back out to the car. Tinker Bell and Vidia hid until they left.

"All clear!" said Tinker Bell. The tinker fairy knew it was time to get back to the fairy camp. "Come on, Vidia," she called, flitting her wings and floating into the air.

"I can't fly. My wings are wet!" Vidia said, her face red with anger.

"That's right," Tinker Bell said. "Sorry. I guess you'll have to walk back."

Vidia crossed her arms in anger. Would she ever get back to the fairy camp?

Old Man Octopus

"You're it!" Nemo tagged Sheldon, who was hiding next to a big mollusk.

"Aw, man!" Sheldon swished his tail. "I'm going to get you next time, Nemo."

"Only if you can find me," Nemo teased.

Nemo swam away, scanning the reef for a good hiding spot. Sheldon would be out to get him for sure. Finally he came to a dark cave in the coral. "Too dark," he shivered, looking into the spooky opening. "It'll be perfect."

Mustering his courage, Nemo swam inside. At first he couldn't see anything. Then, as his eyes adjusted to the dark, Nemo saw a large eye open on the cave wall. What could it be?

Another eye opened. Then the entire wall began to move.

"O-O-Old Man Octopus!" Nemo stammered as eight long arms oozed off the cave wall. Nemo and his friends told stories about Old Man Octopus at sleepovers. In the stories, Old Man Octopus sneaked up on little fish and gave them a terrible scare. "S-sorry to disturb you, sir."

Nemo swam toward the cave's entrance. Then he noticed something amazing: The octopus's arms were changing color . . . and texture! Instead of matching the brown bumpy cave wall, now they looked more like the reddish coral at the bottom of the cave.

"You didn't disturb me, boy. Tell me, what brings you to this corner of the reef?"

The octopus's voice was slow and kind, and Nemo's fear melted away.

"Hide-and-seek, sir," Nemo answered politely. "But I wouldn't need a cave if I could camouflage myself like you!"

Old Man Octopus laughed. "Hide-and-seek, eh? One of my favorites. The camouflage does come in handy, but nothing beats a cloud of ink when you want to make a break for base!"

"You can shoot ink clouds, too?" Nemo was so excited, he forgot to be quiet.

"I hear you, Nemo!" Sheldon shouted.

"Are you ready to swim for it?" Old Man Octopus whispered with a wink.

Nemo nodded. He high-fived one of Old Man Octopus's tentacles. Then, in a burst of inky blackness, he darted out of the cave, past Sheldon, and all the way back to the barnacle base. Safe!

The Prettiest Flower

One morning, Bashful went out to pick the prettiest flower he could find. Suddenly, he heard a noise just over the hill.

"*Ah-choo!*"

Bashful climbed the hill and saw his friend on the other side.

"These darn flowers are making me sneeze," said Sneezy. "But it's worth it—because I've picked the prettiest flower for Snow White's hair." He showed Bashful the white orchid he'd picked.

"That sure is pretty," said Bashful. "But I've got a flower for her, too. It's even prettier."

Bashful showed Sneezy the rosebud he'd picked. Then he blushed pinker than its petals.

"*Ahhh-choo!* Yours is pretty, too," said Sneezy. "Let's go home and see which one Snow White likes best."

On the path back to their little cottage, Sneezy and Bashful came upon Doc, Happy, and Sleepy. They were all arguing about something.

"Snow White bikes liolets," insisted Doc. "I mean, she likes violets!"

Happy laughed. "No. She likes daisies!"

"I think she likes muuuuuums," said Sleepy with a yawn.

When the Dwarfs arrived at their house, they saw Dopey.

"Dopey, what do you have behind your back?" Doc asked.

Dopey showed them a yellow tulip.

"*Another* flower!" cried Happy.

When the Seven Dwarfs went inside, they found Snow White in the kitchen.

"We all wanted to thank you for being so good to us," said Doc. "So we each picked a flower for your hair."

"Now it's *your* turn to pick the flower you like best," said Grumpy.

Snow White felt terrible. She loved all the Dwarfs, and she didn't want to hurt any of their feelings by choosing one flower over another.

"I have an idea," she told them. "Put all of your flowers down on the table and go outside for five minutes. When you come back in, I'll be wearing the flower I think is the prettiest."

The Dwarfs went outside. When they came back in, they gasped in surprise. Snow White had made a flower crown! She'd found a way to wear all their flowers at once.

"I love every one of your flowers!" she told them. "Just like I love each and every one of you!"

MARCH
30

Pooh's Neighborhood

"I say, it's a splendid day in the neighborhood!" cried Owl.

"Which neighbor wood are we talking about?" asked Pooh.

"*Neighborhood*," said Owl. "The place where we live and where all our neighbors live and are neighborly."

"Oh," said Pooh. "It is a splendid day in it, isn't it?"

"Now I'm off for an owl's-eye view!" Owl said as he flew away.

As Owl flew off, Pooh began to think about what it means to live in a neighborhood. He thought perhaps he would bring a neighborly present to his closest neighbor, Piglet. Pooh went inside his house and took a honey pot out of his cupboard.

When he reached his Thoughtful Spot, Pooh suddenly had a thought: I could take the path straight to Piglet's house. Or I could go up the path and around the whole neighborhood. And sooner or later the path would take me to Piglet's house, anyway. So that's what he did.

As he walked the long way to Piglet's house, Pooh came across each of his neighbors in turn. He joined Kanga and Roo for a snack at the picnic spot and collected some carrots from Rabbit. After lunch and a longish snooze at Christopher Robin's house, he soon reached Eeyore's Gloomy Place.

Eeyore was feeling sad, so Pooh offered him a nice lick of honey. But the honey pot was empty! Pooh had eaten all the honey on his journey through the neighborhood.

Pooh walked away from Eeyore's house glumly. Before long, Owl flew over.

"I've seen our whole neighborhood today," Pooh told him. "But now I have no neighborly present left for Piglet."

"The bees have been quite busy at the old bee tree lately," said Owl. "Perhaps you can get a fill-up there."

So they walked together until they came to the old bee tree. Up, up, up Pooh climbed. Owl had a thought, and he told Pooh to go to the very top of the tree and look around.

"Our neighborhood!" cried Pooh. "Our beautiful home!" The Hundred-Acre Wood was spread out below him.

"That's the owl's-eye view," said Owl grandly.

Then Pooh filled the honey pot once more, and he and Owl went to Piglet's house for supper.

Who's Tricking Whom?

Rapunzel was feeling very pleased with herself. A stranger had climbed in through her tower window, and she had managed to knock him out and lock him in her wardrobe!

Rapunzel had lived in a tower her whole life. Her mother, Mother Gothel, always told her that the outside world was way too dangerous for her.

But now Rapunzel had defended herself against an intruder! Rapunzel looked around the room and noticed a satchel Flynn had dropped when he fell. She reached inside and pulled out a gold crown covered with jewels.

Pascal, Rapunzel's chameleon, looked on curiously as Rapunzel inspected the strange object. She tried slipping it over her wrist, but it fell right off. Then she placed it on top of her head. It fit perfectly!

Rapunzel gazed into the mirror. Something seemed familiar. . . .

"Rapunzel! Let down your hair!" Mother Gothel called out.

Rapunzel quickly hid the crown. Then she threw her long hair out the window so that Mother Gothel could climb up into the tower.

"I have a big surprise!" the wicked woman exclaimed. "I'm going to make hazelnut soup for dinner. Your favorite!"

Rapunzel looked at her wardrobe. She had a surprise for Mother Gothel, too. But when she started to speak, Mother Gothel thought she was going to ask about seeing the kingdom's floating lights.

"Enough with the lights, Rapunzel," she shouted. "You are not leaving this tower! Ever!"

Rapunzel was shocked. Realizing that she would never get out of the tower unless she took matters into her own hands, she quickly came up with a plan.

"Oh, of course," Rapunzel said. "I just wanted to tell you that instead of leaving the tower, I would much rather have some mother-of-pearl paint for my birthday."

Mother Gothel frowned. To make this paint she would have to collect shells from a shore three days' walk away. Finally she agreed and set off.

From the top of her tower, Rapunzel watched her mother heading off into the distance. She smiled. In her own way, she had managed to trick Mother Gothel.

Who's Fooling Whom?

Lilo had only had her new dog, Stitch, for a little while. Already he had managed to break just about everything he touched and gotten Lilo's sister, Nani, fired from her new job.

On April Fools' Day, Lilo decided that, for one day, she was allowed to be a pain in the neck to *him*! She got started first thing in the morning. She left a whoopee cushion on Stitch's chair at the breakfast table. When he came in to eat and sat down, a very loud and very rude noise reverberated around the kitchen.

Lilo laughed and shouted, "April Fools'!"

Stitch shrugged. He made rude noises all the time. He wasn't embarrassed one bit.

After lunch that day, Lilo handed Stitch a cream-filled cookie. Only she had replaced the filling with toothpaste mixed with pickle juice. Stitch took a bite.

"April Fools'!" cried Lilo.

Stitch took another bite . . . and another . . . and another, until he finished the cookie. Then he licked his lips. *Ewww!* thought Lilo. Stitch would eat anything!

Later that day, Lilo smeared some of Nani's eyeliner around the eyepieces of her binoculars. She pretended to see something interesting out on the water. "Check out that huge wave!" she said. Lilo held the binoculars up to Stitch's eyes so he could look through them. When she pulled the binoculars away, Stitch had a dark ring around each of his eyes.

"April Fools'!" cried Lilo.

Stitch had no idea that he looked so silly, and even if he had, he wouldn't have cared.

"You're no fun to fool, Stitch," said Lilo that night. Then she pulled back the covers on her bed and climbed in. For some reason, she couldn't extend her legs all the way.

"Hey!" Lilo exclaimed. "Someone short-sheeted my bed! Nani!"

Nani poked her head into Lilo's room. "What's going on?" she said.

Nani looked as if she didn't know what Lilo was talking about. But that only left . . .

No way, thought Lilo. Stitch was just a dog. Lilo looked at him, sitting at the foot of her bed, wagging his tail. There was no way he could have short-sheeted her bed.

Was there?

A Bedtime Story

It was bedtime in the little cottage in the woods. Snow White kissed each Dwarf good night as she tucked him into bed.

"Wait! Wait!" called out Happy before she blew out the candle. "Please tell us a story."

"Very well," said Snow White, smiling. She settled down at the foot of the beds and began. "Once upon a time, there lived a happy little princess—or rather, a mostly happy little princess, but for a single person: her stepmother, the Queen."

"Bah!" grumbled Grumpy with a sneer.

Snow White sighed. "You see, no matter what the princess did—no matter how hard she worked or how good she tried to be—the Queen did everything in her power to make the princess sad."

"Poor princess," murmured Bashful.

"Every night, the princess wished for a charming prince to find her and whisk her away. And then one day, a prince finally did!"

"Really?" exclaimed the Dwarfs.

"Yes!" Snow White told them. "He rode right up to her castle and even scaled the wall to meet her. And, oh, was he ever charming! But here is the sad part: the very next day, the Queen's huntsman took the princess into the forest and told her to run far away and never return."

"So, did she?" Sleepy asked sleepily.

"Yes," Snow White replied. "She ran and ran until she could run no farther. Only then did she realize that she was terribly lost and lonely—with no friend in the world and no place to go."

"Poor princess," Bashful whispered softly.

"That's what the princess thought, too," Snow White said. "For just a minute. But then she discovered that she wasn't alone at all. There were chipmunks and squirrels and deer and rabbits and birds . . . all sorts of forest creatures there to help her. They took her to the sweetest little cottage you ever did see, where she met the most faithful friends a princess could ever have."

"And what happened next?" grumbled Grumpy.

"Well, they lived happily ever after, of course!" Snow White replied. "What did you think?"

Tangled

A Question of Charm

Rapunzel had been kept in a hidden tower her whole life. Her mother had told the girl that the outside world was far too dangerous for her so that Rapunzel would never try to leave.

But Rapunzel had defended herself against an intruder! A strange man had climbed in through the tower window, and she had managed to knock him out with a frying pan and lock him in her wardrobe! Now that Rapunzel had proven that she could take care of herself, she had a plan.

Every year on her birthday, Rapunzel saw strange floating lights in the sky. Her dream was to leave her tower and see the lights up close. Rapunzel held up her frying pan, ready to hit the man if he turned dangerous. Then she opened the wardrobe.

Wham! The intruder fell out onto the floor, still knocked out. Rapunzel tied him to a chair with her enormously long hair. Then her pet chameleon, Pascal, licked his ear to awaken him.

Rapunzel looked at him suspiciously. "Who are you, and how did you find me?"

The young man suddenly smiled his most attractive smile. "I know not who you are, nor how I came to find you, but may I just say . . . Hi. How ya doin'?"

Rapunzel just stared at him. Finally the intruder told her his name was Flynn Rider.

Suddenly Flynn realized that his bag was missing. Inside was a crown he had stolen from the palace! "Where is my satchel?" he asked.

"I've hidden it!" Rapunzel said. "I'm prepared to offer you a deal."

Rapunzel showed him the picture she had painted of the floating lanterns.

"Tomorrow evening they will light the night sky with these 'lanterns.' You will act as my guide, take me to these lanterns, and return me home safely. Then and only then will I return your satchel to you."

Flynn tried to charm Rapunzel once again. "All right, listen! I didn't want to have to do this, but you leave me no choice. Here comes the smolder." He gave her his most charming face as he stared deeply into her eyes.

But Rapunzel still just stared at him. Finally, Flynn gave in.

Rapunzel was delighted. Finally, after all these years, she was going to see the floating lanterns!

Who's in Charge?

"Now, Dory," said Marlin, "you have to promise you'll keep a close eye on Nemo while I'm gone. Can you do that?"

"I can do that!" Dory said confidently.

But Marlin was a little worried. Everyone knew that Dory usually forgot things.

"Remember," Marlin instructed, "Nemo needs to do his—"

"Science homework, practice playing the conch shell, and clean the anemone," interrupted Nemo. "I got it, Dad."

Finally, Marlin waved good-bye and swam off to do his errands. As soon as he was gone, Dory began swimming in circles around the anemone. "Nemo, betcha can't catch me!"

"Dory, come on," Nemo called to her. "I have to do my science homework."

Nemo explained his assignment to Dory: he had to find an abandoned hermit crab shell to bring in to class the next day. So Nemo and Dory swam around the reef. Before long, Nemo spotted one.

"That's great!" replied Dory. "Now we can play!"

"No, Dory," Nemo said. "Now I need to practice playing my conch shell."

Dory and Nemo swam back to the anemone, where Nemo put his hermit crab shell away and got out his conch shell. Dory kept time while he played the songs that he needed to memorize for band practice.

"Thanks, Dory!" Nemo said at last. "We're done."

"Yippee!" Dory cried, swimming around Nemo. "Now it's playtime!"

But Nemo remembered their work wasn't finished yet. "Not quite, Dory," he said. "I have to clean the anemone before I can play."

"Clean?" Dory said with a frustrated sigh.

Nemo shrugged. "Dad said I should do it before he got home," he replied.

Together, Dory and Nemo cleaned up the zooplankton crumbs. When they were finished, the place was spotless.

"Thanks for helping me, Dory," said Nemo. "That went fast with the two of us working together!"

"You're welcome," Dory replied. "So, what do you want to do now?"

Nemo laughed. "What do I want to do now?" he echoed. "I want to play!"

"Play, huh?" Dory said, weighing the idea. "Now that's a crazy idea. I like it!"

A Little Help

"This is bad," fretted Cogsworth the clock, pacing at the bottom of the castle's staircase. "Bad, bad, bad!"

"What is wrong, my friend?" asked Lumiere the candelabrum.

"The Beast hurt Belle's feelings," said Cogsworth. "Then Belle hurt the Beast's feelings. Now they're sulking in their rooms."

"Ah, that *is* bad," said Lumiere. "We will never be human again unless the spell on the Beast is broken. And the spell won't break until Belle falls in love with him."

"Well, there's no chance of that happening now!" cried Cogsworth.

"Nonsense," the candelabrum said. "Sometimes love just needs a little help. . . ."

Lumiere knocked on Belle's bedroom door. "Mademoiselle," he called sweetly. "I am here to tell you that the Beast is very sorry about what happened."

"He is?" asked Belle.

"Oh, yes," said Lumiere. "Now, do you wish to see your surprise?"

The door slowly opened. "My surprise?" asked Belle.

At that very moment, Cogsworth was standing outside the Beast's bedroom door, his gears quaking with fear. Gathering his courage, he finally knocked.

"Go away!" roared the Beast.

Cogsworth wanted to! But instead, he called, "Master, I am only here to tell you that Belle is very sorry about what happened!"

After a long pause, the Beast said, "She is?"

"Oh, yes indeed," said Cogsworth. "Now, follow me to see your surprise."

The door slowly opened. "I have a surprise?" asked the Beast.

Lumiere and Cogsworth led Belle and the Beast into the large drawing room. The room had been filled with fresh flowers from the greenhouse. In the middle of the room stood Plucky, the golden harp.

"Ohhhhh," said Belle and the Beast when they heard the beautiful harp music.

"You're sorry?" asked Belle.

"I am," the Beast admitted.

"I am, too," said Belle.

They smiled at each other. Things were looking up.

"R U Slee-P?"

Alice was lost in Wonderland. As she wandered around, she came across a blue Caterpillar blowing smoke letters.

"R U slee-P?" asked the Caterpillar.

"Am I sleepy?" Alice scratched her head. "I hadn't thought about it. I'm so worried about getting home, it's hard to think about anything else. I don't know, I suppose."

"U kn-O," said the Caterpillar, puffing out a U and an O in red-and-orange smoke.

"I do?" asked Alice.

"Ye-S, U do," said the Caterpillar. "For instance, have U O-pened your mouth without speaking?"

"Oh! You mean a *yawn?*" asked Alice. "No, I haven't yawned."

The Caterpillar yawned himself and asked, "Have U felt your I-lids gr-O-ing heav-E?"

"My eyelids growing *heavy?*" repeated Alice. She blinked, trying to determine if her eyelids had gained any weight since the morning. "No," she told the Caterpillar, "my eyelids are no heavier than usual."

"I C," said the Caterpillar. Then his own eyelids began to flutter, and his head began to nod.

"Perhaps *you're* the one who's sleepy,"

Alice observed, watching the Caterpillar.

"Y?" asked the Caterpillar.

"You yawned, then your eyelids drooped, and you began nodding off," Alice explained.

"I cannot B slee-P," the Caterpillar replied, "because n-O one has sung m-E a lullab-I."

"I can sing you a lullaby if you like," said Alice. "Hmm . . . let's see. . . ." Ever since she'd entered the world of Wonderland, none of the songs and poems she knew had come out quite right. "I'll try an easy one," she said and sang:

"Tow, tow, tow your rope
Slowly up the wall.
Merrily, merrily, merrily, merrily,
Life is a round ball. . . .
Blow, blow, blow your soap
Bubbles in the tub.
Merrily, merrily, merrily, merrily,
Rub-a-dub-a-dub. . . ."

After she finished, Alice asked the Caterpillar, "How did you like it?"

"Come back l-A-ter," said the Caterpillar. "U may B right. I am the slee-P one."

And with that, the Caterpillar fell fast asleep.

A Barrel of Monkeys

Mowgli and his pal Baloo were taking a lazy afternoon stroll through the jungle when they decided they were hungry.

Mowgli knew what to do. He shimmied up a tree, plucked a bunch of bananas, and tossed them down to the bear.

"That's my boy!" Baloo cried proudly.

But as he was scrambling back down, Mowgli spotted a flash of orange, black, and white.

"Shere Khan!" Mowgli whispered to Baloo. "We've got to get out of here!"

The tiger hated men and wanted Mowgli out of the jungle.

The two friends didn't know which way to turn. Now that Shere Khan had their scent, it would be almost impossible to lose him. Then they heard a lively beat drumming its way through the jungle.

"Oh, no," said Mowgli. "King Louie and his crazy band of monkeys. That's all we need!"

Baloo's eyes lit up. "That's exactly what we need, Little Britches!"

Still clutching the bananas, Baloo and Mowgli ran toward King Louie's compound. When they arrived, Baloo disguised himself as an orangutan. The monkeys were so busy dancing and singing that they didn't notice his disguise.

The bear quickly found a huge empty barrel and filled it with the bananas.

"Look!" cried Baloo, peering into the barrel. "Lunch!" The monkeys ran over and jumped right into the barrel! They greedily ate the feast, tossing peels out as they made their way through the bunch.

Baloo signaled to Mowgli, who came out of hiding. "Come and get me, Shere Khan!" the Man-cub taunted.

Within seconds, the tiger appeared in the clearing, a fierce gleam in his eye.

"Hello, Stripes," Baloo greeted him cheerfully. Then the bear picked up the barrel, heaved it, and sent King Louie's troop flying at Shere Khan.

The now-angry monkeys landed on the tiger's back, where they frantically jumped up and down, pulling on his tail and ears. Mowgli and Baloo watched as Shere Khan raced back into the jungle, trying to free himself from his shrieking passengers.

"Like I always say," Baloo declared as he grinned at Mowgli, "there's nothing more fun than a crazy barrel of monkeys!"

The Dance Lesson

"Just imagine," said Cinderella excitedly. "There's a ball at the palace tonight in honor of the Prince, and every maiden in the land is invited. That means me, too!"

All of Cinderella's animal friends clapped and chirped. They loved their Cinderelly.

"Oh, dear," said Cinderella with a sigh. "There is so much to do! And I can only go if I finish my chores."

Suddenly, three loud shrieks came from somewhere downstairs.

"Cinderellllllaaaa! Come down here immediately and help us get ready for the ball!" her stepsisters cried together. And so Cinderella got to work helping her sisters.

Hours later, Cinderella began her other chores. There was so much to do. How would she ever be finished in time for the ball?

Suddenly Jaq had an idea. "I know!" he said to the other mice. "We help-a Cinderelly!" The mice nodded in agreement. Soon everyone was happily cleaning and singing.

As she worked, Cinderella began to imagine the evening ahead. She would wear her mother's beautiful gown. The ballroom would come alive with music and dancing. The handsome young Prince would bow before Cinderella and ask her to dance. . . .

Suddenly Cinderella looked up, alarmed. "Oh, no!" she cried. "I don't even know how to dance!"

"Don't you worry, Cinderelly!" Jaq smiled reassuringly. "Us show you! Easy as pie!"

With that, Jaq bowed before Perla and extended his hand. "Dance, please, missy?" he asked.

Perla blushed as she took Jaq's hand. Soon the two mice were gliding across the floor.

"See?" said Perla. "Not so scary."

Using her broom as an imaginary partner, Cinderella danced and twirled gracefully around the room. She led everyone across the floor, sweeping and cleaning as they went. Then the mice collapsed on the floor, laughing.

"Good-good, Cinderelly!" said Jaq, beaming. "Lucky Prince gets to dance with Cinderelly."

"Thank you all so much," Cinderella told her friends. "With your help, tonight might be the night that all my dreams come true!"

Jin's Treasure

After Mulan had saved China from the Huns, she had returned to her village. She helped out her family the way she always had, and in time, people forgot how brave Fa Zhou's daughter really was.

One day, a group of frightened children came running toward her.

"Help! Help!" they shouted. "Our friend Jin is trapped in a cave!"

"Hurry—take me to him!" exclaimed Mulan. Then she called to her little dragon friend. "Mushu, you've got to come, too!"

The children led Mulan and Mushu to the other side of the mountain.

"A boulder has fallen, blocking the entrance to the cave," explained Wang, the blacksmith. "It will take muscles of steel to move this boulder."

"Yes!" agreed Chung, the carpenter. "If you want to do something useful, go back to the village and fetch us some water."

Mulan returned to the village, but not to fetch water. Instead, she found a shovel and ran back to the cave. Soon, Mulan began to dig at the base of the boulder. Slowly but surely, she formed a tunnel beneath the rock. When the tunnel was finished, Mulan and Mushu climbed under the boulder and into the cave.

"Boy, am I happy to see you!" the boy, Jin, exclaimed.

"We're happy to see you, too!" said Mulan. "But what made you come in here?"

"I saw something shiny and I wanted to know what it was," Jin explained.

Mulan looked around. "You mean that?"

There, in the back of the cave, lit up by Mushu's fire, were many shiny objects. The cave was full of treasure!

"Think of what this fortune could mean for our village!" exclaimed Mulan.

"Come on!" Jin said. "Let's go and show the others." They each grabbed an armful of treasure and headed for the tunnel.

As the pair emerged from the cave, followed by Mushu, the crowd let out a cheer. Then they noticed the gold and jewels.

"What have you found?" asked Wang.

"It's treasure. Now I'll go back to the village and fetch some water," Mulan said, grinning. "I'm pretty thirsty after all that digging."

All Shapes and Sizes

It was a great day for the Oozma Kappas. Mike, Sulley and the rest of the team had taken fourth place in the second event of the Scare Games. It was the first time anything had gone right for Mike since arriving at school. It meant that Dean Hardscrabble couldn't kick Mike out of Monsters University—yet!

Mike had been kicked out of the Scare Program, but he'd made a deal with Dean Hardscrabble. She would let Mike and the rest of the Oozma Kappas back in the Scare Program if they won the Scare Games. But if they lost, Mike had to leave school forever.

That night, the OKs went to a party at the Roar Omega Roar house. The OKs were nervous. They had never been to a party before, but everyone gave them a warm welcome. It felt great—and a little strange. Their classmates weren't usually this nice to them.

The OKs started to relax and have fun. Suddenly, paint showered down on them, followed by confetti, flowers and stuffed animals. The entire room burst into laughter. The OKs looked ridiculous.

The next day, photos of the humiliated Oozma Kappas were everywhere. They were even in the school newspaper.

"Real Scarers look like us, not like you," Johnny told Mike. "But if you really want to work at Monsters, Inc., they're always hiring in the mailroom."

That gave Mike an idea. He ran after his teammates. "Guys, I've been doing this all wrong," he called. "We're going on a field trip!"

Squishy's mom drove them all to Monsters, Inc. Mike led the others onto the roof, where they had a perfect view of the Scare Floor.

"Take a good look, fellas," Mike told his friends. "See what they all have in common?"

"No, not really," Squishy replied.

"Exactly," said Mike. "The best Scarers use their differences to their advantage."

Just then the security guards spotted them. The OKs started to run, but they weren't fast enough. Sulley picked them all up and carried them back to the car!

The OKs drove home feeling inspired. They knew now that monsters of all shapes and sizes could be Scarers. It was their differences that made them great at what they did!

How Rose Dozed

The moon hung high in the sky, and the stars twinkled around it. It was late at night, and Briar Rose was supposed to be sleeping. But with all those owls hooting and the frogs in a nearby pond croaking, who could sleep? After tossing and turning for hours on end, Briar Rose woke up Flora, Fauna, and Merryweather to see if they could help.

"I've got the solution!" Fauna exclaimed. "You need to count sheep."

"Lie down now, dear," Flora joined in, "and picture a fence. Then imagine sheep jumping over it one by one, and don't lose count!"

Briar Rose lay back and did as they said. But when she got to sheep 544, she knew it wasn't working.

Briar Rose went back to her aunts. "No luck," she said.

"Oh, dear," said Flora. "We'll have to think of something else instead."

"Sleep, schmeep!" Merryweather chimed in. "The night has its own brightness, twinkle, and shine. It's such a shame to sleep through it all of the time!"

"But if Briar Rose doesn't sleep at night, she'll be tired during the day,"

Fauna told the other good fairies.

"Good point," Briar Rose agreed.

"Well, then, try reading a book! Reading always puts me to sleep," Merryweather said with a yawn.

"But I like reading," Briar Rose protested. "I'll never fall asleep."

There was a pause as each of Briar Rose's aunts thought and thought about how to help her.

"I know a way to help you sleep!" Fauna said suddenly. "All you have to do is think good thoughts about the day that's passed and hope for the happy things that tomorrow may bring."

"Is that true?" Briar Rose asked.

"Absolutely!" Flora agreed.

"Now, close your eyes, dear," said Merryweather, "and we'll see you in your dreams."

Briar Rose wasn't sure at first, but Flora, Fauna, and Merryweather had never let her down before. So she lay back and closed her eyes. She remembered her favorite parts of that day, then thought about the wonders tomorrow would bring.

And wouldn't you know, pretty soon, she was lost in her dreams.

Lizzy's Fairy House

Tinker Bell was a very curious tinker fairy. She always wanted to investigate everything—and nothing interested her as much as the mainland. Humans had such unusual inventions!

The fairies had recently arrived to bring summer to the mainland. Almost as soon as Tink touched down, she saw a car speeding down the road. She couldn't help herself. She had to take a closer look. Soon the car stopped in front of a house. The driver got out and went inside with his daughter, Lizzy. This was Tinker Bell's chance. She quickly flitted beneath the car's hood!

As Tink played with the car, Vidia appeared. Pulling on a lever, Tink accidentally soaked her friend with fluid from the car. Since Vidia couldn't fly with wet wings, the two headed back to the fairy camp on foot. As they walked, Tink spotted a row of buttons lined up like stepping-stones. She started picking them up.

"I'm not carrying this . . ." Vidia began, but then she spotted something that made her stop in her tracks. It was a fairy house that the human girl had made!

Tink was excited.

"Tinker Bell, we're not supposed to go near human houses!" warned Vidia.

But Tink didn't care. She went inside and looked around, delighted by the tiny furnishings.

"It's perfectly safe," Tink called.

"Oh, really?" asked Vidia. Then, to teach Tinker Bell a lesson, she whipped up a gust of wind that slammed the door shut!

Tink didn't mind. She was having fun exploring.

Suddenly, Vidia saw the human girl approaching. She pulled on the door to let Tink out, but it was jammed shut!

"Tink, someone's coming!" cried Vidia. "Get out of there!"

Tink ignored her. She was sure Vidia was just trying to scare her.

Vidia hid, watching as Lizzy got closer. "Oh, no! What have I done?" she cried as the little girl peeked into the house.

"A . . . a fairy . . ." Lizzy whispered. The little girl snatched up the fairy house and raced inside to her bedroom. What was Tinker Bell going to do now?

A Lady's Touch

Late one night, Lady's ears perked up and her eyes flew open with a start. The baby was crying! Lady climbed out of her basket, pushed open the swinging door with her nose, and tiptoed up the front stairs.

Inside the nursery, Jim Dear and Darling were trying to calm the baby.

"Oh, Jim, I just don't know what's the matter with him!" said Darling.

Jim Dear sat groggily at the edge of the bed, looking at his wife helplessly. "Well, we know he isn't hungry," he said, "since we've just given him a bottle." He massaged his temples as though they hurt. Then he noticed Lady, who had walked tentatively into the bedroom. "Hello, Lady," he said to her.

Lady took a few steps closer to the cradle, where Darling was laying the baby down. His little fists were closed tight, and his shrieks had turned into loud sobs.

"We just don't know what's the matter with the little guy," Jim Dear said wearily to Lady. "We've fed him and changed him, and I've sung him every lullaby I know. Maybe you can figure out what's bothering him!"

That was all the invitation Lady needed. She jumped up onto the bed and peered into the cradle. The baby opened his eyes and looked at Lady. His cries dropped to a whimper, and he reached out to touch her. His tiny hand grabbed hold of her ear and tugged. Lady winced, but held still. With her chin, she began to rock the cradle, and with her furry tail, she beat a rhythmic *thump, thump, thump* on the bed.

"Ga!" said the baby as he broke into a gummy smile. Still holding Lady's ear, the baby giggled.

"Oh, look, Jim Dear!" cried Darling delightedly. "Lady has gotten him to stop crying!"

"I just don't know what we'd do without you, Lady!" Jim Dear said gratefully.

Rock, rock, rock went the cradle. *Thump, thump, thump* went Lady's tail.

Soon the baby's eyelids grew heavy, and then his eyes closed. Tears still streaking his little round cheeks, he relaxed his grip on Lady's ear, smiled, and fell asleep.

New Friends

Carl had flown his house to South America with thousands of balloons tied to it. A boy named Russell had accidentally come with him. It was quite the adventure! The two had met a strange, bird named Kevin and a talking dog named Dug. But Dug's leader, the explorer Charles Muntz, had captured the bird. Russell was angry at Carl. Carl had promised to protect Kevin, but he had let the bird go in order to save his house from a fire.

Now, Carl sat inside, looking at his wife, Ellie's, adventure book. He had promised to take her on an adventure to Paradise Falls, but sadly, she had passed away.

Ellie's book was full of pictures of their life together. Finally Carl realized that their life had been the true adventure.

Suddenly, Carl heard something. He hurried outside and saw Russell gripping a bunch of balloons. He was going to help Kevin.

Carl knew he had to help Russell. He began throwing things out of the house to make it lighter. Carl was on his way when he heard a knock at the door. It was Dug. Together they set out to rescue Russell. Then they saw the boy being lowered out of Muntz's airship! Carl grabbed the garden hose and, using it like a rope, he swung over to the airship and saved Russell.

Once Russell was safe, Carl and Dug went back for Kevin. They set the bird free, but suddenly Muntz appeared with a sword!

Carl fought him and finally escaped. He made it back to the house when—BANG! The balloons began to pop.

The house plunged downward and landed on top of Muntz's airship. As Carl fell out of the house, Muntz ran inside to grab Kevin.

Carl knew he had to save his friends. The house was about to fall off the edge of the airship! Carl told Russell and Dug to hold on to Kevin, and then he waved a big bar of chocolate. Kevin *loved* chocolate. The big bird jumped onto the airship, saving Russell and Dug at the same time. Muntz's foot got caught in some balloons, and he drifted away.

"Sorry about your house," Russell told Carl.

"You know," said Carl, "it's just a house." He had friends now. That was more important.

Piglet's Pink Eggs

Winnie the Pooh had dropped in to visit Piglet, who was busy dyeing Easter eggs. "Easter is coming up, you know," Piglet explained.

On Piglet's kitchen table were six little cups. Pooh peered inside them. Each one held a different-colored dye. Then Pooh noticed a basket filled with some eggs Piglet had already dyed. Every one of them was pink.

"Would you like to dye the last egg, Pooh?" Piglet asked.

"Oh, yes," Pooh replied. "I would like that very much."

Piglet showed him how to place his egg in the wire dipper and how to use the dipper to dip the egg into the cups of dye.

"What color should I dye my egg?" Pooh asked.

Piglet smiled. "That's the fun of it, Pooh," he said. "You can choose any color you want!"

Pooh dipped his egg into the cup filled with yellow dye. He let it sit in the dye for a few minutes, then lifted it out again.

"It worked!" cried Pooh. "Piglet, look! What do you think of my yellow egg?"

"Oh Pooh, it's great," Piglet said. "It's b-bright . . . a-and it's sunny . . . and, well, it's very, very yellow, don't you think?"

Piglet was quiet for a moment. Then he cleared his throat.

"D-do you think . . . I don't know for sure, mind you. But do you think it could maybe use a little bit of, say, pink?" Piglet said.

"I think you're right," Pooh said. So he dipped his egg into the cup filled with pink dye. He let it sit there for just a few seconds before lifting it out. The little bit of pink dye on top of the yellow dye made the egg look pinkish-yellow.

"Hmm," said Piglet. "That's very pretty. But—if you don't mind my saying so, Pooh—I think it could use just a little more pink."

"Okay," said Pooh. So he dipped the egg back into the pink dye. This time he let it sit for five whole minutes before lifting it out. More pink dye on top of the yellow-and-pink color made the egg look as pink as pink could be.

"Well, what do you think?" asked Pooh.

"Perfect!" Piglet exclaimed.

They let Pooh's egg dry. Then Piglet put it in the basket with all the other pink eggs.

"Well, what do you know?" said Piglet. "It fits in so nicely!"

A Perfect Spring Day

"What a lovely spring morning!" exclaimed Snow White, opening the windows to the Dwarfs' cottage. The sun was shining, the birds were singing, and the sweet smell of flowers filled the air.

Snow White stepped outside to get some fresh air and found all of her forest friends gathered around the cottage. "Why, I do believe it's a perfect day for a walk in the woods," Snow White told her friends.

Together, they headed off to enjoy the many sights and scents of spring.

Before long, Snow White and her friends came upon a field of tulips swaying in the breeze.

"Oh, I must pick just a few," the young princess said as she stopped to admire the flowers.

When her basket was filled, Snow White continued into the woods. Soon, she heard a sound. *Quack! Quack! Quack!*

"Why, it's a mother duck and her little ducklings," said Snow White.

Snow White sat down on the bank of the stream and dangled her toes into the cool water. She giggled as she watched the baby ducks drink and splash in the water. They seemed to be having so much fun.

"The Dwarfs will certainly be thirsty when they return home from work," she said. "Perhaps I should bring them some cool water."

Leaning down, Snow White filled her pitcher. Across the stream she saw a perfect gooseberry bush.

"These berries look so ripe and sweet!" said the pleased princess, and she began to pick them.

"Oh, dear. My basket is filled to the brim!" she soon said. "That must mean it's time to head back to the cottage."

As she walked home, Snow White smiled. "This has been such a perfect spring day," she said. "I only wish I could have shared it with the Dwarfs."

When the Dwarfs came home from work that afternoon, they found a note from Snow White telling them to meet her in the meadow. They arrived to a wonderful surprise—a picnic!

Snow White and her friends shared stories about their day over a freshly baked gooseberry pie. It was the perfect end to a lovely spring day!

Ariel's Peace

One day, as Ariel and Flounder were passing by, they heard King Triton speaking to his bravest soldiers.

"The humans are building boats! Humans use their boats to capture sea creatures," King Triton said. "I am sending you to the coast to see how great a danger they pose to our people."

Immediately, the soldiers headed for the coast. "Come on!" Ariel told Flounder. "We're going with them!"

From a distance, Ariel saw some men building a boat near the shore. Others were gathering grain or fishing with big nets.

Suddenly, one of King Triton's soldiers was caught in a fishing net! Tridents in hand, the king's other mer-soldiers swam toward their friend. The fisherman was dumbstruck when he heaved his net onto shore and saw not fish, but the furious merman. The fisherman called to his friends in the fields for help. Grabbing their pitchforks, the farmers raced to defend their comrade.

Where the land met the sea, humans met mer-soldiers, ready to fight. Ariel saw it happening, and she knew she had to stop them.

"Wait!" she exclaimed. Ariel swam between them. She grabbed a trident from a mer-soldier's hand. Before anyone could stop her, she swam up to the human. "We come as friends," she declared, offering up the trident. "These are gifts for you. They will last forever—just as the peace between our people should be everlasting."

The mer-soldiers watched the farmer lay down his pitchfork and smile as he gently took the trident from Ariel.

The farmers and the fisherman quickly freed the mer-soldier from the fishing net. Then a farmer ran back to the fields. When he returned, his arms were full of wildflowers and stalks of grain.

"These are for you," he said, "and your people—from us, your newfound friends!"

Back at the palace, Ariel presented her father with the gifts from the surface world and told him all about the peaceful encounter with the humans. It had been quite a successful day.

Mending the Bond

Deep in the ancient Scottish Highlands, in a kingdom called DunBroch, Princess Merida lived with her family.

Merida's mother, Queen Elinor, wanted her daughter to marry in order to keep peace in their kingdom. But Merida was an adventurous teenager. She wasn't ready to marry.

Angry, Merida slashed a tapestry of her family in half. Then, to make matters worse, she asked a witch for a spell that would change her mother's mind. But instead, it changed Elinor into a bear!

Now, Merida was trying to break the spell. She knew she had to mend the family tapestry. But King Fergus had found Merida and Elinor-Bear in the castle.

Fergus slashed at Elinor-Bear, not realizing she was actually his wife. Elinor-Bear, who was starting to act more like a real bear, struck back, knocking Fergus to the ground. The noise drew the lords and the rest of the clans who were visiting the castle.

As Elinor tried to escape, Merida explained to her father what had happened. But King Fergus didn't believe her. He locked her in the tapestry room for her own safety, and gave the key to the nursemaid.

Merida was desperate to get out. Through the window in the door, she spotted three little bear cubs. They were her little brothers! They'd eaten the rest of the spell cake and turned into bears, too! Merida told the triplets to get the key.

Meanwhile, Fergus and the lords were closing in on Elinor-Bear.

Freed by the triplets, Merida grabbed the tapestry. Then she climbed onto her horse and raced into the forest to save her mother.

Merida finally caught up with the lords just as King Fergus raised his sword to kill the bear. Merida stepped in front of him.

"Are you out of your mind, lass?" Fergus exclaimed.

Gathering all of her strength, Merida swung her sword and chopped off Fergus's wooden leg! King Fergus couldn't understand why his daughter would do such a thing. But Merida was willing to risk anything to save her mother. The bond between them was finally beginning to mend.

In a Tangle

CRASH! Pinocchio was woken from a sound sleep by a noise downstairs. He jumped up and raced to Geppetto's workshop.

"Is anybody here?" Pinocchio called.

"Meow!" It was Geppetto's kitten, Figaro.

"I hear you, but I can't see you!" called Pinocchio.

Suddenly, the puppets above Geppetto's workbench began to move.

"Yikes!" cried Pinocchio, startled.

"Meow!" cried Figaro. He was tangled in the puppets' strings. The kitten tried to get free, but he only became more tangled.

Jiminy Cricket hopped down from the hearth. He rubbed his tired eyes. "What's going on?" he asked.

Pinocchio pointed to the little kitten and laughed.

"Pinocchio, maybe you should help poor Figaro instead of laughing at him," Jiminy said.

"Maybe I should leave him there," replied Pinocchio. "Then Geppetto can see how naughty he's been."

"That's not very nice," said Jiminy. "How would you feel if you were all tangled up?"

Pinocchio sighed. "I guess I wouldn't like it very much." He was about to free the kitten when, suddenly, he exclaimed, "Hey, Jiminy, look at that!"

Figaro's paws were wrapped around the strings in such a way that when his paws moved, the puppets danced!

"That's a neat trick," said Pinocchio. "Figaro can work the puppets!"

The kitten moved his paws some more, and all the puppets danced.

"I have an idea," said Jiminy Cricket. "Do you want to hear it?"

Pinocchio and Figaro both nodded.

The next morning when Geppetto awoke, he got a surprise.

"Look, Father!" Pinocchio said. "Figaro can make the puppets dance!"

Pinocchio winked at Figaro, and the cat leaped onto the puppet strings again.

"Amazing!" Geppetto cried, watching the show. "We can put on a puppet show for all the children of the town!"

Pinocchio was thrilled to see Geppetto so happy.

"But when did you discover Figaro's talent?" asked Geppetto.

"Last night," said Pinocchio, "when I found him in your workshop . . . uh, hanging around."

The Easter Egg Hunt

The Easter holiday was quickly approaching, which meant one thing: the annual Pelekai Easter egg hunt! Lilo couldn't wait to begin painting eggs.

"This is my favorite part," Lilo said. "I'm going to paint one pink with purple polka dots!"

"I'm going to draw mosquitoes on mine," said Pleakley, grabbing a crayon.

"Blue!" cried Stitch, dunking his egg violently in the cup of blue dye.

Later, while everyone washed up, Nani went down to the beach to hide the twenty-five eggs. Whoever found the most would win a prize!

The sun shone on the brilliant white sand as Lilo, Stitch, Jumba, and Pleakley searched high and low for the eggs. As the afternoon sun began to sink, everyone gathered to count the eggs. Jumba had six eggs, and so did Pleakley. Stitch had six, too. Then they finished tallying Lilo's eggs. ". . . four, five, and six!"

But that added up to only twenty-four. There must be one more egg hidden somewhere on the beach! So they split up and went looking for the last egg.

Finally, Lilo spotted something under a hibiscus bush.

"Everybody, come quick!" she cried. "I think I've found the last egg!"

Nani, Jumba, and Pleakley came running.

"Look," said Lilo, "it's a huge foil egg. The biggest chocolate egg I've ever seen!"

"It sure is," said Nani. "This is the prize, Lilo, and since you all found the same number of eggs, it looks like you all get to share it!"

"But where's Stitch?" said Lilo. "He should be here, too!"

Suddenly, the huge chocolate egg began to twitch. It rattled and shook, and then—

Stitch popped out of it, yelling, "Ta-daaa!" Bits of chocolate scattered all over the place.

"Wow!" cried Lilo. "Did you guys plan that?"

"No, Lilo," said Nani, completely confused and a little disturbed. "I have *no idea* how Stitch got in there without breaking the foil."

"My secret!" said Stitch cheerfully. He began munching on a piece of the chocolate egg.

Nani and Lilo smiled and shrugged, and then they all sat down and ate bits of chocolate egg while they watched the sun set over the water.

Two Frogs Instead of One

Tiana had just discovered a frog on the balcony of her friend Charlotte's room. Then the frog had started to talk!

"I did not mean to scare you," apologized the frog. It jumped onto a piece of furniture to take a closer look at Tiana, who was dressed in Charlotte's clothes and looked like a princess.

Downstairs, Charlotte's costume ball was going on.

"Please allow me to introduce myself," he said. "I am Prince Naveen of Maldonia. One minute I am a prince, charming and handsome, and the next thing I know, I am tripping over these!" The frog pointed to his webbed feet.

Terrified, Tiana grabbed a large book from a shelf.

"If you're the prince, then who was that waltzing with Lottie on the dance floor?"

Tiana had seen Prince Naveen dancing at the ball downstairs. She got ready to throw the book at the frog.

"Wait! I know that story!" the frog interrupted, looking at the cover of the book—*The Frog Prince*. "My mother

had the servants read it to me every night!"

Naveen leafed through the pages of the book. As he read, he realized that he knew what to do. Tiana had to kiss him!

"I do not kiss frogs," replied Tiana.

But the frog was not done. "Besides being unbelievably handsome, I also come from a fabulously wealthy family," the frog said. "Surely I could offer you some sort of reward. A wish I could grant, perhaps?"

Tiana thought. This might be her only chance of finally being able to own the restaurant she had always dreamed of owning with her father.

Tiana closed her eyes. She took a deep breath and—*smack!*—she planted a quick kiss on the frog's pursed lips.

When she opened her eyes again, she had turned into a frog, too!

"Do not panic!" begged Naveen.

Tiana, furious, did not reply. She tried one of her new talents, and leaped—*boing!*—right at Naveen's throat!

"You know," said Naveen. "If you're going to let every little thing bother you, it is going to be a long night!"

Chore de Force

Cinderella watched as a blue-and-pink-tinted bubble floated up from her bucket. "Isn't that pretty?" she said. Gus, Jaq, and the rest of Cinderella's mouse friends nodded in agreement.

"I bet it would be fun to float around in a bubble all day! I could see whole cities at a time, bounce on clouds, and soar with the birds," Cinderella said dreamily.

Suddenly, Cinderella laughed. "What am I doing?" she said. "I should stay focused on my chores."

Cinderella finished cleaning the windows and prepared to mop the floor. She plunged the mop into a bucket of soapy water, then dragged it across the floor. As the mop slid across the slippery floor, she suddenly realized . . .

"This is like dancing! How I love to dance!" Gus and Jaq copied Cinderella as she twirled around the room with the mop. "What fun!" she cried happily.

Then Cinderella caught herself. "Oh, my. Did I say that aloud?" Maybe I just need to get away from all these bubbles, she thought. Ironing should do the trick!

She was ironing away and humming merrily to herself when she realized how dark the sky had grown. "Look at the time!" Cinderella exclaimed. "I've been daydreaming the day away and haven't even started dinner."

Cinderella hurried to the kitchen, where she chopped and minced and grated and stirred. "I don't know where this day has gone," she fretted as she added ingredients to her stepsisters' favorite soup. "I've got absolutely nothing done!"

Cinderella's stepsisters, Anastasia and Drizella, barged into the kitchen.

"Where's my laundry?" barked Anastasia.

"Done," Cinderella said.

"And my ironing?" Drizella added.

"Done," Cinderella replied again.

"Did you mop the floors?"

"Wash the windows?"

"Make our dinner?"

"Done, done, done!" Cinderella said gaily.

The sisters marched out of the kitchen, muttering with displeasure.

And there Cinderella stood, all alone in the kitchen once more. As she stirred the pot of soup, she thought, I guess I did get a lot done, after all!

The Mysterious Book

"What are you looking at, Belle?" Chip asked.

Belle smiled at the little teacup. "Oh, you caught me daydreaming, Chip," she said. "I was just looking up there." She pointed to the highest shelf in the Beast's library. On the shelf was a single book.

Belle had wondered about that book since the day the Beast had first shown her the library. The trouble was, none of the ladders quite reached the shelf. So the book had remained a mystery.

Belle's curiosity had grown until she could hardly stop thinking about the book. She explained the problem to Chip, who went straight to his mother. Mrs. Potts called a meeting of all the enchanted objects. As soon as she told them about the book, they wanted to help Belle.

"What we need is a plan," Cogsworth said.

"Yes!" Lumiere cried. "And I've got one!"

That evening, the enchanted objects gathered in the library. First the Stove stood at the base of the shelves. The Wardrobe climbed on top of him. Soon a whole tower of enchanted objects stretched almost to the top shelf.

Finally Lumiere started to climb. He stretched as far as he could. . . .

"What on earth are you doing?" Belle exclaimed from the doorway.

"Oh, mademoiselle!" Lumiere cried. "You're just in time—voilà!"

With that, he finally managed to reach the book, knocking it off the shelf and into Belle's hands.

A moment later, the tower collapsed in a heap!

After Belle made certain that everyone was all right, she opened the book.

"Oh!" she said when she saw the first page.

"What is it?" Chip asked breathlessly.

Belle smiled sheepishly. "I can't believe it! I've already read this one."

The enchanted objects sighed. Had all their work been for nothing?

"But thank you anyway!" Belle said quickly. "It's one of my favorites—it's full of far-off places, magic spells . . . well, let me show you!"

Soon all the enchanted objects were gathered around as Belle read the book to them. And wouldn't you know? It became one of their favorite books, too!

Dig Deep!

Mike and Sulley woke up early and leaped out of bed. They needed to get ready for the next event of the Scare Games. Mike and Sulley were part of Oozma Kappa. Their fraternity was full of students who had failed out of the Scare Program. But the two were sure they could win the Scare Games. Their team had survived the first two events. Now they had three more to go. Mike was determined to lead his team to victory. If they lost, he'd have to leave the university. His dream of becoming a Scarer would be over.

The third event was called Don't Scare the Teen. The OKs successfully worked their way through a maze by scaring all the cutouts of human children and hiding from the cutouts of the teens. Only their biggest rivals, the RORs, made it out of the maze before them. That meant there were only three teams left for the fourth event: ROR, HSS, and OK!

The Hide and Sneak event required all of the competitors to hide in a dark house while referees searched for them with flashlights.

The referees soon discovered HSS— but no one else. The OKs had made it to the final event. They would be competing against the RORs for the Scare Games trophy!

As Sulley headed home from the fourth event, he spotted Dean Hardscrabble, the head of the Scare Program. It had been her decision to kick Mike and Sulley out of the program.

"When we get back," Sulley said to her, "I hope there'll be no hard feelings."

But Dean Hardscrabble told Sulley that she doubted they would win. Mike just wasn't scary enough.

Sulley wondered if Dean Hardscrabble was right. He decided to teach Mike how to be scary.

Sulley told Mike to forget what he had read about scaring in books. He needed to stop *thinking* scary and start *feeling* it.

Mike tried a heartfelt roar.

"Let the animal out!" Sulley coached. "Dig deep!"

Mike gave it all he had. It was an improvement. Sulley just hoped it would be enough to win. He would find out soon.

The battle for the trophy was about to begin.

Leaving the Tower

Flynn Rider wanted his satchel back—the crown he had stolen was inside! Flynn had been running from the palace guards when he had stumbled upon Rapunzel's tower. He wanted to hide inside, but Rapunzel had tied him up and taken his stolen crown. She had been locked in the tower her whole life, and she wanted to know why there were floating lights in the sky every year on her birthday. Now she refused to give him the crown unless he took her to see the lights.

For the first time ever, Rapunzel set a foot on the grass below the tower. It was wonderful! Overcome with excitement, she began to roll around on the ground.

"I can't believe I did this! I can't believe I did this!" she shouted.

But Rapunzel also felt guilty for betraying Mother Gothel, who she believed was her mother. The woman had told Rapunzel she must stay in the tower forever, because the world was too dangerous a place for such a delicate girl. Rapunzel didn't know that Mother Gothel only wanted Rapunzel's magical hair, which kept the wicked woman young forever.

Rapunzel's excitement soon faded and she began to cry. How could she have betrayed her mother like this?

Flynn saw the chance to get hold of his satchel without fulfilling his part of the bargain. He murmured, "Let me ease your conscience. This is part of growing up. A little healthy rebellion, a little adventure. . . . Does your mother deserve it? No. Would this break her heart and crush her soul? Of course. But you've just got to do it."

"Break her heart?" Rapunzel asked. "Crush her soul?"

"Like a grape," Flynn said.

Rapunzel looked sad. Flynn led her back to the tower, saying, "I'm letting you out of the deal. Let's just turn around and get you back home. I get my satchel, you get back a mother-daughter relationship based on mutual trust."

Rapunzel suddenly froze. "I am seeing those lanterns," she insisted, and turned around and stormed away from the tower.

It seemed that Flynn was stuck. He would have to take Rapunzel to see the lights after all.

Make Believe

The fairies were busy bringing summer to the mainland when Tinker Bell had left the safety of fairy camp to follow a car along a road. She wanted to see how it worked.

Vidia had followed Tink, trying to get her to come back. She knew fairies weren't supposed to go near humans. But Tink hadn't listened. On the way back to camp, Tink found a fairy house that the little girl who had been in the car had made. Tink was exploring it when Vidia accidentally trapped her inside!

Just then the girl appeared. Her name was Lizzy. She looked through the window of the little house. She had finally found a fairy!

Lizzy took the fairy house, with Tink inside, up to her room. Then, to keep Tinker Bell safe from the family cat, Lizzy put the fairy inside a birdcage.

Vidia watched from the window. She thought Lizzy was keeping Tink prisoner! She had to get help!

Meanwhile, inside the house, Lizzy let Tinker Bell out of the cage and showed off her collection of fairy artwork. But as Lizzy described what was going on in each picture, Tink realized that the little girl had her fairy facts all wrong!

Tink tried to explain fairy life to the girl, but all Lizzy heard was a jingling sound. "So that's how fairies speak!" she exclaimed.

Tink went over to the fairy house to fix the door. "Why, you're quite the little tinker, aren't you?" asked Lizzy. Tink pointed to herself, then rang the little house's fairy bell. "Tinker Bell?" Lizzy cried. "What a lovely name!"

Just then, Lizzy's father came upstairs to fix some leaks in the roof. Tinker Bell hid.

Dr. Griffiths was a scientist. He wanted his daughter to be just like him. He gave Lizzy an empty field journal. "You're very talented, my darling," he said. "I'm sure you'll be able to fill it with your own scientific research." Then, satisfied, her father went back to repairing the house.

Lizzy sighed. She hadn't wanted to put Tinker Bell in danger by telling her father about the fairy. But she hoped one day she could convince her father that fairies really did exist!

Together Again

Merida was a free-spirited princess. Her mother, Queen Elinor, had wanted Merida to be a proper princess and marry in order to keep peace in the kingdom. But Merida had refused to choose a suitor. Instead, she had fought with her mother, slashing a tapestry of her family in two.

Soon after, a witch had given Merida a spell that had turned Queen Elinor into a bear! Now, Merida just wanted her mother back.

A riddle from the witch had told her to "mend the bond torn by pride." So Merida had sewn the tapestry back together.

Merida's father, King Fergus, and the other clansmen had chased Elinor-Bear into the forest, not realizing she was really the queen.

Suddenly, another bear appeared. "Mor'du!" Merida said with a gasp.

Mor'du closed in on Merida. Bravely, Merida raised her bow and arrow. With a deafening roar, Elinor-Bear charged at Mor'du, shoving him away from her daughter.

The two bears fought until, at last, Elinor-Bear pushed Mor'du against a huge stone. The stone fell, crushing Mor'du beneath it.

In the silence that followed, Merida draped the mended tapestry over her mother. But nothing happened. Merida watched as Elinor-Bear's eyes turned cold and more bearlike.

"I want you back! I just want you back, Mum," Merida said. "I love you!"

Suddenly, Merida felt a hand brush her hair. She looked up and saw her mother smiling down at her. When their bond was repaired, the spell had been broken. Elinor had changed back into the queen!

Back at the castle, Merida and Elinor began a new tapestry, one that would forever record the story of the challenge they had faced—and conquered—together.

Later, they watched as the clans sailed for home. Queen Elinor would never again doubt that Merida's strong, free spirit was that of a proper princess, and the future Queen of DunBroch.

As for Merida, she had finally come to appreciate her mother's strength and courage. She knew now that she wouldn't change a thing about her.

Lend Me Your Ears

"I think I can, I think I can, I think I can," chugged Casey Junior the circus train. The train moved slowly around a bend. "I think I can. I think I . . . *Achoo!*" he sneezed. Suddenly, he came to a halt. "I know I can't," he admitted finally.

The animals and the performers poked their heads out of their train cars, wondering what was wrong.

"Casey Junior here has a very bad cold," the engineer said. "He's going to need some rest before he can take us any farther."

The Ringmaster frowned. "But we're due at the fairground in a few hours. What will we do? After all, the show must go on!"

The engineer just shrugged and turned his attention back to the sneezing, coughing, and spluttering little engine.

The Ringmaster went down the train, swinging open the doors to all the cages and cars. "Come on, everyone," he said. "Might as well stretch your legs."

Dumbo the elephant and his mother, Mrs. Jumbo, took a drink from the bucket of water the Ringmaster had set out. Mrs. Jumbo gazed around. "Looks like we're in the middle of nowhere," she said. "I do hope poor Casey Junior is feeling better soon."

"Me too," Dumbo's friend Timothy Q. Mouse said hopefully.

Just then there was a clap of thunder. Rain began to fall from the sky. The animals and performers ran for the shelter of the circus wagons. Dumbo held on to his mother's tail. Suddenly the wind picked up. The gust caught Dumbo's huge ears and sent him flying backward!

"That's it!" yelled the Ringmaster over the howling wind. "Dumbo, come with me!"

He led Dumbo over to the train, climbed onto the front wagon, and motioned for the little elephant to join him.

"Now spread out those great ears of yours!" the Ringmaster said. Dumbo's ears billowed out, catching the wind like giant sails and pushing Casey Junior along the tracks.

"The show will go on!" the Ringmaster shouted happily.

"I know I can. I know I can. I know I can," chanted Casey Junior. And then he added, "Thanks to Dumbo!"

Woodland Washing

Briar Rose sang as she hung the sheets on the washing line. "Don't you just love the sunshine?" she asked a bluebird who was chirping along with her. The bird chirped a new song in response, and Briar Rose laughed as she pulled her Aunt Flora's red dress out of the basket of clean laundry.

Aunt Merryweather's blue dress was next. Briar Rose was just pegging the shoulder to the washing line when suddenly a pair of cheeky chipmunks leaped onto the line from a tree and raced down the length of it, covering the dresses and the sheets with muddy footprints.

"Look what you've done, you naughty chipmunks!" Briar Rose scolded. She shook a finger at the creatures. "It took me two hours to get those dresses and sheets clean!"

Sighing with frustration, Briar Rose unpegged the sheets from the line and pulled a fresh bucket of water up from the well. Then, taking the washboard and the bar of laundry soap, she began to scrub out the muddy prints. It looked as if she wouldn't get in a walk today after all.

Suddenly, a chattering noise caught her attention.

Looking up, she saw the chipmunks hurrying out of the forest with several other forest animals at their heels. There were two rabbits, four chipmunks, three bluebirds, a deer, a skunk, and an owl.

Briar Rose laughed. "Why, you've brought all your friends! What a wonderful surprise!"

The chipmunks chattered excitedly and the animals all got to work. The birds lifted the sheet into the air so the edges wouldn't get dirty while Briar Rose scrubbed. The deer, the skunk, and the rabbits brought fresh water from the well. And the chipmunks scampered across the laundry soap to get their feet all soapy, then walked across the muddy parts of the sheets until they were clean.

When the washing was done, everyone helped hang the newly clean laundry on the line for a second time.

Briar Rose smiled at her animal friends and gave the chipmunks a little pat.

"Finished at last," she said. "Now we can all take a walk in the forest . . . together!"

A Special Song

King Triton's birthday was in a couple of days, and Sebastian was planning a very special performance. Triton's daughter, Ariel, would sing while the orchestra played a brand-new tune. But they still had a lot of work to do. During rehearsals, a young mermaid named Coral kept accidentally dropping her cymbals.

Sebastian threw down his baton. "Rehearsal is over!" he yelled, storming away.

Ariel comforted Coral and invited her to see all the treasures in her grotto. Ariel told Coral the grotto could be her secret place, too.

A few days later, as Ariel swam into the grotto, she heard someone singing. The voice was strong and sweet. When Ariel arrived, she saw her new friend.

"Coral! You have such a lovely voice! You should be singing in the concert, not playing the cymbals."

The little mermaid shrugged. "I just like singing to myself," she explained. "I've never actually performed for anyone."

The next day at rehearsal, Sebastian made Ariel and the orchestra practice over and over.

"The big day is tomorrow!" the crab said, fretting. "Let's try it again."

By the end of the afternoon, Ariel had lost her voice! Luckily, she knew who could take her place.

"Me?" Coral said when the princess asked her. "But I can't!"

"You must!" Sebastian insisted. "Or King Triton's birthday celebration will be ruined!"

Coral knew her new friend was counting on her. "All right," she said. "I'll do it."

That night, Coral took a deep breath, swam onstage, and started to sing. Before she knew it, the concert was over and the audience began to cheer!

"Coral," said Sebastian, smiling, "from now on, you're going to be a court singer!"

After the show, Ariel found Coral with her family.

"I didn't know you could sing!" one of Coral's sisters exclaimed.

"No one ever would have known if it weren't for Ariel," replied Coral. "She believed in me."

Ariel still couldn't speak, but she gave Coral a big hug. It had been a wonderful evening!

MAY 1

The Missing Vegetables

Of all the things Belle loved about the Beast's castle, the thing she loved the most was the garden in the back. She had read every one of the Beast's books about gardening, and every season she experimented with something new. This summer, she'd decided to try growing vegetables. And now they were ready to be picked. She was planning to use them to make the Beast a salad for lunch.

Belle slipped on her gardening gloves and her sun hat, grabbed her biggest basket, and happily skipped out into the garden.

"First," she said out loud, to no one in particular, "let's get some lettuce!"

But when she bent down to where the lettuce should have been, she found a bed of empty soil.

"My lettuce!" she cried. "Where did it go?"

Bewildered, Belle moved on to where her sweet, tender carrots had been growing.

"Oh, dear!" she cried. "There's nothing here, either!"

And there wasn't a single pea to be found. "I don't understand," she said.

But facts were facts. The garden was empty, and there was nothing she could do . . . but go back to the castle and look for a book about building fences for next summer's garden!

As she walked inside, empty-handed and disappointed, Belle passed Mrs. Potts and Chip.

"What's the matter, dear?" asked Mrs. Potts.

"Oh, everything!" Belle sighed. "My whole garden has been robbed." Then she shrugged. "So much for my salad idea."

"Don't feel sad, Belle," Chip said. "Come and have some lunch."

"I'm not hungry," Belle replied with a sad smile.

"Oh, I don't know," said Mrs. Potts, steering her into the dining room. "You might be . . ."

"SURPRISE!" called the Beast.

"What?" Belle gasped. There, laid out on the table, was what looked like every possible vegetable from her garden, washed and sliced and arranged just so on fancy dishes.

"You've been working so hard in the garden," the Beast explained. "I thought it would be nice if I did something for you. I hope you like it."

Belle smiled. What a treat!

Geppetto's Gift

One day Geppetto was in his workshop painting a clock when he got an idea. "I know what I will do with that pine log I just found," he told his little cat, Figaro. "I will make a splendid puppet!"

He put down the clock and got to work. When he was done making the puppet, he got out his jars of paint and some fabric.

"Suddenly, Geppetto heard a noise outside. He went to the window and looked out. He noticed a little girl walking quietly with her mother. Like the other girls, she carried schoolbooks under her arm. When a group of girls skipped by her, she looked at them shyly.

"That little girl must be new in town. She looks like she could use a friend," Geppetto said. Suddenly he had an idea. "Excuse me, young miss," he called out the window. "I wonder if you could lend me a hand?"

The girl hurried over, tugging her mother after her. Why, an invitation to Geppetto's workshop—how grand!

"As you can see, my friend here needs some eyes," Geppetto said, pointing to the puppet. "But I don't know what color her eyes should be."

The girl thought hard. "Green," she decided.

Geppetto picked up his pot of green paint and painted two big green eyes onto the wooden face.

"Now, what color do you suppose her hair should be?" Geppetto asked.

"Brown," the little girl said with a smile.

Carefully, Geppetto painted brown curls on the puppet's head.

"She'll need a dress," he said next. "What do you think? Red? Green?"

The girl looked down at her own blue dress. "Blue," she told Geppetto.

So Geppetto made a little blue dress for the little puppet. Then he added a smiling red mouth to the puppet's face.

"Now there's just one last thing," Geppetto said. "I'm busy in my shop all day long, and I'm afraid this little lady might be lonely. Could you take care of her for me?"

The girl's face lit up with delight. "Thank you!" she cried. Hugging the puppet in her arms, she carried her out the door.

"Thank you," the girl's mother said. "You know, you'd be a wonderful father."

Geppetto smiled. If only! he thought.

Tony and the Tramp

Tramp licked the last of the tomato sauce from his chin. "So, what do you think, Pidge?" he asked Lady.

"That was the most wonderful meal I've ever had," Lady gushed.

"What did I tell ya?" Tramp boasted. "There's no one in the world who can cook up a meal like Tony!"

"I couldn't agree with you more," Lady said. "Can I ask you a question?"

"Sure thing," Tramp said. "Ask away!"

"I was just wondering," Lady began, "how you and Tony met."

"How I met Tony?" Tramp laughed. "Now that's a story!"

"I'll bet!" Lady said.

"Well, see, it goes like this," Tramp began. "It was a cold and snowy night. I don't think it had ever been that cold before, and I know it hasn't been since. I had been walking uphill for miles. Icicles were hanging from the tip of my nose."

"Wait a minute!" Lady interrupted. "You were walking for miles uphill? In this town?"

"That's right!" Tramp said. "You've never seen the likes of it."

"Exactly!" Lady told him. "You know why?"

Tramp shook his head.

"Because it isn't possible! There are no big hills around here!" Lady said.

"Okay, you're right," he confessed.

"So, then, what's the truth?" Lady asked.

"The truth is," Tramp began, "I wasn't always the slick and handsome devil you see before you."

"Is that right?" Lady was amused.

"And this one afternoon I was being harassed by a group of mangy mutts who outnumbered me ten to one. So I took off as fast as my paws could carry me. And as they were chasing me, along came the dogcatcher. Before he could get me, Tony came running out with a bowl of steaming hot pasta," Tramp explained. "He told the dogcatcher I was his dog. The dogcatcher didn't believe him. But when Tony put the bowl of pasta down in front of me, he had no choice. Let me tell you, I thought I'd died and gone to heaven."

"I can relate to that," Lady said, recalling the meal.

"And the rest," Tramp said, "as they say, is history!"

Good Housekeeping

Snow White and the Prince were going to be married. Her dear friends, the Seven Dwarfs, were filled with joy to see Snow White so happy. But they knew they were going to miss her—not to mention her wonderful cooking and how she kept their cottage so clean and tidy!

Snow White was also worried about how the little men were going to get along without her. She decided it was time they learned how to cook and clean for themselves.

"First, let's see you sweep out the cottage," she said. "Remember to push the dirt out the door and not just move it around on the floor."

The men all grabbed brooms and set to work.

"Don't forget to open the door *first*," Snow White added. Then she moved on to the next task. "Now we'll do the laundry! First you heat the water over the fire, then you scrub the clothes with a bar of soap, rinse them, and finally hang them on the line to dry."

Dopey was first in line. He jumped into the tub and rubbed the bar of soap all over the clothes he was wearing.

"Dopey," said Snow White, "it's easier if you wash the clothes after you've taken them off."

A bit later, the Dwarfs trooped into the kitchen for a cooking lesson.

"Now we're going to make stew," said Snow White. "You take a little of everything you have on hand, throw it into a pot, and let it simmer for a long time."

As Snow White was leaving, Doc said, "Don't worry, Snow White. We're going to be fust jine—I mean, just fine."

The next night, the Dwarfs made dinner and invited Snow White and the Prince to join them. When the guests arrived, Dopey led them over to the large pot simmering over the fire and grandly lifted the lid. An old boot, some socks, a bunch of flowers, and a cake of soap were floating on the top.

"We made it with a little bit of everything we had on hand, just like you said," Sleepy said.

"Perhaps we should go over that recipe again," Snow White said with a laugh.

One Lucky Pup

"Where are we going?" Penny asked.

"This will be fun," Perdy said soothingly as she coaxed the puppies into the car. "I promise."

Roger steered the car down a winding country lane. The puppies smelled all kinds of good things. They smelled hay and flowers. Then they smelled something sweet—peaches!

"Here we are!" Anita opened the car door.

"Where's here?" Freckles asked Lucky.

"It looks like an orchard!" Lucky yipped. He loved to eat fruit.

Roger stretched. "You dogs run and play," he said. "We'll call you when it's time for our picnic."

"Don't eat too many peaches," Pongo barked, but the puppies were already running off.

All morning, the puppies romped and played in the green grass until Pongo and Perdy came to call them. "Time for lunch!" Pongo barked.

"I'm not hungry," Rolly said, rolling over in the grass.

"I hope you didn't eat too much," Perdy said.

The big dogs herded their puppies up the hill toward the spot where Roger and Anita were laying out a picnic.

Perdy scanned the group. "Wait a minute," she said to Pongo. "Where's Lucky?"

The black-and-white pack stopped in its tracks. Pongo counted them. Lucky was definitely missing!

"Don't worry, Mother," Pepper said sweetly. "I have an idea." She turned to her brothers and sisters. "Hey, everyone, she barked. "We have to find Lucky!"

All of the puppies yipped excitedly and tumbled over one another to find Lucky's trail. Soon every nose was sniffing the ground. Penny sniffed around a tree and behind a patch of tall grass. She'd caught the scent!

"Here he is!" Penny barked.

The rest of the dogs gathered around to see the puppy asleep in the grass. Lucky's ears covered his eyes, but there was no mistaking the horseshoe of spots on his back, or the pile of peach pits by his nose!

"Lucky is lucky we found him," said Perdita with a relieved sigh.

"And," Pepper joked, "he'll be *really* lucky if he doesn't wake up with a tummy ache!"

Spring Has Sprung!

Spring had come at last to the forest. *Sniff, sniff*—Bambi could smell the change in the air. The days were growing longer. The nights were getting shorter. Crocuses and daffodils were pushing new green shoots out of the ground. And the forest didn't feel quite as lonely as it had during the cold weather. In just the last few days, Bambi had noticed that there were more animals peeking their heads out of their holes, burrows, and dens.

Early one morning on the first day of spring, Bambi decided to take a walk through the forest. He came upon Mrs. Possum and her children hanging upside down by their tails from a tree branch.

"Hello, Mrs. Possum," Bambi said. "I haven't seen you since autumn. Where have you and your family been all winter long?"

"Oh, we like to spend most of our winter indoors," Mrs. Possum replied. "But now that spring is here, it's so nice to be out in the fresh air again."

Then Mrs. Possum and the rest of her family closed their eyes and dozed off.

Continuing through the forest, Bambi stopped by a tree filled with twittering birds.

"Hello," Bambi said. "Where have you birds been all winter long?"

"Oh, we fly south for the winter, to warmer places where we can find more food," the bird explained. "But we are so happy it's spring once more. It's lovely to be back in the forest and to see all of our friends."

Then the bird joined her voice with her friends' twittering tunes.

Bambi kept walking, meeting old friends at every turn. He came upon mice moving from their winter quarters back into their spring and summer homes. He noticed the squirrels and chipmunks snacking leisurely on nuts, no longer storing them away for the winter. He heard a woodpecker rapping at a pine tree, and he spotted the ducks out for a swim on the pond.

Yes, thought Bambi, it had been a long, cold, difficult winter. But somehow the arrival of spring made him feel that everything would be all right. Everywhere he looked there was life, there were new beginnings . . . and, most importantly, there was hope.

A Deal Is a Deal

An evil sorcerer had changed spoiled Prince Naveen into a frog. Naveen assumed that kissing a princess would change him back, so he went looking for one. When he saw Tiana dressed up for a costume ball, he thought she was a princess. He promised to help her buy the restaurant she so desperately wanted if she would kiss him. But when they kissed, Tiana had turned into a frog instead!

"What did you do to me? I . . . I'm green and I'm . . . slimy!"

The two frogs realized they could not stay in New Orleans. And so they set off for the bayou.

"If you're the prince, then who was that waltzing with Lottie on the dance floor?" asked Tiana.

Naveen explained his story.

"Voodoo? You mean to tell me all this happened because you were messing with the Shadow Man? It serves me right for wishing on stars. The *only* way to get what you want in this world is through hard work," she muttered.

"Hard work?" retorted Naveen, surprised. "Why would a princess need to work hard?"

"I'm not a princess. I'm a waitress."

At these words, Naveen uttered a cry. "Well, no wonder the kiss did not work," he said indignantly. "You lied to me! You were wearing a crown!"

"It was a *costume* party!" Tiana shouted.

Realizing his mistake, Naveen decided to get revenge on Tiana. "Well, the egg is on your face, because I do not have any riches! I am completely broke!" He started to laugh.

"And you had the gall to call *me* a liar?" fumed Tiana.

"I intend to be rich again," said Naveen. "Once I marry Miss Charlotte LaBouff, if she will have me."

Suddenly, hungry alligators surrounded them! Quickly, Tiana took refuge in a hollow log by the water's edge. Naveen begged her to save him.

"Help me get out of the swamp and once I marry Charlotte, I will get you your restaurant."

Tiana dropped a vine and pulled Naveen to safety.

"Well, waitress," Naveen said, "looks like we're going to be here for a while, so we may as well get comfortable."

Tiana sighed. She had just been caught in her own trap!

The Final

It was the final event of the Scare Games. Mike, Sulley, and the rest of the Oozma Kappas were competing against their biggest rivals, the Roar Omega Roars, for the trophy. The RORs were the reigning champions. Could the OKs beat them?

The RORs and the OKs entered the packed stadium. The crowd roared for the OKs. No one had expected them to make it this far, and the crowd was rooting for them.

"It's time to see how terrifying you really are in the scare simulators," said Brock Pearson, the vice president of the Greek Council. "Be warned. Each simulated scare has been set to the highest difficulty level."

One member from each team took their places at the starting line. After four rounds, the RORs had a significant lead over the OKs. It was up to Mike and Sulley to win it for the team.

Sulley went up against Randy, Mike's old roommate. Sulley entered the simulator. He successfully dodged every obstacle in the room, crept up to the bed, and let out a thunderous roar. It was so loud that it shook Randy's simulator. Sulley easily won the challenge. Now the RORs and the OKs were tied!

The last two team members to compete were Mike and Johnny Worthington, president of ROR.

"Don't take the loss too hard," Johnny sneered at Mike. "You never belonged here, anyway."

Mike knew it was up to him. He couldn't let anything distract him from doing his best.

Johnny entered his scare simulator and got a huge scream. Next Mike entered his room.

Mike ruffled the scare simulator curtains and crept along the side of the bed. Then he closed his eye and concentrated. This was it. He took a deep breath, jumped, and let out his most explosive roar.

The robot-child sat bolt upright. Mike's scream can filled all the way to the top. The OKs had won the Scare Games.

The stadium cheered wildly as Mike walked out of the simulator. The RORs were stunned. They had never imagined that they would lose the Scare Games—especially to the Oozma Kappas!

But had the OKs won fairly?

Berry Picking

Briar Rose lived in the forest with her three aunts, Flora, Fauna, and Merryweather.

One morning, Flora called the group together to suggest they go out to search the forest for berries.

"What a wonderful idea," said Briar Rose.

"Yes, indeed," said Merryweather. "If we pick enough, we can make a berry pie."

"If we pick enough," declared Fauna, "we can make enough jam to last us through the whole year."

"Well, we'll never have enough if we don't get started now," said Flora. And so they gathered their berry baskets and set out.

The four berry-pickers followed a shady path through the forest until they came upon a thicket bursting with berry bushes. Without delay, they got to work. But just because they got to work didn't mean their baskets actually got full.

Merryweather, for one, had a terrible time keeping her basket upright. Every time she bent to pick another berry, her basket tipped and out spilled all but two or three berries. Fauna, on the other hand, had an entirely different problem

keeping her berries in her basket— somehow they kept finding their way into her mouth!

As for Briar Rose, her heart and her mind were miles away from her berry basket . . . dancing instead in the arms of a handsome stranger.

"All right, dearies," Flora called as the sun began to sink. "It's time to start back to the cottage. Let's see what you've got."

"Um, well . . ." said Merryweather. "I don't seem to have many berries in my basket."

Flora rolled her eyes and moved on to Fauna. "Let me guess . . ." she said as she looked from Fauna's empty basket to her purple mouth.

"Ah, yes . . ." Fauna said as she guiltily dabbed at a drop of juice on her lips.

Flora sighed. "And you, Briar Rose?" she asked hopefully.

But Briar Rose just looked down sheepishly at the empty basket in her hands. "I'm sorry, Aunt Flora," she said. "I guess I got a little bit distracted."

"Well," said Flora, shaking her head, "no berry pie for us this week, I guess." Then she shrugged. "But we can always have chocolate cake instead!"

Ariel Changes the Tune

Sebastian rapped his claw on a piece of coral and cleared his throat. The mermaid princesses kept talking as if the little crustacean were not even there. With a heavy sigh, Sebastian grabbed a huge conch shell. After a lot of effort, he managed to hoist it to his mouth and blow.

The shell sounded like a giant horn! The princesses looked startled and, to Sebastian's relief, they stopped talking.

"Shall we begin?" the small crab asked calmly.

Sebastian raised his claw and was about to bring it down to start the vocal warm-up when Aquata interrupted him.

"Ariel's not here," she said.

"Oh, Ariel!" Sebastian cried. Ariel was constantly swimming off on her own and holding things up.

"Do you want us to find her?" Arista asked.

"No." Sebastian sighed. "Then you will *all* be lost, and I don't know *what* I would tell your father."

"We wouldn't get lost," Attina protested.

"We *always* show up on time,"

Adella added. The other sisters nodded their heads in agreement.

"Girls, girls!" Sebastian said, trying to calm them. He wished they could go ahead without Ariel, but her voice was by far the most beautiful.

Suddenly, Ariel swam up with Flounder. "I hope you weren't waiting for me," she said sweetly.

"Where have you been?" Aquata put her hands on her scaly hips.

"You're late, and we *still* don't have a song for father!" Attina added.

"We do now!" Ariel said cheerfully. Ariel couldn't tell her sisters, but she had been to the surface. It was forbidden. Her seagull friend Scuttle had given her something very special. A new song!

Ariel began singing the human tune. A moment later, Ariel's sisters began to sing along.

Sebastian closed his eyes and listened to the music wash over him. The song was perfect!

"Where did you learn it?" he asked when they were done.

Ariel looked at Flounder. "A little bird told me," she said with a wink and a smile.

Happy Mother's Day!

One fine May day, Roo hopped over to Winnie the Pooh's house. "I have a problem," Roo told Pooh. "Mother's Day is almost here, and I don't know what to give my mama. Do you have any ideas?"

"Let me think," said Pooh. "Think, think, think. A gift for Mother's Day. . . ." Luckily, Pooh spotted a big pot of honey sitting in his cupboard. "That's it!" he cried. "Mothers like *honey*!"

"They do?" asked Roo.

"Doesn't everybody?" Pooh asked.

So Pooh gave Roo a pot of honey. Roo bounced over to Rabbit's house next. As usual, Rabbit was working in his garden.

"Hello, Roo," he said. "What's in the pot?"

"It's honey," Roo explained, "to give to my mama on Mother's Day."

Rabbit frowned. "No, no, no," he said. "Mothers don't like honey. If there's one thing a mother wants to get on Mother's Day, it's a big bunch of fresh carrots."

"They do?" Roo said doubtfully.

"Oh, yes," said Rabbit. He reached into his wheelbarrow and pulled out a bunch of freshly picked carrots.

"Thanks, Rabbit," said Roo. Then he hopped to Eeyore's house of sticks.

"What do you have there, Roo?" Eeyore asked.

"Some gifts for my mama for Mother's Day," said Roo.

"I suppose some mothers might like carrots," Eeyore said. "And maybe others might like honey. But in my opinion, you can't go wrong with prickly thistles."

"Prickly thistles?" asked Roo.

"Yes," replied Eeyore. "Here, take these. Then Kanga will be sure to have a happy Mother's Day. If that's what she wants."

"Well, thank you," said Roo, tucking the prickly thistles into his pocket and heading for home.

The next morning, bright and early, Roo bounded into the living room.

"Happy Mother's Day, Mama!" he shouted.

"Why, thank you, dear," said Kanga.

"I thought and thought about what to give you," Roo explained. "Pooh said honey. Rabbit said carrots. And Eeyore said thistles. But I decided to give you this," he said, throwing his arms around his mama in a kangaroo-sized hug.

Kanga smiled. "Thank you, Roo. You were right. That's the best Mother's Day gift of all."

MAY
12

Fit for a Princess

Cinderella hummed to herself as she slipped the silver needle through the colorful fabric. She had been working hard on her new quilt for weeks, and it was finally almost finished!

Cinderella knew the quilt would be fit for a princess. The worn fabrics were colorful and soft, and with the cotton stuffing she'd found in the attic, the quilt would be wonderfully cozy. No more shivering under her threadbare blanket!

Gus agreed. He couldn't help but climb between the sewn-together quilt fabric and snuggle into the cotton filling.

Suzy and Perla, who were helping Cinderella with the sewing, giggled. "Go and get us some more thread, sleepyhead," they called. But Gus was already dozing off. The sound of his snores drifted out from between the layers of quilt.

"Gus!" Jaq called. But the snores only got louder. "That mouse hasn't helped with this quilt one bit!" Jaq sighed and went to get the spools of thread himself.

Cinderella was just sewing together the last edge of the quilt when loud footsteps echoed on the attic stairs. It was her stepsister, Anastasia. A moment later, she stormed into the room carrying a fancy blue gown. "My dress was not ironed properly!" she shouted. "Can't you do anything right?"

Then she spotted the quilt. "It's beautiful!" she cried. "And it will look wonderful on my bed!"

Cinderella looked at Anastasia in shock. Would her stepsister really steal her quilt? She knew Anastasia and Drizella could be mean, but that would be downright cruel!

Suddenly, the quilt began to move. A moment later Gus's quivering nose poked out from between the unsewn pieces of fabric.

"A rodent!" Anastasia screamed. She dropped her dress in fright and leaped onto a small wooden chair. "Why, that quilt isn't fit for use in the stable!" she cried.

Cinderella tried not to laugh as her stepsister leaped off the chair and fled down the stairs. Yawning, Gus climbed the rest of the way out of the quilt.

"Well, Gus-Gus," Jaq said, "I guess you did end up helping with the quilt, after all!"

The Good Luck Charm

In ancient China, crickets were believed to be good luck. But on one particular night, long, long ago, Mulan's Grandmother Fa was having trouble remembering that. There was a cricket loose somewhere in her bedroom, and every time she was about to drop off to sleep . . . *Cri-cket! Cri-cket!* the cricket chirped loudly.

"This cricket will bring good fortune to our home," Grandmother Fa said, looking on the bright side.

All was quiet for a few minutes. Then—*Cri-cket! Cri-cket!*

"Ugh!" exclaimed Grandmother Fa, throwing off the covers and getting out of bed.

She lit a candle and began her search. She looked everywhere. But there was no sign of the cricket.

She blew out the candle. She got back into bed and tried to sleep.

Cri-cket! Cri-cket!

Grandmother Fa got out of bed again and relit her candle. She searched in her closet. She looked inside her slippers. She checked under her pillow. But she didn't find the cricket.

One more time, she climbed into bed and tried to sleep.

Cri-cket! Cri-cket!

Grandmother Fa sighed and dragged herself out of bed. She relit the candle. Was there any place she hadn't yet looked?

Just then, a slight movement on the windowsill caught Grandmother Fa's eye. There, sitting on the windowsill, was a tiny cricket. She scooped it up gently and cradled it in her hand.

That's when Grandmother Fa noticed that the window was open. And it looked like a rainstorm was brewing outside.

"Well, little cricket," Grandmother Fa said, "is that why you were trying to get my attention?" Had the cricket been trying to save Grandmother Fa from waking up to a puddle beneath her open window?

"Maybe you're good luck, after all," she said.

She decided she would hold on to the cricket to see if it brought her more luck. So Grandmother Fa pulled out a bamboo cricket cage, gently placed the cricket inside, and put the cage on her bedside table. At last, she'd be able to get some sleep.

Cri-cket! Cri-cket!

Or would she?

A Three-Star Pub

Rapunzel's golden hair had magical healing powers. As a baby, she had been kidnapped by Mother Gothel, who used her hair's magic to stay forever young. The woman pretended to be her mother, and she locked her away in a tower and never let her out.

But one day, Flynn Rider had come along, and Rapunzel had convinced him to take her to see the floating lights that rose in the sky every year on her birthday.

The two walked through the woods together. Suddenly, there was a noise in the bushes. Rapunzel jumped back, terrified. "Is it ruffians? Thugs? Have they come for me?" She hid behind Flynn.

A little rabbit hopped out from the bushes. Rapunzel blushed. If she carried on like this, Flynn would guess that she had never been out of her tower before!

But Flynn had already realized why Rapunzel was scared, and that gave him an idea. He decided that a little pub called the Snuggly Duckling was the perfect place to take her for lunch.

"Are you hungry? I know a great place for lunch," Flynn said.

"Where?" Rapunzel asked.

"Don't you worry," Flynn replied. "You'll know it when you smell it."

Flynn and Rapunzel soon arrived at the Snuggly Duckling. Rapunzel was horrified! The place was full of ruffians!

Flynn was sure Rapunzel would want to go back to the tower now! Then he could take his crown and go on his way.

Meanwhile, Mother Gothel was walking through the woods when she saw Maximus, the captain of the royal guard's horse. She thought the guards might have come for Rapunzel! She raced back to the tower.

"Rapunzel!" she called. But there was no reply. Mother Gothel uncovered a secret entrance to the tower and soon discovered the awful truth: Rapunzel was gone.

Then she saw something glimmering beneath the staircase. It was the crown in Flynn's satchel! There was also a WANTED poster with Flynn's face on it. Now she knew who had taken Rapunzel—and nothing would stop her from finding him!

Scaredy Cats

"Nala!" Simba whispered. "Are you awake?"

"Yes," Nala whispered back, stepping out of the dark cave where she slept with her mother. "Why are you here? You're gonna get us in trouble . . . again."

Earlier, Simba and Nala had gone to explore the forbidden Elephant's Graveyard, where they'd almost been eaten by hyenas.

"Come on," Simba hissed. "Follow me."

Soon the two cubs were on the dark savannah near the base of Pride Rock.

"What do you want, anyway?" Nala asked.

"I just wanted to make sure you weren't still scared," Simba said.

Nala scowled at him. "Scared?" she exclaimed. "*I'm* not the one who was scared!"

"What?" Simba cried. "You're not saying I was scared, are you? Because there's no way I'd be scared of a few stupid hyenas. I wouldn't have been scared even if we ran into a *hundred* hyenas."

"Well, I wouldn't have been scared even if we saw *two hundred* hyenas and an angry water buffalo," said Nala.

"Oh yeah?" Simba said. "Well, I wouldn't have been scared of *three hundred* hyenas, an angry water buffalo, and a—"

"FURIOUS HORNBILL?" a new voice squawked from the darkness.

"Ahhhhhh!" Simba and Nala cried, jumping straight up in the air.

A brightly colored bird stepped out of the shadows. It was Zazu, Simba's father's most trusted adviser.

"Zazu!" Simba cried. "You scared us!"

"I wasn't scared," Nala said with a scowl.

"Me neither!" Simba added quickly.

Zazu glared at both of them over his long beak. "Not scared, were you?" he said drily. "That certainly explains the shrieking."

"You just startled us," Nala mumbled.

Zazu fluffed his feathers. "Listen up, you two," he said. "Everyone gets scared. It's how you respond to it that counts. That's where true bravery lies. Get it?"

"Got it," Simba and Nala said.

"Good." Zazu marched toward Pride Rock. The sun was coming up, and it was time for breakfast. "Now let's get you back home posthaste . . . or I'll *really* give you something to be scared of!"

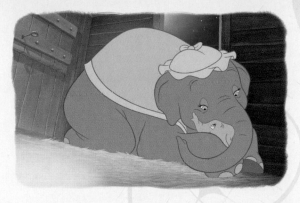

An Elephant Lullaby

More than anything else in the world, Mrs. Jumbo had been longing for a baby elephant of her own. Then, one day, the stork brought her one!

The tiny elephant was the most beautiful creature she had ever seen. Mrs. Jumbo was the happiest animal in the circus. Then it happened: her baby sneezed, causing his ears to unfold. They were extremely large ears, and the other elephants laughed at him.

"Instead of calling him Jumbo Junior," one elephant said drily, "he ought to be called Dumbo!" Mrs. Jumbo ignored their taunts and curled her trunk around her beloved baby.

As the days went by, Mrs. Jumbo grew to love her baby more and more. She played hide-and-seek with him, pretending to be surprised when he hid behind her legs. She played peekaboo with him. She sang him lullabies at bedtime and danced around with him when he woke up.

One evening, Mrs. Jumbo found her precious baby looking terribly sad. She tenderly put him to bed, tucking his large ears around him to keep him warm.

"Don't mind what the others say," she whispered softly. "You are going to grow up to be a fine elephant! Shall I sing you a lullaby, darling?"

As Dumbo nodded, Mrs. Jumbo heard the other elephants talking in the next stall. "Honestly!" one of them was saying. "You'd think he was the only elephant left on earth, the way she pampers him!"

But Mrs. Jumbo ignored them and began to sing:

"Hush, little baby, don't you cry.
Mama's gonna sing you a lullaby.
And if someone should laugh at your ears,
Mama's gonna be here to dry your tears.
Just lay your head down and try to rest.
You're the one that Mama loves the best."

Then she continued to hum and rock her son until his eyelids grew heavier and heavier, and finally he fell asleep.

Mrs. Jumbo hummed for a little while longer, then stood up. The stalls had grown very quiet.

Suddenly, Mrs. Jumbo heard a soft snoring. Her lullaby had put all the elephants to sleep!

MAY
17

A Big Buzz

Flit let out a big sigh. Pocahontas was spending so much time with John Smith that she never had time for him anymore!

Buzzz, buzzz. Flit was grateful that his speedy wings made noise when he flew. At least Pocahontas could hear him—even if she pretended she didn't.

"Look at this, John," Pocahontas said, crouching down in the path. "Fresh deer tracks."

John leaned over to inspect the prints left behind in the mud. Flit buzzed down, too. There were two sizes of prints, large and small.

"A mother and her fawn," John said. He leaned forward for a closer look, accidentally crowding Flit out of the way.

"They're probably looking for food before the snows come, so they'll be fat enough to make it through the winter," Pocahontas explained.

Pocahontas smiled up at him and stood. Flit buzzed up a second later, just as John lifted his hand to push a lock of hair off Pocahontas's face. Once again, Flit was shoved away.

That was it! Flit had had enough of being ignored! He flapped his buzzing wings faster and faster. Then he

began to fly in a circle around John and Pocahontas. *Zzzzzzzzzzz!*

"Do you think he's trying to tell us something?" John asked, leaning toward Pocahontas.

"I don't know," she replied. She leaned in closer to John, too. Soon they were nose to nose, looking into each other's eyes.

Flit gave up. He quit buzzing and flopped to the ground, landing in one of the deer tracks. He was exhausted.

"What was that about, Flit?" asked Pocahontas, scooping him up with a laugh.

Flit was still panting. He wasn't even sure he could fly anymore. He gazed up at Pocahontas, his eyes wide and his shoulders slumped.

"That is one exhausted hummingbird," John said.

Pocahontas stroked Flit's blue feathers, then leaned forward and kissed him on the end of his long, pointed beak. Then she set him gently on her shoulder.

"You just ride here for a while," she told him.

Flit grinned happily as John and Pocahontas continued on through the forest. Mission accomplished!

How to Win at Hide-and-Seek

"Belle!" Mrs. Potts called. "Oh, Belle!"

Belle was sitting in her bedroom, surrounded by a pile of books.

"There you are!" Mrs. Potts cried.

"Hi, Belle," Mrs. Potts's son, Chip, chimed in.

"Hello to both of you. Were you looking for me?" Belle asked Mrs. Potts.

"As a matter of fact, I was," Mrs. Potts told her. "I was just stopping by to inquire as to whether or not you would like some tea."

"Thank you," Belle said. "I would love some."

Mrs. Potts poured Belle a piping hot cup of tea. Belle took a sip and thanked her.

Mrs. Potts soon headed back to the kitchen, but Chip stayed behind. He wanted to play with Belle.

"How about a game of hide-and-seek?" Belle asked the small teacup.

"How do you play that?" Chip asked.

"It's simple," Belle said. "One person hides and the other person tries to find him."

"I can do that!" Chip said.

"Of course you can," Belle told him.

"So, do you want to be the hider or the seeker?"

"I want to be the hider," Chip told her.

"Okay," Belle said. "I'll close my eyes and count to ten. One, two, three . . ."

Chip took off, darting behind the curtains just as Belle called, "Ten! Ready or not, here I come! Hmm, now where could he be?"

Belle looked under the table. "He isn't there," she said. Then she looked in the corner. "He isn't there, either." She looked high and low, but she couldn't seem to find Chip anywhere.

"I give up," Belle said. "Come out, come out, wherever you are!"

Chip silently giggled from behind the curtain, but he was careful not to make too much noise. He was having fun!

"It seems that Chip doesn't want to come out from his hiding place," Belle said. "I guess that means I'll have to eat a slice of Mrs. Potts's chocolate cake all by myself."

When he heard that, Chip jumped out from his hiding place and called out to Belle, "Here I am! Wait for me!"

Where Mowgli Belongs

Mowgli the Man-cub had lived in the jungle his whole life. Then, one day, everything changed. Shere Khan, the man-eating tiger, heard about Mowgli and came looking for him. The wolves agreed Bagheera should take the boy back to the Man-village, where he would be safe. Mowgli was angry; he didn't want to leave his home in the jungle. But he and Bagheera set off on their long journey.

Along the way, Mowgli encountered a python who wanted to swallow him up, a parade of very noisy elephants, and the King of the Apes, who wanted to know how to make fire. Mowgli also made a friend, Baloo the bear.

Mowgli still didn't want to go to the Man-village, so he ran away from Baloo and Bagheera. Once he was on his own, it wasn't long before Shere Khan found him. The tiger gave a loud roar. He leaped at Mowgli, taking the Man-cub by surprise! But Baloo arrived and fought with Shere Khan. Baloo was knocked onto the ground, and Mowgli was worried that he wasn't going to wake up.

But Baloo did wake up! Mowgli laughed and threw his arms around the big bear's neck.

Suddenly, a lightning bolt struck a nearby tree, which burst into flames. Shere Khan was terrified!

Seeing his chance to get back at the tiger, Mowgli picked up a burning branch. The Man-cub tied the branch to the tiger's tail. Shere Khan screamed as he tried to get it off. Then he fled into the jungle—never to be seen again!

Mowgli, Baloo, and Bagheera carried on toward the Man-village. Suddenly, they heard someone singing. Mowgli peered through the trees and saw a young girl kneeling by the river.

Mowgli climbed a tree to have a closer look.

The girl turned and smiled. Mowgli shyly smiled back. When she began to walk off toward the Man-village, Mowgli ran to join her.

Baloo and Bagheera were sad that their young friend was leaving. But they knew he would be happy and safe.

"It's where he belongs," said Bagheera. "Come on, Baloo, let's get back to where we belong."

And so, arm-in-arm, the two friends headed slowly back to the jungle.

Howling at the Moon

Lady had been having a really bad day. First, she'd had a run-in with two nasty cats. Then she'd been put in a horrible muzzle. But because of Tramp, everything had changed.

"It's amazing how a day can start off terribly but end wonderfully," Lady told Tramp as they trotted through the moonlit park. "Thank you for helping me escape that terrible muzzle—and for dinner at Tony's."

"Aw, shucks, don't mention it!" said Tramp. "Hey, you wanna have some real fun?"

"I don't know," Lady said cautiously. While she was very fond of Tramp, she also knew they were very different dogs. Tramp was used to life on the streets, so his idea of fun might be very different from hers.

"Don't worry," Tramp assured her. "This is something I think you'll enjoy."

"What is it?" asked Lady.

"Well, for starters, you have to look up," said Tramp.

Lady did. The sky was filled with stars and a big, bright moon.

"What am I looking for?" she asked.

"The moon, of course!" cried Tramp.

"Haven't you ever howled at the moon?"

Lady laughed at Tramp's suggestion.

"What's so funny?" asked Tramp.

"I'm a practical dog," explained Lady. "I bark politely when the situation calls for it, but I don't see any point in howling at the moon."

"Why not?" asked Tramp.

"Well," said Lady, "what's the use of it?"

"You know, Lady," said Tramp, "a thing doesn't have to be useful to be fun."

Lady thought it over. "Okay," she said. "What do I do?"

"First, sit up real straight," said Tramp. "Then look up at the moon, take a deep breath, and just let all the troubles of your day disappear in one gigantic howl!" He demonstrated: "Ow-ow-OWWWWWWW!"

Lady joined Tramp and howled as loudly as she could.

"You're right!" she cried. "It does feel good to howl at the moon!"

"Stick with me, kid," said Tramp. "I know what's what."

Lady suspected Tramp *did* know what was what, but there was an even better reason for her to stick with him. He'd become her best friend!

Fairy Facts

All the fairies knew that Tinker Bell was too curious for her own good! But now she was in real trouble! She had been captured by a human girl named Lizzy!

Lizzy was excited. She wanted to learn all about fairies. But Tinker Bell soon learned that what Lizzy *did* know was all wrong.

Tink tried to explain fairy life to the girl, but all Lizzy heard was a jingling sound.

"So that's how fairies speak!" she exclaimed.

Tink went over to the fairy house to fix the door. "Why, you're quite the little tinker, aren't you?" asked Lizzy. Tink nodded and pointed to herself, then rang the little house's fairy bell. "Tinker Bell?" Lizzy cried. "What a lovely name!"

Outside, it had begun to rain. Tink couldn't fly with wet wings, so she opened a blank field journal that Lizzy's father had given her. He didn't believe in fairies and wanted Lizzy to record her research about "real" things in it. Tink knew the journal was perfect for Lizzy's fairy facts!

Lizzy wrote the words "Scientific Fairy Research" on the first page. Then she asked questions and Tinker Bell acted out the answers.

Soon the journal was filled with drawings of Tink's fairy friends and Pixie Hollow, and descriptions of the fairies' special talents.

In no time, Lizzy's fairy field journal was complete.

The rain had stopped, too.

Tink knew it was time to go find her friends. Tinker Bell was sad about leaving Lizzy, but excited about going back to fairy camp.

As Tink flew out of the window, Lizzy's father came into the room. Lizzy tried to show her father the journal they had made.

"I made it especially for you, father. It's just like your field journal, it's filled with lots of facts. . . ."

But Dr. Griffiths was too worried about the leaks in the roof to look at Lizzy's book.

Tink saw how sad Dr. Griffiths was that he couldn't spend more time with his daughter. She decided she had to stay and help them. After all, fixing things was her talent!

Homework Helper

Stitch didn't care for weekdays much now that Lilo was back in school. To Stitch they were the longest and most boring days of the week. So you can imagine Stitch's excitement when three o'clock finally rolled around and Lilo's school bus dropped her off.

"Lilo!" Stitch would shriek, racing down to meet her. "Playtime! Playtime!"

Usually, Lilo would toss her backpack onto the porch and they would hop on her bike.

But one day, Lilo didn't drop her backpack. And she didn't run after Stitch.

"Sorry, Stitch," she said. "My teacher says if I don't start doing my homework, she's going to have to have a talk with Nani!"

Stitch didn't understand. "Homework?" he said, peeking into Lilo's backpack.

"Homework," said Lilo, "is math problems and a book report and a week's worth of spelling words that I have one day to learn! Now please, Stitch, be a good alien and shoo."

But Stitch wasn't about to give up so soon. He was back in less than a minute with a basket full of Lilo's favorite action figures.

"You've got to be kidding," said Lilo. "I am not playing super heroes. Can't you see I'm busy?"

This was mighty frustrating! But Stitch loved a challenge. Off he ran again, and this time he came back wearing a catcher's mask and vest and carrying a baseball, a bat, and Lilo's glove.

"Play ball!" Stitch shouted.

Lilo almost got up, but then she shook her head. "No, Stitch." She sighed. "If I don't start these spelling words now, I'll never finish them tonight."

Stitch thought for a second, then dashed off once again. Lilo could hear all sorts of banging and slamming coming from her room. It sounded like Stitch was turning it upside down! Oh, great, she thought to herself. But at least he's leaving me alone. . . .

Then, to Lilo's surprise, Stitch came back again carrying a book of crossword puzzles under his arm.

"Lilo play *and* spell words!" Stitch cheerfully told her.

"Why didn't I think of that?" said Lilo. "Stitch, you can help me with my homework any time!"

Home Sweet Home

As the sun rose above the Seven Dwarfs' cottage, Snow White was already thinking about what to make for supper that evening. She had arrived at the cottage just the day before, after her evil stepmother, the Queen, had driven Snow White from the palace.

Luckily, a group of helpful woodland creatures had befriended Snow White and led her to the Dwarfs' little cottage. Now, for the first time in a long time, she felt safe and happy.

"Perhaps we'll have gooseberry pie for supper tonight!" she told her animal friends as they cleaned the cottage. When they had finished, they left the cottage and headed to the forest to pick berries. With all her friends helping, Snow White quickly filled her berry basket.

"How different life has become," she said to her friends. "I don't miss the grand castle at all. I love living in this funny little cottage. A home doesn't need to be grand to be a happy one! Remember that."

The animals exchanged looks with one another. Then they began tugging at her skirt to pull her to her feet.

"What is it, dears?" she asked them. "Oh! Do *you* want to show me where all of you live? I would love to see!" she said delightedly.

Two bluebirds were first. Twittering excitedly, they fluttered around their nest, which had been built in a little nook of a nearby tree.

"What a lovely nest!" cried Snow White. The birds looked pleased.

The fawns were next. Pulling at her skirt, they brought Snow White to a sun-dappled clearing in a warm glade.

"How cozy!" exclaimed Snow White. The fawns flicked their tails happily.

Next, the chipmunks and squirrels showed her the hollow in an old tree where they lived.

"You all have such pretty little homes," said Snow White as they made their way back to the Dwarfs' cottage. "Thank you for showing them to me. We are all lucky to live where we do, aren't we?" she said with a smile.

And with that, she skipped the rest of the way back to the cottage to start preparing her pie. She could hardly wait until the Dwarfs got home!

A Frog's Appetite

An evil sorcerer had changed spoiled Prince Naveen into a frog. Naveen assumed that kissing a princess would change him back, so he went looking for one. When he saw Tiana dressed up for a costume ball, he mistakenly thought she was a princess. But when he kissed her, Tiana had turned into a frog instead!

Tiana and Naveen, now both frogs, found themselves lost in the bayou. Tiana, working hard as usual, had just finished building a raft to cross the swamp. As for Naveen, he was happy to sing while she maneuvered their makeshift boat.

"I could use a little help!" she grumbled.

"I'll play a little louder!" replied Naveen without moving.

Suddenly, an enormous alligator emerged from the muddy waters! The frogs froze in terror. But he wasn't dangerous. His name was Louis and he was mad about music! He loved the jazz pieces that Naveen was singing.

"I am Naveen, prince of Maldonia, and she is Tiana, the waitress," introduced Naveen.

Tiana explained that they were trying to find a way to break the spell that had transformed them into frogs.

Louis suggested they ask Mama Odie, the queen of the bayou, for help.

Louis was scared to go too far into the bayou, but finally he agreed to guide Tiana and Naveen.

As they traveled, Naveen started to get hungry. So hungry, in fact, that his frog's tongue suddenly shot out all by itself into the path of a cloud of mosquitoes! Then a big firefly landed on a nearby dandelion. This time it was Tiana's tongue that shot out without warning!

Tiana slapped a hand over her mouth. "There is no way I am kissing a frog and eating a bug on the same day!"

But Tiana couldn't fight it; she was a frog now, after all. Her tongue shot out in the direction of the chubby firefly at the same time as Naveen's. They both missed the firefly. Instead, they ended up with their tongues tangled together.

The firefly, whose name was Ray, quickly untangled the frogs. Then he offered to take them to Mama Odie.

Tiana and Naveen were on their way!

Donald Duck Goes Camping

Uncle Donald was taking Huey, Dewey, and Louie camping! When they arrived in the woods and found a camping spot, Huey and Louie helped their uncle put up the tent while Dewey read from a camping guidebook.

"The guidebook says to hang the food locker from a tree," said Dewey.

"I know everything there is to know about camping," Donald said. "The food will be all right on the picnic table."

Just then, two squirrels scampered down from a tree and snatched a bag of peanuts. "Hey!" Donald shouted. "Come back here!"

"The guidebook says it's good to share with little animals," said Louie.

"I don't care what the book says. Those are my peanuts!" replied Donald.

The two squirrels ran along the tree branches and chattered at Donald again. This time, they seemed to be laughing at him. "I'll get even with you!" Donald yelled. He climbed up the tree toward the squirrels. Just as he was about to grab them, they leaped onto a thin branch.

"The book says to stay off small branches!" Dewey cried.

CRRRACK! Suddenly, the branch broke, and Donald fell into the river.

"Help!" Donald cried. "Pull me out!" He tried to swim toward land, but the current was too strong. He spotted a rock and grabbed on to it. "Do something!" he called to his nephews. "Look in the guidebook!"

Huey, Dewey, and Louie started flipping through the book. They only looked up when the squirrels returned—with a beaver! The beaver waddled to a tree that stood beside the river and began to gnaw at it.

"He's trying to help!" Dewey said. "If the tree falls into the river, it might be long enough to reach Uncle Donald."

A few minutes later, the tree fell over with a crash. Donald climbed along the tree trunk toward dry land. Once safely ashore, Donald ran toward his car.

"Where are you going?" his nephews called.

An hour later, Donald returned. His car was filled with presents for the beaver that had helped him, and all the other animals, too. They were delighted and munched on their treats!

A Special Surprise

The underwater kingdom was quiet and peaceful. Every mermaid and merman was in bed fast asleep—everyone, that is, but Princess Ariel and her friend Flounder.

Trying not to make a sound, Ariel and Flounder swam away from King Triton's palace and began their journey toward the surface.

Ariel wasn't going to let anything ruin her plans for tonight. Prince Eric, the prince she had saved in a shipwreck, was having a royal ball. Ariel had a very special surprise for him.

"Swim faster, Flounder!" she cried. Flounder raced to keep up. Just as Ariel and Flounder approached the surface, Ariel saw beautiful lights dance across the water. When they poked their heads out into the air, Ariel and Flounder saw colorful lights explode in the sky above Prince Eric's castle.

"I've never seen anything so beautiful in all my life," said Ariel breathlessly. "The human world is such a wonderful place!"

"It sure is pretty!" said Flounder.

Off in the distance, Prince Eric stood on the palace balcony. He didn't feel like joining in the royal celebration. He couldn't stop thinking about the mysterious girl with the lovely voice who had saved his life in the shipwreck.

Ariel's heart leaped with joy when she saw Prince Eric. "It's time for my surprise!" she said.

"R-r-ready?" asked Flounder.

With a nod, Ariel closed her eyes, opened her mouth, and began to sing. Suddenly, the night was filled with the sweet sound of Ariel's voice.

Hearing her beautiful voice again, Eric's face lit up. "It can't be!" he said.

Eric remained on the balcony, enchanted by the beautiful song filling the night air. When the song was over, Eric looked out across the sea. He hoped to catch a glimpse of the wonderful girl who had saved him. Where could she be?

"Who are you?" he called out into the night. But all he heard was the echo of his own voice.

"I'll be back soon," Ariel whispered as she and Flounder swam toward home. "Just wait and see."

The Power of Dreams

Rapunzel's golden hair had magical healing powers. As a baby, she had been kidnapped by Mother Gothel, who used her hair's magic to stay forever young. The woman pretended to be her mother, and she locked Rapunzel away in a tower and never let her out.

But one day, Flynn Rider had come along, and Rapunzel had convinced him to take her to see the floating lights that rose in the sky every year on her birthday.

On their way to the palace, Flynn and Rapunzel stopped at a pub called the Snuggly Duckling. It was full of horrible ruffians! Flynn hoped the men would scare Rapunzel into going back to her tower.

Suddenly the thugs recognized Flynn. One of them held up a WANTED poster with his picture on it. The thugs seized the thief. They knew they could get a lot of money for handing him over to the royal guard.

"Ruffians, stop!" Rapunzel cried. "Hey, leave him alone! Give me back my guide!"

But no one was listening to Rapunzel. She had to do something.

Finally, she wrapped her hair around a branch and flung it at one of the thugs. It hit him right in the head!

"Put him down!" she shouted. The thugs stopped what they were doing and looked at her.

"I don't know where I am and I need him to take me to see the lanterns because I've been dreaming about them my entire life," Rapunzel said. "Find your humanity. Haven't any of you ever had a dream?" she asked the roomful of thugs.

Everyone was stunned. Who would have believed that such a delicate young girl could get so angry? What's more, she was right!

"I've always yearned to be a concert pianist," one thug admitted, moved to tears.

Little by little, everyone in the pub began to describe his hidden hopes and dreams. One wanted to knit. Another wanted to bake. And one dreamed of falling in love!

Flynn couldn't believe his ears— or his eyes! The girl had managed to win over a room full of the meanest, toughest men in the kingdom! What was he going to do now?

Say Ahhh, Pooh!

"Christopher Robin says it's time for my animal checkout," said Pooh.

"Checkout!" cried Piglet. "Oh p-p-poor P-P-Pooh—you're sick!"

"Sick?" asked Pooh. "No—I'm fine. Though I must say I am feeling a bit rumbly in my tumbly."

"Let's go together," said Piglet. "It's so much more friendly with two."

So Pooh and Piglet climbed the ladder up to Owl's house.

"Christopher Robin, why do I need an animal checkout, anyway?" asked Pooh once they had arrived at Owl's house.

"Silly old bear," said Christopher Robin. "Not an animal checkout—an *annual checkup*. We need to make sure you are healthy and strong."

Rabbit weighed Pooh and then told him to go into Owl's room. Piglet wished him good luck. Once Pooh and Christopher Robin were inside, Owl entered with a flourish. "Well, if it isn't Winnie the Pooh!" he said. "Splendid day for a checkup, isn't it? I say, how are you feeling?"

"A bit flippy-floppy in my tummy, actually," said Pooh.

Owl felt Pooh's tummy. He felt around Pooh's neck and under his arms and said that everything seemed to be right where it should be. Pooh was glad. Then Owl pulled a small rubber hammer from his bag. "Reflex-checking time!" he said grandly.

"What's a reflex?" asked Pooh. Owl tapped Pooh's knee—and his leg gave a little kick! "Oh do that again," said Pooh. "That was fun." So Owl tapped Pooh's other knee, and that leg gave a little kick, too!

Then Owl said, "Sit right here. It's time for your shot."

"I know it will only hurt for a moment, and it will keep me from getting bumps and weasels," Pooh said bravely.

"That's mumps and measles, Pooh," said Owl.

Piglet came in and sat right next to Pooh while he had his injection. When Owl was done, Rabbit popped back in with a bandage for Pooh's arm.

"Wow," said Piglet. "You didn't even make a sound!"

"An annual checkup is no problem for a brave bear like Pooh," said Christopher Robin.

I'm just that sort of bear, thought Pooh with a smile.

A Birthday Surprise

"**G**et up, Jaq! Get up!" Gus cried.

"Go away, Gus-Gus," Jaq mumbled sleepily, and he rolled over.

"No, no, Jaq. Get up. It's a special day." Gus pulled on his tail. "It's Cinderelly's birthday."

Jaq sat up. "Today?" he asked, his eyes growing wide "Today is her birthday?"

Gus smiled and nodded vigorously.

"Well, come on! We haven't got much time!" Jaq cried. "We have a lot to do if we're going to throw a surprise party!"

Soon Cinderella's animal friends were gathered on the windowsill for a meeting.

"We can make a cake!" Suzy and Perla volunteered.

"Watch out for L-L-Lucifer," Gus stuttered. Baking would mean stealing eggs and butter from the kitchen!

"We'll take care of that cat," Mert and Bert said, crossing their arms.

"But we still need a present," Jaq said.

"Something pretty!" Gus cried.

"I've got it!" Jaq sat up straight. "I saw some slippers in the garbage last night when I was looking for food. There's a hole in one toe, but the bottoms were okay."

"We can fix them," the mice said.

It took the mice all day to get ready, but everything turned out beautifully. The sun was setting when they finally heard Cinderella's soft steps coming up the stairs.

"Here she comes!" Gus whispered.

Jaq took a match and lit the candle stump that was stuck in the iced cake. Beside it the slippers were mended and wrapped. A ribbon was twirled into two pink roses, one on each toe. The door opened slowly.

"Surprise!" the mice squeaked. The birds twittered and dropped confetti.

"Oh, my!" Cinderella gasped. "This *is* a surprise!"

"Happy birthday," Gus said shyly.

"It's all so lovely," Cinderella said. "But I'm afraid it's not my birthday."

"It's not?" Jaq's smile vanished. The rest of the mice and birds were silent.

"I'm afraid not, but that's what makes this such a special surprise." Cinderella beamed.

The animals laughed, and they all sat down to share the delicious cake together.

Fairies to the Rescue

Vidia was very upset. Tinker Bell had been captured by a human girl named Lizzy!

The fairies had been busy bringing summer to the mainland when Tinker Bell had flown off to investigate a car.

The car had stopped at a small country house and a girl named Lizzy and her father, Dr. Griffiths, had gotten out.

Vidia had followed Tink to the house. She knew humans could be dangerous and she wanted Tinker Bell to come back to the fairy camp with her. But on their way there, Tink had found a little fairy house. She was excited and had gone inside to explore.

Vidia wanted to teach Tink a lesson. She slammed the door shut with a gust of wind.

Just then, Vidia saw Lizzy walking up the path, but the door of the little house was stuck! Vidia hid as Lizzy picked up the fairy house and spotted Tinker Bell.

The little girl was so excited that she took the house—and Tink—straight home and up to her bedroom.

Lizzy placed the fairy house on the bed and peeked in one of its windows.

But Tinker Bell was nowhere to be seen. "Where have you gone?" Lizzy asked. She took the roof off the house and *ZIP!* Tink darted out.

Mr. Twitches, Lizzy's cat, lunged for the fairy. As Vidia watched from the window, Lizzy put Tinker Bell in a birdcage for safekeeping.

"Don't worry," Lizzy told her. "Mr. Twitches won't bother you in there."

Vidia knew that she had to free Tink, but she couldn't do it alone. She flew toward the fairy camp, but a rainstorm slowed her down.

When Vidia finally arrived, she told her friends what had happened: Tinker Bell had been captured and put in a cage. The fairies had to save her.

"We can't fly in the rain," Fawn said. "And the meadow's already flooded!"

But Clank and Bobble weren't worried about the rain. They had a plan. They would build a boat!

With the tinkers' help, the entire camp set to work creating a hull out of bark, a mast out of reeds and twigs, and a sail out of a lily pad.

It was going to be a challenge, but the fairies were determined to rescue their friend.

The Coziest Carriage

O'Malley, Duchess, and the kittens were visiting Scat Cat, one of O'Malley's oldest and dearest friends.

Scat Cat lived in a broken-down carriage that had once been very grand indeed. But the wheels had fallen apart long ago, the cushions were shredded, and there was a huge hole right in the middle of the worn, tattered roof. Still, as far as Scat Cat was concerned, his home was perfect.

"I feel free here," he told the kittens. "I can come and go as I please. And when I stretch out on the cushions at night, I look up and there are the stars a-twinklin' and a-winkin' back at me!"

A few days later, there was a knock at Madame's door. It was Scat Cat.

"You'll never believe it," he said. "I went into town to stretch my legs, and when I got back . . . poof! The carriage was gone!"

"Naturally, you will have to stay with us!" said Duchess. "I'm sure Madame would be delighted to have you as our guest."

But after only one night, Scat Cat began to feel sad. Everything at Madame Bonfamille's happened according to a strict schedule. Scat Cat missed doing as he pleased.

"You know what I miss most?" Scat Cat told O'Malley and the kittens. "My old carriage. What I wouldn't give to be able to look up at the sky and count the twinklin' stars. . . ."

The kittens decided to help Scat Cat. Madame had been complaining about her old carriage. So Berlioz climbed into it and began clawing at the old cushions. Marie joined him. Soon, the cushions looked just like the ones in Scat Cat's old carriage!

Finally, Toulouse crashed through the carriage roof, making a huge hole.

"Oh, my!" exclaimed a voice. It was Madame. She surveyed the damage . . . and smiled! "At last I have an excuse to buy a new carriage," she said. "Let's take this one out to the junkyard at once."

"I don't believe it!" cried Scat Cat, when the kittens led him to his new home. "It's purr-fect! How can I ever thank you?"

"It was our pleasure," said Berlioz. He flexed his claws. "It's not every day we're thanked for clawing something to pieces!"

The Silent Treatment

The Queen of Hearts loved to shout orders at her royal subjects. She shouted so much, in fact, that it wasn't surprising when she came down with a terrible case of laryngitis.

"There, there," said her husband. "Rest your voice and let me do the ruling for you, my dear." The Queen hardly let the King get a word in edgeways most of the time, so he was looking forward to being in charge for a change.

As they strolled through the royal garden, the Queen noticed that the fence was painted pink instead of the required red. "Off! Off!" the Queen croaked.

But the King just smiled. "The Queen decrees that you may have the day off!" he told the gardeners.

Soon the couple paused to play a game of croquet. The Queen hit the hedgehog ball with the flamingo mallet, and the hedgehog rolled willy-nilly across the lawn. The playing-card wickets knew better than to let the Queen make a bad shot. They jumped all over the grass, making sure the ball passed beneath them.

"I'm undefeated!" the Queen rasped triumphantly.

The King couldn't understand exactly what his wife was saying.

"The Queen says she cheated!" he finally announced.

The entire royal staff gasped. Those nearby ducked as the Queen swung a flamingo at the King's head. "That's enough croquet for today," crooned the King soothingly.

He led his wife to a bench in the shade. The Queen sat down, pointed to the servants hovering nearby, and acted out drinking a cup of tea.

The King stood up and announced, "You're all invited to have tea with the Queen!"

A table was laid with tea and sandwiches. Everyone ate, laughed, and had a wonderful time. The Queen, ignored by everyone, seethed with anger. She grabbed one of the flamingo mallets, then charged the table. Unfortunately, she didn't see the croquet ball in her path. As she tripped, the flamingo's beak plunged into the ground, causing the Queen to pole-vault up and over the table of guests and through her open bedroom window.

"A splendid idea, my dear!" called the King. "A nap will do you good!"

In the Doghouse

"Good morning, Tramp," said Lady, yawning and stretching. She rolled over on her silk cushion. "Wasn't that just the most wonderful night's sleep?"

But Tramp just groaned. His sleep had been far from wonderful. In fact, he hadn't gotten much sleep at all. Last night had been Tramp's first night sleeping in Lady's house—or in any house, come to think of it.

"How do you do it?" he grumbled. "That bed is so soft, I feel like I'm sinking in a feather pool. And between Jim Dear's snoring and the baby's crying, I could barely hear the crickets chirping."

"Oh, dear," Lady said, feeling truly sorry for her mate. "I know!" she exclaimed. "Jim Dear and Darling love you so—I'm sure they'd let you sleep up on their bed tonight. There's nothing in the world better than that!"

But Tramp shook his head. "I'm afraid it's the outdoors I need," he explained. "I mean, I know you grew up this way and all . . . but it's just so much fun to sleep under the stars. And the moon, too. There's nothing to howl at in this bedroom."

That night, as soon as the sun set and the moon began to rise, Lady and Tramp went out to the garden. Happy at last, Tramp turned three times and then plopped down. "Oh, how I love the feel of cool dirt on my belly!" he said with a dreamy smile.

Meanwhile, Lady gingerly peeked into the dark and slightly damp doghouse. Already she missed the comforts of Jim Dear and Darling's room.

Tramp watched as Lady stretched out on the doghouse floor, then got up and moved outside, then back in once again. It was plain to see that, try as she might, Lady just could not relax on the cold, hard ground.

"Don't worry," Tramp announced, "I have an idea."

And with that, he ran into the house. Seconds later, he reappeared with Lady's silk cushion in his teeth. Carefully, he swept the doghouse floor with his tail and laid the cushion down just the way Lady liked it.

Lady smiled and lay down. And do you know what? That night, they both had the sweetest dreams either one had ever had.

The Sweetest Songs of All

"Why is Quasimodo so sad?" asked Hugo.

"Judge Frollo has commanded that he never leave Notre Dame Cathedral," answered Victor. "He's lonely because he has no friends."

Just then Quasimodo appeared.

"Good morning, Quasi!" Hugo cried. "Nice day for ringing bells."

"I guess so," Quasimodo replied, staring at the people far below.

"Cheer up! What do they have down there that we don't have up here?" Hugo asked.

Quasimodo frowned. "I don't know, because I've never been there. But I hear people laughing and singing."

Then Victor spoke. "The sweetest songs of all can be heard in this tower, if you do what I tell you to."

"I will!" Quasimodo cried.

"Then fetch a piece of firewood and a knife from the kitchen," Victor commanded.

Quasimodo quickly returned with both. "I want you to carve statues of lots of different birds," said Victor.

Quasimodo nodded. For two days, he worked. On the third day, he showed Hugo his first carving.

"Wow, that really looks like a dove," said Hugo.

"I'm going to carve a finch next," Quasimodo vowed.

Over the next few weeks, Quasimodo carved hundreds of birds out of wood—larks and thrushes and robins and sparrows. Each statue was better than the last. He worked so hard that he nearly forgot he was lonely.

Finally, he showed Victor and Hugo a carving of a beautiful nightingale.

"It is your best work of all," said Victor.

Quasimodo was so proud that he set his bird on the highest tower so they could all admire it.

The next morning, he was surprised to see two real birds perched next to his statue. More birds soon arrived. Some even built nests. Soon, hundreds and hundreds of birds lived in Notre Dame. They woke Quasimodo with their songs in the morning and they sang him to sleep at night.

Victor had told Quasimodo the sweetest songs of all could be heard at Notre Dame, and he was right. Since that day, birds have always lived in Notre Dame Cathedral.

The Prince's Dream

The Grand Duke was worried about Prince Charming. The Prince had finally met the girl of his dreams, but she'd run away. And now it was impossible to reason with the Prince.

"You must bring her back!" the Prince told the Grand Duke.

"Of course, Your Highness!" said the Duke. "I've already sent the royal guards after her carriage."

But the guards returned without her. The captain bowed to the Prince. "I'm very sorry, Your Highness," he said. "I don't understand what happened. I could see her carriage ahead of us—and an extraordinary carriage it was. It actually seemed to shimmer."

"Then what happened?" asked the Duke.

"We turned a corner and the carriage simply . . . vanished," said the captain.

"I don't even know her name," said the Prince in a daze.

The Duke sighed as he watched Prince Charming's eyes glaze over. The Prince would clearly be distracted until they found this mystery girl.

"Well, for now, you must try to focus on your duties as the host of the ball," the Duke advised the Prince. "The ballroom is still filled with eligible maidens."

The Prince shook his head. "There is no other maiden. Not for me. If only she had left some clue!" he cried despairingly. "Some token to remember her by!"

The Duke rolled his eyes. "Your Highness might try investigating your right jacket pocket, then."

Startled, the Prince stuck his hand into his pocket and withdrew a glass slipper. He had been so distracted by his newfound love for the mystery girl that he had completely forgotten about the tiny glass slipper she had left behind on the stairs! He looked at the slipper, then at the Duke.

"I . . . I . . ." the Prince stammered.

"I suggest you allow me to see to the arrangements," the Duke said kindly, taking the slipper. "We'll find your mystery lass, Your Highness."

The Prince nodded gratefully, then turned toward the window and gazed out into the night. Somewhere out there, his princess was waiting for him. "Dreams can come true," he murmured. "After tonight, I'm sure of it."

The Fairy Boat

Tinker Bell loved humans—or, at least, she loved human things! But now Tink was in trouble. She had been exploring a fairy house in the meadow when she had been *captured* by a human girl named Lizzy!

Vidia, who had seen the whole thing happen, thought the girl was going to hurt Tink. And so she set off to get help.

What Vidia didn't realize was that the young girl was actually being very kind to Tinker Bell. Lizzy loved fairies and wanted to learn more about them. In fact, Tinker Bell was happily teaching the little girl everything she knew.

If Vidia had known that, she might have taken the time to wait out the storm that had just broken. Instead, Vidia, who couldn't fly in the rain, ran across the field and arrived at the fairy camp soaked to the bone.

"A little girl has kidnapped Tinker Bell, in the old house, on the other side of the road," Vidia cried. "We have to hurry and save her!"

But the fairies couldn't fly in the rain!

Clank and Bobble, two tinker-talent sparrow men, had an idea. They would build a boat. Soon all the fairies were gathering materials. Even the forest insects helped. Nothing was too much work to rescue everyone's favorite tinker fairy!

The fairies used a piece of bark to form the shell of the boat, a bendy stick as the mast, and lily pads as sails. Soon the boat was finished. All the rescuers needed to do now was climb aboard!

In no time, the boat was sailing through a channel in the middle of the field. The channel was actually a deep wheel track filled by the rain, but for a fairy, it was the perfect size to sail down.

Then, suddenly, the ground dipped down. The channel was transformed into a waterfall! The current rushed the boat downstream!

Vidia tried to reverse the boat by commanding the wind to blow in a circle. But the storm was stronger than her powers, and the boat soon crashed down the waterfall, breaking into pieces.

With no boat, the fairies would have to carry on by foot. . . .

Just Like Everyone Else

There was wild cheering in the stadium at Monsters University.

The Oozma Kappas had won the Scare Games!

The OKs hoisted Mike Wazowski, their team leader, up into the air. He had gotten the loudest scream of any of the competitors in the scare simulator.

Mike was delighted, but he was also relieved. It meant he could rejoin the university's Scare Program. Dean Hardscrabble had kicked Mike and Sulley out after they had accidentally broken her famous scare canister. But she had agreed to let the whole team join if they won the Scare Games.

For Mike, this was a special moment. He had proven to everyone that he had what it took to become a top Scarer.

Alone a few minutes later, he went back into the simulator to relive the moment. He turned to the robot-child and said, "Boo!"

Once again, the robot screamed.

"I knew I was scary. I didn't know I was that scary," Mike told Sulley, who was watching from the doorway.

Mike bent down to look at the settings on the simulator. Someone had changed them from "hard" to "easy." It was Sulley!

Mike was hurt and angry.

"You said you believed in me, but you're just like everyone else!" he yelled and stormed away.

As Sulley wandered across campus, students congratulated him on his win. Even the RORs, the best fraternity on campus, asked him to join them. Sulley felt awful. He knew he didn't deserve their praise.

Meanwhile, Mike snuck over to the Door Tech department and stole a key to the lab where students tested doors to the human world. He was going to prove to everyone once and for all that he was scary.

Back on campus, Sulley confessed everything to Dean Hardscrabble.

"You did what?" she exclaimed. "I expect you off campus by tomorrow!"

Suddenly, the alarm sounded in the Door Tech Lab. Dean Hardscrabble flew off to investigate.

Sulley's heart sank. He was sure it was Mike who had set off the alarm, and that meant he was in serious trouble.

Sulley had to help his friend!

The Frog Hunt

An evil sorcerer had changed spoiled Prince Naveen into a frog. Naveen assumed that kissing a princess would change him back, so he went looking for one.

Prince Naveen saw Tiana dressed up for a costume ball and mistakenly thought she was a princess. But when he kissed her, Tiana had turned into a frog instead!

Now the two frogs were in search of a way to break the curse. Deep in the bayou, they faced countless dangers. But of all the predators, the most frightening were the hunters—even the alligators were wary of them. Fortunately, Tiana and Naveen knew they could count on the help of the friends they had met along the way.

"My name's Raymond, but everybody calls me Ray!" announced the large firefly who had just joined them.

Ray offered to show Tiana, Naveen, and their alligator friend Louis the way to Mama Odie, an old voodoo woman who lived in a boat stuck in a tree deep in the bayou.

Tiana blazed a trail through the bushes while Louis followed her, trying to escape the pricker bushes. Suddenly—

whoosh!—a net swooped down and scooped up Naveen.

Three frog hunters—Reggie, Darnell, and Two Fingers—were out to capture the two frogs, and Reggie had Naveen in his net!

"No, no, no!" Ray said, panicking. "A bug's got to do what a bug's got to do!" he cried as he shot straight up Reggie's nose.

Quickly, Naveen escaped while Ray was blown out of the hunter's nose. Meanwhile, Darnell and Two Fingers had captured Tiana!

Naveen leaped in to save her. While Naveen diverted the men's attention, Tiana jumped out of her cage. Naveen and Tiana jumped all over the place, and in the end, the hunters only succeeded in knocking one another out.

"These two ain't like no frogs I ever seen. They smart!" Reggie marveled to his friends.

"And we talk, too!" Tiana called to him.

The hunters opened their eyes wide, speechless. Then they screamed in terror and ran off!

It was a frog hunt they weren't likely to forget anytime soon.

DUMBO

Telephone

"Did you hear the news, my dear?" one of the circus elephants said to another.

"What is it?" the second elephant asked.

The first elephant looked around carefully to make sure that no one was listening.

"Well," she whispered in the second elephant's ear, "you know Mrs. Jumbo's son, Dumbo? A little bird told me that his first show was a hit! Everyone loved the 'Building on Fire' act. Dumbo leaped off a platform twenty feet high. And they're going to raise it up much higher next time!

"But don't tell a soul!" the first elephant warned.

As soon as the first elephant turned away, the second elephant turned to another of her friends. "Listen, dear," she said. "You'll never believe what I just heard!"

"What is it, dear?" the third elephant asked.

The second elephant lowered her voice to a whisper. "It's Dumbo—twenty clowns had to hit him with a tire to get him to leap off a platform!"

The third elephant gasped. "Oh, my! That is big news!"

"But don't breathe a word to anyone!" the second elephant exclaimed.

Soon the third elephant was talking to another friend. The fourth elephant gaped with amazement as she listened.

". . . and so Dumbo set the platform on fire, and it took twenty clowns to put out the flames," the third elephant confided.

The fourth elephant told a fifth, and the fifth told a sixth. Soon the whole circus was buzzing with the news of Dumbo's first clown show.

A little bird was flying over the Big Top when he saw a pair of elephants chattering below. "Good day, ladies," he said. "What's the word around the circus this evening?"

"It's Dumbo," one elephant said excitedly. "It seems he fell off a platform in the last show and hit twenty clowns. Now they're talking about setting him on fire next time!"

The little bird didn't stick around to hear the end of the discussion. "I can't wait to spread this news!" he squawked, fluttering back up into the sky. "Wait until everyone hears—they'll never believe it's true!"

A Game of Robin Hood

"Let's play Robin Hood!" Skippy shouted to his friends Tagalong, Toby, and Sis.

"All right," agreed Tagalong. "I'll be Robin's best friend, Little John. Toby can be the mean old Sheriff of Nottingham!"

"Well, then, I will be Maid Marian," said Sis.

Robin Hood was loved by the people, because he robbed from the rich and gave to the poor. Nowadays many people were needy, for they were taxed heavily by the Sheriff of Nottingham. Everyone knew that the Sheriff was in league with the evil Prince John, and that they used the tax money for their own gain. Prince John's brother, King Richard, was the true king of England. But King Richard was fighting in the Crusades far away. He couldn't protect his people, so someone else had to—and that someone was Robin Hood!

"Hands up, sirrah!" said Skippy gleefully. He and Tagalong pretended to raid Toby's carriage. "We shall lighten your wallet today and give it away to the worthy citizens you have been taxing so heavily."

"Drat! My evil plans have been foiled again!" snarled Toby, handing over his pretend money.

"One day I'm going to get you, Robin Hood!" Toby continued.

Skippy laughed. "You'll never find me, Sheriff!" he cried. "If you come into Sherwood Forest, we will give you such a whipping that you'll wish you'd never heard of Robin Hood!"

Sis giggled, then ran over to a table and climbed up on top of it.

"Oh, Robin! Robin!" she cried. "Help me, my darling, my own true love! That mean old Prince John has locked me up in this high tower! He heard that we are in love, and he intends to prevent us from ever being together!"

Suddenly, the children froze. Someone had chuckled from behind the door of a nearby cottage. "Uh-oh," Skippy whispered. "We're toast. It's got to be the Sheriff of Nottingham!"

"He'll lock us up and throw away the key!" Toby said, his voice shaking.

Just then the "Sheriff" stepped out from behind the door. It was Robin Hood!

"Keep up the good work, kids!" he said with a merry laugh. And then he bounded away into Sherwood Forest.

Into the Tunnel

Rapunzel's golden hair had magical healing powers. As a baby, she had been kidnapped by Mother Gothel, who used her hair's magic to stay forever young. The woman pretended to be her mother, and she locked her away in a tower and never let her out.

But one day, Flynn Rider had come along, and Rapunzel had convinced him to take her to see the floating lights that rose in the sky every year on her birthday.

Flynn was cunning. He had tried to frighten Rapunzel by taking her to a horrible pub full of thugs. He thought this would make her want to return to her tower and give up on the idea of seeing the floating lights. Then he could take his crown and go on his way! But Flynn hadn't counted on Rapunzel charming the ruffians!

"Find your humanity," Rapunzel cried out. "Haven't any of you ever had a dream?

Little by little, everyone in the pub began to describe his hidden hopes and dreams. One wanted to knit. Another wanted to bake.

Suddenly the royal guard appeared. They were looking for Flynn.

"Where's Rider? Where is he?" demanded the captain of the guard. He was followed by Maximus, his horse. The horse had nearly caught Flynn before, and he was still hot on his trail! Luckily, Flynn and Rapunzel had time to slip behind the counter before anyone saw them.

The landlord leaned toward Flynn and grabbed him by the arm. The young thief was sure he was about to be turned in to the royal guard. But instead, the ruffian lifted up a heavy trapdoor hidden behind the bar and whispered to them, "Go, live your dream."

"I will," Flynn replied.

"Your dream stinks. I was talking to her!"

"Thanks for everything!" said Rapunzel.

Flynn slipped into the dark tunnel first. Rapunzel took a deep breath and plunged into the dark behind him.

The landlord closed the trapdoor. Flynn and Rapunzel were on their own now!

Castle Cleaning

It was a particularly warm and sunny April morning, and Belle and Chip the teacup were gazing out of a castle window at the blue sky and the budding trees and plants.

"Well, Chip," Belle said, "it is spring at last. And you know what that means, don't you?"

Chip hopped up and down in excitement. "It means we get to play outside?" he asked.

Belle laughed. "Well, yes, that too," she replied. "But first it's time to do some spring cleaning."

Belle got together a few cleaning supplies. "I think I'll start in the dining room," she said. She pulled the silverware out of the silver cabinet and began polishing a fork.

"Ooh!" exclaimed the enchanted fork. "Careful! Ouch! Not so hard around the tines!"

"Oh, dear!" said Belle. "I'm sorry." She gently polished the rest of the utensils.

Next, Belle gathered all the dishes. But when she dipped the first enchanted dish into the soapy water in the sink, it cried out, "Ahh! Too cold! Too cold! Stop!"

Belle gasped, apologized, and hurried to add more warm water to the sink.

After finishing the dishes, Belle went to the library to take a break from her cleaning. Chip hopped in behind her. "Oh, Chip," Belle said wearily, "spring cleaning in this castle is a challenge. I'm not used to cleaning enchanted objects!"

Chip giggled. "And I guess we're not used to it, either. We always just clean ourselves!"

"Clean yourselves?" said Belle.

That gave her a great idea. If the enchanted objects could clean themselves, they could clean other objects, too!

Belle called the enchanted objects together. "I wonder if I could ask your help with a little project," Belle began.

Soon Belle had a small army of enchanted objects cleaning everything else in the castle. In a few short hours, the entire castle had been cleaned, and Belle and Chip were relaxing in the library.

"Well," Belle said as she sank into a comfortable chair, "you know what they say: Many hands make light work. And a little enchantment never hurt, either!"

Boy's Best Friend

Like all little boys, Pinocchio wanted a puppy. And, like all little boys, he promised to feed it and walk it and do everything and anything required to care for it.

"Puppies are a lot of work," Geppetto told his son. "And puppies like to chew things, like slippers—and wood." The wood carver glanced over at the rows and rows of wooden toys on his workbench. "No, I don't think a dog is a good idea," he said finally.

That afternoon, when Pinocchio returned from school, Geppetto had a present waiting. The boy wasted no time in opening the box. Inside was a wooden dog.

Not wanting to hurt Geppetto's feelings, Pinocchio thanked his father and placed the toy on his bed.

A few days later, as Pinocchio was walking home from school, he heard a puppy whimpering in an alleyway. "Why, you look just like the wooden dog my father carved for me," Pinocchio said. He wondered what he should do with the puppy. "Well, I can't leave you here all by yourself," he decided.

The boy went home and tied the dog to a tree a few doors up the street. Then he sneaked the puppy a bowl of food and went back inside.

After Geppetto had fallen asleep, Pinocchio slipped outside and scooped up the dog. "Now, you're going to have to be very quiet," he warned.

But once inside, the puppy sprang from Pinocchio's arms and made a dash for Figaro!

"Look out!" cried Pinocchio.

Suddenly, Geppetto appeared in his nightclothes. "What's going on here?" he asked.

"Well . . ." Pinocchio began. Just then, the puppy sprang onto Pinocchio's bed, knocking the wooden dog beneath it. Geppetto blinked. The puppy looked just like the toy he had made for his son!

"Could it be?" the toy maker asked. "Pinocchio! You wanted a puppy so much that the Blue Fairy must have turned your toy dog into a real one!"

Pinocchio was thrilled. But he knew he had to tell his father the truth.

"Well," Geppetto said as he watched the pup carrying the wooden dog around the house, "I suppose we have room for two dogs here—especially if one of them walks the other!"

Listen with Your Heart

It was a clear, crisp day. Pocahontas had just finished visiting with Grandmother Willow. Now she was climbing to the top of a high mountain with her friends Meeko the raccoon and Flit the hummingbird.

Soon the friends came to a fork in the path.

"Which direction should we take, Meeko?" asked Pocahontas.

The raccoon pointed to the wider, flatter path, which made Pocahontas laugh.

"Let's try this one!" she said, pointing to the narrower, steeper route. They climbed and climbed, and the path grew narrower and steeper.

As Pocahontas sat down on a large tree stump to catch her breath, the winds suddenly picked up. Then the clouds moved in, and rain poured down on them.

"Uh-oh," said Pocahontas, jumping to her feet. "We can't stay here, and it's too slippery to climb back down. We need to keep moving!"

Pocahontas paused. Where should they go? "I need to listen," Pocahontas said to herself. "I must listen with my heart to the spirits all around us, and they will keep us safe."

Pocahontas tried to listen, but it was hard to hear anything over the pouring rain and rushing winds.

Suddenly, she heard them. The spirits spoke to her! They told her to climb a little higher, just a bit, and there she would find shelter.

"Come on, Meeko! Come on, Flit!" she called over the wind and rain. "We'll find shelter just a little way up!" Sure enough, the friends found an opening in the rocks just a bit higher up the path. Between the rocks was a small cave, and inside it was warm and dry.

The storm soon passed, and the sun came out. "Come on!" Pocahontas cried to Meeko and Flit. "Let's go see what it looks like at the top!" They hurried the rest of the way up the trail until they came out on a wide, flat ledge. Far below, they could see the forest and, beyond it, the sparkling blue sea.

"You see, Meeko? See, Flit?" said Pocahontas. "We're seeing the world in a different way. Isn't it beautiful?

"And just think," she said, more to herself than to the other two, "if I hadn't chosen that unexplored path, I would never have heard the spirits talk to me!"

The Flying Blueberries

Everyone in the ant colony was in a good mood. The grasshoppers had been driven off once and for all, and none of the ants had even been hurt! But Flik's amazing fake bird had taken quite a beating, and the Blueberries were determined to fix it.

"Fixing that bird is a big job," said Mr. Soil, Dot's teacher, "but I know the Blueberries can do it."

The Blueberries stared at the fake bird. It was one big mess!

"I'll be back in a little while to see how you're doing," said Mr. Soil.

With a cheer, the Blueberries went to work. Some picked new leaves to cover the frame. Others glued those leaves into place with sticky honey. After hours of hard work, the bird was fixed.

"Let's sit in it!" Dot said.

Just as the Blueberries crawled inside the bird, the wind began to blow. Suddenly, the breeze caught the fake wings. The bird took off!

It was up to Dot to save the day. She hopped into the pilot seat and took control.

The Blueberries flew around Ant Island once, then twice. Soon they weren't afraid anymore.

"Look!" screamed Rose. "Real birds are attacking the worker ants!"

Dot jiggled the controls. The fake bird dived out of the sky and frightened the real birds away.

"Hooray!" yelled the Blueberries.

"Don't cheer yet!" Dot cried. "This contraption is out of control!"

With a bump and a crash, the bird hit the ground and skidded to a halt.

"It's wrecked again!" said Rose. "And here comes Mr. Soil! He's going to be so mad."

But surprisingly, Mr. Soil was smiling.

"You're heroes!" he told them. "You saved the worker ants."

"But the bird is wrecked again," said Rose.

"And you can fix it again, too," Mr. Soil replied.

"And here is a merit badge for you, Princess, in honor of your first flight," Mr. Soil continued.

Dot was confused. "I've already made my first flight," she said, fluttering her tiny wings.

"Ah, but this is a special badge," Mr. Soil replied. "It's for making your first flight not using your wings, but using your head!"

A Prizewinning Pair

Max and his dad, Goofy, were sitting at the breakfast table. Max looked at the funny pages, while Goofy leafed through the other sections of the newspaper.

"Listen to this!" said Goofy. "Channel Ten is sponsoring the Father and Son of the Year Contest. The father and son who can prove that they have achieved something truly incredible together will appear on national TV."

"Too bad Bigfoot ruined that video we took of him last summer," said Max. "Hey, I know! Why don't we go back and find him again?"

"Okay, Maxie. Count me in!" said Goofy.

Goofy and Max packed their bags and got into their car. They reached the campsite that night, pitched their tent, and went to sleep. Soon they were awakened by a loud crash.

"It's him!" cried Max. "Get the camera!"

But when they poked their heads out, they saw it wasn't Bigfoot at all, but Pete and P.J.

"I'm sorry," said P.J. "I told my dad about your trip, and now he wants us to win that prize. We're out here looking for Bigfoot, just like you two are."

The next day, Pete set up a barbecue with several juicy steaks.

"This will lure him out for sure," he told P.J.

The trick worked. In a matter of minutes, Bigfoot crashed through the trees and made a beeline for the meat. "Tackle him, P.J.!" yelled Pete.

Though he was scared, P.J. did as he was told. Bigfoot threw him around while Pete turned on the camera. "The judges are going to love this!" cried Pete.

"Help!" P.J. begged.

Goofy and Max heard P.J.'s cries and came running from the lake. Without saying a word, Goofy jabbed the monster in the backside with a fishing lure while Max threw a fishing net over the monster's head.

"You were awesome," Max told Goofy.

"Right back at you, son," Goofy replied.

Back at home, Pete turned in the video. The judges had decided Goofy and Max deserved the award! But on the day they were to appear on TV, Goofy and Max decided to go to the beach together instead. They realized they didn't need anybody to tell them what an incredible father-and-son team they were.

They knew it already!

Invincible Mushu

After helping Mulan defeat the Huns and restore the Fa family honor, Mushu had been given back his old job as family guardian. He helped guard the temple of the Fa ancestors.

One day, Mushu was sunning himself on the temple roof when a big cricket waddled up. He seemed to be staring right at Mushu.

Mushu frowned. "Who you lookin' at?" he said to the cricket.

The cricket flicked out his tongue. Mushu was offended.

"Oh, yeah?" he said. "Stick your tongue out at me, will you? Well, get a load of this!" Puffing out his tiny chest, Mushu spat out a miniature burst of fire, no bigger than the flame of a match.

The cricket just blinked.

"Not good enough for you, eh?" Mushu said. "All right, tough guy. Try this on for size!"

Mushu cleared his throat dramatically. Taking a deep breath, he opened his mouth and spat a bigger flame at the cricket.

The cricket crouched, lowering his chest to the ground. Then he straightened his legs. Then he crouched again. The cricket was doing push-ups, as crickets often do.

"Oh-ho!" Mushu shouted. "Think you're tough, do you? Well, Mr. Scales for Brains, I didn't spend time in the Imperial Army for nothing!"

And with that, Mushu crouched down and began to do push-ups, too.

". . . ninety-eight . . . ninety-nine . . . one hundred!" Mushu counted, panting. He leaped to his feet and began to run circles around the cricket. "Just ask anyone; I'm the dragon that defeated hundreds of Huns. I could eat you for lunch, small fry."

The cricket just sat there. Then— *Snap!* The cricket snatched up a fly that landed on Mushu's nose.

"Ahhhh!" Mushu screamed. He was so startled, he leaped backward . . . and fell off the roof. He landed on the ground in a puff of dust.

"Ha-ha-ha-ha-ha-ha-ha!" The air filled with the sound of roaring laughter. The ancestors had seen everything.

"Cheer up, Mushu," one ancestor said. "It looks like you have a new friend."

Sure enough, the cricket had followed Mushu down from the roof. "Well," Mushu said, "I always did want a pet."

Street Cats

"Oh, Mama!" said Marie dreamily. "Paris is so pretty in the morning! May we please go explore just a bit?"

"All right, darlings," their mother replied. "But just for a few minutes. Madame must be missing us terribly. Be sure to stick together!"

The kittens passed a doorway to a jazz hall, where the previous night's party appeared to be still in full swing. "Oh, yeah!" said Toulouse as he danced in the doorway to the swinging beat.

"Come on, Toulouse," said Berlioz crossly. "I'm hungry!"

A few steps down the block, a fish seller was just setting out his wares in the window of his shop. The fishmonger smiled at the kittens through the window, then came out of his shop and tossed them each a sardine. "Here you are, my pretty cats!" he said to them.

The kittens meowed a thank-you and gobbled up the tasty treat. "The streets of Paris are the coolest place on Earth!" said Berlioz as they continued walking. "I don't want to go back to Madame's house!"

"Berlioz! You mustn't speak like that!" said Marie. "You know how much

Madame needs us. . . ." Suddenly, she broke off. Her brothers followed her gaze, which was directed at the window of a fancy pet shop. "Oh, my!" she cried out delightedly. "Look at those!" In the window of the shop were several jeweled cat collars, all in different shades of the finest leather. Marie thought they were the most beautiful things she'd ever seen— especially the pink one.

"I must say, the streets of Paris are a wonderful place!" Marie said dreamily.

Just then, they heard a deep barking. A moment later, a huge dog came bounding around the corner. The kittens froze. Then all three of them turned and scampered back down the street in the direction of their mother and Mr. O'Malley, with the dog hot on their heels.

"Paris is a fine city," said Berlioz, panting, as he raced down an alley. Darting behind some trash cans, the kittens were able to lose the snarling dog.

"Yes," replied Marie. "But I'm not sure how I feel about the Parisians— particularly the canine kind!"

Goofy Goes to the Doctor

Mickey woke up early and checked the date. Today Goofy was supposed to go to the doctor for a checkup.

Mickey found Goofy and brought him back to the Clubhouse. Daisy stopped by, and Mickey told her why Goofy looked so glum. Daisy decided this would be a good time for her to play Dr. Daisy. She explained to Goofy that the doctor would examine parts of his body.

Goofy asked, "Does that hurt?"

"Nope. Not a bit," said Mickey.

Next Daisy said that the doctor uses a stethoscope to listen to heartbeats. Daisy listened to Mickey's heart. Goofy asked what it sounded like.

Daisy said, "It goes *lub-dub, lub-dub.*"

Then Willie the giant arrived. He wanted to help, too.

"When I go to the doctor," said Willie, "my favorite part is getting to stick out my tongue and say *AHH* so the doctor can examine my throat."

Willie showed them how he did it. *"AHHHH!"*

"Oh, boy," said Mickey. "Thanks, Willie. We get the idea!"

Goofy was starting to feel better. "So that's it?"

Daisy explained that was most of it, but that he might need to have a shot, too. She told him that sometimes the doctor gives you a shot of medicine to stop you from getting sick. That made Goofy nervous.

"I have a thinking trick that I use when I get a shot," said Mickey. "I close my eyes and think about things that I like; then I count them. Can you guess what I think about?"

"Hot dogs!" said Goofy.

"You betcha," said Mickey. "By the time I count three of them, it's all over."

"Say, that is a neat trick," said Goofy. "I think I'll count hot fudge sundaes!"

At last it was time for Goofy and Mickey to go. Daisy explained they might have to sit in the doctor's waiting room for a little while, so it was a good idea to take a book or a toy. Goofy grabbed several—just in case.

Goofy felt a lot less worried, and his trip to the doctor wasn't scary at all. Hot diggity dog!

Rabbit's Frightful Garden

Rabbit woke up bright and early. He had a lot of work to do in his garden. There was just one problem. Rabbit had lent all his tools to his friends—and they hadn't returned them.

Meanwhile, Pooh and Piglet were enjoying breakfast with Kanga when Roo bounced in with a bunch of wildflowers.

"Thank you, Roo!" Kanga exclaimed, giving him a kiss. "Let me just trim these."

She rummaged around in a kitchen drawer, where she came across Rabbit's gardening shears. "Oh, no," Kanga said. "I never returned these to Rabbit after I borrowed them."

"That reminds me," said Piglet, "I still have Rabbit's rake. And, Pooh, I'll bet you still have Rabbit's shovel."

The friends decided the neighborly thing to do would be to return Rabbit's tools right away. When they arrived at Rabbit's house, though, their friend was not at home. He was on his way to *their* houses to get his tools back!

"Rabbit's garden could use some work," Kanga said. "Why don't we take care of it for him as a way of saying that we're sorry for keeping his tools for so long?"

Everyone agreed that this was a splendid plan.

When they had finished working, they spotted some birds hungrily eyeing the harvest.

"This garden needs a scarecrow!" cried Roo.

The work crew sprang into action, and soon a towering scarecrow was planted right in the middle of the garden. "Won't Rabbit be surprised?" Piglet said proudly.

When Rabbit returned home a few minutes later, he couldn't quite believe his eyes. First he looked at the vegetables, all neatly picked. Then he looked at his garden tools, which had mysteriously reappeared. Finally, he looked at the strange scarecrow, which seemed to be looking right back at him!

"D-d-d-did you do this?" he stammered to the straw man. Just then, a gust of wind knocked over the rake resting on the scarecrow's arm.

Convinced his garden was haunted, Rabbit turned and ran for his life.

"Ahhhhhhhhh!" he screamed as he rushed past his friends.

"I *told* you he'd be surprised," said Piglet.

A Big Surprise

One spring morning, Snow White visited the Dwarfs' cottage to leave them a surprise. She knew the Dwarfs worked hard, and she wanted to make sure that when they got home that day, they didn't have to do any more work.

After the Dwarfs had left for the mines, Snow White and her animal friends hurried into the cottage and set to work. The birds chirped while they picked up crumbs. The squirrels used their fluffy tails to dust. And the chipmunks washed and dried the dishes. With so many helpers, Snow White had the downstairs gleaming in no time. Next, they went upstairs and made the beds. Before long, every inch of the Dwarfs' cottage was neat and tidy.

Back inside the cottage, Snow White and her friends fixed supper. There was soup to be simmered and bread to be made. Before she knew it, the late afternoon sun was casting long shadows across the windowpanes.

Tweet! Chirp! A bluebird was singing outside the window. That was the signal that the Dwarfs were almost home.

Snow White and the animals hurried outside, hid, and peeked in through a window. When they got inside, the Dwarfs could not believe their eyes. The floors were swept, the room was tidy, and there was even a freshly baked pie cooling on a windowsill!

"What is that delicious smell?" Doc wondered.

"Look!" cried Grumpy. He went to the pot of soup.

The Dwarfs were confused. They tried to guess which Dwarf had done this.

Doc noticed that Happy's smile was especially big. Was he keeping a secret? Dopey pointed out that Sneezy seemed supersneezy. Maybe because he had dusted and swept the cottage?

Snow White giggled as she listened outside the window. "They'll never guess that we did it," she whispered to her animal friends.

After a long workday, their tummies pleasantly full, all Seven Dwarfs were ready to go to sleep. When they climbed the stairs, the Dwarfs found one last treat: seven neatly made beds. As they drifted off to sleep, the Dwarfs decided to tell their good friend Snow White about this wonderful surprise the very next time they saw her.

Lucky's Last Laugh

It was getting quite late at Pongo and Perdita's house, but their darling little puppies were still not asleep. That was because Lucky wouldn't stop talking!

"And then," he was saying, "there was the part at the very beginning, when Thunderbolt jumped across that canyon. Whoosh! Like a rocket!"

"Yes, Lucky, we remember," his sister Penny said. "How could we forget? You've reminded us a hundred times!"

"Yeah! It was so great! And then there was that part when—"

"Lucky!" wailed Rolly. "We all watched the same episode of *Thunderbolt* tonight. You don't have to tell us about it."

"Yeah, I know, but I just wanted to tell you about that great part when Thunderbolt found the little girl, then ran back to tell the sheriff—"

"Lucky! It's late! We want to go to sleep!" barked Patch.

Lucky laid his head on his paws. "Okay," he said. "I'll be quiet."

All the puppies closed their eyes.

"Oh! But what about the part when the sheriff told Thunderbolt to climb up that cliff, and he got to the top, and he grabbed that rope with his teeth, and he pulled up the little girl—"

"Lucky!" yelped Pepper. "We don't care about Thunderbolt. Go to bed!"

"Right." Lucky sighed, lying down once again. Then he suddenly sat up. "Wait a sec! Don't care about Thunderbolt?"

"We mean," said Freckles, "that we want you to be quiet so we can go to sleep!"

"You mean," said Lucky, "you don't want me to tell you about the last part where Thunderbolt ran back to the mountains and into that cave and found that amazing thing?"

"Yes!" Lucky's brothers and sisters shouted together.

"Oh. Okay," said Lucky. "Good night."

And with that, Lucky closed his eyes. For a minute, everyone enjoyed the silence. Then Penny sat up.

"Hey, wait a minute," she said. "What thing did he find?"

"Yeah," said Patch. "I missed that."

"Me too," said Rolly. "What was it exactly that he found, Lucky? Tell us."

But there was no answer. Lucky was fast asleep. And now the *other* Dalmatian puppies were wide awake!

A Muddy Rescue

The fairies were on the mainland to bring the season of summer. Tinker Bell had found herself with no work to do, because all of her inventions were working perfectly. She had nothing to fix, so she had entertained herself by flying after a car! She had followed it all the way to a house where a little girl named Lizzy lived with her father. But as she headed home, Tink had accidentally been captured by Lizzy!

The fairies had to save their friend. But there was another problem: a storm had started. The fairies couldn't fly in the rain, so they built a boat and set off to rescue Tinker Bell.

What the other fairies didn't realize was that Tink was fine! She had decided to stay and help Lizzy spend more time with her father.

Back on the fairy boat, the rescuers were in a panic. They were heading straight for a waterfall!

Silvermist, a water fairy, reached into the waterfall. She was able to make the water rise up so that the drop wasn't as steep, but the boat still crashed onto the shore and broke apart. The fairies would have to continue their mission on foot.

Finally Vidia spotted the muddy road that led to Lizzy's house. She helped her friends across, but then got stuck in the mud herself! Silvermist, Fawn, Rosetta, and Iridessa grabbed her and pulled. Suddenly, they saw the lights of a car coming toward them!

"Pull! Pull!" Rosetta cried, but Vidia was trapped. And worse, the mud was sucking the other fairies down, too!

Iridessa knew what she had to do. Walking toward the car, she held up her hand and bounced the headlight beams back at the driver. He thought another car was coming straight for him and slammed on his brakes.

Moments later, the driver got out of his car. "Hello? Is somebody out there?" he asked.

Fawn grabbed his shoelace and instructed the others to hold on tight. When the driver turned to leave, he pulled them all out of the mud!

The fairy friends were relieved. They made sure everyone was okay, then continued on their way to rescue Tinker Bell.

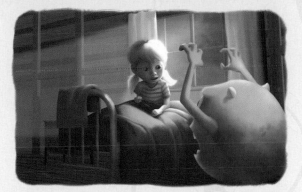

You Look Funny

Mike Wazowski was a monster on a mission. He was trying to prove that he deserved a place in the Scare Program at Monsters University. Mike's fraternity, Oozma Kappa, had just won the Scare Games. But Mike had learned that his teammate, Sulley, had cheated. He had changed the settings on the scare simulator to easy for Mike's turn. He didn't think Mike was scary enough to win on his own! Mike was determined to prove him wrong.

Mike broke into the Door Tech Lab at the university. He grabbed a door and placed it in the docking station—the portal to the human world. All he had to do now was walk through it and perform a real Scare on a human child.

Mike quietly entered the room. He rolled across the floor and ruffled the curtains. Then he crept closer to the child's bed. He could hear her stirring. Mike leaped up.

"*ROAR!*" he cried as ferociously as he could.

The child just looked at Mike and smiled. "You look funny," she said.

Mike couldn't believe it. His Scare hadn't worked. Everyone was right. He really *wasn't* scary after all.

Suddenly Mike realized that he wasn't in a child's bedroom at all. He was in a big room . . . and it was full of kids . . . and they were all looking at him. Mike had walked into a cabin full of campers!

Back in the Door Tech Lab, Dean Hardscrabble and her guards were holding back a crowd. "No one goes through that door until the authorities arrive," she announced.

Sulley arrived at the lab and told the OKs that it was Mike who had entered the human world without authority.

"But he could die out there!" cried Squishy.

Sulley wasn't going to let that happen. He would rescue Mike—but he needed the OKs' help to lure the guards away from the door.

Mike's friend Don quickly created a distraction. While the guards were dealing with him, Sulley charged toward the door. Hardscrabble spotted him at the last minute.

"Sullivan, don't go in there! It's extremely dangerous!" she cried.

Sulley knew the dangers, but he had to save his friend.

Friends Forever

Experiment 626 was a blue creature from a distant planet who was punished for being very naughty and destroying everything around him. One day, he escaped his planet in a police cruiser and headed straight for Earth!

On the tiny island of Kauai was a little girl named Lilo. She found it hard to make friends and was very lonely.

One night, Lilo had a fight with her sister, Nani. Lilo went to her room and slammed the door shut. Out of her window, Lilo saw a falling star and made a wish: "I wish for someone to be my friend," she whispered.

The falling star that Lilo had seen was actually Experiment 626's ship crashing on the island! A truck driver found him and took him to an animal shelter. All the other animals were scared of 626, but he didn't care. He scrunched two of his four arms in toward his torso so he would look more like a dog. That way, he'd be adopted and have a place to hide from the aliens who were chasing him.

The next day, Nani decided to take Lilo to the shelter to pick a new pet.

"Hi!" Lilo said when she saw 626.

"Hi," the creature replied, and then he gave her a hug. Lilo walked back to the front room and told Nani she'd found the dog she wanted.

"He's good," she said. "I can tell. His name is . . . Stitch."

They took Stitch home even though Nani thought he looked strange. Nani was glad Lilo finally had a friend.

At home, however, Stitch began to tear things apart and cause trouble for Nani.

"We have to take him back," Nani said.

"We adopted him!" Lilo cried. "What about *ohana*? Dad said *ohana* means *family*! And family means—"

"Nobody gets left behind," Nani finished. "I know."

She remembered how welcoming her parents had been and how important family was to them. She changed her mind. She would give Stitch another chance—for Lilo's sake.

From then on, Lilo and Stitch stuck together through anything that came their way. Lilo helped Stitch learn how to behave, and Stitch became the friend that Lilo had wished for on a falling star.

An Extraordinary Secret

Rapunzel had magical hair with healing powers. She had been kidnapped as a baby by the evil Mother Gothel, who used her hair's magic to stay young forever. The woman locked Rapunzel away in a tower and never let her out.

But one day, Flynn Rider had come along, and Rapunzel had convinced him to take her to see the floating lights that rose in the sky every year on her birthday. The two had been in a pub, the Snuggly Duckling, when the royal guards arrived looking for Flynn! The ruffians in the pub helped them to escape into a secret passage beneath the floor. Now they were fleeing through the passage!

Meanwhile, in the Snuggly Duckling, Maximus the horse led the royal guards straight to the secret passageway. The horse and the guards all charged into the tunnel.

Flynn and Rapunzel raced out of the tunnel and skidded to a stop at the edge of an enormous cavern. Rapunzel lassoed her long hair around a rock, swung through the air, and landed on a stone column. Flynn spun around and fought off Maximus and the guards!

Then Rapunzel threw Flynn her hair and held on as he leaped off the cliff.

Rapunzel and Flynn weren't safe yet. Maximus had a different plan— with one kick of his hoof, he brought down a dam leading into the cavern! Water quickly came flooding into the space.

The guards were swept away by the raging flood. Flynn and Rapunzel ducked into a cave, just as a stone column crashed to the ground, closing off the entrance. They were trapped!

Water quickly began to fill the cave. Flynn cut his hand trying to dislodge the large rocks surrounding them, but the boulders wouldn't budge. There was no way out.

"This is all my fault!" sobbed Rapunzel. "I'm so sorry, Flynn!"

"Eugene. My real name is Eugene Fitzherbert," Flynn admitted. "Someone might as well know."

"I have magic hair that glows when I sing," Rapunzel said.

The thief stared at her in shock. Then, suddenly, Rapunzel realized that her hair might actually be able to save them!

Maybe they would be okay after all.

Together Is Better

The Beast paced up and down his castle's long hallway. *Click, click, click* went his claws against the marble floor.

"It's been hours," he grumbled. "What do you suppose she's doing in there?" the Beast asked Lumiere.

"Reading," Lumiere replied. "After all, monsieur, it is the library."

"I know it's the library!" bellowed the Beast. "I know my own castle!"

Suddenly, the library doors burst open. Belle stormed out. She looked around the hallway.

"What is going on?" she asked.

"It's the servants," lied the Beast. "They make too much noise."

"Don't blame them," said Belle. "*You're* the one who's been clicking your claws for hours."

"I have not," said the Beast. "You were hearing things."

"And then you started bellowing," said Belle.

"So what if I did?" roared the Beast. "It's my castle!"

A door opened, and Mrs. Potts rolled up on a serving cart. "Anyone care for tea?" she asked.

"Not me," huffed Belle.

"Me, neither," huffed the Beast.

"Oh, come now. Just a spot?" asked Mrs. Potts, rolling her cart into the library.

Belle and the Beast followed her in and sat down.

"Why were you so angry?" asked Belle, sipping her tea.

"I was bored," said the Beast. "I guess I . . . missed you."

"Why didn't you just say so?" Belle asked.

"Because . . . I didn't think you missed me," said the Beast.

"I just love to read," Belle said.

"I know," said the Beast.

Belle thought for a moment. "I have an idea," she said. "How about we read together?"

Belle picked out a book about a princess and a dragon. First Belle read aloud to the Beast, and then the Beast read aloud to Belle.

"That was fun," said the Beast.

"Yes," said Belle. "Let's do it again tomorrow night."

In the hallway, Lumiere sighed with relief.

"Maybe now we'll get some peace!" he said to himself.

Mowgli's Nap

Baloo stretched, leaned against a tree trunk, and scratched his back as he slid to the ground. "Am I ever sleepy," he said. "I think it must be time for an afternoon snooze."

"Good thinking, my friend." High above them, stretched out on a branch, Bagheera the panther dangled a paw. His golden eyes were half closed in the heat of the day.

"A nap? Not for me!" Mowgli shook his mop of dark hair. "I'm not tired."

"Now, hold on a second there," Baloo said. "Don't you want to go hunting with us after it cools off? You're going to need energy."

"I have plenty of energy," Mowgli insisted. "I have energy right now!"

"You may have energy, but if you use it now, you will not have it to use later," Bagheera said wisely.

"Listen to the cat." Baloo yawned. "He knows what he's talking about." And with that, Baloo pulled Mowgli onto a pile of leaves and held him down with one great paw.

"I have energy for now *and* later," Mowgli grumbled.

"Good nap, Man-cub," Bagheera purred at the scowling Mowgli.

A moment later, the panther and the bear were sleeping soundly. As soon as Mowgli heard their snores, he hoisted up the arm that was pinning him down.

"Good nap, yourself," Mowgli whispered. And he tiptoed off to swing in the trees and drop sticks on the animals below.

Baloo's snores shook the jungle for an hour, perhaps two, before Mowgli returned to the shady napping spot again. He'd had a grand time in the treetops, but the sun and the swinging had tired him. The great gray bear looked so soft and peaceful lying against the tree that Mowgli couldn't help himself. He curled up against his friend and closed his eyes.

Not two minutes later, Bagheera awoke and stretched his inky paws. The panther flicked his tail under Baloo's nose.

"I'm up. I'm up and ready to go!" Baloo sat upright. Then, spying Mowgli, the bear gave the boy a good shake. "How about you, Man-cub? You awake?"

But the only sound that came from Mowgli's mouth was a loud snore.

A Royal Friend

A crowd of girls looked on
excitedly as Cinderella's
coach came to a stop outside
of their school. The headmistress
hurried to open the door. "Welcome,
Your Highness!" she exclaimed.

"It's so nice to see you all again,"
said the princess.

Everyone was happy to see
Cinderella. But no one was more
excited than a little girl named Emma.

Later that afternoon, when it was
time for her to go, Cinderella made an
announcement. "In one week, there
will be a party at the castle—held in
your honor."

The next day, the headmistress
took the girls to the meadow near the
royal estate. While her classmates ran
and played, Emma noticed several
seamstresses walking toward the castle
gates. Emma ran up behind them and
slipped inside!

She wandered the hallways until
a seamstress saw her and called out,
"Are you here for a fitting? Come in!
Stand here, dear." She began draping
fabric around Emma. When Cinderella
stopped by, Emma was wearing one of
the dresses.

"You look beautiful!" exclaimed
Cinderella. The princess invited Emma
to have tea with her.

"It must be wonderful to be a
princess," Emma said between bites
of a cookie. "You get to wear fancy
clothes and go to parties all day!"

Cinderella laughed. "There's more
to being a princess than clothes and
parties. Help me this afternoon and
see what a princess really does."

That afternoon, Emma and Cinderella
put together baskets of goods to donate.
Then they delivered the baskets to
orphanages. When they arrived back at
her school, the headmistress gave Emma
a big hug.

"Where have you been?" she cried.
"We've been so worried!"

Emma apologized. "I just wanted to
be a princess for a day," she said.

Hearing that, Cinderella decided
Emma should help plan the party. So
Emma helped to bake the cake.

"Because you've worked so hard, I'm
going to make you an honorary princess
for the evening," Cinderella said.

Emma was thrilled. She was going
to be Princess Emma for one magical
night!

Tink Causes Trouble

The fairies were on the mainland to bring the season of summer. Tinker Bell had found herself with no work to do, because all of her inventions were working perfectly.

The curious fairy had entertained herself by flying after a car! She had followed it all the way to a house where a little girl named Lizzy lived with her father.

Vidia had tried to teach Tink a lesson, trapping her inside a tiny fairy house that Lizzy had made. But then, the little girl discovered Tinker Bell. Vidia flew back to the fairy camp to get help.

But what Vidia didn't realize was that Tinker Bell had become friends with Lizzy. She was happily teaching Lizzy all about fairies.

Tinker Bell had also seen how sad Lizzy was that her father had no time for her. He was too busy trying to fix the leaks in their roof.

Tinker Bell decided she would fix the leaks herself. She flew into the attic and rigged up a system to take the water back outside.

As she finished, Tink couldn't help but notice a butterfly fluttering in a jar on Dr. Griffiths's desk. The scientist had caught it earlier to study. Seeing the poor creature trapped, Tink felt terrible. She decided to set it free.

Later, Dr. Griffiths came by to check on his daughter. "All the leaks have stopped," he said. "It's as if they mended themselves."

After he had gone, Tinker Bell tried to get Lizzy to show her father the fairy field journal. But when Lizzy got downstairs, her father was very upset.

"The butterfly is gone," he said. "I was going to present it at the museum tonight. Since there is no one else in the house, it must have been you. Tell me the truth."

"I could tell you, father," Lizzy declared, "but you wouldn't believe me."

"Very well," Dr. Griffiths said, "off to your room. I'm very disappointed in you."

Tinker Bell felt bad for getting Lizzy into trouble. She wanted to show herself to Dr. Griffiths, but Lizzy wouldn't let her new friend put herself in danger. Tinker Bell would have to find another way to fix things.

The Longest Day

"Could I have everyone's attention, please?" called Woody. "Today is Andy's last day of school. And you know what that means. . . ."

Summer meant the toys would get to play with Andy all day. They wanted the fun to start right away, but they had to wait until Andy came home. One by one, the toys suggested ways of passing the time. Buzz Lightyear made up a game of laser tag.

"But it's still only morning," Rex protested when the game was over. "This is the longest day of my life!"

"Don't worry, Rex," Buzz said. "There are plenty of other things we can do."

The toys decided to play knights-and-dragon in the castle Andy had built the night before. Rex played the dragon and pretended to attack the castle, letting out a roar. Then, suddenly, Andy's puppy, Buster, came skidding into the room and attacked it for real!

"Bad Buster!" Woody said as the dog ran out of the room. He hurried over to the mess. "We're going to have to rebuild the castle so it looks exactly like it did before."

The toys worked together restacking the blocks. When they were done, the castle looked as good as when Andy had built it!

By three o'clock, the toys were all waiting anxiously for Andy. "I'm positive this is the last day of school," Woody said, climbing onto Andy's desk. Then he spotted a note. "Oh, I'm sorry, guys," he said. "It appears there's a party after school."

"So what time will Andy get here?" asked Rex.

Woody didn't know the answer.

Suddenly, the toys heard the happy shouts of children playing. Woody looked out the window and saw lots of kids in Andy's backyard. Andy's entire class was here for the end-of-school party! No wonder it had taken him longer to get home, Woody thought.

Footsteps thundered up the stairs, and Andy and his classmates burst into the room.

"Wow! Great toys!" a boy shouted as he picked up Buzz and Rex. The other kids grabbed more toys until Woody and all his friends were part of the celebration.

This is going to be the best summer ever! Woody thought happily.

A Visit to the Castle

"All right, men," Doc said. "Here we are. Now, all we have to do is go up and dock on the floor—that is, knock on the door!"

The Seven Dwarfs had just reached the castle where Snow White lived. They had been so busy in the mines that this was the first time they'd had a chance to visit Snow White since she had married the Prince.

"Time's a wastin'," Grumpy said. He knocked firmly on the tall wooden door.

A moment later, a guard opened it. "Er, good day," the castle guard said. "New servants around the back, please."

"Oh, we're not flu nervants," Doc spoke up. "Er, we're not new servants. We're here to see the princess!"

"Yes! The princess!" the other Dwarfs agreed. Dopey nodded eagerly.

The guard looked doubtful. "*You're* here to see the princess?"

He looked them over. The Dwarfs stood up straight, glad that they'd remembered to wash that morning.

Finally the guard shook his head. "I'm sorry," he said. "You don't look like the sort of visitors that would interest the princess."

And with that, he began to shut the door.

But Grumpy held the door open. "Mark my words," he growled. "If you don't tell the princess we're here, there'll be trouble."

"Who is it?" a sweet voice called from inside the castle. "Who's at the door?"

"Never mind, Princess!" the guard called. "It's just some strange little men who claim they know you."

"Little men?" Snow White cried, rushing forward. She peered around the door past the guard, and her lovely face lit up with joy. "Why, Doc, Grumpy, Sleepy, Dopey, Happy, Sneezy, even dear Bashful!"

Bashful blushed deeply. "Gosh," he said. "Hello, Princess."

The guard looked surprised. "You mean you know these fellows?" he asked Snow White. "I thought they were just riffraff."

"Riffraff?" Snow White cried. "Why, no—they may look a little different, but they're just like royalty to me! They're my very best friends."

The guard apologized to the Dwarfs. Then Snow White invited her friends into the castle for a nice, long visit.

Dinglehoppers and Jibbermutts

Ariel sat on a rock, talking with her friends Scuttle the seagull and Flounder the fish. She loved visiting the surface, although she knew it was dangerous for mermaids to venture there. Her father would definitely not approve, but then, these days, he seemed to disapprove of so much of what she liked to do.

"What's it like on land, Scuttle?" she asked.

"Land?" echoed Scuttle. "Oh! Land! Yeah, well, it's great on land. I know all about humans."

"Like what?" Ariel asked eagerly.

"Well! For instance . . . you know all about the dinglehoppers they use to comb their hair, right? And the snarfblatts that they make music with?"

"Yes," said Ariel.

"Well, did you know that they also have these strange rectangular objects with sheets of paper inside? They're called jibbermutts. Humans like to throw them to one another," Scuttle explained.

"Oh, Scuttle," said Ariel breathlessly. "Would you fly up to Eric's window and come back and tell me what you've seen?"

Scuttle flew off. While he was gone,

Ariel lay back on the rock in the warm sunshine, dreaming of what life must be like on land. Soon, Scuttle returned.

"Did you see him?" asked Ariel eagerly. "What was he doing?"

"Yep, I saw him!" Scuttle replied importantly. "He was trying to eat with a dinglehopper! And he had a jibbermutt, but it almost looked like he was trying to read it instead of throwing it like he's supposed to. Ariel, I don't think your prince is too bright."

Ariel sighed dreamily, imagining her handsome love. She did wonder why he would try to use a dinglehopper to eat, though.

"Don't suppose you'd want his dinglehopper for your treasure chest, would you?" asked Scuttle with a mischievous glint in his eye.

"Oh, Scuttle! You didn't!" shouted Ariel.

"Yup. Just as soon as he set it down, I flew in through the window and grabbed it. Boy, was he surprised!"

Ariel clutched the dinglehopper to her chest. "I'll probably never know what it's like to live on land, but no matter what happens, Scuttle, I will treasure this forever!"

Tag!

Early one morning, Simba woke up ready to find Nala and continue their game of tag. The night before, when their mothers had made them stop, Simba had been It—which was a terrible way to go to bed!—and he was eager to tag Nala and make *her* It as soon as possible. But when he arrived at the pride's meeting place, it seemed everyone was there except for Nala.

"Where's Nala?" he asked his mother.

"I heard her mother say she wasn't feeling well," Sarabi replied. "They're staying in the cave and resting until she's better."

"But she has to come out," protested Simba. "I'm It and I have to tag her!"

Sarabi smiled. "I'm afraid you'll just have to wait, little Simba," she said.

"But that's so boring!" Simba groaned.

"You can play by yourself for a little while," she reminded him.

"Aw, all right," Simba sighed.

First, Simba tried hunting grasshoppers. Then he tried scaring giraffes. Next he went to check out the watering hole. But it wasn't as busy as usual. Finally, he tried just lying down and finding pictures in the clouds. But that was Nala's favorite game, and it made him miss her.

Simba rolled over and swatted a bright wildflower with his paw. "Tag, you're It," he said halfheartedly. Suddenly, an idea popped into his head.

With newfound energy, Simba picked as many flowers as he could carry in his mouth and made his way back to the pride's cave.

"Dees ah fur Nana," he mumbled through his mouthful of stems. Simba dropped the flowers at Nala's mother's feet. "These are for Nala," he repeated. "I hope she feels better really soon."

"Oh, thank you, Simba," the lioness said. "But why don't you give them to her yourself? She seems to be feeling much better. Nala!" she called.

Out came Simba's friend, smiling and looking very glad to see him. She sniffed at the pretty flowers. "Are these for me? Gee, thanks, Simba." Then she turned to her mother. "Can I go out to play with Simba now, Mama?"

"I don't see why not," said her mother.

"Grrreat!" said Nala.

"Yeah, grrreat!" said Simba. Then he reached out and gently tapped her with his paw. "Tag! You're It!"

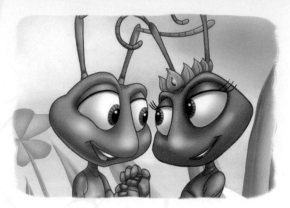

Flik's Big Date

Flik loved Queen Atta very, very much. So he decided to plan the most romantic evening for the two of them an ant could possibly imagine.

"I'll pick you up at eight tonight," Flik told Atta when he met her in the anthill early that morning. Then he hurried off to get ready for their big date.

First, there was the dinner to plan: sprouted wheat with sunflower seeds and wild truffles and free-range millet on a bed of dandelion greens.

Then Flik went down to the creek to find the perfect leaf for a romantic moonlit cruise.

"This elm leaf should do," Flik said as he tied the leaf to a root near the shore. "And I'll use this twig as my oar."

"How's it coming?" he asked the circus bugs, who were back for a visit and busy practicing their instruments just up the hill from the creek.

"Brilliant!" Slim replied. "Just brilliant. Don't worry about a thing. It's all under control. We'll have Atta's favorite song memorized by tomorrow night, no problem!"

"But our date is *tonight*!" said Flik.

"Told you so," said Francis.

"Don't worry," said Slim. "Remember, we're professional entertainers. You want an orchestra to dance to, you'll have an orchestra to dance to."

"Are you sure you wouldn't like some magic instead?" Manny the Magician asked. "I have found that nothing inspires romance in a lady quite like cutting her in half."

"Um, I think I'll stick with the dancing," said Flik.

Speaking of inspiring romance had reminded Flik of something. He needed to get the fireflies set up.

"Come on, guys!" he called to glowing insects he'd hired for the evening. "I want some of you in the trees, some of you along the water, and the rest of you over there by the picnic blanket. . . . Perfect!" he said as their abdomens lit up the quickly falling night. "Everything is set to go!"

Suddenly, Flik looked down at his watch, and his heart skipped a beat. "Oh, no! It's eight o'clock!" he yelled. "I've really got to go!"

Can you believe it? Flik was so busy getting everything ready, he'd almost forgotten to pick Atta up for their date!

The Masquerade Ball

"Where could she be?" Cinderella asked.

Cinderella and her new husband, the Prince, were holding a masquerade ball. Cinderella had sent a special invitation to her Fairy Godmother, who had promised to come. But the ball had started almost an hour ago, and Cinderella still hadn't seen any sign of the cheerful little woman.

"Don't worry, my love," the Prince said. "I'm sure she'll . . . What's this?"

A messenger handed Cinderella a note.

Never fear—I'm here, my dear. Just seek and you will find which mask I am behind!

Her Fairy Godmother was playing a trick on her!

"I'll find you," Cinderella whispered.

Was her Fairy Godmother wearing that beautiful unicorn costume? Was she the milkmaid standing by the fountain? The dancing harlequin clown? The fuzzy brown bear? Cinderella felt a little dizzy as she turned around and around. How would she ever find her Fairy Godmother in the crowd?

Cinderella looked around thoughtfully. When she turned back to the fountain, the milkmaid was gone! Instead, someone in a butterfly mask was standing there.

"Looking for someone, Princess?" the butterfly said in a deep voice.

"No—never mind," Cinderella said.

She wandered away, still searching. But she kept thinking about the twinkling eyes behind the butterfly mask. Then she remembered something—the milkmaid had the same twinkling eyes! Could it be . . . ?

Cinderella hurried back to the fountain. But there was no sign of the milkmaid *or* the butterfly. The only person standing nearby was wearing a beautiful pink princess costume.

Cinderella stared at the princess. Mischievous eyes twinkled behind the gold and pink mask. Suddenly, Cinderella laughed out loud.

"Aha!" she cried. "I caught you!"

She pulled off the mask. Her Fairy Godmother smiled back at her.

"You win!" she exclaimed. "How did you find me?"

"I almost didn't, the way you kept magically changing costumes," Cinderella said. "Then I remembered how you magically changed my outfit not too long ago—and I figured it out!"

A Wonderful/Terrible Day

"What a wonderful day!" Mickey Mouse said to himself. He hummed as he strolled through the outdoor market.

"I'll take that cheese and a loaf of bread," he told the market vendor.

"You're just in time," the vendor replied. "That was my last loaf!"

Meanwhile, Donald Duck was just leaving his house. "What a terrible day!" he said in a huff. He had overslept and woken up with a crick in his neck. He hurried to cross the street, but had to stop for traffic at an intersection.

"I'll take a loaf of bread," he told the vendor at the market.

"Sorry," the vendor replied. "I'm sold out."

"Sold out?" Donald's eyes bulged out of his head. "Sold out?"

Down the block, Mickey Mouse was having a friendly chat with Goofy. "How have you been, Goofy?" he asked.

"Fine," Goofy said as he peeled a banana. He ate the whole thing in one big bite, then dropped the peel on the ground.

Back in the market, Donald sulked. He was hungry!

"This is so unfair!" he said. Slumping his shoulders, he started off toward the park at the end of the street. But a few steps later, he slipped on a banana peel.

"*Ooof!*" Donald fell to the ground with a thud. Scowling, he got to his feet.

Not far away, Mickey was spreading out his picnic blanket in the park. All around him, children were laughing and playing.

"Hey, kids!" he called with a friendly wave. He took a big bite of his cheese sandwich and chewed happily. "What a wonderful day," he said again.

Donald kicked a small pebble on the sidewalk. His tummy growled loudly. Suddenly—*thunk!*—a ball hit him in the head.

"Watch it, kids!" Donald shouted. He rubbed his sore head. "What a terrible day."

Then Donald heard a familiar voice call out, "Hey, Donald! Come have a cheese sandwich with me!"

Donald saw Mickey waving to him from under a tree. Donald wanted to stay mad. But the truth is that no duck can resist a cheese sandwich! And so he smiled and ambled over.

Maybe it wasn't such a bad day after all!

Curses, Jafar!

Jafar wanted to be Sultan. But that meant he had to marry Jasmine. And so he set off to find the princess.

He found her in the palace gardens, playing with Rajah. "Good afternoon, Princess," said Jafar.

"Go away," Jasmine told him. "You're no different from my father and Prince Ali. You all treat me like some kind of prize to be won."

Rajah growled in agreement. "All right, I'll go," said Jafar. "I just wanted to let you know that I do understand you. You feel trapped here," he cooed. "What you really want is to see the world."

"That's true," she told him. "But I make no secret of wanting freedom, or of wanting to travel. You'll have to do better than that."

"I could show you the world," Jafar promised, "*after* you marry me and I become Sultan."

Jasmine still didn't trust Jafar, and neither did her tiger. Rajah growled again.

"Don't you wish to see the world's wonders?" asked Jafar.

"Like what?" Jasmine asked.

"The ocean for one," said Jafar. "You've only seen the desert. But I will show you a place where blue waves stretch forever."

"Really?" said Jasmine, her eyes widening, impressed despite herself. "What else?"

"The mountains," said Jafar. "The land around Agrabah is flat and brown. But I'll show you mountains that touch the clouds."

"I . . . I . . ." Jasmine said, looking into the spinning eyes of the wizard's cobra staff. She didn't realize Jafar was hypnotizing her!

With a huge growl, Rajah leaped between Jasmine and the wizard's staff. Jafar jerked back, and the eyes on the staff stopped spinning.

Jasmine shook her head and said, "I think you should go."

When Rajah growled again, Iago, Jafar's parrot, cried, "Aacch! You heard the lady!"

Outraged, Jafar left.

"Don't take it too hard," Iago told his master on the way out. "There's a very good reason your trick didn't work—a four-hundred-pound reason with long, razor-sharp teeth!"

Belle's Royal Wedding

Belle's wedding was just days away. Everyone at the castle was busy preparing for the special celebration.

As she got ready for her big day, Belle thought back to when she had first arrived at the castle. It had been so frightening—everyone had been under a magical spell. The Prince had become an angry Beast, and the servants were enchanted objects. But over time, Belle had become friends with the staff. Then she and the Beast had fallen in love. Now she couldn't wait to marry her Prince!

Meanwhile, the Prince was preparing for the wedding, too. "I am the happiest man in the world!" he said to Lumiere and Cogsworth. "And I want Belle to be the happiest woman!

"How can I show Belle how much I love her?" the Prince continued. "I know! Let's find a special gift for her in the village!"

Lumiere and Mrs. Potts wondered how they could show their love and appreciation for the young couple, too. Together, they came up with a plan. . . .

Finally, the wedding day arrived!

During the ceremony, the Prince gave Belle his gift: a blank journal. "You can

fill it with all the adventures we will have together," he said.

After the ceremony, the newlyweds walked into the ballroom. The staff had laid out a huge banquet!

"Thank you!" said Belle. "But there is so much! I'm not sure even our whole household can eat all this food!" she joked.

Mrs. Potts and the other servants smiled and led the couple into the garden . . . where the entire village was waiting to surprise them!

"I took the liberty of inviting them on behalf of the household," said Lumiere. It was the staff's gift to Belle and the Prince.

"It's a magnificent gift!" the Prince said. He couldn't stop smiling. He and Belle were both thrilled to welcome everyone into their home.

As the couple shared their first dance, a shout went up from the happy crowd: "Congratulations!"

Belle and the Prince knew that their wedding had been a perfect celebration— for everyone.

With so many friends gathered around them, it had been the most magical day ever.

Lost and Found

Lady stretched and rolled over. It was so cozy up on the window seat. Sunlight shone through the glass and glinted on her diamond-shaped name tag.

Lady sighed contentedly. The tag was her most prized possession. Besides her owners, of course. Jim Dear and Darling were very good to her. Just last night, they had given her and Tramp steak bones to munch on.

The bones! Lady had almost forgotten them. Leaping off the window seat, she hurried to the kitchen. Luckily, the bones were right where she'd left them— next to her food bowl.

Lady began to carry the bones into the garden. It took three trips, but soon the bones were lying in a heap on the grass. Then she got to work.

Dig, dig, dig. The soil piled up behind her as Lady dug yet another hole. She carefully nosed the last bone into its hole and covered it with soil. After prancing delicately on top to pat down the earth, she collapsed in an exhausted heap. Burying bones was hard work!

Suddenly, Lady realized that something was missing. She gingerly felt her neck. Her collar! It was gone!

Panicked, Lady searched the garden for the collar. It was nowhere to be found.

I must have buried it with one of the bones! Lady realized with a jolt. She looked at all the freshly filled-in holes.

Tramp will help, Lady thought. She ran inside to get him. He was playing with the puppies, but he ran outside as soon as he heard what was wrong.

Soon the two dogs were busy undoing all of Lady's hard work.

"I see something shiny!" Tramp called.

Lady was by his side in an instant, but it wasn't the collar. It was just an old bottle cap. Lady dropped her head sadly.

Lady and Tramp got back to digging. Finally, just as dusk was falling, Tramp found a thick blue band with a golden tag—Lady's collar!

Lady let out a happy bark. Then she carried the collar into the house and sat down at Jim Dear's feet.

"Your collar came off, Lady?" Jim asked as he fastened it around Lady's neck. "It's a good thing you didn't accidentally bury it with your bones!"

Faith, Trust, and Pixie Dust

The fairies had come to the mainland to bring the season of summer. But Tinker Bell had found herself with no work to do, because all of her inventions were working perfectly. With nothing to fix, she had entertained herself by flying after a car! She had followed it all the way to a house where a little girl named Lizzy lived with her father.

Vidia had tried to teach Tink a lesson, trapping her inside a tiny fairy house that Lizzy had made. But then the little girl discovered Tinker Bell. Vidia panicked. She hadn't meant to put Tink in danger. She flew back to the fairy camp to get help.

The fairies had set off at once to save Tinker Bell. So far they had sailed through the flooded meadow, survived a boat crash, and rescued Vidia from being stuck in the mud.

"I was just thinking if Tink were here," said Silvermist, "how not quiet it would be right now. I really miss her."

"Tinker Bell getting trapped is all my fault," Vidia admitted. "I am so sorry."

To Vidia's surprise, the other fairies weren't upset with her.

"Tink can get into plenty of trouble by herself," Rosetta declared.

The friends gathered around and chanted the fairy motto: "Faith, trust, and pixie dust!"

Vidia loved feeling like she was part of the group. She usually liked to be by herself, but she was finally beginning to understand the importance of friendship.

Back in Lizzy's room, the little girl was feeling sad. "I wish I were a fairy just like you," Lizzy told Tink. "Then I could fly around with the other fairies all the time." Tink knew how to make Lizzy's wish come true: pixie dust!

She told Lizzy to close her eyes and spread out her arms. Then Tink hovered above Lizzy's head and showered her with pixie dust. It was time for some flying lessons!

Lizzy was so happy to have a friend like Tinker Bell. She knew her father loved her and wanted to spend more time with her, but he found it hard to believe in magic and especially in fairies.

Lizzy hoped that one day she could change his mind.

Start Being You!

Mike was in big trouble. He had snuck into the human world to prove that he was scary. But instead of scaring a human child, he had found himself in a cabin full of campers who thought he was cute!

Meanwhile, back in the Door Tech Lab at Monsters University, Sulley had snuck past the guards protecting the door Mike had used. He had to save his friend!

Sulley slipped through the door into the human world and found himself in an empty cabin. Where had Mike gone?

Looking out the window, Sulley saw a group of rangers gathered in the dark outside. Realizing that Mike must have fled to the nearby forest, Sulley made a break from the cabin. The rangers shined their flashlights on him as he disappeared into the trees. They thought they'd seen a bear.

Sulley found Mike sitting by a lake.

"You were right," Mike said sadly. "The children weren't scared of me. I thought I could show everybody I was something special . . . but I'm just not."

Sulley told Mike that he had messed things up his entire life, too. "You're not the only 'failure' here," he said.

Together, the two made it back to the cabin. But when they opened the door back to Monsters University, they found that it was an empty closet. Dean Hardscrabble had shut it down from the other side.

Meanwhile, the rangers were getting closer. Mike had a plan.

As the rangers entered the cabin, Mike and Sulley turned on a fan, shook the shutters, and fluttered the curtains. This unnerved the rangers. Then Mike slammed the door, which made them jump. Next they clawed on the walls and toppled the bunk beds over like dominoes.

The rangers screamed.

Finally, Mike gave Sulley the signal. The big blue monster rose up menacingly and let out a deafening roar.

The petrified rangers screamed . . . and screamed . . . and screamed.

At the Door Tech Lab at the university, the humans' screams filled the scream can to the brim. In fact, they filled all the scream cans in the room!

Suddenly the light above the door turned red. The door burst open and Mike and Sulley flew through it.

A Refreshing Cup of Tea

"*Twinkle, twinkle, little bat!
How I wonder what
you're at!
Up above the world you fly,
Like a tea-tray in the sky.*"

The song came from behind the tall tree with the mitten-shaped leaves. Alice knew it could only have been sung by one person: the Mad Hatter!

"Oh, bother!" Alice sighed. Truly, the Hatter and his friends were among the last creatures she wished to see.

"And yet," Alice went on to no one but herself, "a nice cup of tea would be quite refreshing. . . ."

In the clearing, the Hatter, the March Hare, and the Dormouse were sitting, much as they had been upon Alice's last visit, around their ample tea table.

"A-hem . . ." Alice made her presence known to them by clearing her thirsty throat.

"Well!" exclaimed the Hatter. "If it isn't our dear, dear old friend! I say, what was your name again, dear old friend?"

"Alice," Alice patiently replied.

"Well, have a seat, Alice, dear!"

"Thank you," said Alice. "I *could* use a cup of tea."

"And how would you use it?" the Hatter asked. "Carefully, I hope."

"Very carefully," Alice assured him.

"Ah, well, that's good. And that's also bad."

"Bad?" Alice asked.

"You heard him!" said the March Hare. "Can't you see? We have no tea!"

"No tea?" asked Alice, gazing about at the table.

"No tea?" sobbed the Dormouse, stirring from his sleep. "No tea!"

"There you go upsetting him again!" shouted the Hare.

"I didn't . . ." Alice began. Then she remembered how useless it was to argue with a hare who was mad. Instead, she left the March Hare to his shouting, and the Dormouse to his crying, and the Hatter to his . . . whatever it was he was doing . . . and walked over to the stove. Finding a tin of fragrant tea leaves, she dropped some in an empty teapot and filled it with hot water. Then she reached for the cleanest cup she could find and filled it.

She was tempted to offer her hosts a cup as well. But on second thought, she decided, perhaps it was better to just . . . go.

Dining Under the Stars

An evil sorcerer had changed spoiled Prince Naveen into a frog. Naveen assumed that kissing a princess would change him back, so he went looking for one. When he saw Tiana dressed up for a costume ball, he mistakenly thought she was a princess. But when he kissed her, Tiana had turned into a frog instead!

Now the two frogs were traveling through the bayou in search of a way to break the curse.

Along the way, the two had met Louis the alligator and Ray the firefly.

After a long day of walking and an adventure with some frog hunters, everyone was starting to get hungry.

"How about swamp gumbo?" suggested Tiana.

"That'll do!" said Louis.

Naveen leaned against a tree, his feet up on a mushroom. He placed a leaf on his knees as a napkin, and added, "Sounds delicious! I'll start with a pre-dinner cocktail and something to nibble on while I wait, thanks."

"Oh no, no, no, Your Royal Highness!" protested Tiana immediately, handing Naveen some mushrooms. "You are going to mince these."

Tiana went to gather the other ingredients. "Are you mincing?" she called.

With a sigh, Naveen slowly began slicing a mushroom.

Tiana chuckled, amused. "Step aside, mister," she said. "Watch and learn." And taking the knife, she quickly sliced the mushroom. Then she handed the knife back to Naveen.

"I've never done anything like this before," said Naveen. "When you live in a castle, everything is done for you."

Naveen chopped the mushrooms, and soon the swamp gumbo was ready.

Suddenly, Ray raised his eyes to the sky, seeing the evening star. "There she is. The sweetest firefly in all creation— Evangeline!" He sighed. "So far above me, yet I know her heart belongs only to me!"

Ray began to sing softly, and Naveen invited Tiana to dance. "Oh, no," she said. "I don't dance."

"If I can mince, you can dance," he retorted. Tiana gave in, and Naveen led her in a gentle waltz, guiding her steps.

"Lottie's getting herself one heck of a dance partner," Tiana told Naveen. "We best be pushing on."

Homeward Bound

"Welcome back to our humble abode," Dodger told Oliver. He and his pals had "rescued" the little kitten from the town house he had been living in with his new owner, Jenny, and brought him to the barge where they lived.

"But I want to go back to Jenny's," Oliver explained.

"Jenny? So, all of a sudden you have a thing against dogs?" Dodger said. "And after all we've done for you!"

"No, no, I don't have a thing against dogs," Oliver explained.

"Then why in the world would you pick Jenny over New York's coolest canine?" Dodger asked.

"It's not you—" Oliver started to say.

"Oh, I get it," Dodger interrupted, circling around Oliver. "You're all about money now. Got a taste of the finer things in life, and now you wouldn't want to be seen slumming with the likes of us dogs."

"That's not true—" Oliver began.

"Well, I'll tell you one thing money can't buy," Dodger barked. "Freedom!"

"Freedom?" Oliver asked.

"Yeah, on the street you can do what you want, when you want to. Then, if you want to just kick back with the gang at Fagin's, that's cool, too. See what I mean? The freedom to choose instead of being locked up in that big house, doing whatever Jenny wants when she wants it," Dodger said.

"It's not like that!" Oliver protested.

"You could have all the freedom in the world, but instead, you're leaving us for a better cut of prime rib," Dodger said accusingly.

"No, that's not it at all," Oliver explained to his friend. "I like it at Jenny's. It's comfortable, and I get lots of love. Jenny needs me, and I need her, too!"

Dodger thought about this for a moment. "You know what, kid? I can't argue with that. Stay with Jenny if you want."

"Okay." Oliver suddenly felt kind of sad. "We can still be friends, though, right? Even though we see things differently?"

"Sure," Dodger agreed.

"And, you'll come visit?" Oliver asked.

"Visit?" Dodger considered this for a moment. "Absatively posolutely!"

Oliver grinned. It was the best of both worlds. What more could a kitten ask for?

Tiger Lily

It was a hot summer night in Never Land—so hot, in fact, that the poor Lost Boys couldn't sleep. And so it was decided that instead of trying to stay in their hideout in Hangman's Tree, Peter Pan and the Lost Boys would camp out for the night in the wild wilderness.

"It's dark out here," said Cubby.

"And awful quiet," said Tootles.

"Won't you tell us a story, please, Peter?" asked Slightly, who was shivering in his fox suit despite the sticky heat.

"Very well," agreed Peter. "If it will make you all be quiet! I will tell you the story of the very first time I ever camped out in the wilderness—which, by the way, was the first time I met Tiger Lily.

"I had made myself a fire, a great big one, 'cause it was fall and the nights were getting cool. I'd just laid my head down on a patch of nice, soft moss, when all of a sudden I heard a rustling in the shadows."

The Lost Boys gasped. *"Indians?"*

But Peter shook his head. "Not Indians," he told them. "That's what I thought at first, too. No, this was something bigger. It was a bear! It

jumped out of the trees, growling and waving its big paws in the air like Captain Hook swattin' blue flies. I've never seen such a mean, angry beast, before or since!"

"So wha-wha-what did you do?" asked Slightly.

"Told him to get lost, of course. To scram! But he just kept charging.

"Well, I'm not going to lie to you; I started to get nervous. And then, there she was—Tiger Lily, as quiet as a mouse. Without a 'hi' or 'how do you do,' she grabbed a stick from my fire and waved it at the bear. The next thing I knew, the bear had turned around and was running off crying! I suppose Tiger Lily saved my life that night," said Peter.

"Um . . . Peter?" said Cubby, peering out into the darkness. "Do you know what ever happened to that bear?"

Peter thought for a moment.

"Nope," he said and shrugged. "Probably still out there, wandering around, I guess."

Peter Pan yawned a big, mischievous yawn.

"Now stop yer yammerin' and close your eyes and go to sleep already!"

A New Friend

Mulan was painting in her bedroom when she heard a noise in the old cypress tree outside. She looked up. High in the branches was a tiny gray kitten.

"Oh, you poor thing. Are you stuck?" Mulan asked.

"Meow," replied the little kitten.

Mulan grabbed hold of the lowest branch and pulled herself up into the tree. The climb was not easy, but at last she reached the kitten. Cradling it in one arm, she climbed back down to the ground.

"There," said Mulan, catching her breath. "Now you can go home."

But the kitten would not budge.

"Very well, suit yourself," said Mulan, scooping up her flowers. "I'm late already and really should get home. Try to stay out of trees, little one!" And with that, she turned to go.

"Meow, meow, meow!"

Mulan looked down at her feet to find her new kitten friend trotting close beside her.

"Well, well!" Mulan laughed. "It appears the Fas are going to have a little house guest!"

But not everyone at Mulan's house was pleased to have company. Namely Mulan's dog, Little Brother. Especially when the kitten walked in and lay down on his silk cushion!

"Ruff! Ruff! Ruff!" he barked.

"Now, now," Mulan said. "Our friend here has just been through quite an ordeal. Be a good host and let her rest, won't you?"

But then the kitten did something even harder to forgive: she walked right over and drank out of Little Brother's dish!

"Grrrr! Grrrrr! Grrufff!" protested Little Brother.

"Oh dear," said Mulan. "She's probably thirsty, too. Here, kitty," she said, setting down a bowl of milk. "Have some of this."

Imagine Little Brother's surprise when that tiny kitten pushed the dish of milk all the way over to him with her little black nose!

"Meow," said the kitten, giving it one more push.

"Look, Little Brother!" exclaimed Mulan. "Isn't she sweet? She wants to be your friend."

And, from that moment on, that's what she was!

A Talented Mouse

"Look, Dumbo," Timothy Q. Mouse said, pointing to the newspaper. "There's another article about us in here!"

Mrs. Jumbo, Dumbo's mother, peered over Timothy's shoulder. "What a nice story," she cooed. "Too bad the picture isn't better—why, I can hardly see you, Timothy!"

Timothy peered at the paper. "Hey," he said, scanning the story. "This article doesn't mention me at all!"

"It's all right," Mrs. Jumbo said soothingly. "Everyone knows how important you are."

But Timothy wasn't so sure. "Am I really that important?" he said. "It's Dumbo who has the talent—not me."

Timothy wandered away sadly. "I have to figure out a way to get famous on my own," he muttered. "But how?" Suddenly, he snapped his fingers. "I've got it!" he cried. "I'll learn to fly, too! That way Dumbo and I can be famous together!"

Timothy climbed to the top of the tallest circus tent. Dumbo had learned to fly by jumping off things. Timothy just hoped it would work for him, too. He rubbed his hands together.

"Here goes nothing," he muttered.

He leaped off the tent and looked down. The ground seemed very far away.

"Uh-oh!" Timothy gulped. What had he done?

The ground got closer and closer. Timothy squeezed his eyes shut. . . .

Suddenly, he felt himself being whisked upward. Opening his eyes, he saw that he was clutched in Dumbo's trunk.

"Whew!" he gasped. "Thanks, buddy!"

Dumbo smiled at his little friend. He set Timothy in his cap. Timothy settled into the familiar spot. Flying was much more fun when Dumbo's ears did all the work!

Soon they landed beside Mrs. Jumbo.

"Oh, Timothy!" she cried. "You're safe! When I saw you fall, I was so worried. . . . Dumbo and I don't know what we'd do without you."

Timothy blinked. "Never thought of it that way," he mused. "Maybe I'm not front-page news, but who cares? I know I'm important, and my friends know it, too. That's what matters!"

Timothy smiled. He had plenty of his own talent, and that was good enough for him!

The Two Tigers

Princess Jasmine and her pet tiger, Rajah, were riding through the busy streets of Agrabah when they came upon a big, colorful circus tent. The tiger's eyes opened wide as he stared at the circus poster.

"That looks like fun," Jasmine said to Rajah. "But we really should be going. It's almost time for lunch."

Back at the palace, the tiger hardly touched his food.

"What do you think is wrong with Rajah?" Jasmine asked.

Aladdin shrugged. "Maybe a nice long carriage ride would make him feel better," he suggested.

Soon Jasmine, Aladdin, Abu, and Rajah were riding through Agrabah in the royal carriage. As they rolled past the circus poster, the tiger suddenly perked up.

"Hmmm," Aladdin said. "Maybe we should take Rajah to the circus."

Inside the circus tent, the announcer said, "I now present Mallika—the star of our show!" Out walked a beautiful tigress. Jasmine saw Rajah's face light up. He was in love!

When the show was over, Jasmine and Aladdin took Rajah to meet Mallika. The two tigers were very happy to be together—and clearly did not want to be apart.

"Can Mallika please come live at my palace?" Jasmine asked the circus owner. "She would be very happy there."

"I'm sorry, Mallika is our star," the owner replied. "Without her, we wouldn't have a circus."

That night, there was a knock at the palace door. It was the circus owner—and a very sad-looking tigress.

"Ever since Rajah left the circus, Mallika won't eat," the circus owner said. "Even though she's the star of my show, I want her to be happy. So I've come to give her to you."

The two tigers ran to each other and gently touched noses. Jasmine and Aladdin were very happy for Rajah and Mallika. But they felt bad for the circus owner. Without his star tigress, the circus would surely close.

Suddenly, Jasmine had an idea.

The very next morning, the circus tent was moved right next to Jasmine's palace! Mallika could perform at the royal circus every day and come home to Rajah every evening. It was perfect!

Small Fairies Come in Big Packages

Princess Aurora's wedding to Prince Phillip would take place in just a few days. The three good fairies, Flora, Fauna, and Merryweather, wanted to give her the perfect gift. They stood in front of an enormous box, trying to decide what to put in it.

"How about a pretty dress for Princess Aurora to wear on her honeymoon? Something pink!" Flora said decisively.

"What about a grand carriage?" Fauna suggested with a smile.

Flora shook her head. "King Stefan is already having a carriage made for them. No, let's give her a dress."

"I've got it!" Fauna cried. "A flock of doves that we'll release just as Aurora and Phillip come out of the church. Perfect!"

"A tiara to wear with her wedding gown—that's what Aurora needs," Merryweather piped up. "With three jewels: one red for Flora, one green for Fauna, and one blue for me. It will remind our sweet princess of how much we love her."

The three fairies argued back and forth for what seemed like hours.

"Why can't we give her a—" Merryweather began, but as she waved her arms, trying to get the other fairies' attention, she lost her balance and fell right into the big box! Flora and Fauna didn't notice.

"We'll give her both!" said Flora finally.

They pointed their wands at the box, showering it with sparkles—*zzzing!* A huge piece of satin ribbon appeared, wrapped itself around the box, and tied itself into a big bow.

Flora and Fauna put on their capes, ready to deliver the gift to Aurora. But where was Merryweather?

"Oh, well, perhaps she went on ahead," said Flora. "Let's be on our way."

At the palace, Flora and Fauna placed the gift before the princess. When Aurora untied the ribbon, Merryweather burst out of the box. She presented the princess with a beautiful tiara that sparkled with red, green, and blue jewels.

"Oh, thank you, my dears! It's perfect!" Aurora said with a gasp.

Merryweather smiled. "That's exactly what I thought!" she said.

Follow Your Heart

Pocahontas was an Indian princess. One day as she was visiting with her father, Chief Powhatan told his daughter, "Kocoum has asked for your hand in marriage."

"But he's so serious," Pocahontas replied unhappily.

The young woman was troubled. She went to see the ancient tree spirit, Grandmother Willow, to ask for her advice.

Pocahontas told Grandmother Willow about a dream she kept having, where she saw a spinning arrow. "The arrow you see is pointing you down your path," the wise spirit told Pocahontas.

Soon, a ship filled with English settlers seeking gold appeared on the shore. Pocahontas met one of the settlers, John Smith. She and the settler soon grew to care for each other.

Then John learned that the other settlers wanted to attack the Indians. Pocahontas and John set off to talk to Chief Powhatan to see if peace could be reached between their people. Along the way, an Indian warrior attacked John. Another settler shot the warrior, but John took the blame. He was taken prisoner. The Indians decided John would die for his crime.

"I'm so sorry!" Pocahontas cried to John. "It would have been better if we'd never met. None of this would have happened."

"Pocahontas, I'd rather die tomorrow than live a hundred years without knowing you," John Smith told her.

Pocahontas was heartbroken. Then her raccoon friend, Meeko, handed her John's compass. Looking at it, Pocahontas saw the spinning arrow that she had dreamed about. Now she knew which path to follow.

Quickly, she ran to the village and stopped the Indians from harming John Smith. She was willing to give up her own life to protect him. Chief Powhatan laid down his weapon, but the settlers had arrived and were shooting at the Indians.

John Smith jumped in front of the Indian chief, taking the bullet himself.

John Smith had to return to London to have his wounds treated. "No matter what happens, I'll always be with you," Pocahontas told him.

Then she kissed him good-bye— forever.

The Good Thing About Rain

"Rise and shine!" cried Pongo. One by one, he nudged each of his fifteen Dalmatian puppies with his nose. Most of the puppies yawned and stretched. But Rolly just rolled over and slept on.

"Aw, come on, Rolly," Pongo whispered in the pup's ear. "It's morning! Don't you want to go out?"

At the mention of the word *out*, Rolly was instantly wide awake! And he was not alone. As if by magic, the sleepy group had become a pack of jumping, barking puppies. They raced together through the kitchen to the back door, where they jumped up and down, waiting for Nanny to let them out into the garden.

"Okay, here I come," said Nanny as she made her way across the kitchen. Then she flung the door open wide and stepped out of the way to let the puppies race past. But they didn't move. It was raining!

"Oh, go on," said Perdita, trying to nudge the pups out the door. "It's only a little water."

But they wouldn't budge!

The next morning, Patch awoke with a start. With a few sharp barks,

he helped Pongo wake the other puppies. Within seconds, all fifteen were crowding around the back door. Nanny again rushed to let them out. And once again, the puppies were very disappointed to see raindrops falling.

When Nanny opened the door the next morning, the puppies were so surprised to see the sun shining that they didn't know what to do! Then, springing into action, they tumbled over one another in their rush to get out the door. They raced off in different directions, ready to explore.

But then, almost at once, all fifteen puppies froze in their tracks. They looked around at one another, then down at themselves. What was this stuff getting all over their spotted white coats? It was brown. It was wet. It was squishy. It was mud! And it was *fun*!

From the doorway, Pongo and Perdita looked out at their muddy puppies and laughed.

"You know what this means, don't you?" Pongo asked Perdita.

Perdy nodded. "Baths."

Pongo smiled, watching the frolicking puppies. "Let's not tell them just yet," he said.

Wherever You Go, There You Are!

"Oh, dear! Oh, dear!" said
Amelia Gabble. The goose
and her twin sister, Abigail,
had been waddling along the road to Paris
when Amelia suddenly stopped.

"What's wrong?" asked Abigail.

"Just look and you'll see," said Amelia.
Stretching out one big white wing, she
pointed to a fork in the road ahead.

Behind the geese, O'Malley, Duchess,
and her three kittens gathered together.

"I wonder what's wrong," said
Duchess.

"Guess I'd better find out," said
O'Malley. He sauntered forward. "Ladies,
ladies, what's going on?" he asked.

"We know this is the road to Paris,"
Amelia explained. "But we don't know
which way to turn. I think we should go
right," said Amelia.

"And I think we should go left," said
Abigail.

"Mr. O'Malley, are we lost?" asked
Marie in a small, frightened voice.

O'Malley smiled down at the little
white kitten. "Lost? What's lost? I don't
know the meaning of the word."

"I do," said Berlioz. "If you're lost, then
you don't know where you are."

"But you know exactly where you are,"
said O'Malley. "You're right here—with
your mother and me and the Gabbles. So
how could you be lost?"

Duchess shook her head. "Mr. O'Malley,"
she said, "if we want to get to Paris and
we don't know the way, then I do believe
that we are lost."

"But Paris is just a place," said O'Malley.
"And places are easy to find."

"Look, Mama, look!" Toulouse shouted.
"I see something over that hill. It's the
top of the Eiffel Tower!"

"Why, you're right, Toulouse" Duchess
said.

"Nice going, little tiger," said O'Malley.
Then he turned to the Gabble sisters.
"Well, ladies, looks like Paris is thataway!"

Pretty soon the whole group arrived in
Paris.

Marie sighed with relief. "I'm glad we're
not lost anymore."

"Aw, honey," said O'Malley, "someday
you'll understand. Places may come and
places may go, but when you're a free spirit,
you can never be lost."

"Never?" asked Marie.

"Never," said O'Malley. " 'Cause
wherever you go, there you are!"

Marie nodded. She liked the sound of
that!

In Hot Water

Ariel could hardly believe that her plan was going so well. She had convinced Ursula, the sea witch, to change her from a mermaid into a human. She had paid for the transformation with her voice, but that didn't matter. All that mattered was being with Prince Eric, the human prince she had fallen in love with from afar.

"Come along, my dear," a female palace servant said, leading Ariel into a spacious room with sky-blue walls.

Ariel almost tripped on the edge of a rug. She still wasn't used to her brand-new legs. She put one hand into the pocket of her sailcloth dress to make sure that Sebastian was still inside. Her crab friend had come along to watch over her.

"All right, let's get you cleaned up first," the woman said. "It'll be time for dinner soon."

As the woman bustled about, Ariel had a chance to look around the room. There were large windows along one wall and an ornate lantern hanging from the ceiling. There was also a large, shell-shaped bath filled with water. Ariel watched curiously as the servant threw some white powder into the bath. Suddenly, the water fizzed with a huge pile of bubbles! Ariel gasped, delighted, as bubbles floated up out of the water toward the ceiling. She raced forward and leaped right into the bath, splashing water and bubbles everywhere. Forgetting that she couldn't breathe underwater anymore, she dived beneath the bubbles. She came up coughing and wiped the water out of her eyes.

"Ahhhh!" Sebastian sputtered, swimming out of her pocket. He spat out a mouthful of bubbles. "What do these humans do to nice, clean water?"

The servant looked alarmed. "Oh, my! Did I see something move in there?"

Ariel shook her head, quickly shoving Sebastian back into her pocket.

"Well," the servant said. "You can't take a bath in that dress. Let's hang it up to dry."

Ariel was a little worried about Sebastian, but she did as the woman said. Soon the sailcloth dress was hanging on a towel rack. Oh, well, Ariel thought. I'm sure Sebastian can take care of himself!

Eeyore Beats the Heat

Eeyore sighed.

"Something the matter, Eeyore?" asked Roo.

"Oh, it's just that it's so terribly hot," replied Eeyore. "If I weren't stuffed with sawdust, I think I would melt."

"Well, come with me!" squeaked Roo. "I'm going to the swimming hole to cool off."

But Eeyore shook his head. "Can't do, Roo," he said. "Not with my sawdust and all. . . . I'd probably just sink. And that's if I'm lucky."

So Roo, who felt sorry for Eeyore, but who was also eager to swim, continued on his way.

Soon another friend came along. And this friend was Winnie the Pooh.

"You're looking a little warmish, Eeyore," Pooh said.

"Same to you," said Eeyore with a sigh. "Same to you."

"Ah," said Pooh, "but I am off to catch a breeze—and pay a call on some bees—with my trusty balloon here. Care to join me?"

"No, thanks, Pooh," said Eeyore. "I never did like feeling like the ground was missing. And I expect that with my luck, the balloon would probably pop."

"I understand completely, Eeyore. Wish me luck, then, won't you?" Pooh replied.

"Good luck, Pooh," said Eeyore. "As if anything I ever wish comes true."

The next friend to come upon Eeyore was little Piglet.

"Hello there Eeyore," said Piglet. "Whoo! Are you as uncomfortably hot as I am?"

"Oh, no," said Eeyore. "I'm sweltering."

"Poor Eeyore," said Piglet. "Why don't you come play in the cool mud with me?"

But once again, Eeyore shook his head. "Afraid mud is not an option, Piglet," he said. "Once I get dirty, I'll never get clean. No. Go enjoy yourself on this hot day like everyone else. All except me. As usual. I'll just suffer."

And suffer poor Eeyore did . . . until not too terribly much later when his friends all returned with something sure to cool off even Eeyore on this sultry day.

"Guess what we've brought you, Eeyore!" Roo squealed with delight.

"It's ice cream," whispered Pooh.

"Ice cream, huh?" Eeyore sighed. "I suppose I'll have to eat it all before it melts."

And do you know what? He did!

A Professional Thief

Mother Gothel was angry. Rapunzel—the girl she had kidnapped and kept hidden her whole life—had dared to leave the tower! Even though Mother Gothel had warned the girl about the dangers of the world outside, Rapunzel had still followed that thief Flynn Rider into the forest!

Rapunzel had hair with magical healing powers. Mother Gothel needed her so she could stay young forever.

Mother Gothel followed Rapunzel's trail to a pub, where Rapunzel had befriended a group of ruffians.

How can I persuade Rapunzel to return to the tower now? wondered Mother Gothel. She will never believe my stories about monsters anymore!

Mother Gothel went on thinking. Soon she had hatched a plan. Spying on the ruffians at the pub, she had discovered that the Stabbington brothers had been Flynn's partners in crime. But Flynn had tricked them by keeping a crown they had stolen for himself.

Mother Gothel had found Flynn's crown hidden in Rapunzel's tower. She decided to make an offer to the brothers. Mother Gothel gave them the crown.

"If that's all you desire, then be on your way," she said. "I was going to offer you something worth one thousand crowns. And that wasn't even the best part. It comes with revenge on Flynn Rider."

Mother Gothel had gotten the Stabbingtons' attention. She offered to give them Rapunzel! But first, they had to make Rapunzel think that Flynn had betrayed her. The brothers agreed.

Later, Mother Gothel found Rapunzel in the forest.

"How did you find me?" Rapunzel asked.

"I just listened for the sound of complete and utter betrayal and followed that," Mother Gothel replied scornfully. "We're going home, Rapunzel. Now."

But Rapunzel did not want to go. She told Mother Gothel of her adventures. "I even met someone," she said.

"Yes, the wanted thief. I'm so proud," Mother Gothel said. She held up the crown. "This is why he's here! Don't let him deceive you. Give it to him, watch, you'll see!"

Then Mother Gothel ran off before Flynn returned.

Rapunzel sighed. She knew her mother was mistaken. But could she prove it?

The Fairy Chase

The fairies were on the mainland to bring the season of summer. Tinker Bell, finding herself with no work to do, had decided to chase after a car!

Vidia had tried to teach Tink a lesson, trapping her inside a tiny fairy house. But then the little girl who made the house had discovered Tinker Bell. Vidia panicked. She hadn't meant to put Tink in danger. She flew back to the fairy camp to get help.

Vidia thought that Tinker Bell was being held prisoner by the girl, whose name was Lizzy. But, in fact, Tinker Bell was just keeping Lizzy company. She could leave anytime she wanted! She was simply waiting for the weather to get better, because no fairy can fly with wet wings.

With Vidia's help, Tinker Bell's friends organized a rescue mission to save her. They had braved the rainy weather and almost been run over by a car. Finally they arrived at Lizzy's house.

The fairies carefully crept into the kitchen.

"Tinker Bell is upstairs. The little girl has her in a cage," Vidia said.

"There's also a large human in the house who doesn't like creatures with wings."

Suddenly, the cat that lived in the house spotted the fairies. He bounded after them through the kitchen.

The little fairies looked much tastier to the cat than the mice in the attic. But they were also a lot more clever.

The fairies jumped onto the kitchen table and defended themselves.

The fairies knew they had to get to the stairs so they could look for Tinker Bell. Vidia had a plan: she sprinkled the plates and cups in the kitchen with pixie dust.

The dishes started to float in the air. Vidia jumped from a cup to a plate, managing all the while to steer clear of the cat's claws.

Meanwhile, the other fairies sailed around the living room on the plates, distracting the cat.

While the other fairies chased the cat out of the house, Vidia finally reached the stairs. Her friend was upstairs, and she needed help. Vidia knew it was up to her to save Tinker Bell!

Team Wazowski and Sullivan

Mike and Sulley had entered the human world without permission and found themselves stuck. Now they needed to think fast!

Dean Hardscrabble, the head of the Scare Program at Monsters University, had turned off the power to the door they had used. Now there was only one thing to do. Mike and Sulley needed to generate enough scream power to activate the door from the human side.

With Mike's brains and Sulley's fearsome roar, the two monsters made the humans around them scream and scream and scream!

Suddenly, the light above the door in the Door Tech Lab at the university went on. The humans' screams filled the scream can to the brim. In fact, they filled all the scream cans in the room!

"Impossible!" Dean Hardscrabble said just as Mike and Sulley exploded through the door.

"How did you do this?" Dean Hardscrabble asked in disbelief. But Mike and Sulley didn't have a chance to answer. CDA (Child Detection Agency) agents burst in and led the two away.

Mike and Sulley and were expelled from the university. But it wasn't all bad news. Their friends in Oozma Kappa were being allowed to join the Scare Program, just as Dean Hardscrabble had promised if they won the Scare Games.

"You're the scariest bunch of monsters I've ever met," Mike told them. "Don't let anyone tell you different."

Everyone hugged. Then Mike and Sulley were on their way.

"So what now?" Sulley asked Mike.

Mike thought for a moment. "For the first time in my life, I don't really have a plan," he said.

Just then Dean Hardscrabble appeared with a copy of the school newspaper. They were on the front page. "You surprised me," she admitted. It was clear that she admired their epic Scare.

Mike looked at the newspaper. Next to their photo was an ad for mailroom workers at Monsters, Inc. Suddenly Mike had a new plan!

The friends got jobs working in the mailroom at Monsters, Inc.

Team Wazowski and Sullivan were on their way!

To the Rescue

Snow White and her prince spent nearly every day together. But one morning, the Prince told Snow White that he had an errand to take care of. He saddled his trusty steed, Astor, and bid Snow White farewell.

That afternoon, Snow White spotted a cloud of dust on the road. Astor was returning. But where was the Prince?

Snow White's tender heart filled with dread. Surely the Prince is in trouble, she thought.

Astor stamped her hoof on the ground and nodded toward her empty saddle.

"Do you want me to get on?" Snow White asked. Again, Astor nodded.

The princess barely had time to sit down before Astor was racing down the road toward the forest.

Astor ran deeper into the woods with Snow White tugging uselessly at the reins. If only she knew that the Prince was safe!

Then, suddenly, Snow White spotted a piece of red cloth caught on a sharp thorn. Could it be? It was! A scrap torn from the Prince's very own riding cloak! And that wasn't all. As they continued through the forest, Snow White found his hat dangling from a tree!

The princess gripped the reins with one hand. She clutched the Prince's hat and concentrated on thinking hopeful thoughts. Finally, they emerged into a sunny clearing, and Astor slowed to a stop. Snow White spotted the Prince lying on the ground. She slipped out of the saddle and raced across the clearing. Breathless, Snow White reached the Prince just as he sat up and stretched.

"What a nice nap!" he said. "I hope you're hungry!"

Snow White was bewildered. Next to the Prince lay a lavish picnic spread out on a soft blanket, and the Prince was as happy and healthy as ever!

"I knew Astor would get you here quickly," he said, beaming. "Tell me, are you surprised?"

Snow White paused for a moment to catch her breath. "Oh, yes, very surprised," she said at last, smiling. She picked up an apple and offered it to Astor. "And," she added, "I'm very glad you have such a dear and clever horse!"

Show-and-Tell

"Please?" pleaded Lilo. "He'll be good. I promise!"

"Oh, all right!" Nani said crossly.

Lilo had been pestering her big sister all morning to let her take their pet, Stitch, to dance class for show-and-tell. Nani was worried it would cause a lot of trouble. The girls her age were not kind to Lilo, who had trouble fitting in. As a result, Lilo tended to lash out at them and get herself into trouble. And her strange pet, Stitch, was the same way. Nani was convinced that the strange creature they picked up at the pound wasn't even a real dog.

When they arrived at dance class, Nani gave her little sister a quick hug. "You behave yourselves!" she said.

"You'll behave yourself," Lilo said to Stitch. "I know you will."

"All right," said the dance teacher. "What have you brought today, Lilo?"

Lilo stood up. "This is my dog. His name is Stitch. I got him at the pound."

"He sure is ugly!" said Myrtle.

"Now, Myrtle, be nice," the teacher said.

"Can he fetch?" Myrtle asked. She threw a water balloon that she had brought for show-and-tell right at Stitch!

Stitch caught the balloon and threw it back at Myrtle.

"No!" yelled Lilo, throwing herself in front of Myrtle, accidentally knocking the other girl over. The water balloon hit Lilo and broke, sending water flying everywhere!

"Oh, Lilo," said the teacher, "I think it's time for your pet to go home."

Lilo picked up Stitch and ran outside. "You got us in trouble today," Lilo said to him. "Why did you throw that water balloon at Myrtle?"

Stitch growled.

"Oh, that's right," said Lilo, "you don't do fetch. How could I have forgotten?" She looked thoughtful. "How about we play catch instead? That's almost the same thing as fetch, but there's an important difference. Fetch is something you play with a pet, and catch is something you play with a friend. I think you're more my friend than my pet, Stitch."

Stitch nodded eagerly and held up a ball.

Lilo smiled, and the two friends spent a lovely afternoon together playing catch.

Mama Odie to the Rescue

The evil sorcerer, Dr. Facilier, had changed Prince Naveen into a frog. With the help of a magic talisman, he had made Lawrence, a valet, look like Prince Naveen so that he could marry Charlotte, the richest young lady in New Orleans. This way, the sorcerer hoped to get his hands on the girl's fortune!

But Dr. Facilier had a problem. The talisman was running out of power. He needed Naveen's blood to keep it going. And so he called on his evil shadow spirits to bring him the frog.

The clawed beasts soon found Naveen's tracks in the bayou. They grabbed the frog and carried him away.

"Tiana!" Naveen shouted.

Tiana and her friends Louis the alligator and Ray the firefly tried to hold on to Naveen. But no one could fight against the forces of darkness . . . except a powerful voodoo priestess!

Whoosh! Mama Odie made the evil Shadows disappear. "Not bad for a hundred-and-ninety-seven-year-old blind lady, hey?" she said, laughing.

Mama Odie and her snake, Juju, lived in a swamp boat that was wedged between the branches of a tree. Tiana and Naveen asked the wise woman if she could make them human again.

"Ya'll want to be human, but you blind to what you need," she said to Naveen and Tiana as she stirred her pot of gumbo.

"What we want, what we need—it's all the same thing, yes?" Naveen insisted.

"No! You listen to your mama now. You got to dig a little deeper to find out who you are."

Still Mama Odie knew that the frogs would have to learn that the hard way. "Gumbo, gumbo, in the pot! We need a princess. What you got?" Mama Odie conjured an image of Charlotte and her father in the tub of gumbo.

"Lottie!" said Tiana. "But she's not a princess!"

Then Tiana realized something. "Big Daddy's King of the Mardi Gras parade. So that makes Lottie a princess!"

"Does that count?" asked Naveen.

"Yes it does," said Mama Odie. "But only till midnight. You only got till then to get that princess to kiss you!"

Naveen blushed. Yes, a kiss from Charlotte would suit him very well! Especially if it could make him human again.

A Manner of Speaking

Bambi and his mother were out for a summer's walk. As always, they stopped by the rabbit den where Thumper lived.

"And how are you today, Thumper?" asked Bambi's mother.

"I'd be better if my mom didn't just give me a dumb old bath," he said.

"Thumper! Mind your manners!" his mother scolded him.

Bambi and Thumper were given permission to play hide-and-seek, and so they headed off into the woods.

Bambi turned his back to Thumper, closed his eyes, and started to count. "One . . . two . . ."

"Save me! Help! Bambi, save me!" Thumper cried suddenly. Bambi whirled around to see Thumper hopping toward him with a terrified look on his face. A moment later, a mother bear emerged from a nearby cave with three small cubs toddling behind her.

Though he was terrified, Thumper *still* managed to make a rude comment. "That's the meanest-looking creature I ever saw!"

"I beg your pardon?" the mother bear said. "First you come into my home and disturb my children, and then you call me mean? I think you owe me an apology!"

"Do it!" whispered Bambi. "Apologize."

"I'm s-s-sorry you're mean," Thumper stammered.

"Thumper!" Bambi cried. "That isn't funny."

Thumper looked confused. "I wasn't trying to be funny," he said.

"Try again!" the mother bear boomed.

"Um . . ." Thumper tried again. "I'm, um, sorry I disturbed your cubs . . . and, um, you look just like a momma bear should look . . . which is big. And nice."

Before the mother bear let Thumper and Bambi go, she said, "Like I always tell my children: manners are important! You remember that."

Bambi and Thumper ran home as quickly as they could. When they arrived at Thumper's, his mother said, "Just in time for a nice lunch of greens."

Thumper was about to tell his mom how awful he thought the greens tasted, but he changed his mind. "Thank you, Mama. That sounds wonderful," he said.

Thumper's mother beamed. "What lovely manners! I guess you have been listening to me, after all!" she said, as pleased as could be.

AUGUST 1

The Crown of Diamonds

On Aurora's seventeenth birthday, the queen led her to a huge portrait hall.

"Why, Mother! Is that you?" Aurora exclaimed, pointing to a portrait. In it, the queen was wearing a crown with a pink heart-shaped diamond.

"Indeed. I was seventeen," said the queen. "It's a tradition that on a princess's seventeenth birthday, this crown is to be passed down by her mother and worn until the princess becomes queen. However, the princess must solve three riddles," her mother said with a smile.

Just then, the three good fairies, Flora, Fauna, and Merryweather, flew in.

Flora recited the first riddle: "To the eye, it's a treat; to the nose, a delight; to the hand, it can be quite a fright. Though few think to taste it, its sweetness still shows. To this first riddle, the answer's a . . ."

"Let's see," said Aurora. "'To the eye, it's a treat; to the nose, a delight.' So it's pretty and smells good. 'To the hand, quite a fright.' Like a thorn—on a rose. That's it! It's a rose!"

"Very good!" exclaimed Fauna. "And now for the second riddle: Some plant it, some blow it away, some do it several times in a day. Some may blush getting this on their cheek. Can you guess what it is?"

"It's a kiss, isn't it?" Aurora laughed. She kissed each fairy, causing them to blush.

"Now it's my turn!" Merryweather exclaimed. "What only gets stronger the longer it lives? Some say it's blind, some say it's true, some simply say, 'I feel this for you.'"

Aurora thought hard. Just then, Prince Phillip walked by.

"Happy birthday, my love!" he called.

Instantly, Aurora knew the answer. She hurried up to her mother's sewing room.

"I've solved the riddles!" Aurora exclaimed. "The answer to the third riddle is love."

The queen proudly placed the crown on Aurora's head.

That afternoon, Aurora had her portrait painted so it could be hung in the portrait hall alongside her mother's.

"Happy birthday, Aurora," her mother said warmly. "And may you have many more!"

Chief Mischief-maker

Like all raccoons, Meeko was curious—and that often got him into trouble. And though Pocahontas had a lot of patience when it came to her small furry friend, other members of the tribe were not as understanding.

"Pocahontas, you must teach that animal how to behave!" Chief Powhatan exclaimed when he caught Meeko playing with the tribe's peace pipe.

"Don't worry," Pocahontas told Meeko. "They can't stay mad at you for long. Tomorrow is your birthday, after all!"

Meeko chattered excitedly. He loved his birthday—especially opening presents!

Meeko slipped into Pocahontas's tent and spied his wrapped present. He wasted no time unwrapping it and discovered . . . a headdress just his size, filled with beautiful feathers!

Meeko couldn't wait to try it on. He didn't want to be discovered, so he grabbed his gift and scampered off toward the river. There, he put on the headdress. The raccoon gazed happily at his reflection.

But as he was admiring himself, the headdress fell into the water! The raccoon fished it out and headed back to the village.

On the way, the headdress caught on some bushes, and some feathers were pulled out. Then Meeko tripped over a log and landed on his gift, and even *more* feathers fell out! By the time he reached the village, only one feather remained in his once-beautiful headdress.

Meeko knew what he had to do. He found Pocahontas and showed her what was left of the present.

"Meeko, I am proud of you. You had the courage to admit what you have done," she said. "But you must try to do better."

On his birthday, Meeko behaved perfectly all day. That night, Pocahontas presented him with a gift. It was the headdress, but now it had two feathers instead of one. "For every day that you are able to stay out of other people's belongings, we will add another feather," she said.

Meeko was grateful to Pocahontas for being so understanding, and he was determined to make her proud. He would do his best to fill the headdress—but he knew it would probably take him until his next birthday!

Death-Defying Dale

One morning, Chip and Dale woke up to find a giant red-and-white-striped tent just outside their tree. The chipmunks were curious, and so they went over to the tent and peeked through the door.

Inside, a man was shouting through a megaphone.

"Ladies and gentlemen!" he cried. "Welcome to the World's Greatest Circus!"

The chipmunks tiptoed inside. They watched a silly clown with orange hair and a big red nose turn somersaults. Nearby, a lion tamer cracked his whip at a lion. And high overhead, trapeze artists tumbled though the air.

Dale smelled something delicious. There on the ground, right by the center ring, was a bag full of peanuts! Dale's tummy rumbled. He needed a snack. Chip and Dale hurried over to the peanuts.

Chip was about to take a bite when he realized someone—or something—was standing behind him. He turned around and his eyes opened wide.

It was a huge elephant!

Chip squeaked in surprise and ran away, but Dale was face-first in the sack of peanuts and didn't hear him. Just then, the elephant reached into the sack with its trunk, looking for a peanut. But it didn't grab a peanut—it grabbed Dale!

"Aroooooo!" the elephant trumpeted. With a flick of her trunk, she flung Dale away.

"Eeeek!" Dale squeaked as he sailed through the air. He was headed straight for the lion's open mouth!

Dale closed his eyes.

Whoosh! Suddenly, something scooped Dale out of the air. He opened his eyes. One of the trapeze artists had accidentally grabbed Dale as he flipped through the air.

Dale sighed with relief.

But a second later, the trapeze artist let go. "Eeeek!" Dale cried as he fell right into a bucket of popcorn.

Dale popped out of the popcorn. Suddenly, a spotlight shone down on him.

"Ladies and gentlemen," the ringmaster announced. "Please give a round of applause to our surprise guest, the Death-Defying Chipmunk!"

Learning to Fly

Tinker Bell was upset. She had released a beautiful blue butterfly that her friend Lizzy's father had trapped in a jar. Now, Dr. Griffiths was angry with Lizzy. He though *she* had set the butterfly free. He had sent Lizzy to her bedroom as punishment for not telling the truth.

Tinker Bell knew it wasn't fair that Lizzy was being punished for the fairy's actions, but what could she do to make it up to her?

"I wish I were a fairy!" Lizzy said. "Then I could help the flowers bloom, and I could talk to the animals. That would be so fun!"

The girl spun around, imagining she was hovering in the sky. That gave Tinker Bell an idea. She had gotten Lizzy in trouble, and it was up to her to cheer the girl up.

Tinker Bell tinkled in her little voice and gestured for Lizzy to close her eyes and stretch out her arms. Then Tink sprinkled her with fairy dust.

Lizzy's feet lifted off the floor and she began flying all around her bedroom!

"I'm flying!" Lizzy said, laughing happily.

Soon she was soaring across the room and even walking on the ceiling. But Lizzy wasn't used to flying and she kept knocking things over. She made such a racket that Dr. Griffiths came to see what was going on.

Tinker Bell quickly hid in Lizzy's fairy house. Lizzy did her best to hold on to the back of a chair to keep both feet on the ground!

"What's going on in here?" Dr. Griffiths demanded. "Look at this room! It looks like a cyclone hit it! How did you get footprints on the ceiling?" her father continued. "The truth this time."

"Well, I . . ." began Lizzy. "I was flying. My fairy showed me how."

"You've got to stop this nonsense!" Dr. Griffiths insisted. "I believe in what is real . . . and it's about time you started doing the same." He took Lizzy's fairy drawings down from the wall and put them in the trash.

Tinker Bell had had enough. She flew out of the fairy house and straight at Dr. Griffiths's face!

What would happen to Tinker Bell now?

Dot Rules

Atta was exhausted! Ever since she had taken over as queen, she had not had a moment's peace. There were so many decisions to make and disagreements to settle.

Princess Dot didn't like her big sister being so tired and cranky all the time.

"Why don't you just take a day off?" Dot asked.

"But who will run the colony?" Atta said irritably.

"I will. I am a princess, you know," Dot said.

The next day, Dot began her reign. The first problem arose when their mother's pet, Aphie, ate some leaves that were going to be used to build a rain shelter.

"You need a time-out!" scolded Dot. She put Aphie in a pen for ten minutes. When he came back out, he was a model aphid.

Later, she found Cornelius and Thorny disagreeing over the best way to transport seeds.

"I want you to cooperate and come up with a solution," Dot said. A short time later, Thorny and Cornelius reached a compromise. It turned out they were *both* right!

Flik was the next ant to receive Dot's help. "I can't seem to get this new ant mover to work," he complained.

"How long have you been working on it?" Dot asked.

Flik thought for a moment. "Since I woke up," he answered. "I worked right through breakfast and lunch."

"Flik," Dot said, "you can't think properly if your body doesn't have fuel. You need to stop and eat something. And why don't you take a nap while you're at it?"

Dot had a lot of advice to share with her subjects that day. She reminded Mr. Soil's conservation class that everyone should have a turn to speak. She insisted that the ant boys pick their toys up off the ground. And she firmly told her mother that there was no whining allowed—even if she was upset about Aphie getting a time-out.

By the end of the day, both Atta and her mother had to admit that the colony had run smoothly with Dot in charge.

"What's your secret?" asked Atta.

"It was easy," Dot explained. "Time-outs, cooperating, taking naps, and taking turns—I learned it all in my Blueberry troop!"

Dance, Daddy-o!

Deep in the jungle at the temple ruins, the monkeys and their ruler, King Louie, were always looking to have a swingin' time.

"Let's have a dance-off!" King Louie suggested to the monkeys one evening.

"Hooray!" the monkeys cheered.

"What's a dance-off?" one monkey asked.

"You know, a contest," said King Louie. "An opportunity for everyone to get down, strut their stuff, cut a rug! And whoever lays down the smoothest moves is the winner!"

"Hooray!" cheered the monkeys.

King Louie rubbed his chin. "The first thing we need is some music," he said, pointing at the monkey musicians. "Hit it, fellas!"

The musicians blasted out a jazzy tune, blowing through their hands like horns, knocking out a beat on some coconuts, and drumming on a hollow log. Soon, all the monkeys were gathered around the musicians, tapping their toes and shaking their tails.

King Louie moved his hips from side to side. He waved his arms in the air. He closed his eyes so he could really feel the beat.

"Dance, daddy-o!" one monkey cried.

King Louie boogied and bopped like he had never boogied and bopped before. Then, when the song was over, he stopped dancing and scrambled back onto his throne. "Now it's time to choose the winner!" he said.

"But King Louie . . ." one monkey began to object.

All the other monkeys were thinking the same thing: Didn't you need more than one dancer to have a dance-off?

"Oh, silly me," said King Louie with a chuckle. The monkeys looked at one another and smiled, expecting that the king had realized his mistake. But King Louie said, "Of course, we need a judge! Who will judge?"

Everyone raised their hands. King Louie looked around, then said, "I choose . . . me!"

"Hooray!" the monkeys cheered.

"And as the judge, I will now choose the winner of the dance-off," King Louie continued. He looked around at all the monkeys. "Now, let's see. I choose . . . me! Let's hear it for the winner!"

"Hooray!" the monkeys cheered, because, after all, King Louie was their king—and a pretty swingin' dancer, too!

Looks Can Be Deceiving

Yao, Ling, and Chien-Po missed Mulan. They had become friends in the army—although when they had first met her, Mulan had been disguised as a young man.

Now Mulan's three friends decided they would go to her village and follow Mulan in whatever adventure she might embark on next.

"But what if Shan-Yu is seeking revenge?" Ling said. "He might be looking for us. After all, we did help Mulan defeat him."

Yao thought they should disguise themselves. So the friends donned kimonos, wigs, and makeup and set out for Mulan's village, looking like a trio of women.

When they arrived, the Matchmaker instantly approached them. "And who would you lovely ladies be?" she asked. The Matchmaker was desperate. There weren't many single women in the village, and she had a list of bachelors a mile long to marry off!

"Visitors from far away," said Chien-Po, speaking in a high voice.

"And are you unmarried, ladies?" the Matchmaker asked.

Ling looked at his friends. "We're

unmarried, all right!" he said.

"Well, let me be the first to welcome you to our village," the Matchmaker said, ushering them into her house. "Would you like some tea? Perhaps you would like to pour?" she asked Yao. He tried to remember the way his mother served tea at home. Yao set out the cups and poured as daintily as he could.

"Cookie?" the pleased Matchmaker asked Chien-Po, holding out a plate. Chien-Po resisted the urge to grab a fistful of cookies. Instead, he chose one, stuck out his little finger, and ate it in small bites.

Next the Matchmaker asked Ling what his favorite pastime was.

"Wrestling," he answered. Then, seeing the shocked look on the Matchmaker's face, he added quickly, "Yes, I find that resting keeps my complexion lovely." He batted his eyelashes.

The Matchmaker led the three back outside, just as Mulan was riding into the village. "Stop! You can't marry them off!" Mulan cried, seeing her friends with the woman.

"I certainly can," said the Matchmaker. "Unlike you, Mulan, these three are real ladies!"

Belle and the Castle Puppy

Belle was strolling through the castle garden one day when she saw a puppy huddled outside the castle gates. He looked cold and dirty.

"Oh, you poor thing!" Belle cried. "Let's get you warmed up and fed!"

Belle brought the puppy inside and gave him a bath. When he was clean and dry, the puppy ate a bowl of warm stew.

All the enchanted objects were happy to have a guest. All but the ottoman. He remembered when he had been a real dog. What if Belle liked this dog more?

"Do you want to play?" Belle asked, letting the puppy outside.

A while later, the Beast walked up to Belle. "Someone has dug up my roses!" he exclaimed. Then the Beast saw the puppy. "Get rid of him—NOW!" he roared as he stomped away.

Just then, the ottoman ran past Belle and into the forest. His legs were all muddy! Suddenly, Belle understood.

The ottoman dug up the roses! He just wanted some attention, too, Belle realized.

The puppy raced after the ottoman, barking playfully.

"What if they get lost?" Belle said worriedly. "I have to bring them back safely."

"I'll come and light your way," Lumiere volunteered.

"Puppy! Ottoman!" Belle called, holding up Lumiere.

She heard barking and followed the sound to a clearing. The ottoman and the puppy were surrounded by wolves!

"The puppy is protecting the ottoman!" Lumiere exclaimed.

Quickly, Belle put Lumiere on the ground and lit a large stick.

"Get away! Get away!" she shouted, swinging it toward the wolves.

Just then, the Beast showed up, roaring loudly. The wolves yelped with fear and ran away.

Later that night, everyone settled by the fireplace. Belle watched the Beast stroke the ottoman and feed biscuits to the puppy.

"May the puppy stay until I can find him a home?" she asked.

The Beast cleared his throat. "His home is here—with us," he answered gruffly.

Belle smiled. The Beast was really starting to show a gentle side.

The Storm

One summer afternoon, Jenny invited Dodger and his gang to go on a picnic with her and Oliver in Central Park.

"Go play with your friends," Jenny told the kitten.

As Jenny, Fagin, and Winston the butler unpacked the picnic basket, they didn't notice that the animals were romping farther and farther away. Suddenly, thunder boomed and rain poured down. Then lightning struck a tree.

"I must get you home!" Winston insisted, rushing Jenny out of the park.

"Where's Oliver?" she cried.

"Don't worry," said Fagin. "Dodger will take care of him."

In the morning, Dodger woke up under a tree. Oliver had climbed it when the storm had started. The rest of the gang ran to find shelter, but Dodger had stayed with Oliver all night.

"Hey there, kid!" Dodger called. "You ready to go home now?"

"Yes!" said Oliver, climbing down. "And I've made a new friend. He says he's lost. Maybe Jenny will adopt him, too."

"Wow," said Dodger. "I didn't know cats could grow so big!"

"I'm a bear cub," the creature said.

"Where did you come from?" Dodger asked.

The bear started to cry. "I don't know!" he wailed. "I was scared of the storm, so I climbed a tree. Then a big wind blew me out of the tree. The next thing I knew I was out here on the lawn. So I climbed this tree and met Oliver. Can you help me find my mama?"

Oliver shook his head sadly. "I'm afraid I don't know where bears live in New York City."

"Wait!" Dodger said. "I think I do." He took Oliver and the cub to a fancy entrance with a big iron gate that read CENTRAL PARK ZOO. When the zookeeper saw the cub, he rushed over and led him back to his mother.

"Mama!" cried the bear cub. The mama bear hugged her cub close, and Dodger smiled down at Oliver.

"Time to get you home, too."

When Jenny saw that Oliver was safe and sound, she kissed and hugged him— and Dodger, too.

"Thank you, Dodger!" Jenny cried. "You're my hero!"

"Mine, too," said Oliver. "A friend like you makes even the scariest storm *bear*able!"

Stackblackbadminton

Ariel was a guest at Prince Eric's castle. After dinner she went into the drawing room with Eric and Grimsby to relax.

"My dear, do you play?" Grimsby asked Ariel. He pointed to a table. On it sat a red-and-black-checkered board. Ariel couldn't answer because she had exchanged her voice for legs, but she nodded eagerly.

"I'll make the first move," Eric said, and he slid a black disk from one square to another.

That seems simple enough, thought Ariel. The game seemed similar to a merpeople game called Conch. She reached over and pushed the same black disk to a third square.

Eric laughed. "No, no. I'm black. And you're red. *You* move the *red* pieces."

"Perhaps I should show the young lady?" suggested Grimsby.

He took Ariel's seat, and the two men moved the disks all over the checkered board. Suddenly, Ariel heard a flapping sound at the window. It was Scuttle!

Ariel pointed at the men and shrugged.

"They're playing Stackblackbadminton, a popular human game," said Scuttle.

Ariel's eyes widened. That sounded like something she had better learn if she wanted to fit in to Eric's world.

"You see those disks?" asked Scuttle. "Those are *chips*. At the end of the game, players stack their chips. Then the dealer—the person *not* playing—"

Ariel pointed to herself.

Scuttle nodded. "Yes. It's up to you to end the game by collecting all the chips off the board."

Ariel smiled. She would show Eric she *did* know how to play.

She walked right over to the two men. They seemed to have finished playing. They were staring hard at the board—and there weren't many chips left on it. So she bent down and swept all the pieces off the board.

Eric and Grimsby yelped. The little mermaid grinned. Eric didn't think she knew how to play his game, but from the stunned look on his face, she'd given him quite a surprise!

Ariel smiled and began to lay the chips out as if they were shells in a game of Conch. This Stackblackbadminton game was all right, but she couldn't wait to teach Eric and Grimsby how to play a *really* good game!

The Good Old Summertime

The Seven Dwarfs were on their way back home after a long day at the diamond mine. Each swung a shovel in one hand and a bucket in the other.

As they marched through the forest, Happy enjoyed the sounds of the birds singing and the warmth of the summer sun on his face. "Summer is such a wonderful time of year!" he exclaimed.

"Oh, yeah?" snapped Grumpy. "What's so wonderful about it?"

"Well . . . the days are longer," said Happy.

"The days are hotter," complained Grumpy.

Doc spoke up. "I like the summertime, too. It's a very healthy season."

"Healthy?" said Grumpy. "This heat?"

"Look at all the fresh vegetables and fruit you can eat all summer long," said Doc. "Like the melons on those vines. They're as big as Dopey's head!"

Dopey grinned and nodded.

Grumpy rolled his eyes and said, "Dopey's a melon-head, all right!"

"Don't be such a grump!" scolded Doc.

"Yes, cheer up! Summer's a great season," Happy said with a grin.

"It's too hot, I say," Grumpy insisted.

"And all those blooming plants make Sneezy sneeze even more!"

"Yes," said Sneezy. "Sorry, but . . . *Ahhhhhh-choo!* . . . I think Grumpy's right."

"No, he's not," said Happy. "Summer's the very best time of year."

"It's too hot, I say!" repeated Grumpy.

By this time, the Seven Dwarfs had reached a small bridge running over a brook.

"Well, if it's too hot for you, Grumpy, then I have a special warm-weather remedy," said Doc, stopping in the middle of the bridge.

"Yeah?" snapped Grumpy. "What is it?"

Doc motioned for the other Dwarfs to gather around him. They blocked Doc from Grumpy's view as he leaned over and filled his bucket with cool water from the stream.

"Well?" said Grumpy. "Are you going to give me your special remedy?"

"Of course," said Doc. With a big "Heave-ho!" Doc dumped his bucket of water over Grumpy's head. *Splash!*

"That should cool you off," said Happy.

Grumpy sputtered with surprise. But he had to admit, the soaking actually did cool him off!

A Monstrous Mix-Up

One morning at work, Mike Wazowski opened the door to his locker to find a note taped inside. It said: *Mike: Roses are red. Violets are blue. I have got my eye on you! Sealed with a kiss from . . . Your Secret Admirer.*

Mike showed the note to his best friend, Sulley.

"Who do you think it could be?" Sulley asked.

"I have no idea!" Mike replied.

Mike's mind was racing. Who could his admirer be?

Just then, Mike heard his least favorite voice. "Wazowski!" It was Roz, the humorless and strict Dispatch Manager, sliding up behind them. "You owe me some paperwork!" she said.

"Oh . . . right," said Mike. "I'll get that to you ASAP, Roz. See ya." He and Sulley turned on their heels and hurried on down the hallway.

"All right, Wazowski," Roz called out to Mike, shaking her finger. "But remember: I've got my eye on you. I'm always watching. . . ."

Mike and Sulley froze in their tracks and stared at each other.

"Did she just say—" Sulley began.

"'My *eye* on you'?" Mike said, recalling the wording in the note.

Sulley gulped. "Your secret admirer is *Roz?*"

"NOOOOOOOO!" Mike's scream filled the hallway just as Celia came sauntering around the corner.

"Hi, Mike," she said batting her eye at him. "Rough morning?"

"Oh. Hey, Celia," Mike replied sullenly, still traumatized by the idea that Roz liked him.

"Gee," said Celia, "I thought my note would make your day."

Mike stared at her. "*Your* note?" he said, stunned. "Celia, you're my secret admirer?"

She sighed. "Wasn't it obvious? 'I have got my eye on you'? As in, I have one eye, just like you?"

A wave of relief swept across Mike's face.

"I was going to ask you if you wanted to go out sometime," Celia continued. "But if you don't want to . . ."

Without a word, Mike leaped into Celia's arms and clung to her tightly. "Thank you, thank you, THANK YOU!" he exclaimed.

Celia giggled. "So . . . I guess that's a yes?"

How Does Your Garden Grow?

Alice had eaten a mushroom that made her shrink. Now, everything around her was gigantic!

"The Caterpillar said one side of this mushroom will make me bigger and the other will make me smaller," Alice told a nearby dandelion.

"Which do you want?" asked the dandelion. "To grow bigger or smaller?"

"Bigger!" cried Alice.

"Put your roots in the ground and turn your leaves to the sun," said the dandelion. "You'll grow bigger in no time!"

"But I'm not a flower," said Alice.

"Of course she's not," said a daffodil. "She's a bug!"

Suddenly, Alice heard another voice. "Little buuuug . . ." it sang.

Alice placed the mushroom pieces in her pocket and approached the plant. Its flower buds looked very strange—like split green kidney beans with fine hairs around the edges.

"Get in," said the plant eagerly.

Alice climbed inside one of the strange buds. Immediately, she felt the bud begin to close up tight, trapping her inside!

"What kind of plant are you?" cried Alice.

"A Venus flytrap," said the plant.

"But I'm not a fly," Alice protested.

"Doesn't matter," said the flytrap. "I eat other bugs."

"I'm not any kind of bug!" cried Alice, banging on the springy green walls.

The flytrap just laughed. "I can tell you're going to be a tasty treat, little bug," it mumbled.

"You know," said Alice angrily, "it's not polite to talk with your mouth full! Why, if I were my normal size, I'd—"

Normal size? she thought. Suddenly she remembered the pieces of mushroom in her pocket. She pulled out the two pieces. Taking a chance, she bit into one.

All at once, Alice began to grow. She got bigger and bigger and burst out of the flytrap.

Still angry, she peered down at the flytrap. It looked completely harmless now, no higher than her ankle. She gave it a glare, and then went on her way.

The flowers watched her go. "That was the biggest bug I ever saw," said the violet, in a quaking voice.

"I can't believe I let it go," the Venus flytrap said wistfully. "That bug would have been breakfast, lunch, and dinner for the next fifty years!"

Just Believe

The fairies of Pixie Hollow had been bringing summer to the mainland when they had heard a car pass by on a nearby road. Curious, Tinker Bell had followed the car and been discovered by a girl named Lizzy.

The fairies thought Tink was in danger and set off to rescue her. But just as Vidia arrived upstairs, Tink had shown herself to Dr. Griffiths! Tink wanted to prove to him that fairies existed!

Dr. Griffiths was shocked. He tried to capture Tink in a glass jar. He wanted to show off his discovery to his coworkers. At the last moment, Vidia pushed Tink out of the way. Dr. Griffiths captured Vidia instead!

"I must get this to the museum right away!" he declared.

"Father, you can't do this!" Lizzy cried—but it was no use. Dr. Griffiths ran out of the house, jumped into his car, and drove off.

When the other fairies reached Lizzy's room, Tink told them that Vidia was in danger. The fairies had a problem: it was still raining. The fairies couldn't fly with wet wings. But if they couldn't fly, how would they rescue Vidia?

Tink had an idea. "We can't fly," she said, "but I think I know somebody who can. . . ."

The fairies swirled around Lizzy and showered her with pixie dust.

"All aboard!" cried Tink as Lizzy rose into the air.

Shortly after nightfall, the twinkling lights of London came into view.

"There he is!" Lizzy cried, spotting her father's car.

Tinker Bell flew toward the car and bravely darted into the engine. After some quick tinkering, she stopped the car. Dr. Griffiths jumped out and raced toward the museum on foot. Tinker Bell— and Lizzy—were right behind him.

"Father!" Lizzy called.

Dr. Griffiths turned to see Lizzy flying through the air. "Lizzy . . . you're . . . flying! I don't understand," he continued.

"You don't have to understand," the little girl told her father. "You just have to believe."

Dr. Griffiths's eyes filled with wonder. "I do believe," he said, handing the jar to Lizzy. Dr. Griffiths hugged his daughter tightly. She had been right about fairies all along. . . .

Toys in Paradise

Andy ran around his room, throwing clothes into a bag. His best friend's family was going on a vacation to Florida and they had invited him along.

When Andy left the room, his toys came to life.

"I'd give anything to go on a tropical vacation," said Bo Peep. "Just think of it. The sandy beaches, the warm sunshine . . ."

"Hey, I've got an idea," said Jessie. "Why don't we make our own tropical paradise, right here in Andy's room?"

The toys searched the house for the things they needed. Sarge and the Green Army Men found a potted plant. Hamm and Rex raided the kitchen for Buster's water dish and some sponges. Bo found a doll's umbrella in Molly's room. Soon all of the supplies were gathered in Andy's room.

"Next stop: paradise!" Jessie exclaimed.

The toys got to work. In no time at all, they had created their own tropical paradise. Woody and Buzz stretched out on the lounge chairs they had made out of shoe box tops and sponges.

"Aah. This is the life," Woody said.

But something was missing—an ocean breeze!

Jessie climbed onto Andy's dresser and flipped a switch. Within seconds, the wind picked up, blowing Andy's things everywhere. It was a storm! The toys ran for cover as the beach chairs flew across the room.

"It's okay!" Jessie called. She flipped off the switch and the wind stopped. "It was just the fan. I wanted to make our palm tree sway in the breeze. Is everyone okay?"

"Almost everyone," Woody said. He pointed toward the bed, where Rex's tail was poking out from under the bedspread. It took a while for the toys to convince Rex to come out of his hiding place. He was still trembling with fear!

"Don't worry, Rex," Woody said. "There won't be any more storms here today."

The toys put the umbrella back in its place, shading the lounge chairs from the sun.

Rex walked back over to the beach. "I hope Andy has a great trip," he said. "Paradise can definitely be fun . . . as long as you're with good friends!"

The Wedding Gift

Aurora was busily preparing for her wedding day.

"If you please, Your Royal Highness, what did you have in mind?" the dressmaker asked Aurora.

"Well . . ." Aurora began.

"You'll want white, of course," the dressmaker broke in.

"Actually," Aurora said, "I—"

But the dressmaker wasn't done yet. "And you'll want a train!"

That wasn't what Aurora had in mind at all. But before she could say anything, the fairy Merryweather spoke up.

"But what if she doesn't want a dress that color?" she said, pointing to one of the samples. "What the dear girl needs is something blue," Merryweather said.

"Oh, no!" Flora scolded. "A wedding dress shouldn't be blue. It should be pink!"

"Just a minute, now!" King Stefan declared. "I hereby decree that the color of the gown be left to the bride."

Aurora smiled at her father. Then the king went on. "The most important thing is that the dress be covered with lots of jewels!"

"Why, of course, Your Supreme Highness," the dressmaker said. "Lots of jewels."

Aurora sighed. While her father and the dressmaker talked about various designs, she felt a soft hand take hold of hers.

"Come, darling," her mother said, smiling at her. "I have something to show you."

Together, they walked into the queen's dressing room. Aurora watched as her mother pulled out a long, simple, beautiful gown, edged with delicate lace and tiny pearls.

"This was my wedding dress when I married your father," the queen explained. "And it was my mother's before me. I had hoped one day you'd wear it—if you'd like to."

"Oh, Mother!" Aurora exclaimed. "It's just what I had in mind!"

Moments later, Aurora went downstairs, wearing her mother's wedding gown.

"Ooh!" The fairies gasped.

"Perfect!" declared her father.

Everyone agreed that the dress looked as if it had been made especially for Aurora—and, in a very special way, it had been.

The Heart of a Champion

Life at the palace was a dream come true for Cinderella. She particularly loved that her dear old horse, Frou, lived there, too.

One day, an invitation arrived. "You are hereby invited," read the Grand Duke, "to attend this year's annual Royal International Horse Show, to be held exactly one week from today. Please choose one member from your royal household to represent you in the competition."

Everyone decided that Cinderella should compete! And although there were lots of fine horses to choose from, Cinderella wanted to ride her old friend, Frou.

"My dear," said the King, turning up his nose, "if none of my horses suit your fancy, I can have a hundred more champions here by morning!"

"Frou may be old," said Cinderella, "but he has the heart of a champion!"

And with that, she saddled Frou and swung herself onto his back.

Every day for a week, Cinderella and Frou trained. But Frou kept making mistakes. No matter how sweetly Cinderella urged him on, he missed nearly every jump.

At last, it was the night before the royal horse show.

"Please don't worry," Cinderella told Frou. "You're going to be wonderful."

But Frou didn't quite believe her.

Just then, Cinderella's Fairy Godmother appeared! "My dear," she whispered, "you know Frou can win, and I know Frou can win, but our friend Frou doesn't know it at all. What he needs is confidence."

And with that, she raised her magic wand and waved it at Frou. To Frou's amazement, a glass horseshoe appeared on each of his hooves!

"With these horseshoes, you'll never miss a step," the Fairy Godmother told Frou, sneaking a wink at Cinderella. "And while I'm at it," she added, waving her wand again. Instantly, a golden saddle appeared on Frou's back and Cinderella's simple dress became a beautiful riding outfit.

The next day at the horse show, Frou looked like a true champion! He held his head up high and cleared every jump with ease. And it was all thanks to the magical glass horseshoes—or so Frou thought.

Special Delivery

Roger and Anita had a lot of puppies, and that meant they needed a lot of food. Every Thursday, a truck pulled up full of dog food. And every Thursday Rolly waited by the window for the truck.

One Thursday, Rolly and Pepper noticed that the back of the truck had been left open. "Are you thinking what I'm thinking?" Pepper asked Rolly.

Rolly nodded. "Snack time!" Rolly and Pepper made a dash for the truck and leaped into the back. Pepper clambered up onto the pile of bags and sniffed around. There had to be some loose food somewhere. . . .

"Bingo!" Pepper cried. "Rolly, up here!"

Rolly was there in an instant. *Slurp, slurp, crunch!* The two puppies were so busy eating that they didn't see the truck driver come out of the house.

Slam! He closed up the back of the truck. A second later, it was rumbling down the road.

"Uh-oh," Rolly whispered.

After what seemed like a very long time, the vehicle lurched to a halt. The back door opened, and the driver began unloading bags of food.

Pepper and Rolly jumped out of the van while he wasn't looking. They ran and hid behind the house.

"What do you two think you're doing?" a gruff voice asked.

The puppies spun around. A big bulldog was looking down at them.

"This is my property," the dog said. "It's time for you to scram."

"You don't scare me," Pepper said boldly. "You're not half as bad as Cruella."

The bulldog's mouth fell open. "Do you mean Cruella De Vil?" he asked. "You must be Pongo and Perdita's puppies! I heard about your adventures over the Twilight Bark! Your parents must be worried about you. I'd better get you home!"

Luckily, Pongo and Perdita were out that day and didn't realize what a pickle Rolly and Pepper had gotten themselves into. But there were ninety-seven puppies waiting in the front yard as Rolly and Pepper arrived with their escort.

"Wow," said Lucky, after he'd heard their tale. "Were you scared of that big mean bulldog?"

"No way!" Pepper said. "That bulldog was all bark and no bite!"

A Yummy Dream

Winnie the Pooh stepped into his house and sat down with a sigh. He and Piglet had been out on a long walk through the woods. Now Pooh was tired. And, more importantly, he was hungry.

"My tummy feels very rumbly," Pooh said aloud. He got to his feet and went over to his honey cupboard. There was only one pot of honey inside.

"Oh dear," Pooh said. One pot of honey was not very much. He sat down and began to eat. He ate every last sticky drop. But when he was finished, his tummy was still feeling a tiny bit rumbly.

"Well, I suppose there's nothing left to do but go to bed," Pooh said sadly. He put on his nightshirt and his nightcap and climbed into his cozy bed. A minute later, Pooh's snores filled the air. And dreams began to fill his head—dreams of honey, of course.

Pooh stood before the honey tree. It was so full of honey, it was oozing out of the trunk! Then, suddenly, a purple heffalump appeared behind him.

"Mmmm," the heffalump said, licking his lips. The creature stuck his long trunk into one of the honey pots and gobbled up all the honey inside.

"Those are my honey pots!" Pooh cried. He tried to sound brave, even though he was just a little bit scared. The heffalump looked very big and very hungry.

The heffalump just stared at Pooh. Pooh looked at the honey pots. There were a lot of them. Some were full, but most were still empty. Pooh looked at the honey tree. It was still overflowing with honey.

"I have an idea," Pooh said. "Let's fill the honey pots together, then share a nice snack."

The heffalump nodded excitedly. He picked up a honey pot with his trunk and carried it over to the tree. Pooh did the same, and the sweet, sticky honey dripped into the pots.

When all of the pots had been filled, Pooh and the heffalump sat down together. They ate and ate until all the pots were empty and their tummies were full.

When Pooh awoke the next morning, to his surprise, his tummy wasn't even the slightest bit rumbly. Just then, he remembered his strange dream. It *had* been a dream—hadn't it?

Bedtime for Duchess

"Come, my precious ones!" Duchess called to her kittens, "It's time to go to sleep."

"Oh, Mother!" Toulouse complained.

"But I'm not tired!" Marie joined in.

"I'm not going to sleep," Berlioz added. "Nighttime is when things start happening for us alley cats." Berlioz crouched down low and pounced on an imaginary opponent.

"Now, now, it's been a long day," Duchess said. "I don't want to hear any more protests."

"We need a bedtime story!" Marie insisted.

"A story? I'm sorry, darlings, but it's way past your bedtime, and I'm just too tired tonight," replied Duchess.

"Then why don't we tell you a story?" Toulouse offered.

"Once upon a time . . ." Marie began.

"There was a big, mean, ferocious alley cat," Berlioz continued.

"Berlioz!" Marie protested. "It's not supposed to be scary. She'll have nightmares!"

"Sorry, Mama," Berlioz said.

"That's quite all right," Duchess said.

"Now, where were we?" Toulouse asked.

"Once upon a time . . ." Marie began again.

"Yeah, once upon a time there was this kitten," Toulouse said. "He could paint like no other kitten."

"And that's because the model for his paintings was the most beautiful kitten you've ever laid eyes on," Marie added.

"Give me a break!" Berlioz said, grumbling under his breath. He and Toulouse snickered.

Marie was not amused. "Can we please get back to the story?"

"Okay, okay," Berlioz continued. "This kitten was a painter by day and a smooth-talking, alley-hanging hepcat by night. He was—"

Suddenly Toulouse tapped Berlioz with his paw. Berlioz couldn't believe Toulouse was interrupting him. He was trying to tell a story! Then he saw why Toulouse had stopped him. Duchess had fallen asleep!

Berlioz, Toulouse, and Marie each gave their mother a kiss good night.

"Good night, Mama," said Marie.

"Good night, Mama," said Toulouse.

"Good night, Mama," said Berlioz.

Then all three curled up beside Duchess and promptly fell asleep, too.

Jasmine's Jewel Thief

"This is so much fun!" Jasmine cried. She and Aladdin were flying over the desert on their favorite flying carpet.

Jasmine leaned against Aladdin and reached up to smooth back her windblown hair. But as her fingers brushed past her ears, she noticed that one of her earrings was gone!

"What is it?" Aladdin asked when he saw Jasmine searching the carpet.

"It's nothing. Just an earring," Jasmine said. She tried stay calm, but her eyes gave her away.

"Just an earring?" Aladdin said. "Didn't your father give them to you?"

"Yes," Jasmine confessed. "They're my favorites. At least, they were."

"Are," Aladdin said firmly. "We'll find the other one."

Back at the palace, Aladdin and Jasmine looked everywhere. They searched their chambers, the gardens, even the fountains. They were about to search the kitchen when Aladdin saw Abu scamper by.

Aladdin looked at the monkey suspiciously. "You haven't seen a shiny gold earring, have you?"

Abu shrugged, but he wouldn't look Aladdin in the eye. Aladdin knew the monkey was up to something.

"Are you sure?" Aladdin asked sternly.

Slowly, Abu motioned Aladdin to follow him. When he saw the monkey's bed, Aladdin almost started to laugh. Why hadn't he noticed before how lumpy it was?

Abu pulled back the covers and Aladdin laughed out loud. Abu's bed was covered with shiny objects! There were spoons, goblets, and coins. And from beneath his small pillow, Abu pulled out Jasmine's earring.

Aladdin shook his head and smiled at Abu. "You don't have to scavenge anymore. We live in the palace!"

Aladdin and Abu brought the earring to Jasmine. "You found it!" she cried, leaning down to give Abu a kiss. The little monkey blushed.

"Here, Abu, take this ring as a reward for finding my earring," Jasmine said. She removed a gold ring from her finger and gave it to the monkey, who gave a happy jump and tucked it into his hat.

"Actually, Abu didn't really—" Aladdin began. Then he saw Abu glaring at him. "Well," he continued, amused. "Yes. Um, good job, Abu."

A Stitched-Up Date

Nani was going to the movies with David and had asked Old Lady Kingsley to watch Lilo.

"How is she going to watch us when she can barely see?" Lilo asked. "And," she continued, "do you know what movie Nani and David went to see? *Invasion of the Bug-Eyed Aliens, Part VI: The Sliming*—without us!"

Lilo stood up and said, "Come on, Stitch. Let's go and see the movie ourselves."

Lilo and Stitch sneaked past the snoring Mrs. Kingsley. Lilo opened and shut the front door as loudly as she could. Then, doing her best impression of Nani, she shouted, "We're back, Mrs. Kingsley! Thanks!"

Mrs. Kingsley woke up, tottered to the door, and peered blindly at Lilo. "Is that you, Nani? Well, I hope you had a lovely time."

And with that, the two made a break for the movie theater.

Once they got there, though, they had two problems—money and . . .

"Sorry, kid, no dogs allowed in the theater," the ticket man said.

Lilo had to think quickly. "He isn't a dog. He's my teddy bear."

"He doesn't look like a stuffed animal," the ticket man said.

"They make them very lifelike these days," Lilo fibbed. "My mother is looking for us, and if we don't find her soon, I think I may start to cry."

"Okay, okay," the ticket man said.

By the time the two had gotten into the theater, the bug-eyed aliens had begun the sliming, and everyone was screaming. Lilo and Stitch joined in—perhaps a little too loudly, because Nani and David noticed them right away!

"Excuse me," Nani said as she made her way out of her row and down the aisle, cola spilling and popcorn flying. Nani grabbed hold of Lilo's arm and dragged her out of the theater. David and Stitch were right behind them.

"I'm so angry with you, I'm going to . . . I'm going to . . ." Nani stuttered.

David finished her sentence. "Take you out for ice cream."

"Out for ice cream?" Nani said.

"It's a beautiful night, and I can't think of anything more wonderful than two sisters having ice cream together." David turned to Lilo and Stitch. "Don't you think?"

Should I Stay or Should I Go?

Wendy sat watching Michael and John play with Peter Pan and the rest of the Lost Boys. She was wondering if it was time for them to return home.

"John and Michael seem so happy," Wendy said to herself. "And why wouldn't they? Never Land is such a beautiful place, and flying is so much fun!

"Still," she had to admit, "it is also dangerous. Who knows what sort of trouble we could get into, especially with Captain Hook running about!"

Wendy considered this, then burst out, "What am I talking about? I'm making it sound like it's an awful place, but the truth is, Never Land is the most wonderful place in the world!

"Maybe I really want to stay in Never Land, but in my heart of hearts I know I shouldn't," Wendy suddenly realized. "After all, Mother and Father must miss us terribly.

"That settles it." Wendy stood up abruptly. "We must leave for home immediately. But if I stay—" Wendy stopped herself. "Why, then I'll never have to grow up!

"Then again, I always wanted to be an adult someday," she concluded.

Just then, Peter Pan swooped down beside her. "What are you doing, Wendy?" Peter asked.

"Oh, nothing," Wendy told him.

"Then why don't you come join us?" he suggested.

"I will," Wendy told him. "In a minute."

"All right! But last one there is a rotten—" Peter took off before he could finish his sentence.

"How can I ever leave Peter and the Lost Boys?" Wendy asked herself. "They need me so much.

"But so do our parents," she quickly reminded herself.

Just then Wendy's eyes fell upon a daisy. She bent over and pulled it out of the ground. "Should I stay?" she asked as she pulled a petal from the daisy. "Or should I go?" she asked as she pulled a second petal from the daisy. Wendy did this over and over again until there was only one petal remaining on the daisy.

"Well," she said, "this flower says we should go back home. And I suppose it's right. We'll go back . . . but maybe not just this minute."

Wendy stood. "Hey, Peter, wait up!"

And with that, she flew off after Peter, her mind at ease at last.

True Love

Naveen and Tiana had been turned into frogs by a magic spell. The two had traveled to the bayou and met Mama Odie. The old woman told them that they could lift the spell if Naveen kissed a princess. As luck would have it, Tiana's friend Charlotte was a princess—the Princess of Mardi Gras. But she would only be a princess until midnight.

Now Tiana and Naveen had to find a way back to New Orleans, and fast!

Tiana's alligator friend Louis led the two frogs to the steamship that was coming downriver, taking costume-clad revelers to Mardi Gras. Tiana, Naveen, Louis, and Ray the firefly climbed on board.

Naveen sighed. He would like to have his dream come true, too. Mama Odie had helped him realize something important: what mattered more than anything else to him was Tiana.

"I am in love with Tiana," he confided to his friend, Ray. "I can no longer marry Miss Charlotte LaBouff."

Naveen knew he could marry Charlotte and become rich, but with Tiana he would be rich in love!

"I will find another way to get Tiana her restaurant," he resolved as he prepared a candlelit dinner on the roof of the boat. "I will get a job. Maybe two. Maybe three."

Full of good intentions, he went looking for Tiana.

"I just wanted to show you a little something to celebrate our last night together as frogs," he said, showing her the table.

"All my years, no one's ever done anything like this for me," Tiana said.

Naveen had finally built up the courage to make his declaration when Tiana cried, "There it is!" It was the sugar mill where she wanted to open her restaurant. "Can't you just see it lit up, like the Fourth of July?" she said.

Tiana explained that someone else had bid on the sugar mill. If she didn't come up with more money by the next day, she was going to lose her dream forever.

Hearing these words, Naveen quickly changed his mind. He would rather sacrifice himself and marry Charlotte than cause Tiana any unhappiness. And losing her restaurant would definitely make her unhappy. It seemed he had no choice.

The Show Must Go On

The wind whistled around the Big Top, pulling the canvas tent that Dumbo was holding out of reach of his small trunk.

"I'll get it," Dumbo's mother said as the tent flapped over their heads.

If the weather hadn't been so terrible, Dumbo thought, he could have flown up to grab the edge of the tent. But the whipping wind was too much, even for Dumbo's winglike ears.

At last, standing on her back legs, Mrs. Jumbo caught the canvas in her trunk. She pulled it taut and let the workmen tie it off. But Dumbo noticed several new rips in the fabric.

The Ringmaster had noticed the rips, too. He ordered the clowns to sew them up. "The repairs must be finished by showtime!"

Dumbo felt terrible. All the circus performers, animals, and workmen were working hard in the storm. He had made even more work by letting the canvas get torn. And now the Ringmaster's mood was as foul as the weather!

A blast of cold air blew across the field and whirled the Ringmaster's black top hat off his head.

"That does it!" the Ringmaster yelled.

"There will be no show tonight!"

Dumbo could not believe his ears. The announcement was even enough to wake Timothy Q. Mouse from his nap in a nearby bale of hay.

"No show? I can't believe it!" the little mouse cried.

The rest of the circus folk couldn't believe it, either. They silently continued to set up.

Suddenly, Dumbo noticed something. The Ringmaster's hat was caught on the flagpole, high over the Big Top. Perhaps he could get it for him?

Bravely, Dumbo took off. The wind was strong, but he tucked his head down and flapped his ears hard. When the wind calmed for a moment, the small elephant saw his chance. He grabbed the top hat and quickly flew to the ground.

Shyly, Dumbo held out the hat to the Ringmaster.

"Thank you, Dumbo." The Ringmaster took his hat gratefully. He looked around at all the people and animals still hard at work. He looked a little embarrassed. As he placed the hat on his head, he shouted, "The show must go on!"

The Horse Charmer

Rapunzel had hair with magical healing powers. She had been kidnapped as a baby by a woman who used her to stay forever young. The woman locked her away in a tower and never let her out.

Flynn was a thief who was only interested in getting rich. He had stolen the royal crown, and now he was on the run from the castle guards. But Rapunzel had taken the crown and wouldn't give it back until Flynn took her where she wanted to go.

Now Flynn and Rapunzel were camping in the woods. When they had started their journey, Flynn had just wanted to get back the crown. But now he genuinely wanted to help Rapunzel make her dream come true: to see the floating lanterns being launched tomorrow night.

Flynn awoke the next morning feeling what he thought was rain. *Plip!* A drop of water splashed on his forehead. *Plop!* Another fell on his cheek.

The thief opened his eyes . . . and found himself face-to-face with Maximus, the captain of the guard's horse! Maximus was soaking wet because he had just come out of the flooded tunnel where he had been chasing Flynn the night before.

The two enemies immediately started fighting. Soon the noise of their struggle woke Rapunzel from her sleep.

The horse was holding Flynn by the foot when the girl reached them. Rapunzel took hold of Flynn's arm. Then she turned to the horse. "Easy boy," she said. "That's it. Now sit."

Maximus was enchanted by the pretty young girl, and as Flynn looked on, the horse began to obey her like a well-behaved dog!

"The thing is," Rapunzel told Maximus, "I need you not to get him arrested. Just for twenty-four hours and then you can chase each other to your heart's content. Okay?"

Rapunzel paused and then added, "It's also my birthday . . . just so you know."

Maximus groaned and stretched out his hoof as a gesture of peace. The thief agreed to shake his hoof, wide-eyed in disbelief. He had heard stories about snake charmers, but never about a horse charmer!

Oliver's Sleepover

Oliver couldn't wait. At last, Jenny's limo pulled up to the docks. Even before the chauffeur could open the door, Oliver leaped out the window and began racing toward the barge. Then, remembering Jenny, he stopped, turned around, and waved his paw in her direction.

"Good-bye, Oliver!" she called. "Have a fun sleepover!"

Don't worry, thought Oliver. I will!

This was the first time, you see, that Oliver had been back to the barge since he'd gone to live in Jenny's mansion. And though he loved Jenny dearly, boy, did he miss his friends!

"Tito! Einstein! Francis! Rita!" Oliver called as he ran in to find his four-footed friends waiting for him.

"Hey! What about me?" barked a voice from the back of the barge.

"Dodger!" yelled Oliver. He leaped up on the shaggy dog and gave him a friendly face rub. "It's so good to see you!"

"So how's life in the mansion?" Dodger asked.

"I can't complain," said Oliver.

He told his friends about his latest cruise on Jenny's yacht. "All those fish!" he said dreamily. Then he told them about her house in the country. "The best part is just lying out in the sun! You've got to come over and visit us someday!"

Just then, Fagin walked in with a great big tray. "Oliver, my good friend! Welcome back! I do hope you're hungry!"

Oliver's eyes grew wide as he took in the piles of hot dogs, chicken fingers, and fish sticks (his favorite!) on Fagin's tray. Oliver and the dogs dug in and ate . . . and ate . . . until they could not eat another bite. Then it was time for games!

Fagin dealt out some playing cards.

"I'm gonna stay up all night!" Oliver cried.

"Whatever you say, little buddy," Dodger said. "It's your night."

So they played a little Go Fish, then some Duck, Duck, Goose. Then Fagin told them some of Oliver's favorite spooky stories. When he was done, Dodger turned to Oliver.

"So, what's next, little buddy?" he asked.

But Oliver didn't answer. . . . He was fast asleep!

A Happy Ending

Lizzy lived in the English countryside. One day, she discovered a curious little fairy named Tinker Bell!

Tinker Bell and Lizzy became friends, and Tink realized that the little girl was sad because her father was always too busy to play with her. He was a scientist named Dr. Griffiths, and he didn't believe in fairies. Tink had proven him wrong by showing herself to him! But instead of admitting the truth, Dr. Griffiths had tried to catch Tink and bring her to the museum. Vidia had pushed Tinker Bell out of the way and been captured instead!

Lizzy and the fairies had managed to catch up with Dr. Griffiths just in time and had finally convinced him to believe in the magic of fairies.

Vidia was reunited with her fairy friends and then everyone—including Dr. Griffiths—received a generous sprinkling of pixie dust to fly back home!

The next day, the humans and the fairies enjoyed a picnic together.

"Isn't this pleasant, Father?" asked Lizzy.

"I can't imagine anything better," he answered. "Although chiming Big Ben comes a close second!"

Tink and Vidia sat together, sipping their tea. Before this adventure, Vidia had preferred to be alone. But now, Vidia was learning the importance of friendship. It was only by working as a team that she and the fairies had managed to save Tink from being a museum exhibit!

Not only did Vidia and Tink know each other better now, but they had actually become good friends!

A little while later, everyone settled in to hear Dr. Griffiths read from Lizzy's fairy field journal. Tinker Bell had helped the little girl to fill the journal with facts about fairies—where they lived, what they liked to eat, and much more! It made for magical reading.

Just then, Tinker Bell's friend Terence arrived. He had been delivering pixie dust to all the fairies who were busy working on the mainland.

"Well," Terence said, "you found something to fix after all!"

Tink looked at Lizzy snuggled close to her father.

"I guess I did," she replied with a smile.

Flower's Power

It was a warm summer afternoon in the forest, and a shy little skunk named Flower was playing a game of hide-and-seek. He had been looking for his friends for quite a while.

"Come out, come out, wherever you are!" Flower called. "I give up."

"*Surprise!*" shouted Thumper, bursting out of a thicket. "Here I am! *Ugh!*" Thumper wrinkled his nose. "What's that *smell?*"

Flower blushed bright pink. "Sorry," he said miserably. "I sprayed. It happens when I get scared."

"*Whew!*" Thumper waved his paw in front of his face. "You should warn us before you let out that kind of stink!"

"Well, *you* should warn *me* before you jump out like that," Flower said. "Anyway, it'll go away . . . in a day or two."

But a day or two was too long for his friends to wait. The smell was just too strong!

"Sorry," Bambi told Flower. "I, uh, think my mother's calling me."

"Me, uh, too," Faline gasped. "See you later, Flower . . . in a day or two."

And the next thing he knew, Flower was all alone.

Poor Flower. No matter what his parents said, being a skunk stunk!

And that's why Flower wouldn't have been very surprised if, two days later, his friends had still stayed away. But to his bashful pleasure, there, bright and early, were Bambi and Faline, with Thumper hopping close behind.

"Want to play?" Bambi asked Flower.

"Anything but hide-and-seek!" said Flower.

"How about tag?" said Thumper. "Ready or not, you're It!"

But before the game could begin, a soft *crunch, crunch* of leaves made the friends turn.

"Wha-wha-what's that?" Bambi said, staring straight into a hungry-looking red face.

"That's a fox!" said Thumper.

"A fox?" shrieked Flower. "Oh, no!" He spun around and lifted his tail and buried his head in fear.

The next thing the friends knew, the hungry fox was running away, whimpering and rubbing his nose.

"Sorry," Flower said with a sigh, blushing.

"Don't be!" said Bambi and Thumper.

And do you know what? Flower wasn't!

Ariel's New Move

Ariel had fallen in love with Prince Eric from afar—she was a mermaid living in the ocean, and he was a human living on the land. In order to meet him, Ariel had convinced a sea witch to change her into a human. She had paid for the transformation with her voice.

Once on land, the human Ariel had found her beloved prince! The only problem was that he didn't recognize her. And Ariel couldn't speak to explain who she was. But she wasn't worried. She knew he would fall in love with her.

"Are you hungry?" the prince asked. Eric gestured toward a restaurant and looked at Ariel expectantly.

Ariel smiled and nodded, although she was a little wary of eating. Humans ate fish, and she could not help but think of her best friend, Flounder. But she wanted to please the prince. Surely there was something she could eat that wasn't seafood.

The restaurant was nearly empty. Eric and Ariel sat at a table for two as the owner approached.

"What'll it be, dear?" a woman with warm brown eyes and white hair asked, looking kindly at Ariel.

"She'll have . . . the soup?" Eric looked at Ariel for confirmation. Ariel nodded. "And I will have the specialty of the house."

Ariel was glad that Eric didn't seem to mind talking for her, though she desperately wanted to speak for herself and tell him how much she enjoyed being with him.

Just then, the restaurant's owner sat down in front of a box with black and white keys.

Ariel had never seen a piano before. She had never heard one, either. She was enchanted by the music. She stood and began to sway, but her new legs were so awkward, she stumbled.

Suddenly, Eric's strong arm was around Ariel's waist. With his other arm, he took Ariel's hand in his. Ariel looked startled.

"Haven't you ever danced before?" the prince asked.

Ariel shook her head shyly.

"I'll show you," the prince said, smiling at her. He whirled Ariel around the floor.

The mermaid princess was a natural. She spun and smiled, glad that they had found a way to communicate without words.

The Late Shift

The shift on the Scare Floor at Monsters, Inc., had just ended when Sulley pulled Mike aside.

"Mike, our paperwork is always late," he said. "I'm worried about us getting a bad reputation."

"You're right, Sulley," Mike said earnestly. "From now on, I'm a new monster. You and Celia will be so proud of me—uh-oh . . ."

"What is it, Mike?" Sulley asked.

"Oh, nothing!" Mike grinned. "Sulley, I'll see you later. I've got lots of catching up to do. Paperwork, here I come!"

As soon as Sulley was gone, Mike's smile faded. "What do I do?" he cried. "I have a date with Celia, and I'm already late!" Finally, Mike came to a decision. "I'll catch up tomorrow," he said to himself.

Mike headed for the locker room, whistling a jaunty tune. He had just entered the quiet, empty room when he heard a noise.

"Who's there?" he asked nervously.

"Gagoooo," said the voice.

That was definitely a kid! Mike turned to run—but he tripped over a can of odorant someone had left on the floor and went flying across the room. Footsteps sounded behind him. Mike looked up, expecting to see a human kid. But instead he saw Sulley!

"What gives?" he asked Sulley.

Sulley was laughing so hard, he couldn't even talk. Finally, he said, "I just couldn't resist! After you shooed me out I ran into Celia, who told me about your date. I knew you would rather skip the paperwork than disappoint Celia."

Mike nodded, embarrassed.

"But I told her that you were really behind on your work," Sulley continued, "and I asked if it would be okay for you two to have your date tomorrow night instead."

Mike looked up, surprised. That hadn't even occurred to him. "Did she say yes?" he asked.

"She sure did," Sulley said. "And she also said that since I'm your partner and all, I should really stay here to help you catch up. So, here I am! Now, let's grab some sludgesicles and get to work."

"Okay, Sulley," said Mike. And the two monsters went off to show that paperwork what they were made of.

The Wrong Gift

"Wow, Flounder, everyone's here!" cried Ariel. Mermaids and mermen had come from all over the ocean to wish Ariel's sister Aquata a happy birthday. Unfortunately, Ariel still needed to pick out a gift for her sister.

Ariel and Flounder left the party and swam to her secret cave.

"How about this?" asked Flounder, holding a pretty pink flower.

"Too ordinary," said Ariel.

"Or this?" suggested Flounder, nudging a single gold earring.

"Too small," said Ariel. Suddenly, Ariel noticed a music box. "This is it!" she cried. "The perfect gift! I've listened to this one again and again, and it plays a really beautiful song."

Ariel swam back to the celebration. Beside King Triton, Aquata sat on a clamshell. One by one, the guests presented her with their birthday gifts.

While Ariel waited her turn in line, Sebastian the crab swam by. "Hello, Ariel," he said. "What gift do you have for Aquata?"

When Ariel proudly told Sebastian, his jaw nearly dropped to the ocean floor.

"Are you out of your mind?" he cried.

Ariel's eyes widened. Sebastian was right! King Triton hated humans. And Ariel was not supposed to have anything from their world. That's exactly why she'd kept her cave a secret!

Suddenly, King Triton's deep voice bellowed, "Ariel, you're next."

Ariel hid the present behind her back.

"What gift do you have for your eldest sister?" asked Triton.

"Uh . . ." Ariel began.

"A song!" Sebastian announced.

Ariel racked her brain for a song to sing, and then she hit on it! She opened her mouth and sang the melody from the music box.

When she finished, Flounder swam behind her, replacing the gift in her hand with a beautiful starfish for Aquata's hair.

"It's beautiful!" said Aquata. "And so was your song!"

King Triton smiled approvingly, and Ariel sighed with relief. How she wished her father would change his mind about humans!

"I'd give almost anything to see what the human world is like," she told Flounder. "Do you think my father will ever understand?"

"Maybe he will," said Flounder.

A Relaxing Picnic

"What a lovely day for a picnic!" Snow White cried as she arrived at the Dwarfs' cottage for a visit one spring morning.

"We can't have a picnic," Grumpy said. "We have to work."

"But we've been working so hard in the diamond mine." Sleepy yawned. "Can't we take a day off?"

The other Dwarfs cheered—all except for Grumpy. He just folded his arms and frowned.

"Please don't worry, Grumpy," said Snow White. "A relaxing picnic will cheer you up."

"I doubt it," he grumbled.

"Now, what shall we rake—I mean take—on our picnic?" Doc asked.

"How about some porridge?" said Sleepy with a yawn.

"That's not a very good picnic food," said Snow White. "It's much more fun to pack foods you can eat without spoons or forks."

"How about fruit?" asked Doc.

"And cookies!" suggested Happy.

"And hard-boiled eggs," added Sneezy.

"Wonderful!" exclaimed Snow White. The Dwarfs helped Snow White pack the perfect lunch for their picnic.

"After lunch, we'll want to play," said Snow White. "So you should pack up some things to play with."

They did, and then they were off, hiking through the forest. When they came to a clearing with a babbling brook, Snow White spread a blanket on the grass, and they all sat down to eat.

After lunch, Doc and Happy played checkers, Sleepy took a nap, and Dopey launched an enormous blue kite. Snow White watched Dopey as he ran through the meadow. She clapped when the wind took the kite up in the air. But then the kite lifted Dopey off the ground, too!

"Oh, my!" cried Snow White. "Someone help! Dopey is flying away!"

Grumpy, who'd been pouting by the brook, jumped to his feet. He raced after Dopey. Huffing and puffing, he followed the kite up one hill and down another. Finally, Grumpy grabbed Dopey. Snow White cheered.

Still huffing and puffing, Grumpy collapsed next to the princess on the picnic blanket. "Jiminy Cricket!" he cried. "I can't wait to get back to the diamond mine tomorrow. Relaxing picnics are way too much work!"

Hide-and-Seek

Pixie Hollow was quiet and still. The fairies were playing hide-and-seek, and Tinker Bell was IT!

Tinker Bell looked behind a spiderweb and under a pinecone. Then she saw a bright light shining behind a leaf. Only one fairy glowed that brightly.

"Fira!" Tink yelled.

"You found me!" Fira said, giggling.

Tink couldn't stay to talk. She had other fairies to find!

Tinker Bell started searching again. Bright blue footprints crossed her path. The footprints led over some pebbles and down to the river.

There Tink saw Bess hiding among the pussy willows.

"How did you find me?" Bess asked.

Tink pointed to the art-talent fairy's feet. The bottoms of her shoes were covered in blue paint!

"Oh, drat!" Bess exclaimed. "I spilled some paint in my room today. I must have stepped in it!"

Tink found Silvermist behind a rainspout and Fawn in a bird's nest.

But no matter how hard she looked, Tink could not find Beck.

The fairies explored every garden and searched over the meadow, the lagoon, and the fairy-dust mill.

Tink tugged at her bangs. She was stumped! Beck was usually the easiest fairy to find.

Today Beck was not just an animal-talent fairy— she was a master hider!

Tink was about to yell "Come on out, Beck!" But before she did, a soft sound reached her ears.

Tink followed the noise. It was coming from a hollow log.

She poked her head inside. There she found Beck curled up with a family of hedgehogs!

"Wake up, sleepyhead!" Tink sang out.

Beck opened her eyes and yawned. "You found me already?" Beck asked.

"Already?" Tink cried. "I've been looking for hours! Beck, you are the last hide-and-seek fairy!"

"I am?" Beck asked. "How nice!"

And with that, she rolled over and went back to sleep.

Tink sighed. Beck and the hedgehogs looked so cozy.

Tink pushed Beck over a little. She was tired after all that looking.

As Tink's eyes closed, she heard a voice call, "Tink? Beck? Where are you?"

Oliver Plays Piano

"I've got to get rid of that kitten," Georgette the poodle muttered.

Georgette was used to being the only pet in Jenny's house. But now there was also a little lost kitten named Oliver.

Georgette waited until everyone had gone to bed. Then she tiptoed over to Oliver, grabbed the sleeping kitten, tossed him inside the big piano, and shut the lid. *Bang!*

Inside the piano, Oliver yawned and looked around. He was surprised to find himself in the dark wooden box. He began to move around, trying to find a way out, but every time he moved, his paws hit the piano strings. *Plink! Plunk!*

Oliver started moving faster, hitting note after note and chord after chord. "This is fun!" he exclaimed. *Plunk! Bing! Plink!* "I'm playing piano, just like Jenny!"

Soon, the terrible racket woke everyone in the house!

"What is that horrid noise?" cried Winston the butler. He hopped out of bed and hurried into the living room.

Georgette was standing nearby, doing her very best to look innocent.

"It's that cat!" Winston huffed. "That creature is just too noisy. It's got to go!"

"Success!" Georgette said to herself— until Jenny appeared in her nightgown.

The little girl rushed past the butler and opened the lid of the piano. When she saw Oliver inside, she squealed, "How cute!"

The butler scratched his head. "Cute?"

"Oliver is trying to play a song on the piano," said Jenny, "just like he saw me do earlier today. What a wonderful kitty you are!"

Jenny hugged Oliver, and he began to purr. When the butler saw how much Jenny loved Oliver, his heart melted. "Oh, well," he said. "I guess a little noise isn't the end of the world. Off to bed with you now, Jenny."

"Good night," Jenny said. Then she kissed Oliver's head and told him, "You must go to bed now, too. Let me tuck you in."

Before she left, Jenny patted her poodle's head and said, "Oh, Georgette, aren't we lucky to have a new friend like Oliver in the house!"

"Drat!" Georgette said to herself. "I'd say it's that little fur ball who's the lucky one!"

Month-o-Grams

"What are you doing, Dot?" Flik asked.

Dot was sitting on the floor surrounded by acorns, leaves, dried flowers, sap, and little pots of berry juice.

"I'm making month-o-grams!" she said.

"Oh, right, excellent!" Flik exclaimed. "Month-o-gram, of course!" Then his smile faded. "Uh, Dot? What's a month-o-gram?"

"You've never made a month-o-gram?" Dot asked.

"Apparently not." Flik was beginning to feel sheepish.

"Well, don't worry," Dot told him. "We're in luck! Today's the fifth of the month, and that's exactly when month-o-grams are sent out."

Dot thrust a handful of leaves, some berry ink, and a writing splinter at Flik. "Get started!" she said.

"What do I do?" Flik was nervous.

"Just take the leaf." Dot demonstrated. "Then decorate it and write something nice on it."

"Who do you send month-o-grams to?" Flik wanted to know.

"Everybody!" Dot exclaimed. "The Blueberries send them to our family and friends every month to let them know we care."

Flik and Dot got to work. Soon they were surrounded by piles of month-o-grams, enough for every ant in the entire colony.

"Flik, it's getting late," Dot said. "We had better start delivering these."

Just then, two worker ants rounded a corner and bumped right into each other. They tumbled down, tangled up in a jumble of legs and antennae.

"Hey, watch where you're going," they growled at each other.

"Let's give them a month-o-gram," Dot whispered.

Dot and Flik walked up to the ants, helped them untangle themselves, and handed each of them a month-o-gram of his own.

"Happy September!" Flik and Dot cheered.

The ants smiled broadly. They hugged Dot. They hugged Flik. They hugged each other, and then they strolled off together, leg-in-leg.

"See!" Dot told Flik. "It works!"

Flik and Dot set out to make the rest of their deliveries. They handed a month-o-gram to every ant they saw, spreading happiness and cheer throughout all of Ant Island.

Aurora's Royal Wedding

Princess Aurora and Prince Phillip were to be married. But there were so many things to plan!

"Everything seems well in hand, Your Majesty," said Flora to the queen.

The queen smiled. "Yes, it does, and I couldn't be more delighted. I'll leave you now, Aurora, to enjoy the fun of choosing a cake."

"Thank you, Mother," said Aurora, but she was feeling nervous. She had yet to make any royal decisions on her own.

The royal cooks burst into her room with huge, lavish cakes to choose from. Aurora looked worried.

"What is it, dear?" asked Fauna.

Aurora sighed. "I don't know how to be a princess. What if I'm not a very good one?"

"Nonsense," said Merryweather. "You'll be the finest princess this kingdom has ever seen."

When Prince Phillip came by later, he invited Aurora to join him for a walk.

On their walk, Aurora confided in Phillip. "I'm not sure I know how to act like a princess. I can't even choose a cake!"

Phillip looked at her with love. "My dear, you will be a wonderful princess. But if you're worried, I think I may know someone who can help."

Back at the palace, Phillip spoke to the queen. "Your Majesty," he said, "I think Aurora would like some help—from her mother."

The queen went to find her daughter. "Dear Aurora, I understand that you are worried about being a princess, but being a princess isn't about what you do. Rather, it's about who you are. A princess is honest, thoughtful, clever, and kind. And there is no doubt that you are all of these things."

"Oh, thank you, Mother!" Aurora said. "Now, will you help me figure out what kind of wedding cake we should have? There are so many choices."

The queen smiled. "Your father and I had a very simple cake. I think the same thing would be perfect for you."

On her wedding day, Aurora looked and felt every bit a princess. And the cake was delicious!

A Mother's Touch

Work was piling up in the offices of Monsters, Inc. Celia was out sick with the flu, and there was no one to cover for her. Just then, Mike had an idea.

"I'll call my mom. She'd love to help out," he said.

And so, later that day, in walked Mrs. Wazowski. Sulley and Mike went off to discuss some new plans for the laugh factory, while Mrs. W. made herself at home—very at home. When Sulley and Mike returned at lunchtime, they barely recognized the reception area. Mike's mom had hung ruffled curtains everywhere.

Later that day, Mike rehearsed some new comedy routines. "What do monsters eat for breakfast?" asked Mike. "Anything they want!"

Sulley and Mike laughed until their sides hurt. "I couldn't help but overhear," said Mike's mom. "It might be funnier if you wore a silly hat."

Sulley shot Mike a look.

"Thanks, Mom," said Mike.

A little while later, Sulley and Mike summoned Mrs. W. over the intercom to come to the Laugh Floor. "Um, Mom, do you know anything about this?" Mike asked nervously. He pointed to the card keys, which were now filed by color, making it impossible for anyone to know which card belonged to which door.

Sulley turned and spoke to Mike through gritted teeth. "She's your mother. Do something!"

Just before the day was through, Mike went to the front desk, sat down, and took his mother's hand. He'd never fired his mother before. This wasn't going to be easy!

"Mom, you know I love you. And you make a terrific receptionist, but—"

Just then, Celia walked through the front door.

"Googly Bear!" Celia cried.

"Schmoopsie-Poo! What are you doing here?" Mike asked. "You're supposed to be home in bed."

"I couldn't stand being away from you one day longer," Celia gushed.

Mrs. Wazowski beamed. "He is irresistible, isn't he? Well, I guess my work here is done!" she said, gathering up her things.

Suddenly, Mrs. W. stopped. "Oh, Mikey, what were you about to tell me?"

"Not a thing, Mom," said Mike as he gave her a kiss. "Not a thing!"

Buzz to the Rescue

"There you go, pardners," Andy said as he packed Woody, Jessie, and Bullseye into his backpack. He was taking them to Cowboy Camp. Jessie couldn't wait!

Just then, Andy's mom poked her head into his room. "You know the rules. You can only take one toy to camp with you."

Andy sighed. He lifted Jessie and Bullseye out of the bag and placed them on the windowsill. Then he left his room. Jessie climbed down from the window and flopped into a box full of books.

Suddenly, a Green Army Man yelled, "Red alert!" Someone was coming. It was Molly's babysitter. She picked up the box of books and took it to the attic. The toys looked at each other in shock. Jessie was still inside the box!

"We've got to do something!" Buzz cried.

In the attic, Jessie looked for a way back to Andy's bedroom. But the attic door wouldn't budge. Suddenly, she had an idea. She found a jump rope, made a lasso, and threw the loop over the window lock. Jessie opened the window a few inches and crawled outside.

Just then, she heard someone fiddling with the attic doorknob. Oh, no, she thought. The babysitter! Jessie grabbed the rope and jumped.

But the noise wasn't the babysitter at all. It was the other toys opening the attic door to rescue Jessie. Buzz gasped when he spotted the open window. Then he saw Jessie hanging on to a jump rope.

"Don't let go, Jessie!" he shouted. "I'm coming for you!"

Buzz spread his wings. Then, taking a deep breath, he dove out the window. Jessie looked up and saw her friend falling toward her. Thinking fast, she swung her legs out and caught Buzz. The two toys swung forward—right through Andy's open window! The rest of the toys raced down the stairs to Andy's room.

"We saved Jessie!" Buzz announced.

Jessie laughed. "Saved *me*?" She was the one who had rescued Buzz!

Jessie looked at her friends. They were all smiling. "Thanks, everyone!" she said. "Even though I didn't get to go to Cowboy Camp, this has been the best adventure ever! Yee-hah!"

Writing a Poem

One day in Wonderland, Tweedledum and Tweedledee decided to write a poem about writing poems. So, they put their heads together and set to rhyming:

So you want to write a poem.
You do? Is that true?
Writing poems is usually
Easy to do.
Sun rhymes with fun;
Dew rhymes with shoe;
End sounds like friend,
And other words too.
Pet sounds like net;
That one's no sweat.
Many a word
Will rhyme with day,
Like hay and say
And even bouquet.
Words with long "e" sounds
Are always a cinch.
Bean tree and sweet pea
And flea, at a pinch.
But then there are toughies
Like cousin and buzzin'.
There are rhymes for them,
But they're not dime-a-dozen
Also tricky is icky
And apple and stronger.
Although you can rhyme 'em,
It may take you longer.
There's whoozit and whatsit
And hogwash and hooey.
You try to rhyme those,
And your brain goes kablooey.
So, when writing a poem,
Keep one thing in mind:
Avoid all the hard words
And you'll do just fine!
This poem is over.
This poem is penned.
This poem is finished,
So this is the . . .

Tweedledum looked up. "That's it," he said.

Tweedledee racked his brain. "What rhymes with 'penned'?" he said. "'Bend'?" He tried it out: "'This poem is finished, so this is the bend.' No, no, that doesn't seem right."

Tweedledum took a stab at it. "There's 'pretend'. 'This poem is finished, so this is pretend.' Nah, I don't like it."

Tweedledee sighed. "We'll never think of a good rhyme for the end of this poem."

"You're right," said Tweedledum. "I guess we'll have to leave it unfinished."

So that's what they did. And that was the end.

Jasmine and the Star of Persia

Every night, Jasmine and Aladdin gazed up at the sky. The princess loved stories about the stars.

"What's that star?" Jasmine asked one evening.

"The Star of Persia," said Aladdin. "It's named after a legendary jewel that belonged to a kind and beautiful queen. When she died, they hid the jewel away in a tower, sure that no one would be worthy of its beauty again."

Jasmine's eyes shone. "Is that story true?"

Aladdin shrugged. "I don't know. But there is one way to find out."

The next morning, Jasmine and Aladdin set off on the Magic Carpet. Before long, a tall tower rose from a square in a tiny kingdom. But when they reached the tower, they discovered that it was locked. Without a key there was little chance of getting in.

All of a sudden, a guard spoke up. "What do you want?" he demanded.

"We've heard about the Star of Persia," Jasmine explained, "and we've come to see the jewel."

"That's impossible," the guard said. "No one can see the jewel except a queen

as fair and kind as our own."

"Well," said Aladdin, "this is Princess Jasmine. She's not a queen, but she will be."

"I'm very fair," Jasmine assured him.

The guard's eyes searched the square. "Fair enough to solve the argument happening over there?" he asked.

Jasmine made her way across the square and solved the argument. But the guard still would not let her in. Jasmine decided to get a drink from the fountain and then leave the city.

But Jasmine found the fountain dry. However, as she held a jar under it, a stream of water came out.

"The fountain!" blurted the guard. "It hasn't had water since our queen was alive!"

The people bowed and the guard unlocked the tower door. He led Jasmine to the highest room where the gleaming Star of Persia sat.

The guard offered the jewel to Jasmine. "You have proved you are worthy enough to keep it. But promise to come and visit us whenever you can."

"Oh, I will!" exclaimed Jasmine.

And because she was not only fair and kind, but also honest, she most certainly did.

The Hic-hic-hiccups

"What a day!" Pumbaa said as he led Simba and Timon through the forest. They were headed to the pond.

"What a day, indeed," Timon agreed.

"*Hic!*" said Simba.

"What was that?" Timon cried.

"Don't be scared. It's just that I have the—*hic!*—the hiccups," Simba explained.

"I'll tell you what to do," Timon said. "Forget about it! They'll go away on their own—eventually."

"Forget about it? *Hic!* But I can't roar," Simba explained. And to demonstrate, he opened his mouth really wide. Just as he was about to roar, he hiccupped! "See?" he said sadly.

"Have you tried licking tree bark?" Pumbaa asked.

"Licking tree bark?" said Simba.

"It always works for me," Pumbaa explained.

"That or closing your eyes, holding your nose, and jumping on one foot while saying your name backward five times fast."

Timon watched Simba hop around on one foot, holding his nose with his eyes closed. "Abmis, Abmis, Abmis— *hic!* It's not working!" Simba cried.

"Maybe there's something caught in his throat," Timon offered.

"There's nothing caught in his throat," Pumbaa said.

"How do you know?" Timon asked.

"I just know about these things," Pumbaa answered.

Right on cue, Simba interrupted their argument with the biggest hiccup of all.

"*HIC!*"

And the biggest fly you've ever seen came soaring out of Simba's mouth! It flew right into a tree and crashed to the ground.

The fly stood up groggily and shook itself off.

"It's about time, buddy!" the fly said to Simba.

Simba was about to reply, but he was interrupted by two voices, shouting in unison—

"DINNER!"

The fly gave a frightened squeak and flew off as Timon and Pumbaa both pounced on the spot where it had been just a moment earlier.

Too High a Price to Pay

An evil sorcerer had changed Prince Naveen into a frog. With the help of a magic talisman, he had made Lawrence, a valet, look like Prince Naveen so that he could marry Charlotte, the richest young lady in New Orleans. This way, the sorcerer hoped to get his hands on the girl's fortune!

Naveen mistakenly thought Tiana was a princess, and he kissed her to try to turn himself back into a human—but instead he turned *Tiana* into a frog, too! Although the two were very different, they had fallen in love.

But now the evil sorcerer had managed to capture the frog Naveen! From his balcony, the sorcerer watched the Mardi Gras parade go past. On the main float, Charlotte and the fake Prince Naveen were preparing to get married. The priest had already started the ceremony.

"I object! I object!" cried the frog Naveen, who was locked in a box. He had to stop Charlotte from marrying the fake prince! He bravely managed to launch the box onto the float.

Landing on the float, the firefly heard the frog Naveen calling from inside the box. Ray quickly rescued him and, in a flash, the frog Naveen jumped onto the fake prince and tore the talisman from his neck! The villain changed back into Lawrence.

"Ray!" shouted Naveen. He threw the talisman to the firefly. Ray flew away, but the sorcerer's evil Shadows immediately sprang forward in pursuit.

As the Shadows caught up to the firefly, Ray found Tiana and threw the talisman to her. Tiana tried to run away . . . but the evil sorcerer blocked her way.

With a magic spell, he showed her what her restaurant could look like. "And all you got to do to make this a reality is hand over that little ol' talisman of mine."

But Tiana wasn't so easy to fool. "My daddy never did get what he wanted, but he had what he needed," she said sharply. "He had love. He never lost sight of what was really important, and neither will I!"

As she spoke, she broke the talisman, and the evil sorcerer disappeared into thin air. But had Tiana's dream of opening her own restaurant disappeared, too?

Tree Trouble

Toulouse and Berlioz scampered out the back door of Madame Bonfamille's house. Behind them, Marie trotted in a more ladylike manner, her long white tail swishing back and forth. But even she couldn't stop herself from launching a surprise attack on Toulouse when his back was turned.

"Here I come!" shouted Berlioz as he pounced on his two siblings. Marie escaped, but Berlioz and Toulouse began to wrestle in the leaves.

"I got you both!" Berlioz exclaimed proudly. "I'm clearly the superior pouncer."

"Oh, yeah?" said Toulouse. "If you're so great, let's see you climb to the top of that oak tree." He raised his chin, gesturing to the towering tree above them.

"Gladly," Berlioz replied. He nimbly leaped onto a low branch and began to climb up, up, up the huge tree.

Soon Berlioz was perched on the highest branch.

Toulouse licked his paw. "All right, so you're a good climber," he called up to his brother. "You can come down now."

Berlioz didn't move.

"I said you can come down," Toulouse repeated.

"I—I can't," Berlioz replied. His voice sounded shaky. "I'm stuck." He began to howl. Soon his brother and sister were yowling, too.

It only took a few minutes for Madame Bonfamille to open an upstairs window. She and Duchess stuck their heads out to see what all the noise was about.

"My goodness!" Duchess cried when she spied Berlioz. "What on earth are you doing up there?"

"Don't you worry; we'll be right out to help you," Madame Bonfamille said reassuringly.

A few minutes later, she and Duchess appeared in the yard, followed by a very grumpy-looking Edgar carrying a long ladder.

"Just climb right up and get him, won't you, Edgar?" Madame Bonfamille asked.

Edgar scowled and mumbled something about foolish felines. But he leaned the ladder against the tree trunk and began to climb.

Before long, Berlioz was safely on the ground once again.

Berlioz snuggled against Duchess. He had learned his lesson. He wouldn't give in to any more of Toulouse's challenges . . . at least not ones involving trees!

Patch and the Panther

One dark night, fifteen Dalmatian puppies sat huddled around a black-and-white television set. They watched as Thunderbolt, the canine hero, crept through a deep, dark jungle. Suddenly, Thunderbolt pricked up his ears. The puppies held their breath. Two yellow eyes peered out of the bushes. It was a panther!

"How will Thunderbolt escape the hungry panther?" the TV announcer asked. "Don't miss next week's exciting episode!"

"Aww!" the puppies groaned, disappointed that their favorite show was over.

"All right, kids. Time for bed," Pongo said, shutting off the television with his nose. He watched as the puppies padded upstairs and settled down in their baskets. Then he switched off the light. Moments later, the sound of soft snores filled the room. The puppies were fast asleep.

All except for one. Patch was wide awake. He was still thinking about Thunderbolt and the panther.

"I wish some ol' panther would come around here," Patch said to himself. "I'd

teach him a thing or two."

Outside his room, a floorboard creaked. Patch pricked up his ears. Then he crawled out of his basket to investigate.

The floorboard creaked again. *What if it's a panther?* Patch thought with a shiver. *But I'm not scared of any ol' panther,* he reminded himself.

A shadow flickered across the doorway. The shadow had a long tail. Panthers have long tails, thought Patch. Then two yellow eyes peered out of the darkness.

"Aroooo!" Patch yelped. He turned to run, but he tripped on the rug. In a flash, the panther was on top of him. Patch could feel its hot breath on his neck. He shut his eyes . . .

"Patch, what are you doing out of bed?" the panther asked.

Patch opened his eyes. It was Dad!

"I—I was just keeping an eye out for panthers," Patch explained.

Pongo smiled. "Why don't you get some sleep now?" he suggested. "I can keep an eye out for panthers for a while."

"Okay, Dad," Patch said with a yawn.

Pongo carried Patch back to his basket. In no time at all, the puppy was fast asleep.

The Sapphire Ring

It had been one year since the Prince and Cinderella had married. To celebrate, the Prince decided to hold a ball, and he gave Cinderella a gold ring set with a blue sapphire. But the ring was too large. On the morning of the ball, it slipped off Cinderella's finger.

"Don't worry, Cinderelly," her mouse friends Jaq and Gus piped up. "We'll help you find your ring!"

"Where have you been today?" Jaq asked.

Cinderella thought. "Well, the first thing I did was go to my bedroom to write in my diary." So they hurried to Cinderella's room.

"No ring," Jaq said with a sigh.

"Let's try the kitchen," said Cinderella. "I went there next to make a pot of tea." But the only ring in there was a day-old doughnut.

"Perhaps we should try the library. I read there this afternoon," said Cinderella. They searched high and low among the books, but they could not find Cinderella's sapphire ring.

"I also went to the stables to feed Frou. Perhaps I lost my ring in his stall." The three friends sifted through piles of straw. Still no ring.

Cinderella scratched her head. "There's one more place to look," she said. "The garden!"

The friends searched every blossom until Gus exclaimed, "Cinderelly! I see it!" He picked up a shiny blue object. "Sapphire, Cinderelly?" Gus asked.

Cinderella shook her head. It was just a marble.

"Wait a minute," she said as they stopped by the well. "I drew some water from the well. Could it have fallen in there?"

Cinderella lowered Jaq and Gus into the well. "Do you see anything?" she called down.

"Eek!" came Gus's cry from inside the well.

Cinderella pulled up the bucket as fast as she could. "What did you see?" she cried.

"Oh, nothing," said Gus slyly. "Nothing . . . but Cinderelly's ring!"

"My heroes!" cried Cinderella. "Wait until I tell the Prince how you saved our special day!"

At the ball, Cinderella and the Prince raised their glasses to Gus and Jaq, their guests of honor, and thought how lucky they were to have such wonderful friends.

An Uncle Mickey Day

Morty and Ferdie Mouse were oh-so-very excited. Today was their number one favorite kind of day—an Uncle Mickey day! That meant their Uncle Mickey was going to take them out to do all kinds of special, surprising things.

"Uncle Mickey!" the twins shouted when he came to pick them up. "What are we doing today?"

"What *aren't* we doing today, you mean," said Mickey. "I thought we'd start with bowling."

At the bowling alley, Morty and Ferdie discovered that if they rolled the bowling ball together, they could knock at least four or five pins down every time. Then it was off to the park for some hide-and-seek and a game of catch.

"I'm hungry," said Morty when at last they stopped to rest.

"Me too," said Ferdie.

"How about a barbecue?" suggested Mickey.

Mickey led the twins to a grill, where he had set up hot dogs, hamburgers, and buns.

"We love barbecues," shouted Morty as he and Ferdie gobbled down their lunches.

"All finished?" asked Mickey. "We'll have to hurry if we're going to go to the carnival."

"All right!" the boys shouted.

After the carnival, where they each won a prize, the boys told Mickey what a fun day it had been.

"Well, it's not over yet," Mickey told them.

"Really?" said Morty.

"What's next?" asked Ferdie.

That's when Mickey held up three tickets—and three mitts. A baseball game! Oh, boy!

There was nothing in the whole wide world that Mickey's nephews liked better than baseball games . . . and popcorn . . . and peanuts . . . and ice cream. And to make things even better, Uncle Mickey caught a foul ball and their favorite team won. They even got to watch fireworks at the end of the game.

"Wow, Uncle Mickey! Thank you so much!" said the twins when they finally returned home, tired and full and very, very happy. "This has been one of the best Uncle Mickey days ever!"

"Oh, this was nothing," said Uncle Mickey. "Just wait until next time!"

The Father of Invention

There was never a dull moment in Belle's and the Prince's castle. Mrs. Potts and the other members of the household bustled about, and Maurice, Belle's father, was always tinkering away on a new invention.

One morning, Maurice wheeled a complicated-looking contraption into the kitchen and presented it to Mrs. Potts. "Just a little something to make your life easier," he said proudly.

"Thank you, Maurice, dear, but . . . what is it?" the housekeeper asked.

"I call it a plate pitcher," answered Maurice. He took a pile of clean plates and loaded them onto a mechanical arm. Then he positioned the machine in front of the open china cabinet. He pressed a button and stood back proudly.

The plate pitcher began to hurl plates this way and that! They smashed against walls and onto the floor.

"Look out, Mrs. Potts!" shouted Maurice as a plate whizzed by her head. Maurice turned the machine off. "I'll just go work out the kinks," he said.

The next day, Maurice came up with another surprise for Mrs. Potts.

"It's for cleaning the carpets," he explained as he pointed to a large metal box with a big hose coming out of it. "No more beating heavy rugs for you!"

Maurice picked up the hose and flipped a switch. Instantly, curtains, pillows, and lamps were sucked toward the nozzle. "Must have made it a tad too powerful," Maurice admitted.

The following day, Maurice had yet another time-saving device for Mrs. Potts. This one was a laundry machine that flooded the entire ground floor of the castle with water and soapsuds.

"Maurice," Mrs. Potts said gently, "it is very sweet of you to want to make my job easier. But I enjoy it. By taking care of the castle, I'm taking care of the people I love." She looked thoughtful for a moment, then added, "But I have to admit, the one thing I would love is something that would make me a nice hot cup of tea at the end of the day."

"I have just the thing!" Maurice replied with a twinkle in his eye.

Mrs. Potts looked slightly worried. "You do?" she asked.

"Yes," Maurice answered. "Me!"

The Best Gift Ever

Other than Dumbo's mother, Mrs. Jumbo, all the elephants at the circus made Dumbo feel like a nobody. But Timothy Q. Mouse was different. Since the day he and Dumbo had met, Timothy had encouraged Dumbo.

Dumbo was so happy to have a friend like Timothy! He wanted to do something nice for him.

Dumbo decided to give Timothy a gift. At feeding time, he put aside a bale of hay. Then he lugged the hay behind the Big Top and looked around for Timothy. He found him lounging in the shadow of the lion's cage and plopped down the hay bale.

"Hiya, Dumbo!" said Timothy. "What's with the hay?"

Using his trunk, Dumbo nudged the hay bale closer to Timothy.

"For me?" Timothy said. "Wow. Uh . . . thanks."

Dumbo's heart sank as he realized that mice didn't eat hay.

The next day, Dumbo came upon a patch of flowers. He picked a nice big bouquet and took it behind the Big Top to Timothy.

"Shucks, Dumbo," said Timothy.

"You shouldn't have." Tiny Timothy took the bouquet from Dumbo's outstretched trunk and promptly fell over, dropping the flowers everywhere.

Sadly, Dumbo realized the bouquet he'd made was too heavy for Timothy to enjoy.

The next day, under the Big Top, Dumbo spotted a bunch of balloons tied to a seat. Those wouldn't be too heavy for Timothy. They stayed up all by themselves. So Dumbo untied them and brought them to Timothy.

But when Timothy took hold of the balloon strings, the helium-filled balloons lifted him right off the ground! Dumbo quickly reached out with his trunk and pulled Timothy back to the ground.

With a disappointed sigh, Dumbo took the balloons back. Would he ever find a good gift for Timothy? he wondered.

"Dumbo," Timothy said, "I wanted to thank you for giving me the best gift ever."

Dumbo's eyes widened in surprise. What could Timothy mean? Every gift he had given him had been wrong.

"You're my best friend," Timothy said. "And that's the best gift I could ever ask for."

Celia's Bad Hair Day

"Some encrusted evening," Mike sang to himself as he danced around the bathroom getting ready for his date. He could not wait to see his girlfriend, Celia.

After pulling his car into the parking lot of the restaurant, Mike hopped out and hurried inside. But as Celia turned toward Mike, he noticed something. Rather than rustling happily, her hair-snakes were writhing angrily!

Mike decided to ignore the grumpy-looking snakes. "How's my little Schmoopsie-Woopsie?" He leaned in to kiss Celia on the cheek, but the closest snake lashed out at him.

"Yowch," Mike exclaimed, jumping back. "Bad hair day, snookums?"

"Oh, Googly Bear." Celia sighed, running her hand through her serpentine tresses. "It's just awful. I'm out of conditioner, my shower went cold on me, and I've been in an awful tangle ever since. Are they terrible?"

Choosing a seat far enough away from his sweetie to avoid being bitten, Mike looked closer. Celia's snakes glared at him, their fangs bared. He had to admit, they were a little knotted, and they did not have their usual body or luster.

"They're not so bad," Mike fibbed. He blew Celia a kiss from across the table and tried to smile. This was not the romantic evening he'd been looking forward to.

At the next table, a pair of many-armed monsters held hands and hands and hands. They rubbed their warty noses together and whispered sweet nothings into each other's many ears. Mike sighed. They looked so cozy. Then he had an idea.

"Excuse me, my sweet." Mike stood up and approached the couple. When he came back to the table, he was holding a large purple hat. "Amelia, Ophelia, Octelia, Bobelia, and Madge," Mike addressed Celia's snakes. "How would you like to cozy up in this until we can get you untangled?"

Celia's snakes cooed in delight.

"Oh, Googly Bear!" Celia cried. She wound her hair-snakes and stuffed them into the hat. "You even know how to fix a bad hair day!"

With her hair contained, Celia gave Mike a big hug and a well-deserved smooch.

From Dream to Reality

Rapunzel had been locked away in a tower her entire life, but now her dream of seeing the floating lights up close was about to come true, with the help of a thief named Flynn.

Rapunzel had hair with magical healing powers. She had been kidnapped as a baby by a woman who used her to stay forever young. The woman locked her away in a tower and never let her out.

But one day, Flynn Rider had come along, and Rapunzel had convinced him to take her to see the floating lights she saw in the sky every year on her birthday. He hadn't wanted to, but she had taken a crown he'd stolen and wouldn't give it back until he brought her. And finally she was here! Tonight she would see the floating lights rise into the sky. When they had walked into town, Rapunzel couldn't believe her eyes. She had never seen so many people! But the people kept stepping on her long hair.

With the help of three little girls, Rapunzel's hair was soon beautifully braided.

As Rapunzel wandered the kingdom, she came across a painting of the lost princess. She had big green eyes, just like Rapunzel.

Finally, it was time to see the lights. Flynn led Rapunzel to a small boat.

"Where are we going?" Rapunzel asked Flynn as he rowed her to a spot in the middle of the water.

"Well, best day of your life, I figured you should have a decent seat," Flynn answered.

Suddenly, the young girl seemed terrified. If her greatest dream came true, what would she dream about then?

But the king and the queen were already launching the first lantern from their balcony. As soon as Rapunzel saw it, she forgot her fears. It was even more beautiful than she had imagined! Soon the sky was filled with hundreds of lanterns.

Flynn handed her a lantern so they could launch it together into the sky. Looking at Flynn, Rapunzel realized she trusted the thief. She decided to give him back the crown.

But Flynn no longer cared about the crown. He had fallen in love with Rapunzel. He just wanted to make her happy.

Sweeter than Clover

"Hi, Bambi," said a soft voice. Bambi looked up from the grass he was eating. Standing there was the pretty young fawn Bambi had met that spring.

"Hi, Faline," Bambi said. "It's nice to see you!"

"It's nice to see you, too," Faline said shyly.

"Faline!" a young male deer called across the meadow. "Come over and play with me!"

Bambi's eyes narrowed. He didn't like the idea of Faline going off to play with someone else.

"No, don't go," he said. But what can I say to make her stay? he wondered.

Suddenly, Bambi had an idea.

"I want to show you something special," he told her.

"Something special?" asked Faline.

"I know where to find the sweetest clover you'll ever taste," Bambi said. Thumper had shown him exactly where to find it.

"Where?" asked Faline.

"Just follow me!" exclaimed Bambi.

He led her across the meadow to the babbling brook. Then he followed the brook all the way up a steep, grassy hill.

Finally, they came to a big waterfall.

"The sweet clover is right here by this weeping willow tree," said Bambi. He couldn't wait to share it with Faline.

But when they got to the tree, there wasn't one single clover blossom left.

"Oh, that Thumper!" complained Bambi. He shook his head. He felt very silly. He'd brought Faline all this way, and now he had nothing special to share with her! Bambi looked up at Faline, but something else caught his eye.

"Look," he whispered. "Up in the sky!"

Faline looked up and gasped.

Shimmering bands of color had formed an arch over the waterfall.

"It's so beautiful," whispered Faline. "I've never seen anything like it."

"Neither have I," said Bambi. "But I remember hearing my mother talk about it. I think it's called a rain . . . bow."

"It's wonderful!" cried Faline.

"I'm glad you think so," said Bambi, a little relieved. "But I'm sorry you came all this way for no clover."

"Oh, Bambi," said Faline. "I came because I wanted to be with you. And besides, a rainbow is a much sweeter surprise than some silly old clover, anyway!"

Playing School

Now, it just so happened that when the wind changed ever so slightly and the leaves began to turn scarlet or golden, Christopher Robin returned to school. Not so surprisingly, his friends in the Wood felt as if they should really do the same.

But *playing* school, as you might suspect, is not as similar to real school as perhaps it should be. And, after sitting at their desks for what seemed like a good three and a quarter hours (but was really just five minutes or so), Winnie the Pooh and his friends came to the conclusion that something rather important in their game of school was missing.

"Perhaps it's time we had a snack," suggested Pooh.

"I don't think that's the problem, Pooh," said Piglet.

"Our problem," announced Owl, "is that we do not have a teacher. Of course, I am quite happy to offer my considerable expertise."

"Just a minute, Owl," Rabbit broke in. "Why is it, exactly, that we should let you be the teacher? Some might say—myself included—that I'm better suited to the job."

Owl scowled. "You?"

"Perhaps we should have a vote," said Piglet. "I'd like to nominate Pooh."

"Me?" Pooh said. "Why, thank you, Piglet. I gladly accept. Now . . . what's a teacher again?"

"Really!" said Owl, with no small amount of scorn. "A teacher, my dear Pooh, is the someone who stands before the class."

"To give out snacks?" asked Pooh.

"No, Pooh," said Owl. "To give out knowledge."

"Oh," said Pooh. "I don't think I'd enjoy that nearly so much."

"Well, if it's all the same to you, and if anyone cares, I'll be the teacher," Eeyore said glumly. "I probably wouldn't have made a good student, anyway."

"Hi-ho!" said Christopher Robin, returning from a thoroughly enjoyable, and very well taught, day at school. "Whatever are you up to?"

"Playing school . . . I think," said Pooh.

"Only we don't have a teacher," Piglet explained.

"I could teach you. I learned ever so many things today," said Christopher Robin.

"Hooray!" cheered Roo. "Let's start right away!"

The Chase

"Whoopee!" Tod cried as he tumbled head over tail toward the water. He hit the surface with a splash. A second later, his friend Copper landed right next to him.

"It sure is a beautiful day," Copper said.

"Yeah, it sure is," Tod agreed.

Suddenly the friends heard a booming voice.

"Copper!" the voice rumbled. It was Amos Slade, Copper's master. Amos was usually grumpy, but right now he sounded angry. "Where are you, mutt?" he shouted.

Tod silently crawled into a hole between two big boulders by the water. He could tell that Amos had his other dog, Chief, with him. Both the man and the dog wanted to catch Tod.

Copper crept up beside his friend. "I'd better go," he said. "Amos sounds awful mad."

"Why don't you sneak back to your barrel so you're there when he gets back?" Tod suggested. "He can't be mad if you're already home when he finds you."

Copper scratched behind his ear. "But he's right in my path, and Chief is with him. Chief will hear me or smell me for sure."

Tod grinned. "You just leave that to me." He winked at his friend and dashed up the hill, right past Amos and Chief.

"There's that varmint fox!" Amos cried as Chief took off after Tod, barking like mad. Amos gave chase, running as fast as he could on his long, skinny legs.

Tod leaped over branches and darted around trees. More than once, Chief got close, his hot breath on Tod's tail. Finally the fox got away.

"Never mind, Chief," Amos said when he finally caught up. "We'll get him later."

Chief gave a final growl, but Tod had already escaped and was dashing home.

Exhausted, Amos and Chief started home, too. By the time they got there, Tod was napping next door in front of Widow Tweed's fireplace. Copper was sitting in his barrel, waiting for his master.

"There you are," Amos grumbled. He shook his head. "And I suppose you've been sitting here almost the whole time. We could have used your help catching that dang fox—it's almost as if you're trying to avoid hunting him!"

My Side of the Story

Perhaps you know the story of how Pocahontas and John Smith made peace between their people. Well, I've got a much more interesting story for you—mine.

My name is Percival, but my friends call me Percy. Once upon a time, I was the pet pug of a very important man named Governor Ratcliffe. I lived a life of luxury. But life felt . . . well, pretty boring.

That all changed the day we arrived on the shores of America. Ratcliffe was after one thing and one thing only—gold. And Ratcliffe didn't care about the people who lived in this new land.

John Smith cared, but I didn't care much for John Smith. He was always trying to pat me on the head.

Not long after we had arrived in the New Land, I was having a bubble bath when suddenly—*splash!*—a raccoon landed in my tub! Well, if there's one thing my mother taught me, it was to avoid all animals without a pedigree. This wild creature was filthy and uncivilized! The raccoon ate my cherries and then ran off. After that, I had one thing on my mind—revenge!

The next time I saw the raccoon, he was eating bones out of my personal bone collection. So I had to chase him—it was a matter of pride! But wouldn't you know it, the brazen little devil trapped me in a hollow log.

That's when I ran into John Smith and Pocahontas. And guess who was with them? That's right. It was that bone-thieving raccoon! He grabbed a little hummingbird and started waving it at me like a sword. It would have been funny if it weren't so annoying!

And then the weirdest thing of all happened—a tree talked to me! Grandmother Willow said I shouldn't chase Meeko. By chasing him, I had started trouble between us; now it was time to stop the fighting. Of course, I understood immediately.

It took the humans a little longer to get the picture, but it all worked out okay in the end. I decided I didn't need my fancy, highfalutin life, so I became a settler and stayed with my new friends! John, however, had to go back to England.

I knew he would miss me. So when he reached out to pat my head, I actually let him.

Great Minds Think Alike

Tito the Chihuahua stopped suddenly in the alleyway and sniffed the air.

"Why'd you stop, shorty?" Einstein the Great Dane complained, shoving the smaller dog with his huge paw.

"For your information," Tito said, "I was locating our next meal."

Einstein looked confused. "You were what?"

Tito sniffed again. "Check it out, *amigo*." He pointed to an apartment window two stories above them. "Up there!"

Einstein lifted his nose and sniffed. "Meat loaf!" he exclaimed hungrily. "But how are we going to get it? It's way up there!"

"Leave it to me," Tito said.

Tito raced across the alley and climbed up a pile of crates. His plan was to reach a clothesline stretching between two buildings and use it as a tightrope to the windowsill

Meanwhile, Einstein noticed a Dumpster pushed up against the wall of the apartment building. If he climbed up there and stood on his hind legs, maybe he would be tall enough to reach the windowsill.

"Ha," Einstein said, "I'll show you that bigger is better, my little friend."

"Oh, yeah?" Tito glared at Einstein. He grabbed the clothesline and began to wriggle his way across.

Einstein clambered atop the Dumpster. He carefully stretched up, up, up. . . . Both dogs reached the windowsill at the same time.

"Hey!" Tito yelped. Someone had taken the meat loaf inside!

"Darn," said Tito. "But hey, Einstein, that was a good trick with the Dumpster. Do you think you could do it with me standing on your head? Because there are a lot of clotheslines that are too high for me to reach."

"Sure!" said Einstein. "I could lift you up to a clothesline, and— Hey! I smell chicken potpie!"

Sure enough, there, on another windowsill, was a steaming dish. And right under that window was a clothesline—a clothesline that would normally be too high for Tito to reach by himself. But with a little help . . .

Tito looked at Einstein. "Are you thinking what I'm thinking?"

Einstein grinned. "Great minds think alike!"

A Dance with Snow White

No one could remember a more glorious day. The sun was shining, the sky was blue, and the Prince was holding a glorious royal ball for his true love, Snow White. Nearly everyone in the land had come to join in the fun, including seven rather short men who loved Snow White very much. They had never been to a royal ball before!

After a great banquet, the guests entered the ballroom.

"Gawrsh," Bashful said, hiding behind Doc, amazed by the marble and chandeliers.

As the orchestra began to play, the Prince took Snow White in his arms and the happy couple waltzed across the dance floor.

The Dwarfs sighed. They could not take their eyes off of Snow White. She looked so pretty!

"Wouldn't it be wonderful to dance with Snow White?" Happy asked.

That gave Doc an idea. He led the other Dwarfs into the cloakroom and borrowed a few things.

"Sneezy, stand here. Bashful, you stand on his shoulders. Dopey, do you think you can make it to the top?"

When Dopey was balanced on Bashful's shoulders, Doc wrapped a cloak around the tower of Dwarfs and buttoned it around Dopey's neck.

Wobbling, the Dwarf "prince" tottered toward the dance floor. "May we have this dance?" Bashful asked Snow White.

"Of course!" Snow White giggled when she saw the familiar faces peeking up at her from beneath the fabric.

As the song began, Snow White and the Dwarf "prince" lurched and swayed precariously into the middle of the room.

"Yikes!" Sneezy squeaked. "This cloak is tickling my nose!"

Above them all, Dopey was having the time of his life—when suddenly the Dwarfs heard a sound that made their blood go cold.

"*Ah . . . ah . . . ah . . .*"

"Hang on, men!" Doc shouted.

"*. . . CHOOO!*"

The cloak billowed. The Dwarf "prince" was knocked off balance!

"I've got you!" The Prince caught the Dwarfs just before they all came toppling down. Then he turned to Snow White and held out his hand.

"May I cut in?" he asked.

A Child in Monstropolis

James P. Sullivan was a professional Scarer. He was famous for collecting more screams than anyone else. That was important, because Monstropolis was having an energy shortage. The city's energy came from human screams, but human kids were getting harder to scare. . . .

Sulley led the Scarers of Monsters, Inc. onto the Scare Floor. Together, these were the best scream collectors in the business. One of them was named Randall. He was a mean, creepy monster who was very jealous of Sulley.

A conveyor belt dropped a door at each station. When the red signals flashed, each Scarer would walk through his door—and into the room of a sleeping child. Hopefully, the child would let out a good scream!

The red signals flashed, and the Scarers went to work. Their assistants collected screams in canisters outside the bedroom doors. When a child's scream had been collected, the Scarer would walk back through the door and then enter a different child's room. Sulley was filling up scream canisters faster than anyone!

Suddenly, an alarm rang out. A Scarer named George had returned from the human world with a child's sock on his back! A squad from the CDA (Child Detection Agency) arrived to decontaminate him.

When work was finished, Sulley's best friend (and assistant), Mike, rushed to meet his girlfriend, Celia. They had planned a special date. But the company's cranky file clerk blocked Mike's way.

"I'm sure you filed your paperwork," Roz rasped.

Mike had forgotten!

Luckily, Sulley offered to help. He went back to the Scare Floor to get the paperwork.

When he got there, Sulley noticed that someone had left a door behind. And the red light was on! Puzzled, Sulley peeked through the door, but there was no one there.

As Sulley closed the door and came back into Monstropolis, he felt something touch his tail. The Scarer turned around and saw . . . A CHILD!

"AAAAH!" he screamed. Everyone knew human children were deadly. What was Sulley going to do now?

Toys that Go Bump in the Night

Andy was at a friend's house for a sleepover, and the toys had the whole night to themselves. Woody watched as lightning lit up the sky. It was the perfect night for telling scary stories!

Buzz, Rex, and Jessie took turns telling stories. Finally, it was Woody's turn. His story was so scary, it made the other toys shake with fear.

"All right, gang," Woody said when he saw that the toys were afraid. "I think we've had enough stories for tonight. Let's get some sleep."

Woody had just fallen asleep when he felt a nudge. It was Rex. "I heard something! It's coming from under Andy's bed," the dinosaur said.

"You're going to make me get up, aren't you?" Woody asked.

"If it wouldn't be too much trouble," Rex answered.

So Woody and Rex went to check under Andy's bed. *GRRRRRR*, went something beneath the bed. Woody was starting to feel a little nervous, too. He decided to wake Buzz.

"I think we have an intruder," Woody whispered to the space ranger. Just then, another rumbling sound came from under the bed. Rex wailed and then fainted in fright.

Rex's cry had woken the other toys, who gathered in the center of the room. Buzz tried to crawl under the bed, but his space wings shot out and he got stuck. Sarge and his men pulled Buzz back out.

"There's something under there," Buzz said. "And it was definitely moving."

"We'll take over from here," Sarge announced.

The soldiers stormed under the bed. "Halt!" boomed Sarge's voice. "It's one of our own! Switch to rescue-mission protocol!"

The other toys looked at each other, confused. Suddenly, RC shot out into the room!

"What was he doing under there?" Woody asked.

"His batteries are nearly out of juice," Sarge reported. "He just sat there revving his engine, spinning his wheels, and going nowhere."

"I knew there had to be a simple explanation," Rex said. "I don't know what Woody and Buzz were so worried about."

The Midnight Gift

An evil sorcerer had changed spoiled Prince Naveen into a frog. Naveen assumed that kissing a princess would change him back, so he went looking for one. When he saw Tiana dressed up for a costume ball, he mistakenly thought she was a princess.

But when he kissed her, Tiana had turned into a frog instead!

Despite their differences, Naveen had fallen in love with Tiana. He wanted to marry her, but he was poor. If he married Charlotte, the wealthiest girl in New Orleans, he would be rich enough to help Tiana buy the restaurant she had always wanted.

So, although he loved her, Naveen was giving up his dream of marrying Tiana in order to save her dream of owning a restaurant.

"Let me see if I've got this right," Charlotte said to Naveen. "If I kiss you before midnight, you and Tiana will turn human again, and then we gonna get ourselves married, and live happily ever after. The end."

Naveen nodded. "More or less. But remember, you must give Tiana all the money she requires for her restaurant.

Because Tiana, she is my Evangeline," he said, referring to his friend Ray's one true love."

Charlotte clapped excitedly. "Anything you want, sugar," she said. "Now pucker up, buttercup."

Charlotte was about to kiss Prince Naveen when Tiana leaped in between them.

"Wait!" she cried. "Don't do this."

"I have to do this," said Naveen. "And we are running out of time. It is the only way to get you your dream."

She shook her head. She loved Naveen. She didn't want her dream if it meant losing him.

"My dream wouldn't be complete without you in it," Tiana said.

Charlotte burst into happy tears. "All my life I've read about true love and fairy tales. And Tia, you found it. I'll kiss him for you, honey. No marriage required."

But it was too late—the bells had chimed midnight!

Charlotte desperately placed one, two, ten kisses on the lips of the Frog Prince. But she was no longer a princess! Nothing worked.

Tiana and Naveen were stuck as frogs!

Fairy Dresses

Hem was a very happy fairy. Queen Clarion had just announced that there would be a ball in three days, and the sewing talent was dreaming about the dress she would make for herself.

"Hem? Hem? Did you hear me?" a voice asked.

Hem opened her eyes. A group of fairies stood around her.

Tinker Bell shook Hem's shoulder. "So will you do it?" Tink asked. "Will you make me a new dress for the ball?"

"And me?" Rani asked.

"And me?" Fira asked.

All the fairies wanted a new dress. Hem loved making dresses, but she also liked to take her time. Still, she couldn't say no to her friends.

Hem went to Lilly's garden and picked out the perfect flowers for each dress. Then she made her way back to her room and got to work.

Hem sewed and sewed. Finally, on the day of the ball, she finished.

Suddenly, there was a knock on her door. It was her friends.

Hem gave the fairies their dresses and they went to get ready for the ball.

As they left, Hem realized she hadn't made a dress for herself! Hem's eyes filled with tears. It was too late to find a perfect flower for her dress.

Hem picked up a petal from the floor. Then she spotted half a violet. Maybe she didn't need to pick a new flower after all. She could make a dress from the leftover bits!

It was dark out when Hem finished. She slipped the dress over her head and flew to the courtyard.

As Hem stepped into the firefly light, the music stopped. Every eye turned toward Hem. Her dress was a rainbow of color.

Hem's friends quickly gathered around her.

"You look beautiful, Hem!" Silvermist said.

"It's all of our dresses pieced together!" Fawn pointed out.

Hem's glow turned pink all over.

Queen Clarion flew to her side. "Hem, what a lovely dress!" she said. Then she whispered in Hem's ear, "Will you make me one just like it?"

A few hours earlier, Hem hadn't wanted to think of making another dress. But now she felt differently. Now she couldn't wait. "I'd be happy to!" she said.

Tricked

Rapunzel's golden hair had magical healing powers. As a baby, she had been kidnapped by Mother Gothel, who used her hair's magic to stay forever young. The woman pretended to be her mother, and she locked her away in a tower and never let her out.

But one day, Flynn Rider had come along, and Rapunzel had convinced him to take her to see the floating lights that rose in the sky every year on her birthday.

Now Flynn and Rapunzel were floating in the lake by the palace, watching the lanterns light the night. Rapunzel had just given Flynn back the crown he had stolen, but he didn't want it anymore. He only wanted Rapunzel.

Suddenly, Flynn spotted his old partners in crime, the Stabbington brothers, on the shore. Flynn had stolen the crown from them, and he knew they would do anything to get their revenge. He needed to give the crown back to them right away. Flynn turned away from Rapunzel.

"Is everything okay?" she said in surprise.

"I'm sorry. Everything is fine. There's just something I have to take care of. I'll be right back!"

Flynn rowed the boat ashore. Then, telling Rapunzel he would be right back, he ran off with the satchel containing the crown.

"We heard you found something. Something much more valuable than a crown," the Stabbington brothers told Flynn. "We want her instead." The Stabbingtons knocked Flynn out, tied him in a boat, and pushed it toward the castle. Then they rushed to capture Rapunzel!

Rapunzel dodged the Stabbingtons and ran into the forest. Suddenly, she heard a scuffle, and then Mother Gothel's voice. "Rapunzel!"

"Mother?" Rapunzel ran back and found Mother Gothel standing over the unconscious brothers. Rapunzel still thought Mother Gothel was her real mother, and now she believed that Flynn had abandoned her for the crown.

Heartbroken, Rapunzel began to cry. Mother Gothel wrapped her arm around the girl and led her back toward the tower where she'd been hidden her whole life.

Orator Owl

On their way home from a leaf-collecting excursion on a cold, blustery autumn afternoon, Pooh, Rabbit, Piglet, and Eeyore made their way past Owl's house. They could not help but notice the cheerful light glowing in all the windows—a light so warm and so inviting that the chilly group seemed to thaw just looking at it. And so it happened that they soon found themselves warm and cozy in Owl's living room.

"Owl, thank you for having us in to warm up," said Pooh. "It's awfully windy and cold outside."

"Well, it is getting on toward winter," Owl replied. "Naturally that means it will only get colder before it gets warmer."

Owl was just beginning to expound upon the particular subject of frostbite when Rabbit interrupted, hoping to give someone else a chance to talk.

"Yes, Owl," he said. "I know that Piglet was very glad to have his scarf on today, weren't you, Piglet?"

"Oh yes," Piglet said. "Kanga knitted it for me."

Owl cleared his throat. "Ah yes, knitting," he said. "An admirable hobby. Did you know that knitting is done with knitting needles? But they aren't sharp, as one might assume. They are not, for example, as sharp as sewing needles. Or cactus needles, or . . ."

Owl continued with a comparison of many, many different types of needles. An hour later, when Owl seemed ready to jump into a discussion of pins, Rabbit again tried to change the subject.

"Speaking of pins," Rabbit began, "how is your tail today, Eeyore? I hope it is suitably secure and well-attached?"

"Seems secure," Eeyore replied with a shrug, "but it always falls off when I least expect it."

Rabbit saw Owl sit up in his chair and take a deep breath—a sure sign that he was preparing another speech about tails, or expectations, or Rabbit knew not what—so Rabbit decided it was time to go.

Good-byes and thank-yous were said, and soon the four visitors were outside, making their way home through swirling leaves. And all the way home, Rabbit tried to decide who was windier—the great autumn wind or long-winded Owl!

Sillying the Blues Away

"Oh, me, oh, my!" the White Rabbit said as he rushed past Alice.

"Wait! Excuse me!" Alice called to him. But he was gone.

Alice sat down. "I'm never going to get out of here," she said worriedly.

"What's the matter?" a voice asked. "You seem blue."

Alice looked all around but she didn't see anyone. "Where are you?" she asked.

"Is that better?" the Cheshire Cat said as he suddenly appeared out of nowhere.

"Why, yes," Alice replied.

"Would you like some help?" the Cheshire Cat asked.

"You'll help me?" Alice cried.

"Absolutely!" the Cheshire Cat said with a grin. "But you have to do exactly as I say."

"Okay," Alice agreed.

"First," the Cheshire Cat told her, "you have to put on this winter coat."

"But it's spring," Alice protested.

"You promised to do as I say," the Cheshire Cat reminded her.

"Okay." Alice started putting it on.

"Backward!" the Cheshire Cat ordered.

"But . . ." Alice began. The Cheshire Cat started to disappear. "Wait, don't go!" she pleaded. "Here, I'm putting it on."

Once the coat was back on, the Cheshire Cat reappeared. "Let's go for a walk," he said, grinning at Alice.

"But I'm feeling a little silly," Alice said.

"Don't worry," the Cheshire Cat told her. "No one's looking."

But the truth was, Alice could have sworn she heard the bread-and-butterflies laughing at her.

"Now, drink this cup of applesauce," the Cheshire Cat said.

"Don't you mean apple juice?" Alice asked.

"No, I mean applesauce," the Cheshire Cat said. "Drink it while walking around in a circle three times."

By the time Alice had started her second circle, she was beginning to have doubts. "I think you're playing a trick on me," she said. "You're having me do all these things to make me look silly."

"True," the Cheshire Cat agreed, fading away. "But it's awfully hard to feel blue when you look this silly!"

Alice thought for a moment and realized she had to agree. She was still lost, but now she didn't feel quite so sad about it!

Pink or Blue?

On the day of Prince Phillip and Princess Aurora's wedding, no one was happier for them than the three good fairies.

"Such a happy day!" exclaimed Flora from a balcony overlooking the crowded ballroom. "Fauna, don't you agree?"

When Fauna didn't answer, Flora looked over to find her weeping. "Fauna, why are you crying?" asked Flora.

Dabbing her eyes, Fauna said, "I love weddings even more than happy endings! Both make me cry for joy!"

"It is a joyful day," said Merryweather. "Everyone in the kingdom is here. And look at all the wedding presents!"

"Oh, my!" said Flora. "It will take days for the bride and groom to open them all."

"Point them out again, dear," Fauna asked Merryweather. "I had tears in my eyes."

Without thinking, Merryweather used her magic wand to point. *Zzzing!* She accidentally turned all of the white packages her favorite color, blue.

"Merryweather!" snapped Flora. "Change those packages back this instant."

"I don't know," said Merryweather, tapping her chin. "I like them this way."

"Oh, do you?" said Flora. "Well, look again!"

Using her own magic wand, Flora sent a second blast of magic across the room. *Zzzing!* Now the wedding presents were *her* favorite color—pink!

The two fought for some time, changing the color of the presents back and forth.

"Now, dears," said Fauna, trying to make peace, "can't you two get along? Today is a happy day!"

Fauna had had enough. Taking out her magic wand, she waved it around in a circle and chanted: "Presents changing pink and blue, wed your colors, then stay true!"

With a final *zzzing!* Fauna sent her magic spell across the room, and the presents changed one last time.

"What did you do?" cried Flora and Merryweather.

Fauna shrugged. "I simply mixed your colors together and locked them in. Pink-and-blue-striped wrapping paper is all the rage this year," she said. "Now let's all go eat some wedding cake."

"Wedding cake?" said Merryweather. "Hmmm . . . I wonder what color the frosting will be."

Boo!

Sulley was a professional Scarer. He worked at Monsters, Incorporated, in Monstropolis. His best friend, Mike Wazowski, trained him.

One night, Sulley found a door that had been left open on the Scare Floor. A child had come through! Sulley didn't know what to do, so he went to find Mike.

Mike was at a restaurant with his girlfriend, Celia. Suddenly he spotted Sulley waving frantically outside the window. Sulley looked terrified.

Sulley told Mike all about the child. Mike was horrified—especially when Sulley showed him the kid, whom he was carrying inside a bag.

Back in their apartment, Sulley and Mike tried not to touch the child, just in case it was poisonous. Then Mike accidentally fell, and the little girl started to giggle. Strangely, her laughter made the lights burn brighter—until they burned out!

Finally, Sulley realized that the child couldn't hurt them. He put her to bed, but she was afraid to go to sleep.

Sulley realized she was terrified that a monster was in the wardrobe. So Sulley stayed with her until she fell asleep.

"This might sound crazy," Sulley told Mike, "but I don't think that kid is dangerous. What if we just put her back in her door?"

Mike didn't like the idea, but what else could they do?

The next morning, the friends disguised the little girl as a baby monster and took her to work with them. In the bathroom, they overheard Randall— a mean monster who was jealous of Sulley—tell his assistant that he planned to "take care of the kid." Sulley needed to get the child home quickly!

Mike had gone to the Scare Floor to pull up the kid's bedroom door.

"That's not Boo's door," Sulley said when he saw it.

"Boo?" Mike couldn't believe Sulley had named the child!

Suddenly they realized everyone on the Scare Floor could hear them talking! When they stopped, they saw that Boo had slipped away. Would they ever be able to find her and take her home?

Palindrome-Mania

"Hey, Atta," Flik said. "Did you know that your name is a palindrome?"

Atta gave him a strange look. "What's a palindrome?" she asked.

"It's a word that reads the same forward and backward," Flik replied. "Spelled forward, your name is A-T-T-A. Spelled backward, your name is also A-T-T-A. See?"

"Oh," Atta said. "That's neat. I've never heard of palindromes before."

"Really?" said Flik. "I love them. There are other names that are palindromes, like *Bob*."

"Or *Lil*?" tried Atta. "Hey. This is fun!"

"What's fun?" said Dot, who had just run over to them.

"Thinking of palindromes," Atta replied.

"Huh?" said Dot.

"Exactly!" said Flik. "*Huh* is a palindrome!"

Together, Flik and Atta explained to Dot what a palindrome was.

"Oh!" said Dot. "Wait! Let me see if I can think of another one." Dot looked around, hoping that something she saw would spark an idea. She spotted her mother, the Queen, lounging in the shade.

"*Mom!*" cried Dot. "That's one, isn't it?"

"Not bad," said Atta with a wink, "for a *tot* like you!"

"Oh, yeah?" replied Dot with a mischievous grin. "Well, you ain't seen nothin' yet, *sis!*"

Taking turns, Dot and Atta challenged each other to think of more and more palindromes. "*Redder* is a nice long one!" said Flik. "It's harder to think of palindromes that have more than four letters. Believe me, I've spent hours on that. But there's always *Aidemedia*— that's a type of bird, you know. And *Allenella*, of course, which is a category of mollusk . . ." Flik went on to list a longer palindrome for just about every letter of the alphabet.

As he droned on and on and on, Dot and Atta looked at each other and rolled their eyes. Now they were both thinking of the same word, and it wasn't a palindrome: B-O-R-I-N-G.

When Flik was finally through with his list, he looked up at Dot and Atta with a self-satisfied smile. Each of them had a palindrome ready.

"*Wow,*" said Atta flatly, sounding more bored than impressed.

"*Zzz,*" snored Dot, who had drifted off somewhere between *V* and *W*.

The Winter Woods

Seasons come and seasons go—at least that's how it is in the human world. But in a magical place called Pixie Hollow, spring, summer, autumn, and winter exist side by side. The warm fairies live in spring, summer, and autumn, while the winter fairies live in the snowy Winter Woods.

In Tinkers' Nook, the tinker fairies were making snowflake baskets for the winter fairies.

"I can't believe we make the baskets, but don't get to take them to the winter fairies," Tinker Bell said to her friends Bobble and Clank.

"We wouldn't last a day in that cold!" Bobble said.

"Besides, I'm afraid of glaciers," Clank added. "They're so fast!"

Just then, a group of snowy owls arrived to pick up the baskets. One owl brought Fairy Mary a note written on ice.

"They need twenty more baskets for tomorrow's pickup!" she announced.

Tink watched as the majestic owls headed off toward the Winter Woods. How she wished she could go with them!

A few minutes later, the animal fairy Fawn appeared in the tinkers' workshop.

She was chasing after a feisty bunny rabbit.

"Look out!" Fawn cried.

As one of the animal fairies, it was Fawn's job to round up the animals for their trip across the border to the Winter Woods.

Tinker Bell had always wanted to see the Winter Woods. She offered to help Fawn bring the animals to the border.

Soon the two fairies arrived at the border. Fawn told Tink that only the animals were allowed to cross into the Winter Woods.

But Fawn was having trouble getting one of the animals to cross into winter. He was already asleep!

"Oh, no, no hibernating yet," she said. "You do that in winter!"

As Fawn was talking to the animal, Tinker Bell moved closer to the border. The air was freezing, but that didn't stop her curiosity. She was desperate to see the snow-covered landscape and meet the winter fairies.

Tink gathered her courage, took a deep breath—and jumped! Was winter really the white wonderland she imagined . . . ?

A Friend for Phillipe

Belle loved life in the castle with her prince, and she loved her faithful horse, Phillipe. Lately, however, Phillipe had been acting strangely. Belle decided to try to cheer him up. She asked her friends for some help.

First Lumiere helped Belle brighten up Phillipe's stall. They covered the walls with wallpaper and trimmed them with gold.

"Voilà!" Lumiere cried. "What more could a horse ask for?"

But Phillipe just stared sadly out the window.

Next Belle treated Phillipe to a bubble bath fit for a king. "If this doesn't make him smile," Belle told Chip, "I don't know what will!"

But Phillipe was just as glum after his bath—and Belle was just as puzzled. She asked the Prince if he had any suggestions.

"A good walk always cheers me up," the Prince said.

Belle thought that was a wonderful idea. She rode Phillipe to a big, open meadow, but he wasn't interested in galloping.

"Oh, Phillipe," Belle said in despair. "I just don't know what else to do!"

Suddenly, Phillipe's ears pricked up. Belle barely had time to grab the reins before he charged off!

Before long, they emerged into a clearing filled with wild, beautiful horses! Phillipe whinnied, and several of the horses answered him. Finally, Belle realized what Phillipe had wanted—to be with other horses!

All afternoon, Belle watched Phillipe race and play. Soon Phillipe had even made a friend. The two horses grazed, chased each other around the clearing, and dozed together in the warm sun.

All too quickly, the day was over, and the sun began to set. Belle put Phillipe's saddle on him, and they started back to the castle.

Soon Belle heard the sound of hooves behind them. Phillipe's new friend was following them home!

"Welcome to our castle!" Belle told the new horse when they arrived. Then she hurried off to fix up the stall next to Phillipe's.

"There," she said when she was finished. "Now this looks like a stable where a horse—or two!—could really live happily ever after!"

And that is exactly what they did.

Pictures in the Stars

Ever since Mufasa had died and Simba had left the Pride Lands, Timon and Pumbaa had been his only friends—but what fun the three of them had together! One of their favorite things to do after their evening meal was to lie on their backs in the tall grass and gaze up at the night sky, looking for shapes in the stars.

"See, over there, that long, thin, curving outline?" Pumbaa said. "It's a big, juicy, delicious slug!"

Timon cleared his throat. "I hate to disagree with you, Pumbaa my friend, but that's no slug you see up there. That's an elephant's trunk. If you follow that curving line of stars, you see it connects with the elephant's head at one end. And there are the ears," Timon said, tracing it all out with his finger, "and there are the tusks."

Simba chuckled softly. "It's funny that the things you and Pumbaa see in the stars just happen to be the same things that are on your minds," he said.

"Ooh! Ooh! I've got another one!" Pumbaa interrupted. "A big bunch of tasty berries right over there." He pointed at a grouping of stars. "Don't they look good?"

"See what I mean?" Simba said to Timon, gesturing at Pumbaa.

"All right, Mr. Smarty-Pants," Timon replied. "So what do you see in the stars?"

"Well, now, let's see," said Simba, gazing intently at the thousands of tiny points of light twinkling down at them. There were so many that you could see practically any shape that you wanted to in them. It all depended on how you looked at them. But just to get Timon's goat, Simba wanted to find something really bright—something really clear. Something Timon couldn't deny that he saw, too.

At that moment, a shooting star streaked across the entire length of the night sky.

"I see a bright streak of light over there rocketing across the sky!" exclaimed Simba.

"Ooh! Me too!" said Pumbaa. "Timon, do you see it?"

Timon had to admit that he did.

"Yeah, yeah, I see it," he muttered grudgingly. "Ha-ha. Very funny, Simba."

Home Is Where the Heart Is

Tod, an orphaned baby fox, was still getting used to his new surroundings in Widow Tweed's house. Why, Tod was so young, he was still getting used to being a fox!

In the kitchen, Tod's attention was caught by the large box with a door that Widow Tweed kept opening and closing. Each time she opened the door, Tod caught a glimpse of the box's brightly lit interior and got a whiff of all kinds of delicious treats inside!

But when Tod hopped inside the box, unseen by Widow Tweed as she was closing the door, he got a surprise. It was cold inside! And as soon as the door closed, Tod found himself sitting in complete darkness.

Luckily, Widow Tweed heard Tod's whimpers and opened the refrigerator door.

"Why, Tod, how did you get in there?" she said.

Tod hopped out and darted away. Outside, Tod could see his friends Big Mama the owl and Dinky the sparrow chatting on a tree branch. Tod leaned forward to hop outside and join them, but his nose hit something smooth,

hard, and solid. But it was clear; he could see right through it.

Widow Tweed chuckled as she watched from the living room doorway.

"Discovered glass, have you, Tod?" she asked with a kind smile.

Whatever glass was, Tod supposed he'd have to stay indoors. He hopped onto a table and studied a small square object with some knobs on it. He batted one of the knobs. The knob turned all the way around, and a loud noise blared out of the object. Startled, Tod bolted under the sofa.

Widow Tweed rushed over and turned the knob. The noise stopped. Then she coaxed Tod out from under the sofa. "There, there, Tod," she cooed, cradling him in her arms and petting his head. "That's just the radio. You're having a hard time getting used to everything in this strange new place, aren't you? Here, let's have a snack."

It had been a rough morning for the baby fox. But there, in Widow Tweed's arms, Tod felt a comforting, familiar feeling at last. It was the feeling of being warm and cared for.

At that moment, Tod's new home didn't feel so strange after all.

The Mysterious Voyage

Aladdin and Jasmine had just gotten married. Now they were taking a romantic trip.

"Madame, the Magic Carpet awaits you," Aladdin said, bowing before his bride.

"Won't you tell me where we're going?" Jasmine asked.

"I'm taking you to see things you've never seen before," Aladdin replied. "A whole new, exciting world."

Jasmine and Aladdin settled onto the Magic Carpet. Soon they were soaring high above the palace.

After a little while, the Magic Carpet began its descent.

"Are we there?" asked Jasmine.

"Almost," Aladdin said. "Close your eyes. I want this to be a surprise."

Suddenly, Jasmine heard a loud noise that sounded like crashing water.

"Okay. Open!" said Aladdin. "This, Jasmine, is the ocean!"

Jasmine couldn't believe her eyes. The water was a brilliant shade of turquoise. Huge ocean waves crashed onto a white sandy beach while dolphins leaped in and out of the water.

"It's magical!" Jasmine said. She and Aladdin climbed off the carpet and explored the beach. When they were ready to go, Aladdin snapped his fingers. The Magic Carpet appeared, ready to take them to their next destination.

As they approached, Aladdin asked Jasmine to cover her eyes again. Jasmine felt the air grow colder. Suddenly she felt a warm coat around her shoulders.

"You can open your eyes now!" Aladdin said.

Everywhere Jasmine looked, she saw white! "Oh . . . what is it?" she asked, bending down to touch the cold, white powder.

"It's snow!" answered Aladdin. "Isn't it wonderful? It falls from the sky when it's cold."

"It's amazing!" cried Jasmine.

The two spent the rest of the day playing in the snow. They built snowmen and made snow angels. Soon the sun began to set.

"Thank you for bringing me here," Jasmine said. "I never knew there could be anything so beautiful."

Jasmine settled onto the Magic Carpet for the ride home. This trip had been magical, but she knew this was just the beginning of her wonderful life with Aladdin.

OCTOBER
12

Go Fish!

"Okay, small fry," said Baloo the bear. "Today I'm going to teach you how to fish like a real bear!"

Mowgli was delighted. He loved his new friend Baloo.

"Now, watch this, kid," said Baloo as they arrived at the riverbank. "All ya gotta do is wait for a fish to swim by, and then . . ." *Whoosh!* Quick as a flash, Baloo held a wriggling silver fish in his paw. "Now you try it!" he said to Mowgli.

Mowgli sat very still, waiting for a fish to swim by. Then—*splash!*—he toppled headfirst into the water.

"Hmm," said Baloo after he had fished Mowgli out and set him down, dripping. "Maybe I should show you my second technique."

Baloo and Mowgli walked toward another part of the river. This time, the fish could be seen occasionally leaping out of the water as they swam down a little waterfall. Baloo waded a few steps into the water, waited for a fish to jump, then—*whoosh!*—he swiped a fish right out of the air. "Now you try, buddy."

Mowgli waded in just as Baloo had done. He waited for the fish to jump and then leaped for it. *Splash!*

"Okay, plan C," said Baloo after he had fished Mowgli out of the water a second time. "I'll take you to the big waterfall. The fish literally fall into your paws. All ya gotta do is reach out and catch one!"

Mowgli followed Baloo to the big waterfall. Sure enough, silvery fish were jumping all the way down the falls. It would be easy to catch one of these! In the blink of an eye, Baloo held up a fish for Mowgli to admire.

"I'm going to do it this time, you watch me, Baloo!" said Mowgli excitedly. He scrunched up his face with concentration. For an instant, Mowgli actually had a silvery fish in his hands. But a second later, the fish shot out of his grasp and jumped into the water again. Mowgli looked down at his empty hands with a sigh.

"You know what, kid?" said Baloo. "I think you're working too hard. That's not how life in the jungle should be! It should be fun, happy, and carefree. So come on. Let's go shake a banana tree instead!"

Mowgli cheerfully agreed.

OCTOBER 13

Miss Bianca's First Rescue

The headquarters of the Rescue Aid Society was buzzing with activity. Mice from all over the world had gathered together for an emergency meeting. The chairman of the society had to shout to be heard over the hubbub.

"Attention, delegates!" he cried. "I have called this meeting because a canine urgently needs our help." He clapped his hands. "Mice scouts, bring in the distressed doggy!"

Two mouse workers hurried into the room, leading a small dog with a long body and short little legs. His head was stuck inside a dog food can.

Suddenly, the door to the meeting room flew open and a pretty little mouse walked in. She wore a fashionable coat and expensive perfume.

"Oh, excuse me," she said. "I seem to be in the wrong place. I'm looking for Micey's Department Store?" Then she noticed one of the mice holding the can opener. "Dear me, what are you doing to that poor dog?"

"The dog is quite stuck, I'm afraid," the chairman told her. "But don't you worry, miss. We have this situation under control."

The glamorous mouse pushed up her sleeves and marched over to the dog. She kicked the top of the can three times. Then she gave it a swift twist to the left. The can popped off!

"Hooray!" the mice all cheered happily.

The little mouse smiled. "That's how I open pickle jars at home," she explained. "Well, I'd best be on my way."

"Ah, Mr. Chairman?" a voice piped up from the corner of the room. It was the Zambian delegate.

"Yes?" said the chairman.

"I'd like to nominate Miss . . . uh, Miss . . ." The delegate looked at the pretty mouse.

"Miss Bianca," she told him.

"I'd like to nominate Miss Bianca for membership in the Rescue Aid Society," he said.

The chairman turned to the rest of the mouse delegates. "All in favor, say aye!"

"Aye!" all the mice cried.

"Aroof!" the dog barked happily.

Miss Bianca smiled. "Well," she said, "I suppose Micey's can wait for another day."

A Fairy-Tale Marriage

Deep in the Louisiana bayou, there was a lot of excitement. Naveen and Tiana—two frogs who were madly in love—were about to be married.

Naveen and Tiana were really human, but they had been turned into frogs by an evil sorcerer's curse. On their journey to break the curse, they had fallen in love. It had taken the two a long time to realize that there was a difference between what they wanted and what they needed. And what they needed was love! Even though the two were stuck as frogs, they were happy just to be together.

As all of their animal friends watched, Mama Odie, a good and powerful voodoo priestess, conducted the wedding ceremony. At last she pronounced the frogs man and wife.

Naveen took Tiana in his arms and placed a tender kiss on her lips.

Suddenly, a cloud of multicolored sparks began to swirl around them—and they both became human again!

The couple looked splendid. Prince Naveen was wearing a suit, and Tiana had on a long green dress.

The two looked at each other with surprise and astonishment.

Mama Odie laughed. "Like I told ya, kissing a princess breaks the spell!"

"When you married me," Naveen realized suddenly, "you became . . ."

"A princess," Tiana finished with a laugh. "You just kissed yourself a princess!"

"And I'm about to do it again!" Naveen laughed and kissed his princess as their bayou friends all cheered.

Tiana and Naveen returned to New Orleans, where they were married again in front of their human friends and family.

At long last, Tiana opened her new restaurant—Tiana's Palace! The happy couple had bought the old sugar mill and turned it into the best place to go for good food, lively music, and fun with friends and family. They had even found a place for their alligator friend Louis in the band. It was his dream come true.

Tiana had dreamed of owning a restaurant her whole life. It was a dream she had shared with her father. But Tiana's dreams had grown. Now, she realized, she had everything she could ever wish for—and more!

OCTOBER
15

Breakfast—O'Malley Style!

"Mama, I'm hungry," said little Marie.

"I know, my darlings," Duchess told her kittens.

The day before, they had walked for hours to reach Paris. Now, this morning, their empty stomachs were rumbling.

"I wish we were at the mansion," said Marie.

"Hey, now," said O'Malley, their alley-cat friend. "Don't you like my attic pad?"

"Yes," said Marie, "but at the mansion, Edgar the butler brings us our breakfast every morning."

"On a golden tray," said Toulouse.

"Oh, I get it," said O'Malley. "Well, I can't give you the four-star treatment, but I can get you breakfast—alley-cat style."

Duchess and her three kittens followed O'Malley into the bright Paris morning. They trotted along until they came to a little café.

"I've got a little arrangement here," O'Malley told Duchess. He led her and the kittens to the back of the café. Then he jumped onto the ledge of a window.

A young woman in a white apron came to the window and cooed, *"Bonjour, monsieur."* O'Malley jumped back down and went to the back door. When it opened, the young woman put down a saucer of cream and said, "Here is your breakfast, *monsieur.*"

O'Malley called to Duchess and the kittens, "Psssst. Come on over."

"You've brought some friends!" the woman said.

The woman brought out two more saucers of cream—big ones. The kittens raced to the dishes and began sloppily lapping up the cream.

"Children! Children!" cried Duchess. "Where are your manners?"

The kittens looked up sheepishly, thick cream dripping from their furry chins.

"Thank you, Mr. O'Malley," they said. Then Marie kissed him on the cheek!

"Aw, don't mention it," said O'Malley, embarrassed.

"I see I've made a mistake, *monsieur,*" said the young woman in the doorway. "These are not your friends. They are your family!"

Wow, thought O'Malley, she sure got *that* wrong! But then he stopped himself. He did love Duchess and her kittens. Maybe that was what made a family after all.

Banished!

Sulley was the top Scarer at Monsters, Inc. His job was to collect human screams. Mike Wazowski was his best friend.

Now Mike and Sulley were in big trouble. They'd discovered a human girl in Monstropolis! Monsters were very scared of human kids. They thought they were deadly!

But Sulley had grown to like the human child and had named her Boo. He was no longer scared of her. Mike and Sulley had brought Boo to the Scare Floor to send her home—but she had escaped from them! The two monsters had split up to find her, but a mean monster named Randall had cornered Mike. Randall was Sulley's competition for top Scarer! The nasty monster knew all about Boo. He ordered Mike to bring her to the Scare Floor. He said he'd have her door ready.

When Sulley finally found Boo, Mike told him about Randall's plan. Together, they went to the Scare Floor, but Sulley was still worried. "We can't trust Randall!" he told Mike.

Mike disagreed. To prove the open

door was safe, he went right through—and was captured by Randall!

Sulley and Boo followed the monster as he carried Mike to a secret room in the basement. There they learned that he had invented a new machine to capture screams from kids. He was about to try it out on Mike!

Sulley rescued Mike and raced to the training room. He needed to warn his boss, Mr. Waternoose, about Randall. Mr. Waternoose promised he would fix everything—but he was really working with Randall! He shoved Sulley and Mike through a door into the human world. They were banished to the mountains!

Sulley knew Boo was in trouble. He had to get back to Monstropolis. Racing to the local village, he found a door that led home. He rushed to Randall's secret lab and destroyed the machine.

As Sulley raced away with Boo, Mike arrived to help. The two monsters climbed onto the machine that carried doors to the Scare Floor. The power wasn't on, so Mike made a funny face. Boo laughed, and the power surged! It seemed that human children's laughs were more powerful than their screams.

OCTOBER
17

'Ears a Job for You, Dumbo!

It had been a hard day for little Dumbo. It was bad enough that everyone made fun of his ears. But now they had put his mother in a cage!

What made things even worse was that Dumbo didn't have anything to do. Sometimes it seemed that he was the only creature in the circus who didn't have a purpose.

Dumbo heaved a sigh and went for a walk through the circus tents. Soon he found himself among the refreshment stands. Everyone here had a job, too. Some were squeezing lemons to make lemonade. Others were popping popcorn or roasting peanuts. Wonderful smells filled the air.

Finally, Dumbo came to a little cotton candy wagon. Dumbo wanted a taste, but there were so many customers that he couldn't get close enough.

Suddenly Dumbo heard a loud buzzing. Then all the customers waved their hands over their heads and ran away from the wagon. The smell of sugar had attracted a swarm of nasty flies!

Dumbo reached out his trunk to smell the delicious cotton candy.

"Not you, Dumbo!" the cotton candy man cried. "It's bad enough chasing away flies. Do I have to chase away elephants, too?"

Poor Dumbo was startled. With a snort, he sucked cotton candy right up his nose.

Aaaachoo! When he sneezed, Dumbo's ears flapped and something amazing happened.

"Remarkable!" the cotton candy man cried. "All the flies are gone. They think your ears are giant flyswatters!" The cotton candy man patted Dumbo's head. "How would you like a job?"

Dumbo nodded enthusiastically and set to waving his ears. Soon the cotton candy wagon was the most popular refreshment stand in the circus—and had the least flies. But best of all, Dumbo now had something to do to take his mind off his troubles. He was still sad, but things didn't seem quite so bad. And who knew? Perhaps soon he'd have his mother back.

"I wonder what other amazing things those big ears can do," said the cotton candy man, giving Dumbo a friendly smile. "I'll bet they carry you far. . . ."

A Thank-You Present

"I don't know how I can ever thank them," Snow White said to her new husband, the Prince. The two of them were on their way to visit the Dwarfs and give them a special present—a meal fit for seven kings! Snow White looked at the dishes and hampers filled with delicious food. "It just doesn't seem like enough," she said with a sigh. "They saved my life!"

"I'm sure seeing you happy is thanks enough," the Prince said, putting his arm around Snow White.

As the cozy Dwarf cottage came into view, Snow White perked up.

"Yoo-hoo!" she called as she dashed from the coach. "Sneezy? Happy? Bashful?" Snow White knocked on the door, but there was no answer. "They must not be home yet," she said to the Prince. "We'll have just enough time to get everything ready."

Snow White went inside and set the table and tidied the house, humming while she worked. She was so excited to see her friends that she couldn't help checking the windows for a sign of them every few minutes.

As the sun set, the princess began to worry.

"They're awfully late!" she said.

The Prince agreed. It was getting dark. "Perhaps we should go and find them."

At last, Snow White and her prince reached the mine.

Holding up lanterns, they saw at once what the trouble was. A tree had fallen over the entrance. The Dwarfs were trapped!

"Snow White, is that you?" Doc called through a small opening.

"Are you all right?" Snow White asked.

"We're fine, dear. Just fine," Doc told her

"No, we're not," Grumpy said rather grumpily. "We're stuck!"

Hitching his horse to the big tree, the Prince pulled it away from the mine so the Dwarfs could get out.

Snow White embraced each dusty Dwarf as he emerged. She even hugged Dopey twice!

"Now, let's get you home," she said.

Back at the cottage, the Dwarfs were thrilled to see the fine meal laid out on thei table.

"How can we ever thank you?" Doc said, wringing his hat. "You saved our lives."

"Don't be silly." Snow White blushed. "Seeing you happy is thanks enough."

A Helping Paw

The dairy barn was warm and cozy. Ninety-nine exhausted, hungry pups were taking turns drinking warm milk from the motherly cows inside.

"Just look at the little dears," said one of the cows. "I've never seen so many puppies in one place before!"

Pongo, Perdita, and the puppies had just come in from a long and weary march through the cold. It was very late, and the pups waiting for a drink of milk could barely keep their eyes open. The puppies had recently managed to escape from the dreadful old house owned by Cruella De Vil. Cruella was planning to make a fur coat out of their lovely spotted fur.

Luckily, Pongo and Perdita had rescued them all just in the nick of time.

The pups had their dinners and gathered around the collie who lived in the barn, thanking him for his hospitality.

"Not at all, not at all," the collie replied.

"Do you have warm milk for supper every night out here in the country?" asked Rolly.

The collie chuckled. "No, but we do eat very simple country fare. I'm sure it's plainer than the food you eat in the city, but we eat big meals because of all the chores we do."

"And is it always this cold in the country?" asked Patch.

"Well, now," replied the collie. "I suppose most of you come from the city. No, it isn't always this cold, but there are plenty of differences between living in the country and living in the city. Take leashes, for instance. We don't keep our pets on leashes here, the way you do in the city. There aren't as many dogs nearby, but there are certainly other sorts of animals that one doesn't see in the city. Like cows, for instance. And then there are sheep and horses and geese, and . . ."

The collie stopped talking when he heard a tiny snore escape one of the pups he had just been talking to. He looked around and realized that every one of the pups, as well as Pongo and Perdita, had fallen into a deep sleep.

"Poor little things," he said quietly as he trotted outside to stand guard. "They've been through so much. I do hope they get home safely."

Sparkling Wings

Tinker Bell was a curious fairy. She had always been fascinated by the Winter Woods. Only winter fairies were allowed to enter the mysterious area of Pixie Hollow.

One day, Tink accompanied her friend Fawn to the border between winter and autumn. Fawn was helping animals cross into winter. Suddenly, Tink's curiosity got the better of her and she jumped into the Winter Woods.

Tink looked around in wonder at the wintry landscape, admiring the sparkling snowflakes that drifted down from the sky.

Just then, Tink's wings lit up in a burst of colorful light!

At that moment, Fawn looped a lasso around Tink and pulled her back into autumn.

"I told you we're not allowed to cross!" Fawn scolded. Then she realized that Tink's wings were very cold. "We'd better get you to a healing-talent fairy!"

Fawn took Tink straight to a healing fairy, who warmed Tinker Bell's wings under a special lamp. Soon Tink's friends arrived. They were very worried about her!

"Your wings appear to be fine," the healing-talent fairy reported. Tinker Bell's friends were relieved, but Tink wanted to know what had caused her wings to sparkle.

"It must have been the light reflecting off the snow," the healing-talent fairy said.

Tink wasn't so sure. She went to the Book Nook to do some research. As she scanned the bookshelf, Tink spotted a wing-shaped book.

But when Tink opened the book, she discovered that a bookworm had eaten through the pages! The words that were left didn't make any sense.

Tink asked a nearby sparrow man for help. "Do you know anything about sparkling wings?" she asked.

"No, but the Keeper does," he replied. "He is the Keeper of All Fairy Knowledge. He's a winter fairy. In order to talk to him, you have to go to the Winter Woods."

The next morning, Tink tucked her wings under a warm coat and loaded the heavy book into her satchel. She had decided to go back to the Winter Woods! She knew it was dangerous, but she had to find out the truth.

The Helpful Dragon

Princess Aurora and Prince Phillip were out for a ride when a small dragon popped out from behind a tree and ran over to them.

"Oh, he's so cute!" Aurora exclaimed. "Let's take him home. I'm going to call him Crackle!"

"He does seem like a harmless little fellow," Phillip agreed.

When Phillip and Aurora rode into the courtyard, the three good fairies were hanging banners for a ball. King Stefan and the Queen were coming to the castle.

Flora gasped when she saw Crackle. "Dragons can be dangerous!" she said.

"I think he's sweet," Merryweather spoke up.

Just then, Crackle noticed a kitten in a basket of wool. Crackle listened to it purring. Then he tried to purr.

"Purrgrr, purrgrr!" Clouds of smoke streamed from his nose and mouth! Crackle looked sad.

"Oh, Crackle," Aurora said gently. "You're not a kitten. You're a dragon."

Aurora noticed that Crackle still looked unhappy, so she took him to the castle. But King Hubert heard Crackle and rushed into the room. "How did a dragon get in here?" he shouted.

Frightened, Crackle ran to the garden.

Aurora found the little dragon sitting beside a fountain, watching a fish.

Splash! Before Aurora could stop him, Crackle jumped into the water.

"Crackle, you're not a fish!" Aurora exclaimed. "You're not a kitten, either. Do you think no one will like you because you're a dragon?" she asked.

Crackle nodded.

"You can't change what you are," Aurora said kindly. "But you can be a helpful dragon."

Suddenly, thunder boomed. Rain began to pour down.

"I'm afraid King Stefan and the Queen might lose their way," Prince Phillip said.

Aurora looked at Crackle. "Crackle? Would you please fly to the top of the tower and blow the largest, brightest flames you can to guide my parents to the castle?"

Crackle nodded. Soon gold and red flames lit up the sky.

"See?" Aurora told the little dragon later that night. "Never try to be something you're not, because who you are is already wonderful!"

Donald's Pumpkin Patch

"Look at this!" said Daisy as she came into the Clubhouse one day. "This pumpkin won the grand prize at the County Fair!" She showed her friends a picture of the pumpkin.

"Hot dog!" said Mickey. "That is one big pumpkin!"

"Aw, phooey!" Donald said. "I could grow a garden filled with the biggest pumpkins you've ever seen!"

The next day, Donald got pumpkin seeds and threw them on the soil.

"I think it takes more than that to grow a garden," said Minnie.

Mickey nodded. "First you need to make holes in the dirt, put a seed in each hole, and then cover them up."

"That's a lot of work," said Donald.

"Maybe Toodles can help," said Mickey. "Oh, Toodles!"

Toodles showed them a pogo stick, a mirror, and an elephant. Minnie picked the pogo stick to help them make holes for the seeds. Then Donald dropped a seed into each hole and covered them all with soil.

"See, I told you this would be easy," said Donald as he sat down.

"I think it takes more than that to grow a garden," said Daisy.

"A garden needs water," Mickey said. "Water helps seeds grow."

The friends called Toodles again. This time they chose the elephant. The elephant took a big drink from the pond, and then she sprinkled water over the entire garden using her trunk.

"I told you this would be easy," said Donald.

"I think it takes more than that to grow a garden," said Mickey.

Donald was puzzled. "What else is there to do?"

"Plants need sun," said Minnie. "But your garden is in the shade."

Toodles had just one tool left—a mirror. "A mirror?" asked Donald. "How can that help my garden grow?"

Mickey and Minnie placed the mirror so that it reflected the sunlight onto the garden.

Over the next few months, Donald worked hard. When it was time for the pumpkin contest, Donald picked the biggest, most beautiful pumpkin from his garden.

"The prize for the biggest pumpkin goes to Farmer Donald!" Judge Goofy announced.

Where's Tink?

Peter Pan was in a hurry to meet Tinker Bell. They had a date for a game of tag.

"Tink!" he called as he arrived at his hideout. He took off his hat and placed it on the table. "I'm home!"

But there was no reply.

How strange, thought Peter. Tinker Bell was never late.

Peter called her name again as loudly as he could. But still there was no answer.

"Wake up! Wake up!" he shouted to the Lost Boys, who were napping in hammocks. "Tinker Bell is missing!"

"Where would she go?" asked Tootles.

Peter thought for a moment. He knew that Tinker Bell liked to fly around Never Land. And she really liked paying visits to other fairies. But not when she had a game of tag to play with Peter.

"The question," Peter Pan finally declared, "is not where would she go, but who could have taken her!"

"Oooh . . ." The Lost Boys shuddered.

"Do you mean . . ." the Raccoon Twins began.

"Indians?" finished Peter. "I certainly do. I can see it right now: while you were sleeping, a whole band crept into our hideaway and stole our Tinker Bell away."

Then Slightly spoke up. "Or what if it was—"

"Pirates!" cried Peter. "Of course! Those dirty, rotten scoundrels! It would be just like them to lure Tinker Bell outside, ambush her, kidnap her, and hold her for ransom!

"Men!" Peter cried. "We can't just stand here while Tinker Bell suffers in the grimy hands of bloodthirsty pirates. Why, she could be in mortal danger! I hereby declare that a rescue mission be formed at once. What do you say? Are you with me?"

"Hoorah! Hoorah!" the boys cheered.

Suddenly, Peter heard a sound.

Ring-a-ling! Ring! Ring! Rrrring!

"Tink!" Peter exclaimed as his missing—and furious!—friend shot up into the air.

"Where have you been? You had me worried sick!"

Tinker Bell just jingled angrily at Peter. She hadn't been kidnapped. She'd been trapped under Peter's hat the whole time!

Operation Rescue

Rapunzel had hair with magical healing powers. She had been kidnapped as a baby by Mother Gothel, who used her hair's magic to stay young forever.

Then one day Flynn Rider had come along.

Rapunzel had convinced Flynn to take her to see the kingdom's floating lights. Along the way, the two had fallen in love.

Meanwhile, Flynn's former partners, the Stabbington brothers, were out for revenge. They had helped him steal the royal crown, but things had turned sour between them when Flynn refused to share it.

But Flynn had changed since meeting Rapunzel. Now he was trying to return the crown to the brothers. All he wanted was to be with Rapunzel.

There was just one problem. The Stabbingtons no longer wanted the crown. They had learned of Rapunzel's magic hair and wanted her instead!

The Stabbington brothers knocked Flynn out and tied him in a small boat. Then they placed the stolen crown on his knees and sent the boat off toward the castle.

When the guards saw Flynn with the crown, they arrested him and threw him in the dungeon! Rapunzel, meanwhile, had fallen back into Mother Gothel's hands.

Fortunately, Rapunzel's horse friend, Maximus, had seen everything.

Maximus galloped to a pub full of ruffians that Flynn and Rapunzel had visited earlier. Rapunzel had befriended the men. Now Maximus needed them to help Flynn escape so he could rescue her.

The gang of ruffians came rushing into the prison. They fought with the guards and dragged Flynn out into the main courtyard. There, one of them pushed him onto a cart tipped at an angle.

Wham! The ruffian jumped on the other end of the cart, which flipped like a seesaw, and Flynn flew into the air! He flew over the prison wall and landed right on Maximus's back. The horse had been waiting for him.

Flynn patted Maximus, and the horse galloped off toward the tower. But would they be too late to save Rapunzel from Mother Gothel's evil clutches?

Growing Up

One day, Bambi and Thumper were playing in the meadow when they heard a rumbling noise coming toward them.

"Look, Bambi!" exclaimed Thumper. It was a thundering herd of stags.

"I wish I could be a stag!" Bambi exclaimed.

"Well, you know what my father always says," said Thumper.

"I know," said Bambi. "'Eating greens is a special treat. It makes long ears and great big feet.'"

"No, not that!" said Thumper. "He says, 'If you want to hop well, but your hop is all wrong, then you have to practice all day long!'"

"I have to hop all day long?" asked Bambi.

"No!" cried Thumper. "If you want to become a stag, you have to practice!"

Bambi glanced back at two big deer. They suddenly ran toward each other, locking horns to test their strength.

"Lower your head," Thumper told Bambi.

Bambi lowered his head. "Now what?" he asked, staring at the ground.

"Run straight ahead," said Thumper. Bambi ran straight ahead—toward

the trunk of the old oak tree! But before he got there, a voice cried, "Stop!" Bambi did, skidding to a halt only a few inches from the tree trunk.

Thumper and Bambi looked up. Friend Owl looked down at them with big curious eyes. "Bambi, why were you going to butt my tree trunk with your head?" he asked.

"I'm practicing to become a big stag," said Bambi.

Friend Owl laughed and said, "Bambi, the stags have antlers to protect their heads! And becoming a stag is not something you can practice. It's something that will happen to you with the passing of time."

"It will?" said Bambi.

"Of course!" Friend Owl assured him. "Next summer, you'll see. You'll be bigger and stronger. You'll also have antlers— and, I hope, enough sense not to butt heads with an oak tree!

"Now go on, you two," Friend Owl continued. "And don't be in too much of a hurry to grow up. You'll get there soon enough, I promise you!"

"Okay," said Bambi and Thumper.

Then the two friends returned to the meadow to play.

Ariel's Royal Wedding

Ariel loved Prince Eric from the moment she first saw him. And Prince Eric loved Ariel from the first time he heard her sing. Now they were going to be married!

At home in the castle, Ariel realized that there was a great deal of work to be done for the wedding.

Ariel asked Carlotta, the friendly housekeeper, to help make her dress. They worked through the night. Finally it was ready.

"It's so beautiful!" cried Ariel. "I wish my sisters could see it."

The next morning, Chef Louis drew Ariel a picture of the wonderful wedding cake he would make.

"It's perfect!" cried Ariel. "I wish my father could see it when it's done."

As Ariel made all of her wonderful wedding plans, she kept thinking about her family. It was Ariel's dream to spend the rest of her life as a human and as Prince Eric's wife, but she wanted her family close by on her wedding day. Suddenly, she began to feel very sad.

Later that night, Prince Eric noticed a tear in Ariel's eye. "What's the matter?" he asked.

"I just wish—I just wish that my family could be at the wedding," Ariel replied.

"Hmm, I thought you might want that. So I thought we should have our wedding at sea!" Eric grinned. "It's all planned: we'll be married on the royal ship with your family in attendance."

"That's perfect!" Ariel cried.

Soon Ariel met her sisters near the shore. She asked all of them to be her bridesmaids. She asked Sebastian to be the ring bearer. And she asked her father, King Triton, to give her away.

The day of the wedding finally arrived. The ship was covered with beautiful pink and white flowers. The human wedding guests were all seated on deck. Ariel's father used his trident to magically lift him and Ariel's sisters up to the side of the ship. The rest of her merfolk friends looked on from the sea. King Triton led Ariel to meet her handsome prince. The vows were read. The rings were exchanged.

"Kiss the girl!" cried Sebastian. And at last the prince and princess were married!

The Chase

Things at Monsters, Inc. had become a bit scarier than usual! Best friends Sulley and Mike had discovered a human child in their world and were trying to get her home.

Sulley was the top Scarer at Monsters, Inc. He was the best of the best at collecting children's screams to power the city. But thanks to Boo—the child they'd found—he'd discovered that laughs were just as powerful as screams.

Unfortunately, Sulley's boss, Mr. Waternoose, was working with a mean monster named Randall. They had invented a machine to suck screams out of human kids! Sulley had torn the machine apart and raced away with Boo, but Randall was chasing them.

Mike and Sulley made it to the Scare Floor. But to send Boo home, they still needed to find her door. Mike, Sulley, and Boo jumped in and out of bedrooms. When Randall grabbed Boo, Sulley told him, "She's not scared of you anymore." Then, working together, Boo and Sulley beat Randall once and for all.

But Boo wasn't safe yet. Now Mr. Waternoose and the CDA (Child Detection Agency) were controlling the doors. While Mike distracted the CDA, Sulley escaped with Boo. Unfortunately, Waternoose saw everything.

"Give me the child!" he yelled, running after Sulley. Luckily, Mike recorded Mr. Waternoose as he yelled, "I'll kidnap a thousand children before I let this company die!"

Now everyone knew that Waternoose planned to kidnap children. He was quickly arrested!

It was time for Boo to go home. Sulley followed her into her room. He gently tucked her into bed. Sadly, Sulley returned to Monstropolis. The CDA shredded Boo's door. It wouldn't be used for scaring anymore.

Sulley missed Boo. He had one tiny sliver of her door, but the rest had been destroyed. Before long, Mike surprised his pal. He'd put Boo's door back together! It was missing just one little piece. Sulley inserted the piece, opened the door, and saw . . .

"Boo?" Sulley whispered.

"Kitty!" an excited voice replied.

The two friends were reunited at last!

The Best Kitty-Sitter

Duchess and O'Malley had planned a lovely dinner at Paris's finest restaurant.

O'Malley had even found a kitty-sitter for Duchess's kittens. His friend Scat Cat had offered to watch them for the night!

Duchess and O'Malley told Toulouse, Marie, and Berlioz to behave for Scat Cat.

After they left, Scat Cat turned to the kittens. "Listen up, cool cats," he said. "I'm not the regular kitty-sitter, so this isn't going to be a regular kitty-sitting evening. Got it?"

"Yeah!" they all shouted.

Scat Cat had three instruments with him: an upright bass, a trumpet, and a small piano.

"Gather 'round, you cool cats. We're making music!" Scat Cat exclaimed.

He showed Toulouse where to put his fingers on the bass. Next he gave Marie the trumpet and put Berlioz on the piano. Together they jammed for over an hour, having a grand old time.

"Okay, let's go," Scat Cat said.

"Go where?" Marie asked.

"We've got a gig and we don't want to be late," Scat Cat said. "You three cats are going to *perform*, dig it?"

Scat Cat led the three down the block to a club, where he had signed them up for the weekly open-mike jazz show.

"I don't think we can perform tonight," Berlioz said, shaking his head. "We're not very good."

Scat Cat looked at the three kittens. "You have to play from here," he said, pointing to his heart. "You all have soul—you can't teach that. If you miss a note, just keep playing. *Feel* the vibe."

The kittens smiled. "All right," they said. "Let's rock!"

As they strutted onstage, the familiar faces of Duchess and O'Malley greeted them from the crowd. They had been about to return home from their evening when they saw Scat Cat leading the trio into the club.

"One, and a-two, and a-three," Scat Cat counted, and they began to play.

Throughout the club, heads bopped and paws tapped. The crowd was mesmerized.

"This is the best jazz group I've ever seen," O'Malley whispered to Duchess, and the happy couple sat back and let the music take over the night.

Back to the Winter Woods

Tinker Bell lived in a magical place called Pixie Hollow, where all four seasons existed side by side. Warm fairies like Tink were only allowed in the warm seasons, but Tinker Bell had snuck into winter to see what it was like.

Tink loved the snowy landscape, but she was even more amazed when her wings started to sparkle. In the Book Nook, Tink discovered that the only person who could explain why this had happened was the Keeper of All Fairy Knowledge—and he was a winter fairy. Tink had to go back to the Winter Woods!

Tinker Bell wrapped her wings in a warm winter coat and hid inside one of the snowflake baskets that was headed to the Winter Woods. Soon a snowy owl swooped down and grabbed Tinker Bell's basket. As the owl crossed over into winter, Tink felt an icy blast of air.

A few minutes later, a winter animal fairy named Sled appeared. "Ya ready for the drop off?" he asked the owl. The owl hooted nervously and then let go of the basket.

"Look out!" cried one of the fairies below.

Tink's basket crashed. The book that Tink had brought with her flew out of her grasp and onto the ice. As she crept toward it, a giant shadow fell over her. It was Lord Milori, the Lord of Winter!

But Lord Milori didn't see Tink. "That's odd," he remarked, picking up the book. "Return this to the Keeper," he said. "He can send it back to the warm side with his next delivery."

Tink realized that if she followed the winter fairy, she would find the Keeper. When she was sure no one was looking, she slipped out of the basket and into the Hall of Winter. She hadn't gone far before she ran into a snowy lynx! Tinker Bell jumped back in surprise, but the lynx just looked at her and yawned.

Tink found the Keeper sitting behind a desk. Then she noticed the shadow of another fairy—with sparkling wings! Tink's wings began to sparkle, too! There was something very special happening. Tink couldn't wait to find out what it was.

The Shadow Game

Andy loved going to Cowboy Camp. He looked forward to it all year. So did his favorite toy, Woody. One summer Andy decided to take all his *Woody's Roundup* toys with him.

The first night, while the campers were fast asleep, the gang decided to sleep under the stars.

But Jessie didn't want to go to sleep. "Let's play a shadow game," she said excitedly. She jumped up. "Whoever makes the scariest shadow wins!"

Woody and Bullseye thought the game sounded like fun.

"Who wants to start?" Jessie asked.

"Ladies first," Woody replied.

"Yeeeeehah!" Jessie exclaimed loudly. She flapped her arms up and down. "Look, I'm a bat. Nah, that's too easy. I'll come up with something better."

A few minutes later, Jessie motioned Bullseye toward the fire. She put her hands in fists and curled up her index fingers.

"Why, it's a longhorn steer!" Woody exclaimed, pointing to Bullseye's face.

"That's right, pardner," Jessie answered.

Next it was Bullseye's turn. The horse thought for a moment. Then he leaped up and yanked the hat off Woody's head.

"Hey!" the cowboy cried. "Now why would you do that?"

But Bullseye wasn't being rude. He was making a shadow! "It's a mountain lion!" Jessie exclaimed.

"Good one, Bullseye!" the cowboy said. "Now it's my turn."

Woody got up and ran off. A minute later, he returned with a stick. He took his hat back from Bullseye and walked toward a large rock.

"Sssss," he hissed.

"Oooh, a serpent," Jessie said. "That's more frightening than the mountain lion. But I bet I can do one that's even scarier." She tied a couple of sticks to her boot and made a shadow of a monster. "Rrrrrrrrr," she roared.

The shadow looked so real that it frightened Bullseye. He whinnied loudly and hid behind a rock.

"It's okay, Bullseye!" Jessie said. "It was just part of our shadow game."

Bullseye slowly came out from behind the rock.

"Well, Jessie," Woody said. "I think you win after all!"

OCTOBER
31

Dressed to Scare

Cinderella worked from morning until night doing the bidding of her stepmother and stepsisters. In return, they treated her unkindly and dressed her in tattered old clothes.

It wasn't a very fair deal. Luckily, Cinderella had the friendship of the animals in the manor, including two mice named Jaq and Mary.

"Poor Cinderelly," said Jaq as he and Mary watched their dear friend scrubbing the floor. "She needs a present."

"Hmm," Mary replied. "Let's make a new dress!"

"Good idea!" Jaq replied. But he wondered what they could use for cloth. He looked around, then scurried over to a sack of feed and gnawed it open.

"Jaq, no!" Mary scolded. "You can eat later."

"No-no," Jaq explained. "This cloth is for Cinderelly's new dress. See?" He gestured toward the sack.

The other mice joined to help. They cut out the dress in no time, sewing it together with some thread they had borrowed from Cinderella's sewing kit. Then they stepped back to admire their work.

"Too plain!" Mary announced.

"Yes," Jaq agreed in a disappointed voice. "What should we do to fix it?"

The birds in the barn twittered excitedly. They had just the thing! In no time, they strung berries and kernels of corn, then helped the mice stitch them along the hem, sleeves, and neck of the dress.

"There!" said Perla. "Much better!"

With the birds' help, the mice hung the dress on a post in the garden where Cinderella kept her straw hat. Then they went to fetch Cinderella.

Cinderella gazed at the sackcloth dress on the post with her hat perched on top. "Oh, thank you!" she exclaimed. "I've been needing a scarecrow for the garden!"

Jaq opened his mouth wide to explain, but Mary clamped her paw over it. "You're welcome, Cinderelly," she said.

After Cinderella had gone, Jaq frowned. "We sewed a bad dress."

"But we made a good scarecrow," Mary told him, trying to look on the bright side.

"Yes. And Cinderelly's happy!" Jaq agreed.

And to the mice, that was the most important thing of all.

A Working Holiday

Sebastian the crab loved his busy job as court composer for King Triton. He wrote songs, ran rehearsals, and consulted with the king.

One day, King Triton burst into the rehearsal hall and announced, "Sebastian! You need a vacation. I want you to relax and forget about work for a few days. And that's an order."

After Sebastian had gone, King Triton assembled his daughters and the court musicians.

"Sebastian has been my court composer for many years," he announced, "and I've been wanting to honor him with a grand concert. Now that he's away, we can finally prepare a wonderful surprise for him."

Meanwhile, Sebastian was at the Coral Reef Resort. "Well, here I am at the most beautiful spot in the sea," he said to himself. "But I am bored out of my mind!"

When he couldn't sit still any longer, Sebastian decided that he would sneak back to the palace for a few minutes just to see how everything was going.

The crab wandered into the concert hall, where he found the orchestra and Triton's daughters about to rehearse.

"Sebastian!" cried Ariel. "What are you doing here?"

"Oh, nothing," he said. "I forgot my conducting baton. I never go on a vacation without it." He looked at Ariel. "And what are you doing here?"

Thinking quickly, Ariel told Sebastian that they were preparing a last-minute concert for her father.

That was all Sebastian had to hear! He immediately set to work rehearsing the musicians.

Sebastian rehearsed with the band for three days. Then he snuck out of the palace and made a big show of returning, pretending that he had been away on vacation the whole time.

Triton led Sebastian to the concert hall, where the king gave a glowing speech about the crab's many contributions throughout the years. Then the elaborate program of music began. The orchestra played beautifully, Ariel and her sisters sang exquisitely, and King Triton beamed proudly.

"What do you think?" Triton asked.

"It's perfect!" said Sebastian. "I couldn't have done a better job myself!"

A Wintry Walk

"It's so beautiful," Belle murmured as she gazed at the snow outside.

Suddenly, a heavy red cape was draped over her shoulders. "How about a walk?" the Prince asked.

Belle thought that was a wonderful idea.

The Prince smiled mischievously. "You don't want to forget these, now, do you?" He pulled a pair of large snowshoes out from behind a chair.

"Snowshoes!" Belle cried, clapping her hands together. She had often gone snowshoeing with her father when she was a little girl.

Minutes later, Belle and the Prince were in the castle courtyard, strapping the snowshoes onto their boots. Belle gracefully walked toward the gate to the forest, pausing to scatter birdseed for the neighborhood birds. But the Prince was having trouble. He kept tripping over the giant shoes.

"When I was a beast, I just walked through the snow," he said. "I didn't have to bother with silly things like these!"

The Prince stepped forward and tumbled headfirst into a deep snowbank.

"You're thinking too much," Belle said. "It's actually a lot like walking in regular shoes. You just have to keep your feet a little farther apart so they don't get caught up in each other."

"Hmm," the Prince said, stepping forward. But when he lifted his other foot, it caught on the snow, and he fell down again.

Belle stifled a giggle as she helped him to his feet. "Step lightly," she suggested.

"I'll say," the Prince grumbled. He stepped more lightly this time and moved easily across the snow. Soon the Prince was keeping up with Belle, who led him all the way through the forest. They even stopped to pick berries!

When they got back to the castle, they found hot chocolate and cookies waiting for them in front of the fire!

"Oh, good," said the Prince. "Eating! This is one thing I'll always be good at." He picked up a cookie, which broke and fell with a *plop!* into his cup.

"Aw," he said, looking very sad.

"You know," Belle said with a teasing smile, "you aren't so different from the clumsy beast I fell in love with after all, are you?"

The Magic of Friendship

One day, the Seven Dwarfs were visiting Snow White and the Prince at their palace. They were having a picnic.

"Please, help yourselves," said Snow White as she passed out china plates. "One for you . . . and you . . . and . . . Oh, my! Where is Dopey?"

Snow White and the Prince and all six Dwarfs searched everywhere for Dopey. Finally, Snow White spotted him. He had found a caterpillar!

"Dopey, why don't you bring your new friend along?" Snow White suggested.

Everyone enjoyed the picnic. They ate and ate and ate, until every crumb was gone. Then it was time for the Dwarfs to go home. Dopey took his new caterpillar friend with him.

A few days later, Snow White visited the Dwarfs at their cottage. When she arrived, she found poor Dopey in tears! She asked him what was wrong and he took Snow White outside. Then he pointed to a hard, shiny shell hanging from a branch.

"That old caterpillar went in there a few days ago," said Doc. "Now he won't come out."

Snow White shook her head and then wrapped Dopey in her arms. "Oh, Dopey," she said gently, "didn't you know? The caterpillar is changing!"

"Er . . ." Doc began. "Changing into what?"

Snow White pointed to the butterfly and smiled. "Into that!"

Sure enough, the Dwarfs turned and looked just in time to see the little shell crack open. A creature—Dopey's caterpillar—began to push out. Slowly but surely, the small wings began to open.

"It's a *butterfly!*" cried Happy.

Dopey smiled a big smile and held out his finger to his caterpillar friend, now a fancy-looking butterfly! But instead of climbing onto it, the butterfly flew away! Dopey began to cry again.

Snow White tried her best to comfort little Dopey. "Don't worry," she reassured him. "Remember, I went away, too, but I still come back. Being a good friend sometimes means letting your friends go . . . and then letting them return for lots and lots of visits!"

Just then, the butterfly returned. And don't you know, he landed right on Dopey's nose!

Aurora's Slumber Party

Prince Phillip was away for a few days. Princess Aurora was lonely, and so she decided to invite the good fairies to spend the night.

The fairies arrived at the castle with their wands, ready to use their magic.

"We don't need magic to have fun," said Aurora. "There are all kinds of things to do."

"Is anyone hungry? I'll use a spell to make some food," said Merryweather.

"We have bread, butter, strawberries, and cream right here," Aurora pointed out. "You can make a snack without using magic."

"This is fun!" Merryweather exclaimed as she made herself a triple-decker berry sandwich. It looked so good, the other fairies raced over to make their own. When Flora bit into hers, a dollop of cream flew across the room, right onto Aurora's face!

"Oops," Flora said. "I'm sorry, Princess." But Aurora wasn't upset. In fact, it made her giggle.

A little later, Fauna had an idea. "Let's make a treat for the morning," she suggested.

"Why don't we make some cinnamon rolls?" Aurora offered. They made the dough and left it in the kitchen to rise.

While they were waiting, the friends went upstairs. Flora grabbed a pillow and swung it at Aurora. The princess ducked and grabbed a pillow of her own. A few minutes later, feathers covered the room.

"It's probably time to finish the rolls," Aurora said. She and the fairies went back down to the kitchen and saw that the ball of dough had become the size of a table!

"I *may* have used a teensy bit of magic," Merryweather admitted.

"That's all right," Aurora said with a yawn. "We'll have enough for the whole kingdom."

Fauna pulled out her wand. "I think a little more magic would make this a lot faster."

A few minutes later, all the rolls were done. Aurora and the fairies went back upstairs.

"Let's read a story," the princess said.

And so Flora began to read. After a few minutes, everyone grew sleepy.

"This has been a wonderful slumber party," Aurora said. "Good night, fairies."

"Good night, Princess," the fairies replied.

And very soon, they all drifted off to sleep.

Winter Nap

Bambi nosed under the crunchy leaves, looking for fresh grass. There was none. He looked up at the trees, but there were no green leaves there, either.

"Don't worry, Bambi," Thumper said when he saw the confused look in Bambi's eyes. "We find what we can when we can, and we always make it until spring."

Bambi sighed and nodded.

"Besides, it's better to be awake than napping all winter. Yuck!" Thumper hated to go to bed, even at bedtime.

"Napping?" Bambi didn't know that some animals slept through the winter months.

"Sure. You know, like Flower and the squirrels and the bears. Haven't you noticed the chipmunks putting their acorns away the past couple of months?"

Bambi nodded.

"That's their food for the winter. As soon as it gets cold enough, they'll just stay inside and sleep," Thumper explained.

"But how will they know when it's time to wake up?"

Thumper tapped his foot to think. It was a good question. Since he had never slept through the winter, he wasn't sure of the answer.

"Let's go ask Flower," he said.

And so the two friends headed for the young skunk's den.

"Flower, you sleep all winter, right?" Thumper asked.

"It's called hibernation," Flower said and yawned a big yawn.

"Bambi wants to know who wakes you up in the spring," Thumper said.

"You'll be back, won't you, Flower?" Bambi asked worriedly.

The little skunk giggled. "Oh, we always come back. Just like the grass and the flowers and the leaves," Flower explained. "I never thought about what wakes us up. It must be the sun."

Bambi smiled. He didn't know the grass and leaves would come back in the spring, too! He was feeling much better about the forest's winter nap.

Suddenly, Thumper started laughing. He rolled onto his back and pumped his large hind feet in the air.

"What is it?" Bambi and Flower asked together.

"You really are a flower, Flower!" Thumper giggled. "You even bloom in the spring!"

The Overnight Camp-In

It was raining outside, so Mickey and his friends were having a camp-in.

"Okay," said Daisy. "Let's get this campin' started. Hmmm, what's the first thing we would do if we were outdoors?"

"I always like to smell the fresh air," said Minnie.

"That's a great idea, Minnie!" said Mickey. He put a big bouquet of flowers near the fan. Then he turned on the fan. Everyone closed their eyes. They took deep breaths.

"It smells like the outdoors," said Daisy. "But I wish it sounded more like the outdoors, too."

"Maybe a Mouseketool can help!" said Mickey. "The music box makes sounds."

Mickey wound the music box. Instead of playing music, it made noises that sounded like nature.

"If we were camping out here, we'd probably be setting up the tent," said Minnie.

"Let's do it!" said Mickey. "We can set up the tent inside!"

The friends quickly untied the tent. "How can we make the tent stand up?" asked Daisy. "We can't stick the spikes into the floor the way we would into the ground!"

"I guess we need another Mouseketool," said Mickey. "How about these four neckties! Neckties are good for tying. We can use them to tie the spikes at the ends of the tent to things around the room."

And that's just what they did!

"It's time for ghost stories!" said Minnie once the tent was up. Everyone sat in a circle, but it didn't feel spooky enough.

"We need a campfire!" said Daisy. "You can't tell good ghost stories without a campfire."

"Let's get another Mouseketool," said Mickey. "The flashlight! We've got ears! Say cheers!" said Mickey.

Minnie turned off the lights. Then she turned on the flashlight, held it under her chin, and told scary stories.

"I guess we should all get ready for bed," Mickey said.

So they did. But before they got into the tent, everyone lay on their backs, looking up at the ceiling and thinking about what a great time they'd had with their camp-in!

Alice's Mad Manners

"Clean cup! Clean cup! Move down!" The Mad Hatter shoved Alice aside, nearly spilling her tea.

Alice took a new spot and waited patiently while the Hatter and the March Hare poured a fresh round of tea. Alice tried to recall what her mother and sister usually did at tea parties. It seemed to her that they just sat around and chatted. Perhaps, thought Alice, that is what I ought to do, too.

"Pardon me." Alice addressed the March Hare because the Mad Hatter seemed quite busy buttering his saucer. "Our neighbors got a new dog. He's a—"

"A dog? A dog?" the March Hare shouted. "Where?" He hopped up onto the table, upsetting a plate of toast.

"Oh, I'm terribly sorry." Alice stood and tried to calm the poor hare. "I should have known you wouldn't like dogs. Dinah hates them, too, you know. When Dinah sees a dog, she practically climbs the curtains."

"Very sensible!" the Hatter said, waving his butter knife. "Just who is this clever 'Dinah'?"

"Oh, she's my—" Alice stopped herself. She had got into quite some trouble for

mentioning her cat before. The Dormouse had run off in a panic, and the Hatter and March Hare had given chase. She would not make that mistake again. She whispered in the Hatter's ear. "She's my kitten."

"But that's a baby cat!" the Hatter cried.

Just as Alice feared, the Dormouse bolted and the March Hare started hopping about just as soon as the word *cat* was out of the Hatter's mouth.

"Really, my dear. It is most rude to threaten us on our unbirthdays!" the Hatter cried.

"I'm really very sorry," Alice sighed, sinking back into a chair. She was only trying to be polite. Perhaps, Alice thought to herself, in this place it is better to say what you think you oughtn't instead of what you think you ought.

Turning to the Hatter, she said, "This party isn't very fun, and you aren't very nice!"

The Hatter grinned. "Thank you ever so much, my dear young lady. Tea?" he asked.

"Thank you ever so much," said Alice. She was beginning to get the hang of this!

The Prisoner

Rapunzel's golden hair had magical healing powers. As a baby, she had been kidnapped by Mother Gothel, who used her hair's magic to stay forever young. The woman pretended to be her mother, and she locked her away in a tower and never let her out.

But one day, Flynn Rider had come along. Rapunzel had convinced him to take her to see the floating lights that rose in the sky every year. With his help, Rapunzel had learned to stand up for herself. Finally, he had taken her out on a boat to see the lights. They had been as amazing as she dreamed they would be.

But then Flynn had abandoned her.

With a heavy heart, Rapunzel returned home with Mother Gothel. Alone in her room, the young girl thought sadly about Flynn. Even Pascal, her pet chameleon, was finding it hard to keep her spirits up.

As Rapunzel stared at the paintings on her wall, she realized that she had painted the kingdom's emblem over and over. Then Rapunzel thought of the picture she'd seen of the lost princess. They had the same big green eyes.

Suddenly Rapunzel realized that *she* was the lost princess!

Rapunzel confronted Mother Gothel. "I have spent my entire life hiding from people who would use me for my power," she said, "when I should have been hiding from you!"

Rapunzel knew she had to find Flynn. He wouldn't have just abandoned her. Something must have happened!

"What did you do to him?" she asked Mother Gothel.

"That criminal is to be hanged for his crimes," Mother Gothel replied.

Rapunzel fell to the ground, devastated. How could she have let such a thing happen? But as Mother Gothel tried to comfort her, she grew angry.

"You were wrong about the world and you were wrong about me and I will never let you use my hair again," she shouted at her mother.

As Rapunzel headed toward the window, Mother Gothel grabbed her.

"You want me to be the bad guy? Fine. Now I'm the bad guy," she said.

And with that, she chained the girl up. Rapunzel struggled against her bonds, but it was no use. How would she save Flynn now?

A Party of Three

Widow Tweed hummed cheerfully as she decorated her cottage. Tod, the little fox she had adopted not long ago, watched with excitement. This was his first birthday in his new home!

"Now, Tod," said the widow, "who shall we invite to your party?"

Tod jumped on the windowsill and looked over at Amos Slade's farm. Then he jumped on the kindly woman's lap and gazed up at her with big, sad eyes.

"Oh, Tod! Stop looking at me like that. Well—all right! You can ask Copper over just this once!"

Later that afternoon, Tod invited Copper to the party. "I'm not supposed to leave the yard," Copper explained. "I'll get in trouble with my master."

"Don't worry," Tod said. "I've got it all figured out."

Then Tod headed over to Amos Slade's chicken yard. He ran among the birds, causing them to flap their wings and cluck in panic. That was Copper's signal to bark as loudly as he could. Slade burst out of the cabin just in time to see Copper chasing Tod into the woods.

Copper followed Tod all the way to Widow Tweed's back door.

"Quick, scoot!" she said, shooing the two into the cottage.

While Amos Slade wandered around the woods trying to find Tod and Copper, the party festivities at Widow Tweed's were just beginning. The three played hide-and-seek, pin the tail on the donkey, and freeze tag. Tod won every game. Then it was time to cut the cake.

As everyone had seconds, the widow spied Amos Slade coming out of the woods. She let Copper out the back door, where he stood barking ferociously.

"Good tracking, Copper!" Slade cried. "Did you chase that no-good fox all the way through the woods?"

Copper looked up at his master and wagged his tail.

"Copper," the man said, "what's that on your face?" The hound turned his head and quickly licked the cake crumbs off his muzzle.

"Hmmm," said Slade. "Guess I must be seeing things. Let's go home, then, boy."

Inside the cozy cottage, Tod smiled. It had been a wonderful birthday—and sharing it with his best friend had definitely been the icing on the cake!

Ask Nicely

"Steady, Samson," Prince Phillip said absentmindedly, tightening the horse's reins. "No need to hurry. We'll get there soon enough—and I need some time to think."

Phillip had a lot to think about. He was riding through the forest toward the castle of King Stefan and the Queen. Phillip's father, King Hubert, would be meeting him there. So would the girl Phillip was destined to marry.

"I hope I like her," he murmured to his horse. Then another thought occurred to him. "I hope she likes me!" he added. "I'd better make sure I impress her." But how? he wondered.

"I know!" he exclaimed. "I'll make a dramatic entrance. We'll gallop in and slide to a stop right in front of her. That will impress her for sure!" He whistled and gave Samson a little kick. "Come on, Samson! We've got to practice."

The startled horse snorted and gave the prince a dirty look. He planted his hooves and stood stock-still.

Phillip frowned impatiently. "Come on!" he urged his horse. "Go, Samson!" But Samson refused to budge.

"It's like you don't even *want* to help me," Phillip muttered.

Then the prince blinked. "Wait a minute," he said. "Why should you want to help me when all I do is order you around?" He patted the horse's shoulder. "Sorry, old boy."

He reached into his pocket for a carrot. He fed it to the horse, still patting him. Samson finished the carrot and snorted.

Suddenly, he galloped forward. Then he leaped up and kicked out his heels. Phillip hung on tightly, gasping with surprise as the horse skidded to a halt.

Phillip laughed. "Wow!" he said. "Thanks, Samson. That was perfect. I guess all I had to do was ask you nicely! Now if we can just repeat that for the princess . . ."

The prince's voice trailed off. In the distance he heard the faint sound of beautiful singing. He listened carefully. Who would be out in the forest singing like that? The prince instantly forgot the princess. He had to find the owner of that voice!

"Come on, Samson," he said. "Let's go see—if you don't mind, of course!"

A Misunderstanding

One fine morning, Winnie the Pooh found a lovely pot of honey outside his door with a note. "Whoever could have given it to me?" he wondered.

Pooh went to find Piglet, who was chasing butterflies, and together they found Rabbit, Eeyore, and Tigger. The friends decided to ask Owl to read the note. "This letter has been written by Christopher Robin," declared Owl. "He's gone to s-c-h-o-o-l. Skull! We must rescue him!"

To help them find the little boy, Owl came up with a plan. The friends set off with a map and came to a strange forest with scary plants and an enormous boulder towering up in front of them! The travelers found an opening in the boulder. They looked inside and saw it was filled with a tangle of thorny branches. Then they all thought they heard a growling Skullasaurus. Piglet ran as fast as he could out of the forest—leaving his friends behind.

When Piglet rejoined his friends, the hikers went off in search of Christopher Robin again. They discovered a cave that was a maze of crossing paths inside.

"Let's all go off in different ways," suggested Pooh. "One of us is sure to find Christopher Robin."

While the others were having their own adventures, Pooh found some ice crystals that made him look big and scary. He cast a scary shadow over his friends, who heard growling noises that grew louder and louder.

Tigger yelled, "It's the terriblest Skullasaurus ever!"

The friends all ran—including Pooh, who slipped and fell into a deep hole with an icy floor.

"Can anybody hear me?" Pooh called. But they couldn't.

Luckily, the other friends ran into Christopher Robin, and they all went back to rescue Pooh. They lowered a big honey pot down to pull him up!

"You misunderstood my message!" Christopher Robin said. "It said I was going to *school*."

"But what about the Skullasaurus?" squeaked Piglet. "We heard him growling!"

"That's no Skullasaurus," Christopher Robin said with a chuckle. "That's the sound of the rumbly tummy of a hungry-for-honey bear."

Tough Audience

The sticker on the door read *Enter at Your Own Risk.* But Mike wasn't scared. He had never met a kid he couldn't crack up. Tossing his microphone from one hand to the other, Mike sauntered through the closet door to face his audience.

"Hey, how ya doin' tonight?" Mike greeted the kid. The boy in the race car pajamas just glared. "Did you hear the one about the monster who made it in show business? He really clawed his way to the top." Mike paused for a laugh, but the kid was silent.

"All right. I can see you're a tough audience. Enough of the B material." Mike pulled out all the stops. He told his best jokes. He worked the room. But the kid didn't even crack a smile. Mike prepared to let the one about the seven-legged sea monster fly when he heard tapping on the closet door.

Mike pulled the door open a crack. "I'm working here," he whispered.

Sulley poked his head in. "Mikey, you're dying. You've been on for twenty minutes and you're getting nothing. There are plenty of other kids to make laugh tonight. You can come back to this one later."

"No way," Mike hissed. "He loves me. When he laughs he's going to laugh big. I can feel it."

Just then, a rubber ducky sailed through the air and hit Mike in the eye. "See? He's throwing me presents."

"Cut your losses, Mikey. Let this one go." Sulley put a large hairy paw on Mike's head and urged him back through the door.

"I'm telling you, I've almost got him," Mike said through clenched teeth.

"And I'm telling you to give . . . it . . . up." Sulley pulled harder on Mike. Mike grabbed the door frame and braced himself. Suddenly Sulley lost his grip, and Mike flew backward, skidding on the ducky and wiping out.

"Why, I oughta . . ." Mike leaped to his feet, ready to charge Sulley, but was interrupted by the sound of laughing. In fact, the kid was laughing so hard, tears streamed down his face.

Mike high-fived Sulley. "You know, some kids just go for the physical comedy," he said with a shrug.

Snow White's Special Day

With one kiss from the Prince, Snow White awoke. She had long been under a spell of eternal sleep cast by her stepmother, who had been jealous of the beautiful girl. But love's first kiss had broken the spell.

The Prince lifted Snow White onto his horse, and together they rode toward his castle.

As they neared the castle, the Prince helped Snow White down from the saddle. "There's something I must ask before we go through those gates," he said. "Will you do me the honor of marrying me?"

Of course Snow White said yes!

Wedding preparations began right away. The Prince's staff bustled around Snow White, asking questions about flowers and cake flavors and guest lists. Snow White glanced at the Prince nervously, but his smile put her at ease. She knew he would always be there to help her.

That evening, Snow White went to her room. It seemed very large—and quite lonely! She missed her friends. Suddenly, there was a knock at her door.

"Hello, my dear," the Prince said, peeking his head into the room. "I'm not sure about you, but I'm having some trouble planning this wedding—especially finding the perfect ring for you. So I thought I should bring in the best helpers I know."

The Prince opened the door. There stood the Seven Dwarfs!

The next day, as Happy, Doc, Bashful, and Sleepy helped Snow White with the dressmaker, Dopey, Grumpy, and Sneezy helped the Prince search their mine for the perfect diamond to put in Snow White's ring.

When the wedding day arrived, Snow White's animal friends helped her get dressed in her wedding gown. The royal dressmaker couldn't help but smile—the little animals' special touches complemented his work perfectly.

As she stood ready to walk down the aisle, Snow White looked at her seven dear friends. "You know," she said, "I do need to be walked down the aisle. Would you do me the honor?"

The Seven Dwarfs were overjoyed! And so they walked their princess down the aisle and gave her away to the prince of her dreams.

The Secret Gourmet

When the sun shines in New Orleans, the whole town sings and dances. And that was reason enough for Charlotte's father to want to share a meal with friends.

"Charlotte, darling," he said to his daughter one sunny evening, "what would you say to going to eat at Tiana's restaurant?"

The young woman never missed a chance to visit Tiana. They were very fond of each other. And now that Tiana had married Prince Naveen and they had opened a restaurant together, it was even more fun to visit her!

As Charlotte and her father drove down the road, no one noticed their dog, Stella, fast asleep on the back seat.

Stella woke with a start when the car pulled up in front of the restaurant. Usually, she didn't like to leave the house. She was about to bark, but then she recognized the delicious smell of Tiana's cooking.

Suddenly, Stella didn't want to go back to the mansion after all. She snuck quietly into the restaurant kitchen through the door at at the back of the building.

Meanwhile, Charlotte and her father were joining Eudora, Tiana's mother, who was dining with Naveen's parents.

"Five house gumbos, coming up!" Tiana said.

At the back of the room, Louis the alligator and his band were playing jazz music. The atmosphere at Tiana's Palace was fantastic. Charlotte clapped her hands with joy. "We're going to have such an amazing evening! All that's missing is Stella. What a shame she doesn't like going out."

Poor Charlotte! She had no idea what was happening in the kitchen. Tiana's chef had found the dog and was treating her to anything she wanted to eat. Stella could not possibly have been happier.

"We have a secret gourmet in the kitchen," he laughed. "Her appetite does me proud! Serve her as much as she wants—she's my guest!"

Stella barked with happiness. She was a secret passenger in the car and a secret gourmet in the kitchen. It was good to get out of the house after all . . . but only if you were a secret guest!

Simba's Thank-You Present

Simba lounged in the jungle, feeling happier than he'd felt in ages.

"I should do something to thank Timon and Pumbaa," Simba told himself as he watched his friends in the river nearby. "Something really special!" He decided to make them a present. When he saw a piece of bark lying on the ground, he had an idea.

"Ta-da!" he exclaimed a while later, leading his friends to the gift.

Pumbaa blinked. "Thanks," he said. "Er, what is it?"

"A scratching spot," Simba said, flexing his claws. He'd used vines to attach it to a thick tree trunk at shoulder height.

"Gee," Timon said. "Nice thought and all, Simba, but it's a little high for me." He stretched to his full height but could barely reach it.

Pumbaa nodded. "And I don't scratch." He held up one foot. "Hooves, you know."

"Oh." Simba hadn't thought of that.

"Thanks anyway, kid," Pumbaa said.

Simba decided to try again by building them a nice, soft bed to sleep in. He dug a cozy hole in the ground, then filled it with soft things—feathers, sand, leaves, and bits of fur.

"Ta-da!" he cried when he showed his friends.

"What are you trying to do, kill us?" Timon exclaimed. "Prey animals here, remember? If we sleep on the ground, we become somebody's midnight snack!"

Simba sighed. Why couldn't he think of a present they would like?

Suddenly, Simba realized something. "I've got to think like they think," he whispered. Slowly, a smile spread across his face. . . .

A little while later, he called them over again.

"I've got something for you." He pointed to a pile of palm fronds. "This time I think you're really going to like it. Ta-da!"

He pulled back the leaves. Underneath was a mass of wriggling, squirming, creeping, crawling creatures—bugs and grubs and worms of every shape and size . . . and flavor.

Timon and Pumbaa gasped with delight.

"Simba!" Timon cried. "You're a prince! It's just what we always wanted!"

"Yeah, thanks," Pumbaa mumbled through a mouthful of grubs. "You're a real pal!"

Simba smiled. "No," he said. "Thank *you*. Both of you. *Hakuna matata!*"

Survival of the Smallest

Dot and the other Blueberries were heading out for the First Annual Blueberry Wilderness Expedition. Their journey would take them to the thicket of tall grass next to the ant colony. It was only a few yards from home, but to a little ant, it seemed like an awfully long way.

As the group prepared to leave, some boy ants arrived to tease them.

"How do you expect to go on an expedition without supplies?" asked Jordy.

Dot put her hands on her hips. "For your information," she said in a superior tone, "the whole point is to survive using our smarts. Whatever we need, we'll make when we get there."

When the Blueberries reached the tall grasses, Dot consulted her survival guidebook. "Okay," she said, "the first thing we need to do is build a shelter from the sun."

"I know!" Daisy volunteered. "We could make a hut. All we have to do is stick twigs into the dirt side by side to make the walls, then lay leaves over the top for the roof."

The rest of the Blueberries decided this was a great idea. With a lot of teamwork and determination, they completed a shelter to comfortably hold the troop.

"Now," said Dot, looking at the book again, "it says here we need to protect our campsite."

So the girls dug a narrow trench in front of the hut, just as the guidebook instructed.

A short while later, they heard a scream. When they went to investigate, they discovered Reed, Grub, and Jordy at the bottom of the trench.

It was clear to the Blueberries that the boys had been up to no good.

"Girls," said Dot, pointing to the boys, "observe one of the Blueberries' most common natural enemies—though certainly not one of the smartest."

When it was time for the Blueberries to pack up and hike home, the boys were still stuck in the trench. "Say the magic words and I'll get you out of there," said Dot.

"Okay, okay!" Reed, Grub, and Jordy agreed. "Blueberries rock."

Dot lowered a ladder she had expertly made of sticks. "You bet we do!" she said. "'Cause if we can survive you, we can survive anything!"

A History Lesson

Ariel hung her head. The little mermaid had been caught going to visit the surface—again—to see her seagull friend, Scuttle. King Triton couldn't understand Ariel's interest in the human world. Suddenly, the king had an idea.

"You know, Ariel," he said thoughtfully, "you're so interested in learning more about the human world, but I bet you don't know that much about the world you live in!"

Ariel looked up. "What do you mean, Daddy?" she asked, looking confused. "What's there to know?"

"Well," said Triton, "for starters, do you know about the first queen of the merfolk?"

"I guess not," Ariel replied.

Ten minutes later, Ariel and her father were swimming slowly through the Royal Merseum (that's a merfolk museum, you know), and Ariel was discovering that merfolk history was much more exciting than she had ever imagined.

"This is a portrait of Queen Fluidia, the first queen of the merfolk. She was my great-great-great-great-great-great-great-great-great-great-great-grandmother," said King Triton. He gestured at a sandpainting of a regal mermaid holding a pearl scepter. "That would make her your great-great-great—well, you get the idea. Anyway, Fluidia united all the merfolk into one kingdom many years ago to fight an invasion of sharks. The shark army was the greatest, fiercest army the ocean had ever seen, but Fluidia was more than a match for them!"

"Wow," said Ariel. "She sounds fierce."

"She was. She drove those sharks off almost single-handedly, and in gratitude the merfolk made her queen," King Triton said. "You know, you come from a pretty interesting family. And you remind me a lot of Fluidia, Ariel. You have her strength of will. I think you'll do great things—even if we won't always agree on *how* you'll do them."

"Thank you, Daddy," said Ariel.

Ariel felt like her father was beginning to understand her, so she decided not to tell her father that his trident looked like a dinglehopper. Maybe she would tell him some other time!

A Magical Discovery

Tinker Bell was a curious little fairy. She had hidden away in a snowflake basket going to the Winter Woods! It wasn't the first time she had visited winter, either. She had jumped over the border once before and her wings had sparkled strangely. Now she was determined to find out why.

The only fairy with the answer was the Keeper of All Fairy Knowledge, and he lived in the Winter Woods. So off Tink went.

Tinker Bell found the Keeper in the Hall of Winter. He was with a fairy named Periwinkle. As soon as Tinker Bell and Periwinkle stepped near one another, their wings began to sparkle.

The Keeper, whose name was Dewey, couldn't believe his eyes. "In all my years . . ." he marveled. Then he said, "Follow me."

Dewey guided the fairies onto a giant snowflake. A bright light shone down on them. When Tink and Peri put their wings into the light, the chamber filled with pictures! The fairies saw the journey of a baby's first laugh—a laugh that split in two! One half of the laugh traveled to the Pixie Dust Tree on the warm side of Pixie Hollow—where it turned into Tinker Bell. The other half blew into the Winter Woods, and Periwinkle was born.

"That is why your wings sparkle," Dewey said. "They're identical!"

"We're sisters!" Tinker Bell and Peri cried.

Suddenly, the fairies heard Lord Milori's voice. Dewey told Tink and Periwinkle to hide.

"Keeper? Are you in?" asked Lord Milori, the lord of winter. He wanted to talk to Dewey about a strange book that he had found. He was worried that a warm fairy might have brought it to winter. And he was right. It was Tink's book! She had dropped it when she'd landed in the Winter Woods.

"Crossing the border is forbidden," Lord Milori reminded Dewey. "If a warm fairy comes here, you will send them back."

"Of course," Dewey replied.

When Lord Milori had gone, Dewey told the girls that they could spend a little time together before Tink had to go home.

The sisters soon discovered that they had a lot in common. They were thrilled to have found one another.

Starry Night

Bonnie was camping out. She gathered her toys and brought them to the garden. Then she carefully set up her tent and arranged the toys inside.

Just then, her mom called to her. "Bonnie! Dinnertime!"

"I've got to go and eat my dinner. But I'll be back," Bonnie told the toys.

Left alone in the tent, the toys began to explore.

"This is a right comfortable spot," Jessie said, admiring Bonnie's sleeping bag.

"Yes, the accommodations are quite satisfactory," Mr. Pricklepants agreed with a nod.

"Well, shine my spurs!" Woody cried, noticing a camping lantern. He turned it on, and a warm glow lit up the tent. "How about a sing-along," Woody suggested.

Soon all the toys were singing. Then they decided to head outside. They all wanted to explore.

"Look!" Buttercup said.

"The stars are coming out!" Buzz smiled.

"That is the Big Dipper—seven stars that form a ladle shape," said Dolly.

Jessie hopped on Bullseye. "I'm gonna look around the yard!" she shouted.

"Follow me!" called Buttercup. "I'll show you the rose bed."

Trixie turned to the other toys. "Who wants to play freeze tag?" Before anyone could answer, she tapped Rex with her horn. The rest of the toys began running away as Trixie chased after them.

"I'm wiped out," Hamm said a little later.

"How about a shadow-puppet show?" said Mr. Pricklepants.

"Good idea," Woody said, leading all the toys inside the tent.

The toys used Bonnie's flashlight to create shadow puppets on the wall.

"A sleepover wouldn't be complete without a scary story," Mr. Potato Head said. He clicked off the flashlight. "Once there was a toy in a forest. The forest was dark. Very dark."

Suddenly, the toys heard the sound of someone running.

"Ahhh! " Rex shrieked as a huge shadow loomed over the tent. The toys all flopped over and went still. The tent flap opened up. . . .

"I'm back!" Bonnie said, smiling at her toys. "Did you miss me?"

The Desert Race

The Sultan was angry. The Desert Race was coming up, and he was sure Agrabah would lose to Prince Fayiz of Zagrabah!

"I have an idea!" Jasmine said eagerly. "I could ride Midnight in the Desert Race. He's the fastest horse around!"

"Oh, no!" The Sultan looked shocked at the suggestion. "The Desert Race can be dangerous."

"How about if *I* ride Midnight in the race?" Aladdin spoke up.

The Sultan's face brightened. "What a splendid idea!" he cried.

The next day, Aladdin and Jasmine went to the stables. But when Aladdin climbed onto Midnight, the horse bucked and threw him.

Finally, the day of the race arrived. Prince Fayiz rode in on his impressive white stallion, Desert Warrior.

"What an odd-looking horse Aladdin is riding," the Sultan said to Jasmine. But the princess was nowhere to be found. The Sultan shrugged. "We can't wait any longer," he said, and he started the race.

A black horse with a veiled rider took the lead. As soon as they were out of view, the rider threw off the veil. It was Jasmine! "I just had to prove that you were the fastest," she whispered to Midnight.

Aladdin's horse spotted an oasis of water and jumped in. "Now that's more like it!" exclaimed the horse. Aladdin had a secret. His horse was actually the Genie!

On land, Jasmine and Midnight galloped off without a backward glance. Prince Fayiz and Desert Warrior stayed on Midnight's heels, until the horses had to jump a ditch. Midnight sailed over easily, but Desert Warrior skidded to a stop!

Now there was nothing to keep Jasmine and Midnight from winning. Suddenly, Jasmine heard the sound of hoofbeats close behind her. It was Aladdin! Their two horses crossed the finish line at the same time.

"Congratulations!" Aladdin said.

"Same to you," Jasmine replied. "But where did you find such a fast horse?"

"Er . . ." Aladdin looked at his feet.

"Surprise!" the Genie cried, turning back into himself.

"Sorry, Princess," the Genie said, winking. "We were just horsing around!"

The Lost Mice

It had been a chilly night in the attic of the castle. The mice liked it up there, but they needed heavier blankets for the winter. They knew if they told the princess how cold it was, she would help them. But Cinderella was on her way downstairs and didn't hear Jaq calling her name.

The mice sighed as they walked in front of the fireplace in Cinderella's room. They were sure she wouldn't mind if they sat in front of the blazing fire to warm up, so all of the mice gathered around the fireplace and enjoyed the heat.

Soon the new housekeeper came in. When she saw the mice, she shrieked. She didn't know that the mice were Cinderella's friends! She chased them with a broom, and the mice ran out into the hallway, straight into the castle gardener.

"Take them outside!" the housekeeper said.

Meanwhile, Cinderella and the Prince were out riding. As their horses trotted through the countryside, they saw the castle gardener in one of the fields.

"Hello!" the Prince called out. But the gardener did not answer. The Prince turned to Cinderella. "That was odd," he said. "Why wouldn't he answer?"

"Perhaps he was lost in thought?" Cinderella replied.

Cinderella was right. The gardener was thinking hard. The housekeeper had told him to let the mice go, but he was worried about them. It was so cold outside! Finally, he decided to take the mice to the stables.

By that evening, Cinderella was starting to worry. She hadn't seen the mice all day. She was searching the castle for them when she ran into the Prince.

"I'm looking for our new housekeeper. Apparently she threw the mice out of the castle this morning!" said the Prince.

"Oh, no!" Cinderella cried. "Poor dears. They'll freeze outside!"

"Don't worry," the Prince said. He told Cinderella what the gardener had done. Together, Cinderella and the Prince went to the stables and thanked the gardener.

Cinderella was relieved to see her little friends safe and sound. From then on, the mice always had a warm place of their own—in one of the main rooms of the castle. And so did the kind gardener.

Puppy Trouble

Nanny was watching all fifteen Dalmatian puppies.

"Let's get Nanny to take us for a walk!" Lucky said.

Nanny turned and saw fifteen puppies holding their leashes in their mouths.

"Oh, all right, little ones," she said with a laugh.

When they reached the playground, Nanny unhooked their leashes and breathed a sigh of relief as the puppies scampered off to play. They were so busy playing that they didn't see Lucky chase a butterfly over the top of a wall and disappear.

Lucky landed in the back of a fire engine as it started speeding down the road!

"Woof! Woof!" Lucky barked. "I'm a fire dog!"

Lucky enjoyed his ride, but he was glad when the fire engine stopped. He knew that he had to get back to the playground, so he jumped down to the ground.

"A puppy!" someone squealed.

Lucky looked up and saw a little girl pushing a doll stroller. She stroked him.

"You can be my new dolly," the little girl said as she picked him up and put him in the stroller.

Suddenly, the little girl spotted something on the ground. As she bent down to pick it up, Lucky jumped out and ran away as fast as he could.

When he got back to the playground, Nanny and his siblings were just leaving. Nanny looked up at him as he approached her.

"Why, hello, little pup," she said to Lucky. "Too bad you can't come home with us—you're not a Dalmatian."

Lucky was confused, but then he spotted his reflection in a puddle. He was covered with dirt. Nanny didn't recognize him!

Lucky looked around the park and had an idea. He ran over to some children who were playing in a fountain. The children giggled as the little Dalmatian splashed about with them, washing off all the dirt.

Then Lucky ran home. He grinned as he spotted Nanny in front of the house, unhooking his brothers' and sisters' leashes. He joined them just in time!

Later, when Pongo and Perdita came home, they found Lucky sleeping in his basket.

"You see?" Pongo whispered to Perdita. "I told you nothing would go wrong."

Tiana's Royal Wedding

After many adventures and a ceremony in the bayou, Tiana and Naveen were finally getting married properly! They welcomed Prince Naveen's parents, the king and queen, for the wedding. But all too soon, the royal wedding planners cornered Tiana, announcing their ideas for her wedding.

Tiana's head was spinning! They had everything planned out without any input from her.

"I don't want to upset the king and queen, but their wedding planners' ideas aren't right for me," Tiana told her friend Charlotte.

"It's your wedding! You should do what you want," Charlotte said.

So Tiana made her first wedding decision—she asked Charlotte to be her maid of honor!

Then Tiana's mother arrived. "I'd like to make your dream gown for you," she said.

"Oh, Mama! That's perfect!" Tiana exclaimed when she saw her mother's sketch.

After everyone else had gone to bed, Tiana sneaked into the LaBouffs' kitchen to work on the menu with Charlotte.

"I want a taste of New Orleans," Tiana said. "Let's start with gumbo."

Later, Charlotte said, "Tia, every bride needs something old, something new, something borrowed, and something blue. So here's your something blue." She handed Tiana a beautiful blue necklace.

"Charlotte, this is amazing!" Tiana exclaimed. "And perfect."

Finally, Tiana had to tell Naveen's mother, the queen of Maldonia, that she wouldn't be following the royal wedding planners' ideas. Would she be upset?

"Tiana, dear, I'm so glad you are planning the wedding you want! But would you do me the honor of wearing the tiara I wore when I wed the king?"

Everything seemed perfect! The only thing missing was Tiana's father, who had died years ago. The night before the wedding, as she gazed at the Evening Star, Tiana realized that her father would always be part of her.

On her wedding day, Tiana carried her father's favorite old spoon. She wore the new gown from her mother, the tiara borrowed from the queen, and Charlotte's blue necklace. As she kissed Naveen, Tiana knew that love was what made her wedding—and her life—perfect.

The Princess Jewels

Rapunzel had been kidnapped as a baby by the evil Mother Gothel, who needed the girl's magical hair to stay forever young. The wicked woman had locked Rapunzel away in a tower and never let her out. But with the help of Flynn Rider (a thief turned friend) and Maximus the horse (part of the palace guard), Rapunzel was finally free.

And now, away from her tower and Mother Gothel, Rapunzel and her friends were traveling back to the kingdom. As they walked, Flynn told Rapunzel a story.

"When I was a kid in the orphanage, I read a book about a princess who said a tiara symbolized everything a princess should be. The white crystals stood for an adventurous spirit; green represented kindness; red stood for courage; and the round golden crown itself stood for leadership.

"For years, I thought of that tiara. Then one day, I actually met a gal who could wear it. She certainly was adventurous. She also showed kindness to everyone, courage, and definitely leadership. She turned every bad situation into something wonderful!"

"Flynn, are you talking about—"

Rapunzel started curiously.

"You!" Flynn exclaimed. "I'm talking about all those amazing things you did when you left your tower in search of the floating lights."

"But I did all those things when I had long, magical hair!" Rapunzel exclaimed. "I have no idea how to help anyone without magic."

Suddenly, they heard a noise behind them. "Nobody move!" someone shouted. "Hand over your horse!"

"Rapunzel!" Flynn shouted. "Run away!"

But Rapunzel did not run away. Instead, she ran to rescue Maximus. Rapunzel scolded the bandits.

"I'm so sorry," one man replied. "I need your horse to take my son to the doctor."

"Oh, my! Where is he?" Rapunzel asked.

Within minutes, Rapunzel was tending to the boy's injuries. He smiled as he was hoisted onto Maximus for a ride to the kingdom's doctor.

Rapunzel thought of the tiara—adventure, kindness, courage, and leadership. Suddenly, she realized she didn't need her magical hair after all.

Tinker Bell's Bedtime Story

"Shove over!"

"No. You shove over."

The Raccoon Twins were at it again. Peter Pan knew the bickering wouldn't stop until one of the boys had pushed the other out of the hammock.

"Say, Tink," Peter said, "how'd you like to be the new mother to all of us boys?"

Tink looked at Peter like he was crazy.

"Aw, c'mon," Peter said. "You've seen the guys since Wendy left. They're fighting something awful. They need someone to tuck them in at night and tell them a bedtime story."

Tink was silent for a moment.

"I guess I could ask Wendy to come back," Peter said, looking at Tinker Bell slyly.

That did it. The last thing Tink wanted was for Wendy to return!

"Tink is going to tell us a bedtime story," said Peter. The boys settled down. "Go ahead, Tink." Peter smiled. His plan was working perfectly!

Tink sat down and crossed her arms over her chest. She began to jingle.

"Once upon a time," Peter translated, "there was a beautiful fairy who, against her better judgment, lived with a pack of dirty, unruly, silly boys. And the dirtiest, unruliest, and silliest of them all was Peter Pa—hey!" Peter interrupted his translation.

Tinker Bell jingled spitefully at him.

"Okay," Peter said with a sigh, "I know it's your story. Go ahead."

Tink continued, and Peter translated: "One day, as the lovely Tinker Bell was minding her own business, the very smelly and unpleasant Peter Pan—*Tink!*—asked her to tell a bedtime story. Well, Tinker Bell didn't know any bedtime stories, so she went to fetch Captain Hook so that he could tell one."

With that, Tinker Bell flew out the window.

"Tink! Tink, come back!" Peter cried.

Tinker Bell returned and hovered in the window, jingling with laughter.

"That was a dirty trick!" Peter scolded. "And besides, that's no way to tell a bedtime story." He sat down next to the boys' beds. "You have to do it like Wendy did. Like this."

Now it was Tink's turn to smile. While Peter told a bedtime story and the Lost Boys drifted off to sleep, Tink curled up in her own little bed and closed her eyes. Her plan had worked perfectly!

Across the Border

Tinker Bell and Periwinkle were sisters. They lived in Pixie Hollow, but they had never met! Periwinkle was a winter fairy who lived in the Winter Woods, while Tink lived in the warm seasons of autumn, spring, and summer.

The two had just met, but it didn't take the sisters long to discover that they had lots in common.

Peri showed Tink a bundle of items she had collected. "You collect Lost Things, too?" Tink asked, amazed.

Periwinkle laughed. "I call them 'Found Things,'" she said.

Peri spent the rest of the afternoon showing Tinker Bell around the Winter Woods. Then they went to the Frost Forest, where Tink met Peri's friends Gliss and Spike. They all went ice sliding, which was like sledding down an icy roller coaster. Tink had an amazing time!

That night, Tink built a fire to stay warm while she and Periwinkle talked. She told Peri all about the beautiful things in the warm seasons of Pixie Hollow.

Periwinkle wished she could go there, but it wasn't allowed because the warmth might damage her wings.

Suddenly, the snowy floor of Peri's home crumbled beneath them. It was melting from the fire!

At that moment, Dewey, the Keeper of All Fairy Knowledge, arrived with his snow lynx. He rescued Tink and Peri and then said, "Lord Milori's right. Crossing the border is just too dangerous. Let's take Tinker Bell home."

The three fairies went to the border, where Tinker Bell and Peri sadly gave each other a hug good-bye. As the Keeper turned away, Tink whispered to Peri, "Okay, here's the plan. Meet me here tomorrow. There's something I need you to bring."

Tink had a plan that meant they could meet again. Both fairies knew that they might get into a lot of trouble, but now that they knew about each other, they weren't about to let anything keep them apart.

Back across the border, Tink went to see her friends Clank and Bobble. She needed their help. "It's kind of a secret," she told them.

Clank and Bobble loved secrets! So Tink told them all about her long-lost sister.

The Meaning of Thanksgiving

"Here, Stitch," Lilo said. "Hold up this Pilgrim man while I tack up his wife."

Stitch was confused. He was hungry and didn't understand why Lilo was running around hanging up decorations instead of eating.

"It's Thanksgiving," Lilo said. "You're supposed to be very, very hungry before we eat. Just like the Pilgrims, you know."

Now Stitch was even more confused.

"That's where Thanksgiving comes from," Lilo explained. "The Pilgrims were hungry, so the Indians made them a big dinner, and so they were all thankful."

"Pilgrims?" Stitch repeated uncertainly.

"Pilgrims," Lilo said firmly. "The Pilgrims were some people who came across the ocean in these big boats, and . . ."

Just then, Lilo had an idea. "I know how to explain it!" she cried. "Stitch, the Pilgrims were sort of like you—remember how you came to Earth, far, far away from your old planet, in a spaceship?"

Stitch nodded. He remembered that very well.

"Okay," Lilo said, "and remember how you were lost and all alone, and you weren't sure what to do, and everything seemed strange and unfriendly, and then you joined our family, and it was okay?"

"Family!" Stitch cried happily. He nodded again.

"Well, that's the same thing!" Lilo said. "You're like a Pilgrim. And now you're thankful to be here, right?"

"Right," Stitch agreed.

"That's how the Pilgrims felt, too," Lilo said. "They were thankful. So now we celebrate Thanksgiving to remember that. Get it?"

Stitch nodded. He understood about being thankful. He still wasn't sure why Lilo was hanging up so many decorations, and he still wasn't sure why they had to wait so long to eat the turkey he could smell cooking in the kitchen, but he decided it didn't matter. When Lilo left the room to get more decorations, Stitch took a small bite out of the cardboard Pilgrim. By the time Lilo returned, the whole Pilgrim was gone. She looked around in confusion.

"What happened to the Pilgrim?" she asked Stitch.

Stitch grinned at her. There was a tiny piece of the Pilgrim's hat stuck in his teeth. Lilo stared at it suspiciously.

"Happy Thanksgiving!" Stitch cried.

Ariel to the Rescue

"Oh, Eric! This is wonderful!" Ariel said excitedly as she twirled around the ballroom with her prince. "I can dance with you and see the ocean!" Ariel had once been a mermaid, but she had become a human to marry her true love, Prince Eric.

"Do you miss your sea friends?" he asked.

"Sometimes," Ariel replied. "But I love being with you."

A few weeks later, Eric took Ariel to the lagoon. Ariel noticed that it now had a big wall around it. The wall would keep out dangerous sea creatures, but it also had a gate for Ariel's friends to enter. In fact, Flounder had come to visit. Then Ariel saw something in the water.

"Look!" she exclaimed. As they watched, a small dolphin leaped out of the water!

"He's just a baby. I wonder where his mother is," Flounder said. He swam across the lagoon toward the baby, but the dolphin raced away.

"Poor little guy," Flounder said. "He seems scared of me."

"Let me try," said Ariel. Soon she had coaxed the baby to swim over to her.

"I bet his mother is on the other side of that wall," Flounder said.

Sebastian and Flounder searched, but they couldn't find the baby's mother.

That night, Ariel awoke to the sound of thunder. Scuttle flew up to their window.

"Come on, Princess! Flounder needs you, and quick!" squawked the seabird.

When she and Eric arrived at the lagoon, Flounder was trying to calm the frightened baby dolphin. "He needs his mother, Ariel!"

Ariel climbed onto the lagoon wall and called to the sea creatures. "Help me, please! I am Ariel, princess of the seas. I need my father, King Triton."

Below the surface, sea creatures raced to find King Triton. Suddenly, there was a flash of light! King Triton had arrived.

The storm quieted down. The baby dolphin's mother was at the lagoon gate, frantically trying to get in.

"Oh, dear!" Ariel exclaimed. "The gate won't open! She can't get in!"

Eric looked at King Triton and nodded. The sea king raised his trident and blasted down the wall. The dolphins swam to each other, and then the baby went to Triton to thank him.

Ariel was glad that everything was back to normal.

Dumbo's Daring Rescue

"**A**ll right, kid. You're on," Timothy Q. Mouse said from the edge of Dumbo's trunk. Dumbo was ready. He knew what he had to do, because he did the same thing every night. When the firefighter clowns called, Dumbo would leap from the platform and plummet toward the ground. Then, at the last possible moment, Dumbo would spread his tremendous ears and fly. The audience would cheer, and the show would be over.

Taking a step forward, Dumbo began to fall. He sped faster and faster toward the floor of the tent. The audience swam into view. They were screaming and laughing.

Then Dumbo saw something else. There, in the first row, was a little girl sitting all by herself. She was crying and holding on to a stick of cotton candy.

In an instant, the little elephant forgot all about the act. Spreading his ears, he swooped away from the shouting clowns. He scanned the seats intently. Why was the girl all alone? Where were her parents?

"Dumbo! What are you doing?" Timothy clung to Dumbo's trunk as he soared toward the peanut and popcorn sellers. "We don't have time for a snack now!"

Dumbo ignored his friend. The little girl needed help!

At last, Dumbo saw what he was looking for. There, next to the cotton candy stand, were two very worried-looking parents.

"Clara, where are you?" the father called. His voice was lost in the busy crowd. His daughter would never hear him calling!

Dumbo circled the tent again, turning back toward the bench where the little girl sat sobbing.

Swooping low, Dumbo stretched out his trunk and scooped up the little girl.

"Dumbo, what are you doing?" Timothy cried again.

Dumbo sailed back and placed the girl gently beside her parents. Immediately, the little girl's tears were dried. She was safe in her parents' arms!

The crowd went wild as Dumbo soared high over the arena. Even the clowns were smiling.

"Nice work, kid," Timothy said. "Good show."

The Gift Horse

Prince Phillip had just met the woman of his dreams in the forest. Now he wanted to buy her something to show her how much he loved her.

Samson shook his mane and refused to move a hoof. Shopping wasn't his idea of fun. He was tired and wanted to go back to the castle for some oats!

"C'mon, boy," pleaded the prince. "I'll give you some nice crisp apples."

Apples! Samson's eyes widened. Suddenly, he wasn't so tired anymore! With a bright whinny, he kicked up his hooves and took off.

When they reached the village square, the prince scratched his head in thought. There were so many shops. "What sort of gift do you think she will like? Red roses?" he asked, passing a flower shop.

As a horse, Samson didn't care all that much. Yet he did his best to answer and shook his head.

"Yes, you're right," said the prince. "She lives in the forest. She must see flowers every day."

They passed a dress shop, and the prince peered in the window.

"How about a new dress?" he asked Samson.

Samson shook his mane in irritation.

"No, huh?" said the prince. "Girls like to choose their own dresses, don't they?"

They passed more shops: a bakery, a hat shop, and a blacksmith.

Samson sighed. If he didn't help the prince find a gift soon, they could be here all day! With a whinny, Samson took off down the street. The prince yelped in surprise. By the time he'd taken back control of the reins, Samson had stopped in front of a jewelry shop.

"Samson, you're a genius!" the prince cried at the sight of the gems glittering in the window. "That sapphire ring sparkles as beautifully as her blue eyes."

The prince bought the ring, slipped it in his pocket, then mounted Samson again.

"To the castle!" said the prince. "I've got to tell my father I've found the girl of my dreams."

Samson whinnied and took off at a gallop. He didn't know what the king would say to the prince, but he was sure of one thing—he had certainly earned those apples!

A Family Reunited

Mother Gothel was a wicked woman who had stolen a princess when she was just a baby. Though she pretended to love the girl, whom she named Rapunzel, she only truly loved Rapunzel's magical hair, which kept the woman young forever.

One day, Rapunzel met Flynn Rider, a thief who helped her escape. But Mother Gothel found Rapunzel and had Flynn sent to the palace dungeon.

Rapunzel had finally discovered the whole truth: that she was the kingdom's lost princess and that Mother Gothel had kidnapped her.

Just then, Flynn arrived outside the tower. Although Mother Gothel had had him thrown in prison, he had escaped and rushed to Rapunzel's aid. Mother Gothel threw Rapunzel's long hair out the window for Flynn to climb. He hoisted himself up the golden locks, believing it was Rapunzel who had thrown it to him. But when he climbed through the window, it was Mother Gothel who greeted him . . . with a stab in the back!

The young girl promised to do whatever Mother Gothel wanted in order to save Flynn. But Flynn didn't want Rapunzel to sacrifice herself for him. As she bent over him, he picked up a piece of glass from a mirror that had been broken in the struggle and he cut off all of Rapunzel's magical hair!

Rapunzel's hair immediately faded, the golden color turning to brown. With a yell, Mother Gothel began to grow older and older . . . until she disappeared into a pile of dust!

"You were my dream," the dying Flynn told Rapunzel.

As Rapunzel wept, one of her tears fell onto Flynn's face and began to glow! Flynn was healed.

Overcome with happiness, Rapunzel and Flynn finally exchanged their first kiss. Then Flynn brought Rapunzel to the castle, where the King and Queen were waiting. What joy—their beloved daughter had come home, and their family was reunited at last!

In every corner of the kingdom, the people celebrated the return of their lost princess by launching thousands of lanterns into the sky—the same lanterns that had helped Rapunzel to find her way home.

Periwinkle's Trip

Tinker Bell lived in Pixie Hollow. Her sister, Periwinkle, also lived there, but they had just met! Tink was a warm fairy who lived in the parts of Pixie Hollow where it was always spring, summer, and autumn. Peri was a winter fairy who lived in the Winter Woods—and no fairy was permitted to cross the border.

The two had met when, overcome by curiosity, Tinker Bell had snuck across the border. But Tink could not stay long. It was just too cold for her.

Before Tinker Bell left, the sisters came up with a plan for Peri to visit the warm side. They just needed their friends' help.

The next day, Periwinkle arrived at the border with her frost-fairy friends and a glacier fairy. They had a huge block of ice with them.

Tink arrived with her tinker friends, Clank and Bobble, and the strangest-looking contraption the winter fairies had ever seen. It was a snowmaker! Clank and Bobble loaded the ice into the snowmaker, which grated it and turned it into snow.

"You did it!" cried Peri.

Peri flew across the border and into a cascade of snow pouring out of the snowmaker. She loved it! It meant that she could stay cold while she visited the warm seasons.

"This is Periwinkle, my sister!" Tink told her friends. Tink's friends surprised Peri with a rainbow and a field of blooming flowers!

Rosetta gave Peri a flower. "It's called a periwinkle," she told her.

Peri held up the little purple flower and covered it with frost. The others gasped as the flower glistened in the sunlight.

A few minutes later, Peri began to feel very weak. Her wings were wilting! Clank and Bobble realized that the snowmaker was running out of ice. There wasn't enough snow to keep Peri cold. They had to get her back to the border!

As Tinker Bell and Vidia carried Periwinkle into winter, Lord Milori appeared. Tink pleaded with him to help Peri as Vidia gently pulled Tink back to the warm side. Tink was in just as much danger as Peri if she didn't leave.

Tink hoped her sister would be okay. But would she ever get to see her again?

Sledding

Lady stood on the porch as Jim Dear and Darling walked up the front path. Jim pulled a sled, and Darling held their son. They were all covered in snow, rosy-cheeked and smiling from ear to ear.

"That was fun! Wasn't it, Darling?" Jim asked.

"I don't know the last time I had so much fun," Darling agreed, patting Lady on the head.

"But we should get out of these wet clothes before one of us catches a cold," Jim said, leaning the sled against the side of the house.

"I agree," Darling said. And the three of them hurried inside.

Just then, Tramp came walking up the front path. "Hey, Pidge," he said to Lady. "What do you say we take this old thing for a spin?"

"What is it, anyway?" Lady wanted to know.

"A sled!" Tramp told her.

"What do you do with it?" she asked.

"You ride down hills," Tramp said. "Come on. I'll show you. It'll be great! You saw how much fun Jim Dear and Darling had."

Tramp grabbed the rope in his teeth and pulled the sled across the porch and down the steps.

Lady took off after him. "Wait for me!" she cried anxiously.

"Come on, Pidge!" Tramp encouraged her. "Jump on!"

Lady jumped onto the sled, and Tramp pulled her down the snowy street and up to the top of a nearby hill. "What a view, huh?" he said.

"What a view indeed," Lady agreed. "What now?"

"Now, we ride," Tramp said. He pushed the sled forward and took a running leap onto it, sending them racing down the hill.

"Oh, dear!" Lady yelped as they went down the hill, the wind blowing back her ears.

"Just hold on!" Tramp instructed.

Lady squeezed her eyes shut, and Tramp barked with excitement. But suddenly they hit a patch of ice, the sled spun, and they went flying—right into a snowbank!

Tramp jumped to his feet. "Pidge, are you okay?" he asked anxiously.

"Okay?" Lady asked. She was already pulling the sled back up the hill. "Hurry up, Tramp! Let's do it again!"

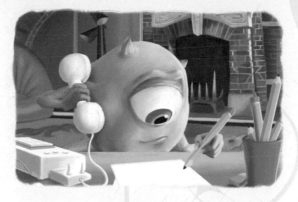

Monster Laughs

Sulley was worried. As the new head of Monsters, Inc., it was his job to make sure the power levels stayed high. But none of the monsters seemed to be getting enough laughs.

"Mikey, we've got a power problem," Sulley said to his friend. "It's been a year since we switched from scare power to laugh power, and the monsters aren't funny anymore. All their routines are old and dull."

Mike thought for a moment. "I got it!" he said, snapping his fingers. "I'll write some new jokes for all the monsters!"

Mike spent the next few nights writing jokes and inventing gags. He made a huge list. Then he gave his jokes to the other monsters.

But things didn't go so well when the monsters took the jokes into the kids' rooms.

A monster called Pauley tried one of Mike's jokes on a little girl.

"Why did the one-eyed monster have to close his school?" he asked. "Because he only had one pupil!"

The girl just gave Pauley and his *sixteen* eyes a blank stare.

"They're terrible!" said Mike. "I need to round them up for some practice. If they can learn to perform the jokes just like me, our power levels will go through the roof!"

"But, Mike, that's the problem," said Sulley. "The other monsters can't perform the jokes like you, because they're *not* you."

The next day, the monsters were feeling downhearted.

Suddenly, a very tall monster called Lanky slipped on a banana skin. When he landed, his arms and legs were all tangled up. Lanky started to laugh. Soon all the monsters were laughing. It was great!

Mike thought for a moment. "That's it!" he cried. "Instead of copying me, you just have to be yourselves! That's how to be funny!"

"That's right," said Sulley. "If you've got sixteen eyes—use them! If you have really long limbs—use them! Be proud of who you are!"

A few days later, the Laugh Floor buzzed with activity. Behind wardrobe doors, kids roared with laughter.

"Great job, Mikey," said Sulley. "Power levels are going back up!"

Buttercup the Brave

"Which horse would you like to ride today?" a stable groom asked Princess Aurora.

Aurora looked around. There were so many horses! It was always hard to choose. But then a fine palomino caught Aurora's eye.

"What's this horse's name?" Aurora asked.

"We call him Brutus, Your Highness," the groom replied.

"Oh, no!" Aurora exclaimed. "That won't do at all. I think I'll call him Buttercup."

The next day, Aurora decided to ride Buttercup to the fairies' cottage. But the moment they entered the woods, Buttercup became a different horse. He began to walk slowly and look around nervously.

"What's the matter, Buttercup?" Aurora asked. "Why, there's nothing to be frightened of!"

By the time they reached the cottage, Aurora was feeling a bit frustrated. How could a horse who was so brave at the palace be so timid in the woods?

Flora, Fauna, and Merryweather hurried out of their cottage. "Oh, what a beautiful pony!" Merryweather exclaimed.

Aurora sighed. "He is beautiful," she said. "But he seems to be afraid of the woods!"

"I'm sure it will be all right," Flora said. "You'll just need to be patient with him."

Soon it was time to say good-bye to the fairies. Aurora and Buttercup began to make their way back through the forest. Suddenly, Buttercup stopped abruptly.

"What is it this time?" Aurora asked with a sigh.

Then she looked ahead and gasped in horror. An enormous mountain lion was blocking their path!

To Aurora's surprise, Buttercup didn't panic or try to run. Instead, he stood proudly and puffed himself up to look even bigger than he was. He planted his hooves and snorted angrily at the mountain lion. Then he marched forward and struck out at the lion with his front hooves!

The lion let out a yowl and raced away. Buttercup had been brave when it really counted.

"Good boy!" she praised him. "You know, Buttercup, I think we make a perfect team!"

The Perfect Gifts

The holidays had always been Cinderella's favorite time of the year. She loved the cheer and good feeling of the season. Every year she cooked delicious holiday treats and crafted small decorations. And she had always managed to set aside time to make some small presents for her mouse friends.

Now that she lived in a beautiful castle, Cinderella found that she enjoyed the holidays even more. This year, Cinderella wanted to give especially wonderful gifts to her mouse friends.

First Cinderella went to the royal kitchen. "My mouse friends like cheese," she told the cook. "Could you make some cheese pudding?"

The cook assured her that the cheese pudding would be the best in the world.

Then Cinderella went to the royal tailor. She told him the mice's favorite colors, and he helped her pick out rich, beautiful fabrics. "I will make mouse outfits the likes of which have never been seen," he said, rubbing his hands together.

Finally, Cinderella went to the royal carpenter. "My mouse friends don't have any nice furniture. Can you help me?" she asked.

The carpenter said he would gladly make tiny beds and chairs and tables for the mice.

The next day, as Cinderella and Prince Charming were having tea, the cook, the carpenter, and the tailor arrived to deliver the presents for Cinderella's mouse friends. Cinderella thanked them and sent them each on their way with a kind word.

The pudding was a beautiful color, the clothes were artfully sewn, and the tiny furniture was grand and elegant. But none of it seemed quite right for Cinderella's mouse friends.

"I don't understand," Cinderella said sadly. "The cook and the tailor and the carpenter are the best in all the land. So why don't I like what they made?"

"Well," answered Prince Charming, "you know your mouse friends better than anyone else. Maybe *you* should make their presents."

"You know, that's a wonderful idea." Cinderella was delighted. "I'm going to make my friends the nicest gifts they have ever received."

Having a Ball

It was almost Christmas, and the puppies couldn't wait!

"Do you puppies know what comes before Santa and dinner and presents?" Perdita asked.

Patch wasn't sure. He sat down on the hall rug to think.

"We have to decorate and sing carols," Perdita said, wagging her tail.

At that very moment, Roger and Anita threw open the door to the study and invited all the dogs inside. Patch blinked. He couldn't believe his eyes. "What's a tree doing in the house?"

"Just watch." Perdy gave Patch a quick lick.

While the dogs looked on, Roger and Anita began to decorate the tree. They hung lights and angels, snowmen and tinsel. Of all the decorations, Patch liked the glittering glass balls the best. Balls were one of his favorite things! He couldn't take his eyes off them.

When the tree was ready, Anita brought in cocoa and dog biscuits. Munching on a biscuit in front of the fire, Patch didn't think the evening could get any better. Then Roger sat down at the piano, and everyone began to sing.

Patch howled along with the others, but he could not stop looking at the balls on the tree. A large red one was hanging near the floor. Patch reached over and gave the ball a pat with his front paw. It swung merrily above him. Looking at his reflection, Patch started to laugh. His nose looked huge!

Penny stopped singing to see what was so funny. "What are you doing?" Then Freckles joined them, then Lucky. The puppies took turns knocking the ball and watching it sway, then—*crash!*—it fell to the floor, shattering.

The singing stopped. Poor Patch was sure the special evening was ruined!

"Oh, dear." Anita scooped the puppies out from under the tree. "Careful, now," she said. "Those balls aren't for playing with."

While Roger swept up the glass, Patch cowered. He knew he was in trouble.

"Maybe I should give you all one gift early," Anita said, smiling.

Patch couldn't believe his luck! Instead of a firm talking-to, each puppy got to rip open a small package. Patch tore off the paper.

Inside was a brand-new red rubber ball!

Variety Is Best

"What in the world is *that*?"

The Queen of Hearts stopped short. It was a crisp autumn day, and she was taking a stroll in the royal gardens.

"What? What is it, Your Majesty?" several of the Queen's servants cried.

The Queen pointed to a tree. "Look!" she commanded. "That leaf. It's red!"

"Yes, my dear," the King said calmly. "You see, it's autumn, when many leaves change color."

The servants quivered, waiting for the Queen's usual cry: OFF WITH THEIR HEADS! But instead, the Queen . . . smiled!

"Red," she murmured. She looked down at her own red outfit. "Yes, perhaps this tree is on to something. Red is a fine color for just about anything." She cleared her throat. "From now on, I want *everything* to be red!"

The servants nodded and ran off in a tizzy. Soon everyone was busy painting things red.

Later, the Queen of Hearts went for another stroll with the King. "Look, my dear," the King said. "Everything is red, just as you wished."

The Queen looked around. The leaves were red. The trunks of the trees were red. The grass was red. Even the castle was red! The Queen frowned. Somehow, all the red didn't look quite as wonderful as she'd expected. "Hmmph," she said. "I don't like it. TOO MUCH RED!" She glared at the servants still holding their red paintbrushes.

"Yellow!" she bellowed. "I want everything *yellow* instead!

"Wait!" the Queen shouted. "I changed my mind. GREEN! No more yellow, GREEN!" Out came the green paint.

"No, PURPLE!" Out came the purple paint.

"No, ORANGE! No, BROWN! No, PUCE! MAGENTA! LAVENDER! NAVY! LIME! PINK! SKY BLUE! TAN! CARNELIAN! CYAN! BLACK! GOLD! CREAM! OLIVE! WHITE! BLUUUUUUUE!"

The Queen stopped to catch her breath. She looked around. "Now that's more like it," she said to the King. "Plenty of variety, just as it should be."

The King blinked. He stared at the purple leaves, the yellow tree trunks, and the pink grass.

"Of course, my dear," he said. "Just as it should be."

The Jewel of the Bayou

Prince Naveen was worried— Tiana's birthday was coming up, and he still hadn't found the perfect gift for his princess! Nothing had seemed special enough for Princess Tiana. But luckily, one morning, Naveen overheard Tiana and Charlotte in the kitchen.

"When my daddy and I used to go fishing in the bayou, we'd sometimes find a piece of swamp amber," said Tiana. "It was the most precious thing!"

"That's it!" whispered Naveen. He met up with the jazz-loving alligator, Louis. They were going to find Tiana some swamp amber!

As the birthday party began, Tiana couldn't find Naveen anywhere. A guest said he had seen the prince down by the old mossy tree in the bayou. Tiana was afraid Naveen was in trouble. She ran to the river and climbed into a rowboat. She saw Naveen in the distance. He dove into the water by the old tree.

"Naveen!" Tiana called out. When the prince didn't reappear, she dove into the water!

She found Naveen in a tangle of roots. Tiana grabbed his hand and pulled him to the surface.

Naveen reassured her that everything was fine and gave her a hug. He opened his hand to reveal a plain, muddy rock. "I was expecting a sparkling jewel, but this is just—"

"Swamp amber!" Tiana exclaimed. She explained that the rock brought back loving memories of her father.

"That is the most precious gift of all," said Tiana.

Back at Tiana's Palace, Mama Odie picked up the swamp amber. "A little sparkle couldn't hurt," she said, tossing the rock into a pot of gumbo. "Gumbo, gumbo in the pot, we need some sparkle. What you got?"

In a puff of magic, the swamp amber became a dazzling golden jewel set in a fine necklace.

"Mama Odie!" Naveen exclaimed. "How did you do that?"

Mama Odie winked at Tiana. "Oh, it's just a talent we have down here in the bayou. We like to take things that are a little slimy and rough around the edges and turn 'em into something wonderful!"

"Like turning a frog into a prince!" Naveen agreed. Then he and Tiana danced the night away.

Woody's Hat

It was Saturday morning, and the toys in Andy's room were waking up. Jessie yawned and stretched. "It's time for *Woody's Roundup!*"

On the show, Woody's hat flew off and Bullseye trampled it! Jessie picked up the hat. It looked pretty ragged.

"I have lots of hats," Jessie told Woody. "Maybe you can find a new one."

Jessie brought Woody all the hats she could carry. There were so many, they tumbled out of her arms.

Woody picked up one of the hats and put it on his head. "What do you think?" he asked.

Jessie smiled. "I think it looks mighty fine."

"I don't know," Woody said. "Do you think it's too brown?"

"How about that one?" Jessie said, gesturing toward a hat with buttons on the band. "It's a lighter brown."

"That one's not brown *enough*," Woody said.

"Hmm," Jessie sighed. She piled more and more hats onto Woody's lap. "There must be a hat here that you like. Keep trying. How about this one?"

"That one is pink!" Woody said. "I'm

sorry, Jessie, but none of those are right for me."

Jessie couldn't believe that Woody couldn't find *one* hat he liked in the huge pile she had brought.

"What we really need is a plan," she told Woody. "Why don't you tell me just what kind of hat you're looking for, then we can try to find it in the pile."

Woody leaned against the fence and thought. "I'd definitely like a brown hat," he said. "Not too dark or too light, but brown is best. It would be nice if it had a wide brim. And it should have stitching around the edge. But I don't think we'll find anything like that."

Sheriff Woody looked hopeless. Then Bullseye pulled Woody's old hat from the pile!

Jessie laughed when Bullseye held up the hat.

"Woody, I think Bullseye found just the right hat!" Jessie called out.

Woody grinned. "This is *exactly* the kind of hat I wanted! How does it look?" he asked.

"It's the best hat in the West!" Jessie replied.

The Reason for the Rule

Tinker Bell and her sister, Periwinkle, both lived in Pixie Hollow, but they had just met. There was a fairy rule that warm fairies, like Tink, lived in the spring, summer, and autumn, while winter fairies, like Peri, lived in the Winter Woods. Neither could cross the border.

Tinker Bell, overcome by curiosity, had crossed anyway. That was when she had met Periwinkle. After a day in the Winter Woods, Tink figured out a way for Peri to visit the warm side: she made a snowmaker. But her plan had backfired and Peri's wings had begun to wilt.

"This is why we do not cross the border," Lord Milori said. "The rule is there to protect you."

"Your rule will not keep us apart!" Tink cried.

"This is not Lord Milori's rule," said Queen Clarion, appearing behind her. "It's mine. I'm sorry."

Tink and Peri were sad. They gave each other one last hug before they parted. Then Lord Milori flew off on his owl, knocking the snowmaker into the stream as he went. But instead of going over the waterfall, the snowmaker got caught on a ledge, creating a small snowstorm out of the ice that flowed into it!

Meanwhile, on the warm side of Pixie Hollow, Queen Clarion tried to explain the importance of the rule to Tink. Lord Milori did the same with Periwinkle.

They told the girls that, long ago, two fairies had fallen in love. One of the fairies was from the warm seasons, while the other was from winter. Every day at sunset, the couple met at the border. One day, one of the fairies crossed the border. He ended up breaking a wing, for which there was no cure. After that, Queen Clarion made the rule to keep all fairies safe.

As Tink listened to the tale, she gazed out the window. It was snowing! Queen Clarion and Tink raced outside.

The Queen stopped at the edge of the stream. Clank and Bobble were desperately trying to free the snowmaker, but the air was already growing colder.

"The seasons have been thrown out of balance," Queen Clarion said worriedly. The snow was freezing the warm side of Pixie Hollow. If the Pixie Dust Tree froze, there would be no more pixie dust! Tink knew she had to think of a plan, and quickly!

DECEMBER
12

A Magical Surprise

It was a lovely day in Agrabah. In the palace garden, Princess Jasmine was pouring a bowl of tea for her pet tiger, Rajah. The problem was, this perfect day was just like *every other* perfect day.

"Sorry to be so glum," Jasmine said to Rajah. "I was hoping to spend some time with Aladdin, but I can't find him anywhere."

Rajah nodded his furry head.

Just then, to Jasmine's surprise, the Magic Carpet zoomed into the garden and stopped in front of her—all alone. Jasmine realized the carpet wanted her to jump on for a ride.

Soon Jasmine was riding high above the kingdom. "Oh, Magic Carpet, it's beautiful up here," Jasmine said with a sigh. "But I'm worried about Aladdin. Can you take me to him?" Jasmine asked. But the Magic Carpet didn't respond.

Taking matters into her own hands, Jasmine urged the Magic Carpet on a search for Aladdin. She looked everywhere she could think of, but still there was no sign of him. Finally, the princess told the Magic Carpet to return to the palace.

Before long, the Magic Carpet landed in the castle garden.

"SURPRISE!"

As Jasmine stood, surprised, all of her friends and family leaped out from behind the bushes, carrying presents. Delighted, Jasmine smiled from ear to ear. But what was this all about? It wasn't her birthday.

Suddenly, Aladdin popped out from behind a large cake. "Happy anniversary, Jasmine!" he said, beaming. "Are you surprised?"

"Surprised?" Jasmine replied. "Of course I am!" Then she added to Aladdin in a whisper, "It's not our anniversary!"

Aladdin smiled and whispered back, "It's the anniversary of the day we first met in the marketplace. I thought it was cause for a celebration."

Jasmine smiled and kissed Aladdin on the cheek. But when she looked at the Magic Carpet, she stopped abruptly.

"Why, you sneaky thing!" she said. She smiled. "You were in on this surprise all along, weren't you?" Then she turned to Aladdin.

"This party is wonderful." This would certainly be a day she would never forget.

Fast Friends

"Here, kitty, kitty," called Penny, peering underneath her bed. "Come on, I won't hurt you." She reached her hand out toward the old orange cat she had seen race into the girls' dormitory room and dart under the bed.

Penny had lived at the Morningside Orphanage for a long time. But in all her years there, she had never known that a cat lived there, too.

"Whatcha doin' under there?" Penny asked.

Surprisingly, the cat answered her. "I'm hiding from the headmistress," he whispered. "Is she coming this way?"

Penny looked up and toward the door of the dormitory. She saw the headmistress poke her head into the girls' room, glance around hurriedly, then head off down the hallway.

"Nope, she's gone," Penny said. "The coast is clear."

Breathing a sigh of relief, the cat came out from under the bed and jumped up onto the windowsill.

The cat was wearing a red wool scarf around his neck and a pair of glasses on his nose, and his long white whiskers looked just like a mustache.

"Thanks," he said. "That was a close one."

"Why was the headmistress after you?" Penny asked him.

"Oh," the cat said with a chuckle, "she got me a while back to keep mice out of the basement." He stretched, yawned, and jumped down to lie in a patch of sunlight on the floor. "But I don't mouse too well anymore. I'm getting too slow to chase anything. I'm not as young and spry as I used to be. Say, my name's Rufus. What's yours?"

"Penny," she replied with a smile. She reached under her pillow and pulled out her teddy bear. "And this is Teddy."

"Well, hello, Penny," said Rufus. "And hello, Teddy."

Quiet little guy, huh?" Rufus said to Penny. "What's the matter? Cat got his tongue?"

Penny giggled. "Teddy's very good at keeping secrets. And so am I. You can come hide under our bed whenever you need to. We won't tell."

"You won't?" Rufus replied. "Aw, that's mighty good of you." And so, feeling safe and secure by the side of his new friends, Rufus closed his eyes and settled down for a catnap.

Manners, Mowgli!

A strange but delicious smell drifted past Mowgli's nose. Turning around, he spied several platters of food. A moment later, people filed in and sat in a circle around the food.

Mowgli had just come to live in the Man-village, and he was about to have his first meal!

Mowgli lunged forward and grabbed a piece of meat. He shoved it in his mouth and chewed. He had never tasted cooked meat before, and it was delicious! As the juice dribbled down his chin, he grinned at the humans surrounding him.

They did not grin back. In fact, they were looking at him in disgust. Surprised, Mowgli's mouth dropped open. A piece of half-chewed meat fell out.

"Disgusting," said an elderly woman.

"Why, he eats like an animal!" said a girl.

Mowgli didn't understand a single word they said. But it suddenly dawned on him that he didn't live in the jungle anymore. Humans did things differently from the jungle creatures. Mowgli sighed. Would he ever fit in here?

Smiling sheepishly, Mowgli finished chewing and wiped his mouth with his arm. Then he sat back and watched the others eat.

Mowgli tried to copy them, with little success. The sharpened stick didn't cut nearly as well as his teeth, and half the food fell off the paddle.

At the next meal, Mowgli watched for a long time before he began to eat. The food was strange to him—warm liquid with soft vegetables. Holding his bowl in one hand, he tried to scoop the broth into his mouth with the paddle. But the soup kept slipping off, leaving him with almost nothing.

Mowgli put his bowl and paddle down with a frustrated sigh. Then, ever so slowly, he picked up the bowl a second time and lifted it right to his lips. Then he took a big gulp of soup, swallowing and smacking his lips.

The others stopped and stared yet again. Then the village elder nodded and lifted his bowl to his mouth and took a long sip, finishing with a lip-smack of his own.

Soon everyone was gulping the broth, slurping and smacking away. Mowgli grinned. It looked like he might fit in after all!

Jazzing It Up

"Now, that's what I call a beat!" O'Malley cried. He tapped his paw to the lively rhythm of Marie's singing. The kitten was really learning to jazz up her musical exercises.

Marie smiled happily. O'Malley was so funny! She was glad he had come to live with her mother and brothers and Madame Bonfamille in the big Paris house.

She was also glad that there was a recital coming up. All of Madame Bonfamille's friends were coming, and some of her mother's and O'Malley's, too. There would be tea and crumpets and salmon and fresh, creamy milk. It was going to be the gala event of the season.

And there was more. None of the guests knew what Marie was going to perform. It was going to be a total surprise, and completely different!

Normally, Marie liked to perform a classical piece by Brahms or Mozart— something sweet and delicate and ladylike. But not this time. . . .

Finally, it was recital day. Marie peeked out from behind the velvet curtain. The parlor was packed with fancy ladies, gentlemen, and cats from all over Paris.

"I hope they like it," she said to herself as she took the stage.

Marie tapped her foot, took a deep breath, and began to sing. . . .

Her voice was loud and clear and slid across the notes like honey.

Madame Bonfamille and the cats smiled and nodded in time with the rhythm. But most of the ladies and gentlemen did not look as pleased as Marie's family.

Scat Cat's eyes narrowed as he pounded his paws on the ivory keys. The romping music echoed off the parlor walls.

As Marie belted out the refrain, she closed her eyes and let the music carry her away. When she opened them, it was her turn to be surprised. Everyone in the audience was moving to the beat, tapping their feet or nodding their heads. They were in the groove!

Marie did a little flip before she and Scat Cat finished the song. When the song was over, the audience jumped to their feet.

Marie and her jazzy performance had received a standing ovation!

Rapunzel's Royal Wedding

Spring had sprung, and Flynn had a surprise for Rapunzel. Maximus the horse and Pascal the chameleon wanted to join them, but Flynn wanted to be alone with Rapunzel.

Dusk fell, and Flynn jumped into a boat with Rapunzel, leaving the other two onshore. The lovely night reminded them of times past. Flynn held Rapunzel's hand and looked into her eyes. He reached into his pocket, and—oops! He did need Pascal and Max after all. They had the engagement ring!

"Will you marry me?" Flynn asked Rapunzel. He couldn't wait any longer; he would give her the ring later.

"Yes!" Rapunzel said happily.

On their way home, Rapunzel wanted to tell everyone their wonderful news! The pub ruffians were delighted. It turned out they had been waiting for a wedding to organize for years! Then the couple asked Maximus and Pascal to be ring bearers. They could not have been prouder to accept!

When it was time to find a dress, Rapunzel was determined to design her own. She sketched and sketched . . . but simply could not make up her mind!

The pub thugs tried to help her, but their dresses didn't seem right, either. Luckily, the Queen arrived.

"Darling," she said. "I want to help you make the perfect dress. Let's go look at the wedding shops in the village, and then we'll work together to design your gown." And that is exactly what they did!

On the morning of the wedding, bells rang throughout the kingdom. Everyone was excited to see the King and Queen happily riding in the royal coach. And Max and Pascal were thrilled—until Max sneezed and the rings flew into the air! The horse and the chameleon chased the rings out of the church and up and down the streets.

Max and Pascal made it back to the wedding just in time for the exchange of the rings—but the two friends were a mess! Luckily, Rapunzel and Flynn didn't mind one bit.

The newlyweds danced their first dance. They took their first taste of their wedding cake. And as they rode away in their wedding coach, Rapunzel cried out happily, "Best. Day. Ever!"

Relaxopolis

It was another cold, blustery day in Monstropolis. Sulley and Mike were on their way to work. Mike sighed heavily.

"What's wrong, little buddy?" asked Sulley.

"I'm sick and tired of winter!" Mike replied. "It's cold, it's windy, and it gets dark early." He thought for a moment. "Sulley, I think I have the winter blues!"

Suddenly, Mike spotted a big billboard. On it was a big pink monster sitting in a lounge chair on the beach, wearing sunglasses and sipping what looked like an ice-cold booberry slushie. In big letters it said Beat Those Winter Blues in Relaxopolis!

Mike stopped in his tracks and grabbed Sulley's furry arm. He pointed at the sign, too excited to say a word.

"That's a great idea!" Sulley cheered. "A week on a tropical island is just what we need!"

Mike and Sulley arrived in Relaxopolis a few days later. They went right to the beach, where they each ordered an ice-cold booberry slushie. As the friends lay down on their lounge chairs on the sunniest part of the beach,

Mike said, "This is the life, isn't it, buddy?"

"You bet," said Sulley. "Do you think you need some of this Monster Tropic sunscream? You'd better be careful. You don't want to get too much sun your first day!"

"I'll just soak up the rays for a little while first," said Mike happily. "My winter blues are just melting away."

After a while Sulley grew bored sunbathing and decided to go for a swim. Then he let some little monsters bury him in the sand up to his neck and built a sandcastle with them.

A couple of hours later, he returned to the lounge chairs, where Mike was sound asleep. Sulley took a closer look. His little green friend had not changed position since Sulley had left. He hadn't put on any sunscream, either. Without meaning to, Mike had burned himself in the sun!

"Hey, little buddy," said Sulley as Mike woke up. "Guess you chased those winter blues away, huh?"

Mike just looked at Sulley sleepily.

"You aren't blue anymore," Sulley explained. "Now you're bright red!"

Cinderella's Royal Wedding

Prince Charming had found the woman he loved, and he wanted to marry her. He bent down on one knee and asked her, "Will you marry me?" Of course Cinderella said yes!

The King was thrilled. In the hallway of the palace, he showed Cinderella a portrait of a beautiful woman. "This is my wife on our wedding day. And you shall wear the same thing. It is royal family tradition," said the King. "There is nothing more important than family traditions!"

Cinderella quietly looked at the Queen's portrait. Her dress and necklace were beautiful . . . but they just weren't quite right.

That night, Cinderella had a dream. In it, her mother told her something important. "Cinderella, my love, whenever you have a problem, if you listen to your heart, it will lead you to the answer."

When Cinderella awoke, she began to search through some of her old trunks. She soon found what she was looking for—a portrait of her mother on her wedding day. Cinderella showed the portrait to the royal dressmaker. "Would it be possible for you to make me a dress like this?" she asked.

Next Cinderella visited the royal jeweler. "Do you think it would be possible to turn this necklace into something a little different?" She explained her plan to him.

Finally the wedding day arrived! The King came to see Cinderella.

"I hope you don't mind, but this is a copy of my mother's wedding dress," said Cinderella. "It honors my family tradition. And with my necklace and veil, I also honor yours, Your Majesty."

The King saw that his queen's pearl necklace had been used to make both a wedding necklace and veil.

"Oh, my dear girl, this is a great honor. You have blended the treasures of two families—and created a new tradition of your own."

The King proudly led Cinderella down the aisle, and Cinderella and the Prince answered the question that all brides and grooms must answer.

"They do! They do!" shouted Gus-Gus.

And so, by following tradition—and her heart—Cinderella had the wedding of her dreams!

First Frost

Bambi blinked sleepily. Something was different. The forest did not look the same. The air was crisp and cold, and everything was frosted and sparkling.

"Jack Frost has been here," Bambi's mother explained. "He's painted the whole forest with ice crystals."

Bambi was about to ask his mother who Jack Frost was and how he painted with ice when he heard another voice—an impatient one.

"Get up! Get up! Come look at the frost!" It was Thumper. He tapped his foot impatiently. "We haven't got all day!"

Bambi scampered out of the thicket. He looked closely at the colorful leaves on the ground. Each one was covered in an icy-white pattern. He touched his nose to a big orange oak leaf. "Ooh, it's cold!" he cried.

"Of course it is!" Thumper laughed.

"I think it's beautiful," said Faline as she stepped into the clearing.

"Me too," Bambi agreed.

"Well, come look at this!" Thumper hopped away, and the two young deer followed, admiring the way the sun sparkled on the frost-covered trees and grass.

Thumper disappeared under a bush.

Then Bambi heard a new noise. Creak, crack.

Faline pushed through the bushes with Bambi right behind her. There was Thumper, cracking the thin ice on a puddle with his feet.

Bambi had never seen ice before. He pushed on the thin ice with his hoof. It seemed to bend. Then it shattered!

Soon the three friends were all stomping on the ice-covered puddles. When all the ice was broken, Faline had an idea. "Let's go to the meadow!"

Bambi thought that was a great idea. The grass would be sparkling! They set out at a run, bounding and racing one another through the forest. But when they got to the meadow's edge, they stopped.

They looked, sniffed, and listened quietly. They did not sense danger—no, the trouble was that in the meadow, nothing was different. There was no frost.

"What happened?" Bambi asked.

"Frost never lasts long," Thumper explained. "It melts as soon as the sun hits it. But don't worry. Winter is coming, and soon we'll have something even better than frost. We'll have snow!"

Mike's Dog Problem

It was business as usual at the new Monsters, Inc. Mike Wazowski was one of the top Laugh Collectors. He told funny jokes and made children giggle a lot. But lately, he was having trouble on the job.

"Oh, no, this kid has a dog!" Mike groaned as he read the paperwork for his next assignment. Mike was terrified of dogs, but no one else knew. He was too embarrassed to say anything.

Mike was pacing the Laugh Floor, trying to come up with a good excuse to skip work, when his friend Sulley arrived.

"What are you waiting for, buddy?" asked Sulley.

Mike couldn't think of an excuse, so he reluctantly walked into the boy's bedroom. He saw the dog and jumped up on a stool to get away from it. The dog ran up to the stool and sat in front of Mike, who got so nervous he couldn't remember his jokes! The boy didn't laugh at all. Mike was very upset. He just couldn't relax when dogs were around. He would have to go back to the Laugh Floor without any laughs.

The next day, Mike was assigned to the same room because he hadn't collected enough laughs. Sulley noticed that Mike didn't want to go, so he snuck in behind him to find out why.

Once inside, Mike tried to tell a joke—but he was so nervous that he froze with fear. Sulley suddenly realized that his friend was afraid of dogs!

That day after work, he asked Mike about it. "I feel like a giant chew toy when I'm near them, like any second they might bite me!" cried Mike.

"Don't worry, pal," Sulley said, and then he taught Mike all about dogs.

"Remember, Mike," Sulley said. "Even though dogs slobber, have big teeth, and make loud noises, that doesn't mean they're scary."

The next day, Mike and Sulley went to a room with a dog. Mike remembered what Sulley had taught him—to stay calm and let the dog sniff him. He took a deep breath. The dog bounded over and sniffed Mike, who tried to relax. The dog was friendly, and Mike began to feel comfortable. Soon he was telling one joke after another! Thanks to Sulley's help, Mike became the top Laugh Collector again—and he even grew to like dogs.

"Maybe I'll get a dog," declared Mike.

"Maybe you should start with a hamster," Sulley said with a chuckle.

A Winter's Tale

One bright, sunny December day, Winnie the Pooh was trudging through the Hundred-Acre Wood on his way to visit his good friend Piglet. Piglet was sick in bed with the sniffles.

"Poor Piglet," Pooh said with a sigh. "What a shame he can't come outside to play in this lovely snow." Then the bear of very little brain came up with a perfectly wonderful idea. "I know!" he exclaimed. "I will bring some snow to Piglet!"

He scooped up a mittenful of snow and formed a snowball. He dropped it into his pocket, and then he made another, and then another. Then he hurried on to Piglet's house. When he was nearly there, he passed Tigger, Rabbit, Roo, and Eeyore heading the other way.

"Hello, Pooh!" called Roo. "Come and build a snowman with us!"

"I'm sorry, but I can't," said Pooh wistfully. "You see, I am bringing some snowballs to Piglet."

Piglet was indeed not well, but he was very happy to see his friend. "Hello, Booh," he said snuffily. "I'b glad you cabe. *Ah-choo!*"

"Poor Piglet," said Pooh. "I'll make tea." He was just putting the kettle on when a large drop of icy water rolled out from underneath his hat and down his nose. This reminded Pooh of something.

"I brought you a present, Piglet!" he cried, snatching off his hat. But there was nothing there.

Puzzled, Pooh ran to his jacket, which he had hung on a hook near the door. There were no snowballs in either of the pockets! But there was a sizable puddle of water on the floor underneath Pooh's coat.

"I don't understand it!" Pooh remarked, scratching his head. "I brought you some snowballs, but they seem to have disappeared."

"Oh, d-d-d-dear," Piglet said with a sigh. "I do wish I could go outside and blay. Could you bull back the curtaids so that I cad see the sdow?"

Pooh hopped up and pulled back the curtains so his friend could see the snow. Both of them gasped when they looked outside.

There, just below Piglet's window, Tigger, Rabbit, Eeyore, and Roo had built a beautiful snowman, just for Piglet!

"Oh, friedds are the best!" Piglet said happily. *"Ah-choo!"*

A Royal Visit

Snow White was very happy. She had married her true love and she lived in a beautiful castle. But she missed her good friends from the forest, the Seven Dwarfs, very much.

"Well, why don't you go for a visit?" the Prince said.

"That would be lovely!" Snow White cried.

Snow White wrote a note to tell her friends that she was going to visit, and she asked a bluebird to deliver it.

At the Dwarfs' cottage, Doc read the note and ran downstairs to tell the others.

"Hooray!" Happy cheered. "Snow White is coming!"

But the other six Dwarfs looked around their messy cottage. "We have a lot to do, men!" said Doc.

"She'll want lunch," Grumpy huffed. "Someone's gonna have to cook!"

"Why don't you and Happy fix somethin' suitable for Snow White to eat?" Doc suggested.

The Dwarfs started to work on their chores right away, but it didn't go very well. Sleepy got tired and lay down. Sneezy kept sneezing as he dusted. And Dopey knocked furniture over as he swept. Meanwhile, Happy and Grumpy couldn't agree on what kind of sandwiches to make.

All too soon, Snow White arrived. The Dwarfs smiled as Snow White hugged each of them and kissed their foreheads.

"Please forgive the mess, Princess," Bashful whispered to her. "We didn't quite get it cleaned up."

"Oh, please," Snow White said with a laugh. "Forgive *me* for giving you such short notice! Besides, I've come to see you—not your cottage."

"Would you care for a ham and jelly sandwich?" Doc offered, holding up a platter. "Or peanut butter and cheese?"

"Oh, how sweet," Snow White replied. "If I had known you'd go to all this trouble, I wouldn't have brought a picnic with me."

"Picnic!" the Dwarfs exclaimed.

"Well, yes. I remembered how much you liked it when I cooked, so I brought some of your favorites. But let's eat your sandwiches first."

The Dwarfs looked at one another, and Doc cleared his throat.

"We can have ham and jelly anytime," he said. "Let's enjoy your picnic and have a great afternoon." And that's exactly what they did.

Tinker Bell's Plan

Tinker Bell and her sister, Periwinkle, had just met. The two had been separated at birth when a baby's laugh had broken in two. One half had landed in the Pixie Dust Tree and become Tink, while the other half had landed in the Winter Woods and become Peri.

Queen Clarion had a rule that no fairy could cross the border between autumn and winter. But Tink and Peri had broken the rule to visit each other. Tink and her friends had built a snowmaker so Peri could stay cool outside the Winter Woods, but now it was making so much snow that the seasons were out of balance. If the Pixie Dust Tree froze, there would be no more pixie dust! Pixie Hollow would die!

Suddenly Tink noticed a flower her sister had covered in frost. It was blooming again. Maybe they could save all the flowers, and the Pixie Dust Tree, by covering *them* with a layer of frost!

Tink flew into winter, but her wings iced over and she fell to the ground. Tink told the frost fairies her plan. Lord Milori, lord of winter, agreed.

"Start at the freeze line and spread out to the other seasons," he ordered. "The rest of you—cover the tree!"

When Lord Milori reached the Pixie Dust Tree, he draped his cloak around a shivering Queen Clarion. It broke her heart to see his damaged wing. Many years ago, the two had been in love.

The fairies waited anxiously as the air slowly warmed. Sunbeams began to stream through the frozen Pixie Dust Tree's branches and the frost melted. The pixie dust started to flow again! The plan had worked!

With the danger over, Tinker Bell admitted that she had broken her wing when she flew into the Winter Woods. Heartbroken, she said a final good-bye to her sister. The two touched wings.

Just then, there was an explosion of sparkling energy. The magic between the sisters healed Tink's broken wing!

From that day on, warm fairies were able to visit winter fairies whenever they liked, with a coating of frost to protect their wings. New friendships formed—and long-lost loved ones were reunited at last!

Donald's Christmas Gift

Christmas was coming to the Clubhouse!

"Do you think Donald will like his present?" Daisy whispered to Minnie.

"Oh, yes," Minnie squeaked in reply.

Donald overheard. "Oh, boy. Oh, boy!" he gasped. "I can't wait to find out what my present is!"

Just then, he saw a card slip out of Minnie's hand. He picked it up and read the name of a nearby bicycle shop.

"Aha!" Donald shouted aloud. "A clue!"

Donald went to the bicycle shop and discovered that Minnie had sold her bicycle to the shopkeeper.

The shopkeeper said that Minnie had been on her way to the bookshop. So off Donald went. At the bookshop, Donald saw that Mickey had sold his rare collection of books about mice!

Next Donald visited the pet shop, where he saw that Pluto had traded in his favorite bone! At the hat shop, Donald spotted that Goofy had sold his hat.

All of my friends are giving up the things that they love just to buy presents, Donald said to himself. Don't they know that Christmas is a time to get presents?

Donald closed his eyes for a minute. He imagined each of his friends holding a Christmas present. They all looked so happy. But they weren't *getting* presents. They were *giving* them!

"That's it!" Donald exclaimed. "I know just what I have to do now."

Donald raced home and put all of his pennies into a big sack. Then he went back to all of the shops and bought back everything his friends had sold! When he was done, his penny sack was empty, but his heart was full. Donald chuckled when he opened his present on Christmas morning—it was a piggy bank for his penny collection! He didn't have any pennies left to put in it, but he loved it anyway. After all, it was the thought that mattered.

"This is a wonderful present," he said. "But you have given me something so much better. You have shown me the true meaning of Christmas, and that's the best gift of all!"

A Merry Christmas

"**M**erry Christmas!" Ebenezer Scrooge crowed as he watched the Cratchit children open all the gifts he'd brought for them.

"A teddy bear!" Tiny Tim exclaimed. His sister had a new doll, and his brother was busy playing with a new train set. And that was just the beginning.

"And there's another present, too," Scrooge said with a twinkle in his eye. "I'll be right back."

Scrooge walked outside. A moment later, he reappeared carrying a big package wrapped in red paper and tied with a giant green bow.

The children ripped off the paper and squealed in delight.

"Father, it's a sled!" Tiny Tim cheered happily.

"I can see that," Bob Cratchit replied, looking up from the turkey he was carving. Scrooge had brought the turkey over that very morning.

"Can we go sledding? Can we? Can we?" the children chorused.

"Of course," Cratchit replied. "But not until after dinner."

"And dinner is ready right now," Mrs. Cratchit said.

"Dinner!" the children shouted as they scrambled to their seats at the table.

Mrs. Cratchit sat down. "I can't remember when we've had such a feast, Mr. Scrooge," she said happily. "Thank you ever so much for all the gifts you've given us."

Scrooge raised his glass in the air. "That's what Christmas is all about," he said warmly. "Happiness and goodwill. Merry Christmas!"

Everyone clinked glasses, then got busy eating.

When they were done with the turkey, Mr. Cratchit said, "Now, how about that sledding?"

Minutes later, everyone was bundled up and ready to go.

Scrooge pulled the children all through town, singing Christmas carols at the top of his lungs.

"Why is everyone staring at Mr. Scrooge?" Tiny Tim whispered to his father.

Mr. Cratchit smiled down at his son. "Because they like him," he said.

"I like him, too," said Tiny Tim. "This is the best Christmas ever!"

The Mysterious Jewel

It was a fine morning, just right for a walk along the seashore. With joy in her heart, Princess Ariel strolled along the beach. Ariel had once been a mermaid, but she had become a human to marry her true love, Prince Eric.

The princess wandered all morning, and she found herself a long way from the castle. Suddenly, she stubbed her toe against a hard object buried in the sand.

"Ouch!" she cried. She dug up a shiny object. It was a jewel!

"Scuttle, go and find Sebastian. Tell him to call my father!" she said.

A moment later, Ariel's father, King Triton, emerged from the sea.

"Father," said Ariel. "I've just found this wonderful jewel, and—"

"Where did you find it?" asked King Triton, amazed.

"On the beach," explained Ariel. "Do you know where it comes from?"

"I'm going to show you something," said her father solemnly. Then he transformed her into a mermaid.

Ariel dove into the water after her father. Soon they arrived at the throne room of his underwater palace.

King Triton showed Ariel a treasure chest without anything inside.

"Many years ago, a tidal wave carried off the treasure of Atlantica," explained the king. "This jewel is the only one that's been found."

"I'll help you find the others!" said Ariel.

First the princess searched the wreck of a ship and collected almost a dozen jewels! Then, with the help of Flounder and his friends, she found even more gems in the coral reef. Soon the Atlantica treasure chest was full to the brim once more, thanks to Ariel.

King Triton opened the chest and took out the stone that Ariel had found on the beach that morning. He had hung it from a beautiful golden necklace! Giving her a kiss on her forehead, King Triton fastened the necklace around her neck.

Soon it was time for Ariel to turn back into a human and return to her castle. That night, Ariel looked out at the ocean, the jewel hanging from her neck. Her family was never very far away, but she found it reassuring to have a little piece of Atlantica with her forever.

Showdown

One afternoon, Jessie was watching *Woody's Roundup* on TV. In the old Wild West, Sheriff Woody and Jessie were talking about who was the best cowpoke.

"I can out-cowpoke you any day," Jessie said with a grin.

Woody knew Jessie was a great cowpoke. But he didn't think she was better than him.

Just then, the Prospector walked over with Woody's horse, Bullseye. Jessie told the Prospector what they were talking about.

Woody sighed. "How about we just say you're as good a cowpoke as I am?"

Jessie grinned. That was all she wanted to hear. She knew Woody was a fine cowpoke.

"Whoa, hold on a rootin' tootin' minute," the Prospector said. "A true cowpoke never backs down from a challenge, Sheriff. How will you prove you're the roughest, toughest cowpoke in the West?"

Jessie suggested they each try to teach Bullseye a trick, but Bullseye wouldn't budge.

"This contest stuff is dumb," Woody said. "What if . . . "

"Woody! Jessie!" the Prospector said. "The new calf just fell into the Rushing River." The two cowpokes quickly climbed onto Bullseye's back and raced to the river. They soon spotted the calf wedged against a rock, struggling and mooing. Jessie grabbed her lasso and threw it neatly around the calf's neck. Woody carefully climbed down, hopping from one slippery rock to the next. He patted the calf and led it back across the river. Meanwhile, on the riverbank, Jessie and Bullseye held the rope so the calf wouldn't be swept downstream.

"Woody saved the day!" Jessie exclaimed when the calf was safely on shore. "He's the bravest cowpoke ever."

"Jessie's the real hero," said Woody. "She lassoed the calf like a great cowpoke."

"Seems we still don't know who is the roughest, toughest cowpoke in the West," said the Prospector.

"Yes, we do," said Woody, grinning at Jessie.

"We're both great cowpokes!" they cried.

A Purr-fect Night for a Stroll

Bernard was sweeping the floor of the Rescue Aid Society when Miss Bianca appeared.

"I'm going for a stroll," she said. "Would you like to join me?"

"Gosh, I don't know," Bernard said. "It's dark out. And it's raining, too!"

"Yes," Miss Bianca said, smiling. "It's the *perfect* night for a stroll!"

Outside, Miss Bianca pulled her collar tight. Bernard opened a big umbrella.

As they walked, it rained harder. Suddenly, Bernard stopped. "Listen!" he cried.

"Meow!"

"It's a kitten," said Miss Bianca. "It sounds like he's in trouble. Look, over there!" she cried, pointing. Under a mailbox, a little orange kitten cowered from the rain. His fur was wet, and he looked very sad.

"Stay back!" Bernard warned. "Cats are dangerous. They eat mice like us!"

"But we've got to help him!" Miss Bianca said.

"Then let me go first!" Bernard insisted. He crept up to the kitten. "Er . . . hello," he stammered. "Are you lost?"

"I'm lost and very hungry!" the cat cried.

"I was afraid of that," said Bernard, eyeing the kitten's sharp teeth and claws nervously.

"Where are your parents?" Miss Bianca asked.

"I'm an orphan," the kitten replied.

"We must help him!" said Miss Bianca.

"I have an idea," said Bernard. "Follow us!"

Bernard took Miss Bianca's arm, and they walked to Morningside Orphanage. They knocked, and old Rufus the cat answered.

"Nice to see you two again," Rufus said. "Who's your friend?" he asked.

"He's Young Mister Kitten, and he's an orphan," Miss Bianca replied.

"He's hungry," said Bernard nervously.

"Here's a nice bowl of milk," said Rufus kindly.

The kitten lapped it up.

"You know," Rufus said, "I could use a helper around here. Would you like to be adopted?"

The kitten threw his paws around Rufus's neck and purred with joy.

Out on the street, Bianca took Bernard's arm.

"See?" she said. "I told you it was the *purr-fect* night for a stroll!"

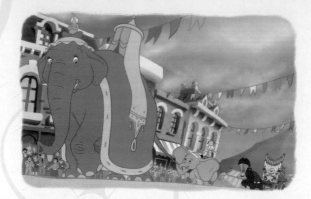

Dumbo's Parade Pals

When Dumbo's circus came to town, the animals and circus folk marched in a big parade. The crowd loved seeing all the circus animals marching down the street.

Suddenly, Dumbo noticed a peanut on the ground. He picked up the peanut with his trunk and ate it. Then Dumbo saw another peanut, and another.

Leaving the parade, Dumbo followed the trail of peanuts all the way to a playground.

"See, the peanuts worked!" exclaimed a little girl with pigtails. "Now we have our own elephant to play with."

"Let's have our own circus," said a boy.

"I'll be the ringmaster!" cried the little girl. "Ladies and gentlemen! Presenting our star attraction—the Little Elephant!"

Dumbo knew just what to do. He stood up on his two back legs. Then he juggled some balls with his trunk. The children cheered.

Soon Timothy Q. Mouse appeared. "Here you are!" he said to Dumbo. "We have to get back to the circus camp to get ready for the show!"

Dumbo nodded and waved good-bye to his new friends.

"I wish I could go see him in the circus tonight," one of the children said. "But I don't have enough money for a ticket."

Dumbo was sorry that the nice children he had met would not be able to go to the circus. That night, he felt very blue as he put on his stage makeup and warmed up his ears. He tucked Timothy into the brim of his hat and climbed onto a tall platform.

"Ladies and gentlemen!" the Ringmaster cried. "I give you *Dumbo, the Flying Elephant!*"

Dumbo leaped off the platform, and his giant ears unfurled. The crowd cheered as Dumbo flew around the tent.

Far below in the crowd, Dumbo spotted his playground friends sitting in the first row! He swept by them, patting each child on the head with his trunk. The girl with pigtails waved at Dumbo. "Your mouse friend gave us free tickets!" she cried.

Dumbo smiled and reached his trunk up to the brim of his hat, where Timothy was riding. He was the luckiest elephant in the world to have such wonderful friends!

Tink Learns a Lesson

Tinker Bell was mad. She and Peter Pan had made plans to explore Skull Cave, but he was still playing Pirate Treasure with the Lost Boys.

When Tinker Bell jingled impatiently by his ear to let him know it was time to go explore, he said, "Just a minute, Tink." So she decided to teach him a lesson.

Tinker Bell flew deep inside a hollow tree.

"Help, help me!" she jingled as loudly as she could. "Peter! Help! I'm stuck!"

A moment later, Peter appeared. He was out of breath from flying to her at top speed.

"What is it, Tink?" he gasped. "Are you in trouble?"

Tinker Bell couldn't help laughing at the worried expression on his face. In fact, she laughed so hard that she fell right out of the tree and landed on the ground.

Peter Pan frowned. "That's not funny, Tink," he said. "I really thought you were in danger! And you interrupted my game!"

He flew away. Tinker Bell stopped laughing. Obviously Peter hadn't learned his lesson yet. He was still leaving her behind to play with his other friends!

Peter was really testing Tinker Bell's patience!

Tink sat down under a mushroom and thought about how to get even with Peter. One last scare that would make him sit up and take notice. But as she thought, she became sleepier and sleepier. She leaned back against the mushroom stem and closed her eyes. . . .

The next thing Tink knew, she had been snatched up by a hungry hawk! Tink jingled and jingled—but Peter didn't come!

"I'm not fibbing this time, Peter!" she jingled. "I'm about to become a hawk's lunch! I'm sorry I ever tried to fool you. This time it's real!"

Then she woke up. Tink was very relieved to discover that she was safe and sound under the shady brim of the mushroom! She took a deep breath.

That was very scary, she thought. I guess maybe I learned my lesson. . . .

Then she thought about it again. Nah!

Countdown to Midnight!

"No sleep till midnight!" Lilo and Stitch chanted, bouncing up and down on Lilo's bed. It was New Year's Eve, and Nani had agreed to let them stay up late.

"Okay, okay." Nani held her hands out. "It's only five o'clock now. Don't wear yourselves out. You still have seven hours until the new year."

"Seven hours! What do you want to do first?" Lilo asked Stitch.

"Surfing!" Stitch cried.

"Sunset surfing it is!" Lilo gave the little alien a high five before turning to Nani. "Okay?" she asked sweetly.

Nani shook her head again. I must be nuts, she thought. "I'll go get my suit."

The three surfed until sundown. Then they headed for home.

"So, what's next?" Lilo asked Stitch. Stitch smacked his lips. "Dinner!"

"Don't worry," Lilo said. "We'll cook."

"Yeah, and I'll clean," Nani muttered.

When they got home, Nani lay down on the couch with her arm over her eyes.

"Ta-da!" Lilo emerged with a huge plate of something steaming and cheesy.

"What is it?" Nani asked cautiously.

"Pizza, Stitch-style!" Lilo said. "With anchovies, peanut butter, and fruit.

Nani cringed.

"Don't worry, Nani," said Lilo. "We left the toothpaste on the side this time, like you asked us to. Plus, there's a milk shake for dessert!"

The three ate the gooey mess, and Lilo and Stitch discussed what was next.

"How about that milk shake?" Nani suggested before Lilo could come up with a noisier, messier, or more dangerous idea.

Stitch grabbed the blender and dumped the milk shake on his head. "Stitch!" cried Lilo. "Oh, well."

Nani shooed the two into the living room and began to tackle the mess in the kitchen. The washing-up took forever. She could not figure out how they'd managed to use so many pots and pans.

She was still elbow-deep in suds when her eyes grew wide with alarm. Something was wrong. It was too quiet!

Nani rushed into the living room. Lilo and Stitch were sound asleep! Nani looked at her watch.

"Five, four, three, two, one," Nani counted down. "Happy New Year," she said softly as she covered the pair with a blanket.

It was only ten p.m.!